the Summer Set

A NOVEL

AIMEE AGRESTI

GRAYDON
HOUSE

**GRAYDON
HOUSE®**

ISBN-13: 978-1-525-82358-9

The Summer Set

This edition published by arrangement with Harlequin Books S.A.

Graydon House
22 Adelaide St. West, 40th Floor
Toronto, Ontario M5H 4E3, Canada
www.GraydonHouseBooks.com
www.BookClubbish.com

Printed in U.S.A.

For my family

the Summer Set

I reckon some of my best leading men have been dogs and horses.

—ELIZABETH TAYLOR

Charlie Savoy - ACTRESS

Charlotte "Charlie" Savoy is a stage and screen actress. Daughter of famed Shakespearean actress Dame Sarah Rose Kingsbury and jazz trumpeter Reggie Fairfield (from whom she's estranged), she was born in New York, New York, but raised primarily in London by her mother after her father left the family to pursue his music career.

Charlie got her start as a teen performing Shakespeare on the London stage then jumped to the big screen, most notably in *Nicholas Blunt's The Tempest*, earning several supporting actress awards (British Independent Film Award, Independent Spirit, Critics' Choice), even more nominations (Oscar, BAFTA, Golden Globe) and anointing her "The Next Big Thing" (*The Hollywood Reporter*).

Despite the accolades, she quickly flamed out, becoming known for erratic behavior when she walked off the set of the psychological action film *Dawn of the Super Id* (one of the most expensive and lowest-earning films of all time). The indie *Midnight Daydream* (a critical darling but box office bomb) was her last film. She now owns an art house movie theater in Boston.

Reputation as a wild child (arrested after jumping off London's Tower Bridge on a dare as a teen)

Dated director Nicholas Blunt

Best friend of actress Marlena Andes (née Marlon Andes)

Legally changed surname to Savoy at age eighteen

Owns North End Cinema in Boston, Massachusetts

1. Midnight Daydream (Charlotte)
2. Nicholas Blunt's The Tempest (Ariel)
3. Illuminate (Haven)
4. Law & Order (Stacy; 2 episodes)
5. A BBC Presentation:
   Live from the Globe Theatre, Macbeth (Lady Macbeth)
6. A BBC Presentation:
   Live from the Globe Theatre, Hamlet (Ophelia)
7. A BBC Presentation:
   Live from the Globe Theatre, Romeo and Juliet (Juliet)

PART ONE

Love is heavy and light,
bright and dark,
hot and cold,
sick and healthy,
asleep and awake—
it's everything except what it is!
—WILLIAM SHAKESPEARE,
ROMEO AND JULIET

STARCROSS EXCLUSIVE:

WASHED UP!: *TEMPEST* STAR
DRIVES CAR INTO BOSTON HARBOR

Actress Charlotte "Charlie" Savoy, 39, best known for her award-winning turn in the classic *Nicholas Blunt's The Tempest*, limped away from a near-fatal crash in the early morning hours of April 24. Paramedics were summoned to Boston Harbor after local fishermen pulled the star from the river.

An eyewitness told *STARCROSS* that Savoy allegedly lost control of her car, which plowed through a barricade. The Oscar nominee reportedly flew through the smashed windshield as her Prius drove off the pier near Boston's Institute of Contemporary Art. "It looked like something out of a movie," the captain of a sightseeing tour boat docked nearby, which was damaged by debris from the flying car, told *STARCROSS*. He intends to press charges for destruction of property and reckless endangerment.

Savoy—who had a meteoric rise in her midtwenties, left Hollywood after a series of flops and now runs North End Cinema on Hanover Street—was treated for multiple lacerations and contusions, according to a source at Massachusetts General Hospital, but is expected to make a full recovery.

Authorities report that speed was a factor in the crash but it remains unclear whether alcohol or impairing substances contributed.

1

SUSPEND YOUR DISBELIEF, AS USUAL

At least Charlie wore her sunglasses in the grainy photo, but they could only do so much. She slammed her laptop shut, as though a cobra might slither out from it. Only to open it again, take a deep breath and lean in to the full horror.

She groaned at the picture of herself, circa one hour ago. She was out of practice with this: it had been years since her photographer-dodging days. The Starbucks sign over her right shoulder indicated the shot had been snapped on the northwest corner of her street during her nearly unrequited search for a cab. That butterfly-bandaged gash slashing her forehead looked even gnarlier in the image. Her cheekbones and chin, battered and bruised, gave her face the uninviting aura of an overripe peach.

She should've just skipped work, she thought, excavating the makeup pouch from her office desk drawer. She swept on enough bronze foundation to erase even her freckles, masked that black-and-blue eye and painted on scarlet lips before returning to the screen.

The play-by-play felt like reading about someone else: it helped to not remember any of it. It *didn't* help that her phone, wallet, purse, keys and pride were all still at the bottom of the river. (She had paid for her cab home from the hospital with the soggy bills in her jeans pocket. And thank God for twenty-four-hour doormen with spare keys.)

But the editorializing: Why did her standard ID always need to be that damn *Tempest*? This must be how it felt for people who shared beloved children with exes they couldn't stand. Also there had been no *substances*—not the illicit kind, at least. And *flops*—plural? It had just been the singular flop, actually, a good movie that just hadn't made any cash.

Sweating now, she tugged off her faux-leather motorcycle jacket—the real one hung in her apartment, drying out like crinkly parchment—and tossed it at the sofa, hitting that framed *Midnight Daydream* poster.

Her door burst open.

"My *God*, you're *alive!*" A flash of zhushed hair and thick hipster frames. Miles, her adoring theater manager/projectionist, threw his arms around her, knocking papers from her desk onto the floor.

Including that letter. The one that had set her off last night before her drive.

"Just like I confirmed for you in the past seventeen emails," she said as he clung to her. He had written all morning after seeing the story and getting no answer on her phone.

"It's all my fault!" He tore himself away—her Frankenstein-stitched left thigh screaming in pain from the motion—and collapsed on her sofa. "I never should've given you the Ambien. I'm like some kind of low-life drug dealer! There's blood on my hands!" He held up jazz hands, his head hung in shame.

"Wow, okay, no—" Charlie laughed, as she always did, at his melodrama.

"But I just wanted to help," he went on, "you *never* sleep and—"

"It's not you, it's me. I totally messed up timing that thing. Rookie mistake." She straightened her leg beneath her long skirt, rotating her ankle. She had even rewrapped it *herself* (one role as a candy striper and she felt qualified). "Don't drive or operate heavy machinery. Message received. I'm fine. Just suspend your disbelief, as usual—"

"And you *still* made me coffee?" he said, producing a North End Cinema–logoed cup. "What is *wrong* with you?"

"Absolutely nothing." Charlie shook her head. "That's what I've been trying to tell you." Charlie made them each a cappuccino every morning at the theater's opulent espresso bar. She saw no reason to abandon her routine today.

"I see what you're doing," he said, taking a sip. "Distraction. Charm. It won't work." He sipped again, then under his breath, muttered, "Why are your cappuccinos so much better than mine?"

"Cardamom," Charlie said, returning to her laptop. She closed out the offending STARCROSS story, pulling up a spreadsheet instead. "And cinnamon."

"WAIT!" Miles barked, regaining her attention. "I mean…" He searched for the words. "If last night wasn't a cry for help I'm supposed to be answering, then what would you call it?"

"I don't know." Charlie exhaled, arms in the air. She really didn't. She wasn't the type to drive into a harbor. At least not anymore. Her mind whipped through her highlight/lowlight reel in flashes like one of those photo montages your phone automatically makes.

It was all pretty well-documented—publicly, internationally, globally. Before her first movie (at age nineteen), she had already: drunk too much; done too much Ecstasy; talked her way into every London club worth going to; danced on too many tables in too little clothing; shaved her head (twice); jumped off London's Tower Bridge on a dare; got arrested; sat in on the drums at Wembley Stadium when she was briefly dating that miserable singer; slept with too many boys…and girls…occasionally at the same time and had it all mean too little; had too few friends; too much talent; and too much hunger.

And then she became successful and was maybe *too* passionate and had artistic standards set too high and possibly had too much bravado, and definitely had too much impulsivity and impetuousness. And then overnight she had…nothing. And now here she was. And that was how that ballad went.

"Not a call you need to answer," Charlie assured him. "Put me right through to voice mail."

"You're sure this isn't about the letter?" he asked, his tone delicate.

"This has *nothing* to do with the letter," she snapped. Of course, it had everything to do with the letter, but she wasn't about to admit that. "I threw it away." Another lie.

"Great!" he said, too peppy, overcompensating. "I just mean… You gave me quite a scare, young lady." Charlie was, in fact, ten years Miles's senior. "So just never do that again, okay?"

"Won't happen again, officer." Charlie nodded, her eyes on that poster of herself lying on a park bench in Boston Common, the title *Midnight Daydream* written as a constellation. Signed by the cast and crew—including Miles, then just a college-aged production assistant.

Charlie grabbed his arm as leverage, rising from her chair on that mangled leg. "Can we go back to talking about important things now, like when you're going to make your move on the guy at the juice bar?" she said, hobbling out into the old-Hollywood glamour of the crimson velvet lobby. She had gutted the place, done a head-to-toe HGTV-worthy renovation after buying it on a whim—like a pack of gum at Stop & Shop—following the night of drunken revelry that was the wrap party for *Midnight Daydream*.

"I know, the protein shakes are garbage but I keep buying them to see him." She felt relief at the return to normalcy.

"Listen, it's not in the shakes to hold our destiny, but in ourselves," she semi-quoted. "And in the meantime, we've got a subtitled Romanian horror film to show." Charlie pushed him toward the entrance.

A guy who looked barely old enough to drink peered inside, hands against the locked glass doors, searching for signs of life. They got a lot of students here, especially on weekends, like last night's weekly *Dawn of the Super Id* screening. She had shown it once as a joke long after its doomed theatrical release and it sold out. So Charlie kept it going and it had become her theater's answer to *Rocky Horror*. They came at midnight every Friday in masks and capes, some handmade from dorm bedsheets. They yelled the terrible dialogue. They sang the theme song. They always left joyous, free, raucous. And when Charlie needed to feel like she was contributing in some way to society, she could at least appreciate having given them a night like that.

She liked to watch the transformation that swept her young audience over the course of that hour and fifty-three minutes. (In addition to its myriad detriments, the film was, in Charlie's estimation, a solid twenty-three minutes longer than it had any right to be.) She just wished she hadn't stayed *last night*. She had forgotten that, at some point, the sleeping pill would, presumably, do what it had been advertised to do. And that she could do something like drive into the river.

"Can't see this stuff everywhere." Miles crossed the lobby to unlock the doors.

Back in her office, Charlie's fingers hovered over her laptop keyboard. Changing her mind, she patted at the floor for the smooth stationery with that neat penmanship. It had been a while since she had received a letter like that: formal, kind, thoughtful. Slouched in her chair, injured leg propped on her desk, she read it again. And again. Always coming back to the closing.

…Without prying, with only reverence and respect, could I ask: Why did you stop doing something you're so good at? And more important: When will you come back? You are missed.

2

I MISSED YOU TOO

Charlie studied herself in her bathroom mirror. In just a week her bruised eye had faded to the dull gray of rancid meat, now easily disguised by concealer. She flat-ironed her raven hair, securing it in a sleek, low ponytail, then rummaged the closet for her most professional-looking getup: that slim black suit, pale pink silk blouse with the bow at the neck and the stilettos she only wore when she felt compelled to impress. Her wardrobe from that perfume ad a decade earlier but *timeless* nonetheless, just like the moniker that had been etched in script on the curved bottle of the fragrance.

Outside, Boston did its best impersonation of her supposed hometown, London. (Though she had lived away from there enough during childhood to have eluded the accent.) The dreary May rain made her think of her mom: the estimable Dame Sarah Rose Kingsbury. News of Charlie's *incident* had warranted mentions in a few celebrity weeklies and, unfortunately, made the hop across the pond. Her mother had called, texted and finally, after no response, emailed: Charlie, Did you receive my voice mail and text? I trust you're alright. Another of your stunts? Please respond. Love, Mum. Her mom's correspondence always scanned like a telegram, full of stops and full stops—much like their relationship itself. Charlie, reveling in being briefly unreachable and not in the mood to answer questions, hadn't yet bothered to replace her phone and had indeed missed the call but wrote back assuring her mom that she was fine, though the accident had not, in fact, been performance art.

By the time Charlie reached the foreboding Suffolk County Courthouse, her lawyer/friend Sam—who had shepherded her through the theater purchase (while questioning her sanity)—was already there pacing, barking into her phone.

"This should be easy," Sam told her, hanging up, hugging her while scrolling her inbox. Sam wore suits and radiated *responsibility*, two things Charlie found comforting in a lawyer. "Be contrite and it should be open-and-shut for community service."

The sterile courtroom's pin-drop silence made Charlie shiver. Next to her, Sam tucked her phone in her bag and rose to her feet, gesturing for Charlie to stand as the judge materialized at the bench. Charlie found it oddly reassuring that the judge was the kind of woman who wore pearls and a frilly collar outside her robe.

"You were okay with my email, right?" Sam whispered, as they sat again.

"What email?" she whispered back.

"My *email*. An hour ago? You have *got* to get a new phone," Sam scolded.

"I know, I know—"

"There was this arrangement, last minute, I hope you'll be amenable to but—"

"What's *that* supposed to mean?" Charlie pleaded.

The judge had begun speaking, so Sam hushed her. Too late.

"Ms. Savoy, this is the part where *I* get to talk." The judge looked up from the paper she had been reading aloud. "Maybe it was different in your episodes of *Law & Order*?"

"No, ma'am, I mean, Your Honor, sir, ma'am, no," Charlie stumbled. She had been wrong about the judge. The woman continued on about the damage Charlie caused and the significant hours of service required like Charlie was the honoree at one of those Comedy Central roasts, albeit one that could end with her in a jail cell.

Until finally, the judge cut to the chase: "…an assignment has presented itself," she said slowly. "Which will make fine use of Ms. Savoy's expertise…" Charlie caught Sam's side-eye. "So Charlotte Savoy shall be required to complete sixty days with the Chamberlain Summer Theater in—"

"NO!" Charlie expelled the word, an anaphylactic response. The judge scowled as though jail might still be an option. "Sorry, Your Honor, I just mean—can I object?" Sam shot her a lethal glare. "It's just that, well—" Charlie tried again as a door at the back of the courtroom creaked open, footsteps echoing. She turned to discover the equivalent of a ghost.

Nick Blunt—director, ex, first love, disappointment, invertebrate—heading her way.

"Mr. Blunt, thank you for joining us," the judge said, unimpressed.

Charlie's posture straightened, heartbeat ticking faster than seemed medically sound. She felt betrayed by her own being, muscles, nerves, ashamed of this reaction.

"Sorry, Your Honor," he said in that deep rasp.

Charlie wished she hated that voice. And it seemed an abomination that he could still be attractive—physically at least.

Rugged with an athletic build, he wore black jeans, a blazer and aviator sunglasses, which he pulled off as he walked (pure affectation since, to her knowledge, it was *still* raining outside), tucking them into the V of his slim sweater.

He took his place beside Charlie, flashing that smile he deployed when he aimed to be his most charming.

"Hi there," he said, as though surprised to be meeting this way.

"Shouldn't you be wearing a cape?" Charlie rolled her eyes, focused on the judge reading again, and returned her body to its proper slouch, recalibrating her expression between boredom and disgust.

"I missed you too, Charlie," he whispered back.

From the corner of her eye, Charlie spotted the sharp beak of that tattoo—the meadowlark—curving around from the back of his neck. It was still there, which gave her a pang of affection, a flare-up she forced herself to snuff out. She imagined how they might look to those few people sitting in the rows behind them. Nick and her with these identical birds inked onto the backs of their necks, midflight and gazing at each other anytime he stood on her right side, as he did now. Mirror images, bookends, the birds' once-vibrant golden hue as faded as the memory of the hot, sticky night she and Nick had stolen away from campus to get them together.

Over the years, she had considered having hers removed or morphed into some other design, but why should she? She liked it. At face value. Charlie sighed again, more loudly than intended, as her mind sped to how this summer would now be.

"Ms. Savoy, is there a problem?" the judge asked, irked.

"Your Honor, I just wondered—is there a littered park or something? Instead?"

"We're fine, Your Honor." Sam patted Charlie's arm in warning.

"Ms. Savoy will report to service June 1." The judge slammed the gavel, which, to Charlie, sounded like a nail being hammered into a coffin.

"I had a client last week who's cleaning restrooms at South Station this summer," Sam said apologetically as they walked out.

Charlie just charged ahead down the hall, an urgent need to escape, her mind struggling to process it all.

"So, craziest thing happened," Nick launched in, catching up to them at the elevator. "I was reading the news and saw about your little *mishap*—" He sounded truly concerned for a moment.

"Don't pretend like you don't have a Google alert on me," Charlie cut him off, stabbing the down button too many times.

"You always were a terrible driver—"

"That river came outta nowhere—"

"But a stellar swimmer—"

She nodded once. She couldn't argue with that.

He went on, "So I made a few calls and—"

"Don't be fooled by...*that*." She waved her hand back toward the courtroom. "You need me more than I need you."

The elevator opened.

"We'll see about that." He let them on first. Charlie hit the button again-again-again to close the doors, but he made it in. "How long has it been, anyway?"

"You know how long it's been," she said as the doors closed so she was now looking at their reflection. It had been six years, three months, two weeks and two days since they last saw each other. At the long-awaited premiere for *Midnight Daydream*— which should've been a thrilling night since a series of snags had pushed the film's release date back two years after filming. But instead of celebratory toasts, it had ended with a glass of the party's signature cocktail—a messy blackberry-infused bourbon concoction the shade of the night sky—being thrown. In retrospect, she thought, there'd been so many signs the movie was cursed.

"You're just mad your self-imposed exile is over." He smirked.

"Always with the probing psychoanalysis." She watched the floor numbers descend, doors finally opening.

Sam scurried out ahead of them. "My work here is done. I'm sure you two have a lot of catching up to do." She gave Charlie an air-kiss before striding off.

"Wait, no, I just need to—" Charlie tried to stop her, but Sam had already hopped in a cab.

"So, I have an office not too far, off Newbury Street, off-season headquarters for Chamberlain—" Nick started.

"Luckily you're usually phoning it in, so I haven't had the privilege of running into you around town." She walked ahead in the cool, pelting rain.

He stayed where he was. "I'd invite you out for a drink—"

"It's, like, 10 a.m. That's too early. Even for you—" She glanced back.

"Summer is gorgeous in the Berkshires, as you may recall," he shouted, sunglasses back on, absurdly, and that smile again. "Welcome back to Chamberlain, Charlie."

3

WELCOME TO CHAMBERLAIN

According to Sierra's official "Chamberlain Summer Shake-speare Theater Apprentice Program" electronic welcome packet, which she had committed to memory, the dorms opened on Monday, May 31 at 10 a.m., just a few moments ago. She had boarded the first bus from Boston to make.it. Yet as she now reached the third floor of Trinity Hall, the gothic fortress that would be her summer home, she felt she had arrived to a show already in progress.

Spirited chatter filled the hallways, that buzzy electricity of new beginnings that always made her queasy. The door of every room propped open, unpacking and instantaneous bonding underway. Her fellow apprentices greeted each other with hugs, comparing notes on where they'd come from. "NYU!"

"Columbia!"

"Vassar!"

"Yale!"

"Boston—BU!"

"Boston—BC!"

And where they were (eventually) going.

"NYC!"

"New York!"

"Off-off-off Broadway!"

"Hollywood, baby!"

At the very end of the narrow corridor, she found her room. Sierra pulled her dark hair from her messy ponytail, deep breath—*Let me be the first one here*—and peeked inside: a leggy blonde lay on one of the twin beds, talking on FaceTime. One half of the room was fully decorated: pictures, theater programs and show posters from NYU productions tacked to the walls; fluffy floor pillows set out; books on the shelves.

Sierra knocked and the blonde looked up from her screen. "Oh, I think my roommate might be here." She eyed Sierra up and down as a girl's voice on the other end signed off.

Sierra smiled cautiously, remained still, like in airport security lines when they pull you aside to wave that metal-detecting wand over you.

"Talk later, love ya," the blonde gushed at the screen, clicking off. She grinned now, as though assessing Sierra's threat level to be low: "Ohmagod, I've been *dying* to get off that call, thank you." She tossed her phone on her fuchsia comforter. "You must be Serena!" She bounced off the bed, slipped on strappy sandals. She wore jean shorts and a tank top.

"Right, sort of, it's Sierra, hi." She smiled, set her bag on the unclaimed bed.

"Sierra, totally, hi." The blonde shook her head, then surprised Sierra by embracing her. "Harlow. Hunter." She said her name like it should already mean something. "C'mon." She took Sierra's hand. "Let's go check out the competition."

"Welcome to Chamberlain." Nicholas Blunt, *himself*, stood at the center of the bare stage. Sierra sat beside Harlow, who had insisted on the front row, though it felt exceedingly close. "You are this summer's acting apprentices. Congrats. You are—" he glanced at the papers in his hand "—thirty, yes, thirty of the finest collegiate thespians from across the country." He rolled up the pages, folded muscular arms, looked out. "Listen, this summer is going to *move*—so fast it'll give you whiplash, every day is a work day here…"

"Nicholas is kind of hot for an older guy, right?" Harlow whispered, proposing it in the manner of a scientific hypothesis. "Like a hot dad on a CW show?"

"I think he's hotter than that," Sierra offered in the same hushed tone, watching him. He was probably mid-to-late forties, since he'd been just twenty-nine when he'd made *The Tempest*, but he seemed younger. "He's like a sexy HBO prestige drama, midlife-crisis-type of a guy." They returned their attention to his words.

"The professional company has three productions from late June through just after Labor Day on *this main stage*." He stomped the last words for emphasis, and Sierra sat straight up. "Name them. Alex—" He called on a boy a handful of seats down from them in the center of the front row.

"*Romeo and Juliet* opens at the end of June. *Midsummer Night's Dream*—July. *The Tempest*—August." Alex's crystal voice projected across the vast space.

Nicholas walked along the stage, stopping in front of them. "…and our four accomplished company members this summer. Name them—" He scanned their row as Sierra's stomach dropped, her throat too dry to produce words. This man had been nominated for an Oscar—how was she going to make it through the summer if she felt this nervous? "You—" He pointed at Harlow.

"Chase Embers, Matteo Denali, Danica Rainier and Charlie Savoy," Harlow answered, proud, fearless, with a gleaming smile.

Nodding in approval, Nicholas Blunt moved on. "*Romeo* opens here in three weeks," he said like a drill sergeant. "This year there's no break. The shows run back-to-back-to-back, which means rehearsing one show while performing another." A collective gasp broke out in the audience. "I know," he answered. "This will only affect most of you in terms of the backstage work. Mornings you're in drama workshop with Professor Bradford. Afternoons you're in your backstage concentration—set construction, lighting, costumes, props…"

"I'm props, you?" Harlow asked softly while Nicholas continued.

"Costumes." Sierra had grossly exaggerated how much she had helped her mom's alterations business at the family resort during off-season.

"I heard that's *a lot* of extra work," Harlow said, dismissive. Sierra just smiled, refocused her attention on the director.

"…so you'll also be called on for everything from picking up trash after shows to delivering food to actors at late-night rehearsals," Nicholas went on. "Assorted odd jobs."

"I'll deliver myself to Chase Embers's place for an odd job," Harlow whispered, which was something Sierra—and half of the room—might be *thinking* but would never say within earshot of Nicholas Blunt.

"I know we don't have to talk about professionalism," Nicholas said, as though he might've heard. Sierra froze, felt her eyes bulge. "Late afternoons and evenings are for *rehearsals*." He paused, giving everyone time to absorb that and to ascribe the full weight of their loftiest dreams onto him. "A select few of you may earn roles on the main stage with the professionals. But everyone's got a chance to get noticed. August 20. The culmination of your summer. This could be the most important date in your career."

August 20. Black Box Showcase. Auditions tomorrow. Sierra had the date burned in her cerebral cortex.

"Talent scouts, casting directors, New York theater, Boston theater are invited to the Black Box Showcase. This is the show put on entirely by you, the apprentices. The directing and writing apprentices will be at your auditions tomorrow. They're staging it. Three one-acts, interspersed with monologues. Every one of you will have a part. So, make us notice you tomorrow, be unforgettable." Nicholas nodded, as though this would be a breeze. "Someone in here might get an agent from it," Nicholas said gravely. "Or get cast in a professional show or be asked to audition for a film that will change your life—"

For a beat, Sierra forgot that this summer would be an artistic cage match and that she sat in a room of to-the-death competitors. Instead, she chose to feel hopeful. The key to stratospheric success lay here, in this building, somewhere. She just had to figure out how to seize it. She watched Nicholas Blunt, like he might telepathically impart these secrets to her.

"And, if that's not inspiring enough, we're taking a trip to New York to see *Abby's Road* on Broadway later this summer." Cheers erupted.

"It's the next *Hamilton*," Harlow oozed at Sierra, as though she didn't know.

"—the highly anticipated musical about Abigail Adams's

role shaping our nation. But first…" Nicholas quieted them down again. "In the spirit of crawling before you can walk, let's tour this place. Crawl out to the lobby and I'll meet you there."

They all rose to their feet and walked to the aisles, but Nicholas interrupted again. "I thought you guys were actors?" He smiled. "Let's see your best *crawl*." With that everyone dropped to all fours and made their way out. Some—like Alex, who shot by doing a quick crabwalk—more agile than others. Sierra instantly regretted wearing a jean skirt. She just hadn't anticipated much physicality today. Mind racing for a way to avoid flashing her peers, she got it: mimicking the swim stroke instead, she coursed ahead of the pack and was first out the door.

—

Afternoon sun blinding her, Sierra stood at the edge of the crowded football field, hand shielding her eyes in search of friendly faces. Her luck had run out. She had successfully made it through the game where the entire extended apprentice class (over one hundred in all, including her acting peers plus the directing, writing, backstage and front-of-house apprentices) organized themselves alphabetically by state (she was one of three people from Oregon, which seemed like solid representation) and a tug-of-war pitting Shakespeare tragedy lovers against comedy fans that had left her with rope burn.

Now Professor Tom Bradford, serious, joyless and wearing a tie, everything Nicholas Blunt was not, had ordered them all to pair up. It seemed a mathematical impossibility that Sierra should end up the odd one out. She had lost Harlow on the way over. Weren't there an even number of them? Yet everyone had instantly attached themselves like at every party she had ever gone to.

Snaking her way through the duos, she stopped near the

southwest corner of the field, one last full slow spin before giving up. But when she completed this rotation, like a planet locked in its axis, she suddenly found the sun.

His name was Robert, according to his preprinted name tag.

"Thank you," she said in relief. He had walked up while her back was turned. Professor Bradford barked something in the background.

"Ohhh no, what's goin' on here? This on the schedule?" Robert said to her, glancing over her head to assess the situation. Tall with dirty blond hair, he had a drawl she didn't expect. Some sort of tattoo peeked out below his T-shirt sleeve. She would've pegged him for set construction, anything demanding a requisite level of brawn, had she not remembered seeing him at the back of the auditorium when she "swam" out to the lobby. Plus, beneath his name it read "Acting."

"Yes," she answered, appreciating that he seemed nervous too. "It was under the euphemism 'All Apprentice Meet-Up.'"

He smiled, opened his mouth to speak, but Professor Bradford's voice boomed:

"Siiilence! Is golden! Look into your partner's eyes and tell them your story, why you're here, without *a single word*. Using ONLY movements! NO voices! Your partner will copy your actions. Take your time, allow them to keep pace, to understand your journey."

A hush quickly fell. Sierra gestured for Robert to go first. She had led a simplistic version of this mirror image game at the kids' theater project she launched last year with a couple drama-major friends, but doing this with peers set her nerves trembling.

Robert closed his eyes, opened them again, shook out his limbs and, as though remembering something, held up his index finger to wait. He peeled the name tag from his shirt, tore off the part that said Robert, crumpled it and tossed it over his shoulder, sticking back on the part with just his last name: Summit.

Was she supposed to follow? It felt bold and dramatic, so probably. She pulled hers off too, and he smiled, so she smiled.

4

WE'RE SUPPOSED TO LIKE IMPROV

Ethan hadn't meant for her to shred her name tag too (and before he had even read it; now he only had her last name: Suarez). It just frustrated him that his tag had his given name—Robert—and not the name he wanted to go by here—Ethan, his middle name—which he had clearly designated on his apprentice application as the name he preferred. It would be his stage name, mark the start of this new life. When they were allowed to talk again, he would explain this to this girl staring at him with kind eyes. Maybe he could make a joke about her "commitment" to the role in destroying her own name tag.

He ran his hand through his hair, tried to figure out what was worth sharing about himself. Oh, wait, but now *she* was running *her* hand through *her* hair—long and shiny, reflective, hickory hued. The gesture looked better when she did it. Her hands hid in her pockets now. Because he had put *his* hands back in *his* pockets, without realizing.

Tell her his story. He placed his hand on the top of his head, as though there was a wide-brimmed hat there, made a motion of taking it off, bowing in greeting. She did the same. He held his hand out horizontally, pointing to the bottom center of his palm—his best approximation of Texas—and then put his hand to his chest. *This is where I'm from for better or worse.* He had slowed his actions and she followed closely enough that it seemed they were, in fact, making these movements at the same time.

He swept his arm out, looking into the field now, then shook his head, shrugged in self-doubt. She did this along with him and he felt understood—which was the purpose of the exercise, but still, it rocked him.

And here was something else: it was a strange thing, Ethan discovered, to gaze steadily into someone's eyes, in complete silence, for this duration of time. To stare into these eyes, which were lighter than her hair—hazel, maybe?—for this long, it seemed impossible to *not* feel something. Maybe that made him a bad actor? Or maybe that made him a *method* actor? Method, sure, that sounded better. Or maybe it wasn't about him and was more about *her.* Which was something he thought he *shouldn't* think about because then he would forget to actually move. He forced his eyes away for a moment, to reset his "motivation," and found that the others seemed less mired in these concerns.

Over her right shoulder, several pairs were leading their partners through what appeared to be cardio work: running, jumping, spinning and finally bowing. Ethan was out of his league here.

Soft fingertips tapped his forearm, bringing him back: she looked at him gently, like waking him from a dream, as Bradford barked at them all to switch roles.

Ethan smiled, relinquishing control. Accepting it, she waved her greeting and showed where she was from on the map of her hand. (It looked to be roughly the Pacific Northwest.) She gestured across the field as he had before but then knelt on the turf, arms over her head like those photos of schoolkids during air-raid drills in the 1950s. After a beat, she sat upright again and shook her head, as though laughing at her fears. He did the same, and felt flattered and entranced by how her story echoed his.

—

"I'm Sierra," she said, as soon as Bradford wrapped the exercise with a classic "Annnnd scene."

"Ethan," he managed to tell her, shaking her hand, before the professor interrupted again. Sierra looked confused—understandably—glancing once more at the remaining half of his name tag, but follow-up questions would have to wait.

"Now! The main event!" Bradford stood on the bleachers. "I call it 'Man Walks into a Room.'" Ethan had been subjected to a version of this exercise enough times to be wary: someone is a host, others join the party, playing roles the crowd shouts out along with an object they're bringing. Sierra exhaled, as one might before scaling a rock wall. So Ethan felt emboldened.

"I know we're supposed to be people who like improv, because we're *here*," he said. All around them people were already shouting (*"Iguana!" "Taser!" "Genius Bar… Genius… Guy!" "Avocado toast!" "Beyoncé!"*). "And we're supposedly 'actors.'" He made quotes around the word. "But, I mean—"

"Yeah, it's not my thing either," she said, sounding relieved to admit this.

Ethan preferred studying a role, slowly absorbing it into his bloodstream. He watched, supportive as so many others threw themselves wildly into the fire. He wished he had that unbridled confidence. Maybe this summer would change him.

"My roommate seems to enjoy it though." Sierra pointed to a blonde hopping onto the bleachers who was instantly anointed "Marilyn Monroe with a chainsaw" by someone in the crowd.

"Sleep with one eye open," Ethan said sarcastically.

The game finally ended with twenty apprentices on the bleachers—none of them him or Sierra—all frozen in various states of zaniness.

—

"So before we go on, I need to know the truth. Who…is… *Robert…Summit*?" Sierra asked pseudo-dramatically, as they walked back en masse from the field, the sun a golden haze beyond the mountains.

"He's still figuring that out," Ethan said, speaking in third person. "But he goes by his middle name, Ethan. At least, when it comes to this kind of thing—acting." He felt a wave of shyness at the admission: he didn't quite feel he had enough theater credits to warrant this. But he had to start somewhere.

"Stage name, sure, I get it," she said, as they walked past restaurants and coffee shops filled with university summer students. "I have kind of an alter ego too. I'm really…an environmental science major." She said it in the lowered tone others might reserve for vocations like *assassin*.

"No, it's too much," he joked, putting his hands up. "We just met."

"I know," she said, cringing. "It's just, this is what I'd love to do." She gestured toward the theater ahead—the historic white-painted brick playhouse evoking a long-ago era with its stately columns and pointed pediment. "But it seems not necessarily, *practical*? I might not be good enough. So while I figure *that* out, I'll also be charting the return of an endangered plant. Don't suppose you heard about the rare chaffseed

THE SUMMER SET • 41

found in Cape Cod a couple years ago? Hadn't been seen in fifty years?" She laughed at herself.

"Uhhh, no." He smiled slowly. "No, I did not."

"Yeah, anyway," she said, sheepish now. "I'm writing my senior thesis on it—"

"Wellesley?" He pointed to the "esley" remaining on her name tag.

She nodded. "So you'll find me roaming Hopkins Forest in my free time and at the end of the summer I have to go to the Cape to check it out. Not exactly soul-awakening stuff..."

"I wouldn't say that..."

She gave him a skeptical look and they both smiled. "But it's the only way I got *funded* to come here," she said. "So it's for my parents, you know, sensible—"

"*That* I can understand. This place is my escape from the *family business*—" he started, infusing the words with a hint of terror.

"That sounds very *Sopranos*," she said.

"Nothing criminal, promise," he explained. "Dangerous but not criminal." They crossed Stratford, their group arriving at the lush gardens of the Quad, set with long tables bearing the necessary barbecue staples—burgers, hot dogs, corn on the cob—expertly arranged, a "Welcome Chamberlain Theater Apprentices!" banner strung between a pair of oak trees. "So, I'm a business major—"

"Harvard?" She glanced at his torn name tag as they reached the buffet line, the volume on the conversations around them dialing up now that the group had compressed.

"I'm a transfer student, so a misfit by definition," he said, self-deprecatingly. He handed her a plate as they made their way down the line. "But my family owns a rodeo. So the bull-riding aspect—"

"Wow, yeah, that qualifies as danger—"

"There you are!" Marilyn Monroe with a chainsaw appeared before them. "I've been looking everywhere for you!" She didn't let Sierra speak: "Harlow. Hunter," she introduced herself, grabbing his arm aggressively enough that he nearly fumbled his plate. "You're rooming with one of my dearest friends, Alex Xing?" she said. "We have a table over here, come!"

As Harlow pulled him away, Ethan caught Sierra's eye and jokingly grimaced.

5

NO SPOILERS

June came too soon, as Charlie knew it would. Though sleep remained elusive, she remained unmedicated but busy enough to avoid thinking about her Chamberlain sentence: so much work to do in order to leave her precious art house behind for two months. She had hired extra staff for the summer to aid Miles—though he seemed more concerned with *her*. *How do you and Nick Blunt plan to coexist for sixty days without murdering each other?* he'd asked her daily. *No spoilers*, she'd always reply, since she didn't actually know. Her relationship with Nick predated her friendship with Miles, but Miles had attended the infamous premiere, so Charlie imagined he had filled in the blanks with a cocktail of tasty gossip and fuzzy facts.

By the time Miles saw Charlie off at South Station though, he had settled into a forced optimism. (*There's no reason you can't enjoy the theater part of this. It's like going back to your roots,* he had encouraged, adding completely unsarcastically, *You have a lot to give*.)

As the bus pulled away, Charlie paged through her tattered copy of *Romeo and Juliet*. Nick had emailed, all business: Charlie, first up is Romeo and Juliet. I trust you're familiar. And then, Your accommodations… followed by an address. He signed it simply, Nicholas, which she found mildly obnoxious. He had worked hard to get *Nicholas* to stick. It was how he had introduced himself all those years ago, as a directing fellow at Chamberlain: *Nicholas*. She had looked him in the eye as she shook his hand firmly. *Really? I think you're a "Nick,"* she had told him. *You'll figure it out soon enough.* She was nineteen, he was twenty-five and speechless. From then on, she called him Nick.

It would be another four years until they made the film that would make them both. (It had been her idea to include his name in the title—*Who do I think I am?* he had asked.) Their actual romantic relationship would take up such a small sliver of her life—just about a year—a little longer if she counted the months he drifted away, lost in his work, distant in miles and in emotion just before their breakup, on a film set of all places. Still, their time together would leave a disproportionately deep mark. She stopped short of calling it a scar because too much of it had been…good.

—

When she finished reading, the bus had just reached those steep, curvy mountain roads she recalled from so long ago. Her thoughts took similar twists and turns to arrive at a place she didn't want to be: on the edge of fear. She had done enough Shakespeare to know what it required of a person. But she hadn't acted, at all, in years: What if it just wasn't *there*? What if it had atrophied like any muscle left unchallenged for too long?

Her breathing too rapid now, she closed her eyes, refocus-

ing. She had played Juliet a thousand times all over London—
the West End, the Globe. And on Broadway, and off Broadway
and off-off Broadway. She exhaled.

Just as fast a more horrific thought shook her: What if Nick
didn't want her for Juliet, but for…Juliet's *mother*? She could
technically *be* Juliet's mother. *But it's not like Juliet was ever really
played by a thirteen-year-old*, she told herself. This was theater—
you just had to *act* young enough. Plus, she looked far younger
than her thirty-nine years. She could do *wide-eyed* when necessary. But, no, even worse: What if she was supposed to be
Juliet's *nurse*? How humiliating was this community service
exercise supposed to *be*? She pulled her Red Sox cap down
farther and closed her eyes, tried to will herself to sleep. She
had been up all night. Again. Packing. Reading. Sketching.
Streaming the latest season of the only show she binged, *Terminal Earth ICU*. Distracting herself. Trying to.

> *On-screen you give the impression of this work being effortless,
> like something you could accomplish in your sleep. Or perhaps
> more akin to breathing: something vital and natural. Most of us
> drama students, I can safely say, will never ascend to that level.
> Which is why I have to ask: Please return to acting? Could
> you look past what reasons you might have had for leaving it?
> You're needed.*

That letter, from a drama student named Robert, drifted
into her thoughts. Somehow asking the same questions that
had kept her up at night for years. Her eyes flickered open
again.

They were nearing their destination, anyway. She could
tell by her favorite sign at the end of a gravel pit on the side
of the road: RUNAWAY TRUCK RAMP. She had asked
her mother back then, two decades ago, seated beside her in

the back of the sedan that had been sent to collect them from the airport, what the sign meant. *That's a device to aid trucks if they're having difficulty braking as they descend from the mountain*, her mother had said in her perfectly posh inflection, eyes not leaving her newspaper. Then added, *If only we had something like that for* you.

Another turn and the bus rattled into the town at last, home of Chamberlain College and the Chamberlain Shakespeare Summer Theater. It was all there still, nestled in this pocket surrounded by mountains: the gothic ivy-covered buildings, the charming Victorian houses, the lively main street, even that sweet little historic log cabin harkening back to the town's first settlers. The one she had broken into with Nick…

This had been a bad idea. On so many levels.

Sixty days. She just had to get through sixty days.

The bus slowed to a stop in front of the old inn. She pulled up her email from Nick, checking the unfamiliar address of her accommodations again. Mapping it on her phone, she followed the route past the inn, along Stratford Road onward through the campus's main quad, still not sure where she was being led.

6

YOU'VE DISTRACTED MS. SUAREZ

Sierra gazed into the harsh fluorescent-lit restroom mirror. She placed the fedora on her head with great care, tucked her chestnut tendrils up into it. Studied her reflection. Then she took the hat off again and chucked it at the wall. She did not belong here. And in a few minutes, everyone else would know that too. Why did she feel this way before every audition? *This* was why she was an environmental science major. She was unequivocally good at that. Didn't the world need more women who were good at science, anyway?

A knock rattled the door. "Is there a Sierra Suarez in there? You're up," came the stiff voice of one of the directing apprentices.

"Yes! Coming! Awesome!" she said. She could feel the butterflies now, the thrill of it! And then something else.

She darted back into the stall. Heaving. And threw up.

Sprinting out again, she glanced once more in the mirror.

"I. Am. Juliet." Kicked the hat up from the floor, gasping when it actually landed in her hands, and pushed through the doors, down the twisting labyrinth through the nearly pitch-black wings and on to the exact mathematical center of the stage. So many faces staring back at her.

"Sierra Suarez, reading for the role of Juliet," she told them. Then spun around, her back to the audience, deep breath, and slowly turned to face them again:

"'Shall I speak ill of him that is my husband?'" She quickly dissolved into the lights and the words until she wasn't quite there anymore.

——

Sierra couldn't remember what happened before Chase Embers—Chase. *Embers!*—burst through the door at the back of the theater and strutted up the aisle toward the directors, collecting all the eyes in the room.

The very fact that she couldn't remember anything meant that whatever *had* transpired between her first words as Juliet and Chase's entrance must have actually been very good. That was how it was if things were going well onstage: her mind knew the lines; her voice knew how to deliver them; her body knew how to feel them. An intersection of reflex, muscle memory, practice. The only time anything came easy.

But with that door opening, sunlight streaming in from the lobby and this divine creature, Chase Embers, slipping out of her fantasies and into her living-breathing reality, a switch flipped and she was aware of the world again. And once that spell was broken, she didn't know how to get it back. She was going to blow this audition.

Who could blame her though? Chase Embers wasn't someone you would ever be able to ignore. So untouchably beautiful it didn't even matter that that wasn't even his real name. She'd had a crush on him for as long as she'd had crushes. As did the whole world. That was how he had famously landed on the Forbes list as a teen. (She was an infant when he was a teen, but she knew every inch of his biography. He was honestly destined for greatness ever since making his film debut as a baby playing Denzel Washington's son in that thriller.) He was now thirty-seven but more gorgeous than ever, the build of an action hero (which he was), lit-from-within glow. It had been announced *after* she got the apprenticeship that he would be here—otherwise the competition to get in would've been even fiercer. She just wished he wasn't here at this particular moment.

"You've distracted Ms. Suarez," Nicholas Blunt said to Chase, loud enough for the room to hear and snicker at her expense.

She realized she had been not speaking for a horrifically long time. Just standing frozen on the stage.

"Ms. Suarez? When you're ready," Nicholas directed her. A few rows back, Chase grinned, talking to an apprentice. She couldn't see who.

"Right, sir." She had no idea where she had left off. Wait, she squinted in the lights, yes: Chase was speaking to Harlow, whose audition had been flawless. Best of the day, so far. Harlow had the confidence *and* the chops. Sierra wished she hadn't had to watch. Why did they have to audition in front of *everyone* like on one of those TV singing competitions? "I'll take it from the top." Sierra turned her back to the audience. She just couldn't remember where "the top" was. Head down, fists opening and closing, grasping for the words. The spotlight burned so hot, sweat trickled down her forehead. She faced front again, cheeks flushed. She knew *Romeo and Juliet* backward and forward. But now it was gone. *Say something! Anything! Preferably from this play!*

"'Tis torture and not mercy. Heaven is here…'" She knew

the minute she started that it was dead wrong. It was Romeo. But she gave in, went through with the whole thing. Then she exited stage left, through the wings, and kept walking until she got outside. Breathing in the sweet June air, sun coating her skin, mountains watching her from the distance, she managed not to cry. Eventually, she returned, through the lobby, listened at the doors for the monologuist to finish and slunk into the back of the orchestra. Just in time.

"Ethan Summit, reading for Mercutio," Ethan said in his faint twang, that same shyness he had on the field. But as soon as he began, he metamorphosed: voice modulated deeper, no trace of his country roots, posture straightened, eyes alive.

Engrossed, she watched, losing herself until a hand squeezed her shoulder, firm and quick: she looked up to see Chase Embers. Walking out the door. He gave her a salute and approving nod before disappearing beyond the theater. It took a few seconds for her to remember to breathe.

7

IF ONLY WE WERE DOING
THE TAMING OF THE SHREW!

When the theater doors crashed open, Ethan thought he might be hallucinating. He had only *just* wrangled his heart back from its breakneck beat, seizing it, slowing it down like he used to lasso wild calves as a kid. That was how this always felt to him: the stage.

"A FUCKING DORM?" a familiar voice shouted.

Ethan—and the entire audience—turned to discover Charlie Savoy stomping up the aisle, eyes set on Nicholas Blunt. Sierra grabbed Ethan's forearm in shock, as though watching the twist in a movie. Charlie passed by, a meteor blazing across Ethan's sky. She looked just as she had in his favorite film, *Midnight Daydream.* Same tangle of long, wavy hair, same red lipstick. He had seen her in person only once, despite weekly visits to her theater. He started going there *before* he knew she owned it, just for the movies you couldn't see anywhere else. But the day after her crash, he'd arrived early, as if staging a one-man vigil, to be sure she was okay, and had been relieved to spot her inside the glass doors.

"If only we were doing *The Taming of the Shrew*," the cos-tumer whispered too loudly to her fellow department heads seated onstage.

Ethan's anger flared. *Don't they know who Charlie is?* An Oscar nominee. An otherworldly talent. The force that had gotten him through high school. He would steal his dad's rusted-out Chevy pickup, make the hour-long drive every Saturday morning to that art house in Austin before his family was even awake, and he would see whatever was playing. *Midnight Daydream* had shown for almost two months straight. It broke his heart when it had finally left. That time had been precious. He could shed the social atrocities he had suffered at school that week and allow her film—about an insomniac outsider—to heal him.

"Seriously, Nick?!" She reached the front row, stepping onto the armrest of an occupied seat and climbing onstage with a graceful leap. This, all of it, was *exactly* what made Charlie exotic, fantastical, worthy of the sites clicked and ink spilled chronicling her.

"Let's take five," Blunt announced to the group. Charlie folded her arms, glared. "Ten, take ten." Then, to Charlie he said, *"You—"* and pointed, signaling for her to come with him. She threw her head back, annoyed. As Ethan watched them disappear offstage, he instantly knew he'd made the right choice declining the American Repertory Theater summer program to come here.

He just couldn't help but wonder what had happened to his letter. The one his friend Miles had insisted on passing along to Charlie. The one Miles said Charlie had never read.

8

PEOPLE FUCKING LOVE ME

Nick didn't want to have to physically turn around to confirm that Charlie was still following. That might show the cracks in his authority. So he simply kept walking out of the theater, into the lobby, down the photo-lined hallway—a who's who of Chamberlain alums—listening for the angry footsteps of her oxfords. Why was she *exactly* as he remembered? Why was he still possibly, probably, kind of, somewhat in love with her even after the irreparable damage she had caused his career? This was a bad idea. Could she tell he was nervous about this? Them? The whole summer?

When he reached his office, he noticed her clip-clop had stopped. He pivoted slowly, prepared to continue their argument in the hallway if necessary. But when he saw what had captured Charlie's attention, he granted her a moment. The theater complex had been redone in the two decades since she had performed here. A gallery of glossy framed photographs now lined the corridor leading to the staff offices: so many accomplished actors on the Chamberlain stage through the years. Their names, shows, engraved in small golden plaques. Their own Walk of Fame. She stood before one of the photos, transfixed. This picture had been blown up nearly poster-size and placed at the center of one wall, anchoring a solar system of smaller photos that orbited it. It showed Charlie, just nineteen, onstage beside her mother in *Much Ado about Nothing*. Both so young, joyful. A celestial glow in the stage lights. That was *that* summer, when Nick had met her.

Only a few paces away from where Charlie stood hung another time capsule. Nick paused before this other photo. He had walked past it every day since arriving a month ago, but hadn't really looked at it. Snapped that same summer, at the opening night party for *Much Ado*, it showed Nick smiling proudly beside his since-departed mentor, Grayson Crestway, world-renowned director and founder of the Chamberlain Summer Theater. The man who had left the theater in Nick's care. That mighty responsibility weighed heavy in Nick's heart, more now than ever.

So ensnared was Nick that he didn't realize when Charlie arrived beside him, gazing at the same portrait. Neither said a word. After a moment, Nick nodded, then moved on toward his office. Charlie followed this time.

"So, now that it's just…us—" Nick sat at his neatly ordered desk, straightened a stack of scripts.

"Look—" she said, not letting him finish. She leaned against the wall. "You know I'm not like that."

He slouched in his chair, trying to appear cool. Trying to *not* keep thinking about that long-ago summer.

"I just want to be treated like everyone else. The actors. I know they're not rooming with apprentices. This place was Airbnb before Airbnb was invented."

He listened as though they were in another courtroom, but he was the judge.

"And yes." She rolled her eyes. "When I was here before I *did* want to be in the dorms, but that's because I wanted to be treated like everyone…then…too. My…peers, or whatever. Which went…not very well, in retrospect, I guess."

He remembered: she had literally been the definition of peerless. An accomplished stage actress at nineteen, here as part of the professional company when the other nineteen-year-olds in the program were students with credits in college shows.

"Are you going to actually say something?" she asked, pulling him from his thoughts. "Or am I doing a one-woman show over here?"

"Right, no." He click-click-clicked his pen. "Listen, if you think you can get along with your castmates——" He cleared his throat.

"People fucking love me," she cut him off.

"If you *think* you can get *along* with your *castmates*," he repeated, scribbling down an address on his personalized stationery. "Then there's a spare room here." He slid the paper across the desk, trying not to smile, then sifted through a drawer.

She grabbed the paper, glanced at it. "Really?" she asked, registering the address. "Is this the same—?"

"Same place. It's still where the company stays." It was indeed the same house where her mother had stayed all those years ago, and she had too—once she got the dorms out of her system. "Your castle awaits." He tossed a set of keys at her— which she caught in one hand—then leaned back in his chair, feet on his desk, pretending to look over notes.

"So you were…always planning? You were just kidding? With the dorm."

He glanced up. She was smiling coyly, hands on her hips.

"Well, look who's gone and gotten himself a sense of humor," she said.

"You're welcome," he said to his notes.

"Thank you." She opened the door to leave.

"Listen," he said, stopping her. "I've got a pack of wild baby thespians to tend to—" he checked his watch "—so go now, but we're not...finished here." He said it with an ease he was proud of. It was obviously an epic understatement. "Dinner, later this week or something?"

"Fine," she said, like it was another sentencing. She started to pull the door shut behind her, but tossed out, "We can talk about how incredibly boring it is that you're doing *Romeo and Juliet*." The door closed.

"Hey!" he called out. "People love *Romeo and Juliet*!" She opened the door, and he continued. "You're the only person in the history of the theater who thinks *Romeo and Juliet* is boring."

"I'm sure that's not true," she said, closing the door as she left, again.

"Don't start with me!" he called out.

She opened the door again and said, "I don't mean boring—Shakespeare was revolutionary in his day, I get it, I'm down. I just mean that I suspect what you, specifically, have planned is excruciatingly boring—"

"Charlie," he cut her off with an exasperated sigh.

"I'm going now." She closed the door yet again.

"Goodbye," he said.

She opened it fast. "We're gonna have to talk about those casting choices." And shut it once more.

"I haven't even told you about the casting!" he shouted through the closed door. Two quick knocks and it opened again, slowly. His heart revved involuntarily. "So we're knock-

ing now, how—" He stopped when he saw his septuagenar-
ian volunteer box office manager, Mary, appear. "Civilized."

"Did you misplace a troupe of young actors, Mr. Blunt?"
Mary asked brightly.

"Oh. Right." He shook his head, gathered his notebook,
the remnants of his iced coffee. His phone rang again. Another familiar number. "I've just gotta—"

"I was hoping Charlie would be in here," Mary said, mischievous.

"Nicholas Blunt here, great to hear from you," he answered
the call. "Tell 'em I'll be right there," he whispered to Mary,
who nodded and let herself out. "No, this is a great time," he
said, sitting down again. "Especially if you've got good news
which—"

He had a splitting headache now and rummaged through
his desk drawer. "Really? Because we've sold out the entire run
already for the first—" he found Tylenol but wished for something more, like Vicodin "—I believe there's no greater proof
that what we're doing is innovative and... Stunt casting?...
That demeans the artistic foundation this theater was built on,
I'm shocked to hear that..." He had actually heard this before.
"We're an award-winning regional..." He squeezed his eyes
shut, kneaded his forehead. "No, the 'glory days' are happening *now*... I'm sorry you feel that way, that couldn't be farther
from the truth...and I respectfully rescind your invitation to
invest in the Chamberlain." He tossed his phone at the door.

9

THE BALCONY IS A GAME CHANGER

Duffel bag slung over her shoulder, Charlie wandered Warwick-shire Way, the main drag with its many new storefronts—yoga and Pilates studios, a day spa, bars, eateries, boutiques—hanging a left on leafy Avon Road, and there it was.

The storybook Victorian home, all turrets and decorative trim. She could feel the house's history but note its transformation: fresh paint, new windows, the crow's nest restored. The once-warped wraparound porch mended, shellacked in an earthy jade hue. A new glider hung there, which likely wouldn't squeak like the old one used to when she sat there with Nick.

As she had walked toward the stage earlier that day, Nick had shape-shifted into that boy she had first met, the aspiring director in Converse shoes, T-shirt, jeans. He was less muscu-lar then, more clean-shaven, his hair wet from an early swim at the lake. Script tucked under his arm, hope in his chest, dreams of making a name for himself.

The front door opened, and on reflex, she darted to the side of the house. To cover, she pulled out her phone, scrolling through texts. From the shadow of a craggy oak, she watched one of her roommates strutting in joggers and a tight T-shirt, yoga mat bag on his fully inked arm: Chase Embers. She groaned, involuntarily, audibly. Luckily, his earbuds were in. He glanced side to side, as though waiting to be noticed, like a heartthrob rolling into the cafeteria in a movie about prom hijinks. He had starred in several of those—and then the dark, paranormal one with Charlie, which had actually been good—before playing a drug-addled college kid in that gritty festival-circuit film everyone loved, his breakout several years ago.

Charlie had slept with him exactly once—at the end of their film shoot—caught up in the finality of it all, young, foolish, drunk and too immersed in their lovesick characters for their own good.

She tapped out a WhatsApp, You'll never guess where I'm staying, and snapped a photo of the porch swing. Everything is the same here, fixed-up, but the same. xx.

Her mother responded instantly: A lot of good memories there, Charlie. This is the first thing you've done in ages that makes any sense. Perhaps this will inspire nostalgia for another relic of the past: home. London is no farther than Los Angeles. It's been quite some time since your passport was stamped. You are always welcome with open arms. Give Chamberlain my regards and don't waste this time, it's a gift. Take good care, will you? Love, Mum.

Always a lacing of guilt to any exchange with her mom. She couldn't exactly hop on a flight anytime soon.

I'll send more photos and let you know how—

"Charlie Savoy," a woman's voice interrupted her text.

Charlie jumped, turned to find a familiar figure at the side entrance. "Danica Rainier," Charlie greeted her.

"Haven't seen you in years," Danica said with no particular warmth. She leaned against the doorframe, long blond hair and maxidress blowing in the breeze, gauzy scarf at her neck. Perfect minimal makeup. She had always been otherworldly beautiful, like the kind of doll psychologists urged young girls not to play with because it would stealthily destroy their self-esteem. Even now, when she had to be fifty or close to it, she still safely qualified as an ethereal goddess. She had enjoyed a brief tenure as America's Sweetheart thanks to two highly successful rom-coms in the early '90s, which still showed somewhere on basic cable nearly every weekend, and that old series enjoying a streaming renaissance thanks to millennials. "I was beginning to wonder whatever happened to you," Danica said in monotone, taking a slow sip from the mug of hot tea in her hands. "I thought you died."

"Glad to be back, from the dead, or wherever," Charlie said, hopping up the steps to the side door, and breezing past Danica into the house. "Not bad here."

Inside, the grand winding staircase was still there, but the hardwood flooring had been redone in a rich chocolate. Walls had been knocked out, opening up the kitchen, dining area and living room. Down the hall, she found the ground-floor bedroom claimed.

"That's Matteo's," Danica reported. "He likes to be near the kitchen—he pretends the entire first floor is his and we're his guests."

"Sounds like him," Charlie said, comforted to know her old

friend would be there. She made her way up the steps lined with framed programs of past shows.

"Your room is the next floor up. I'm on top!" Danica shouted. "Top floor is me!"

Charlie sighed. "Got it!" she called down.

Beside a cluster of vintage Chamberlain posters, she found her floormate's room: bay window, king-size bed, fluffy comforter. Everything immaculate and in place. Very Chase.

She found her own room across from Chase's. She unzipped her duffel, opened the deep top dresser drawer and emptied her bag, pulling out a handful of books and tossing them on the bed, that letter shoved into one like a dagger.

The smallest room in the house, the space had been further cramped by the addition of a spiral staircase leading to a hatch in the ceiling. She pulled out her phone—intending to dash off a snarky text to Nick, comparing this to the dorm she had vacated—but noticed something on one of the steps: a leather-bound copy of *Romeo and Juliet*.

Nick's stationery, clipped to the cover, read: "Before I hear any complaints, you've got a balcony, Juliet." Signed simply "—Nicholas."

Only a few words, but such relief. So she *was* going to be Juliet. She wished it didn't matter, but it did. It meant something that a role like that could still be hers after all this time. She had been hedging her bets in Nick's office, trying to appear like she didn't care. She hoped she had fooled him, hoped he'd read her attitude as confidence.

Climbing the metal coil now, she pushed open the hatch and poked her head up into the late-afternoon sun. The crow's nest, wide enough to fit two people max, offered a perfect view of bustling Warwickshire Way. This escape made it worth having the small room. She felt in line with the mountains surrounding the town, even though they were still much higher. Her body eased, she closed her eyes, let the sun warm her. Then, renewed, she decided to make an effort.

The balcony is a game changer. You're lucky, she texted Nick. The response came immediately: Is that actually a thank you?

Before Charlie could debate whether to write back, a familiar bass voice rang from below: "Hi, honey, I'm hooome!"

10

EVERYONE WHO'S ANYONE WAITED TABLES

"Wait, do you live here too?" Ethan joked as soon as Sierra opened the door to her room. Even though she had unpacked, it still resembled a shrine to Harlow.

"I like to keep a low profile." She rolled her eyes.

"Hang on." He leaned down to study the framed photo on the desk of her surrounded by the kids she taught in her theater program and then grabbed the picture beside it. "I found evidence of your existence." He was quiet for a moment. "So *that's* home?"

She looked over his shoulder at the shot of her standing on the open-air top floor of the grandest tree house at her family's resort. Four stories, winding staircases, twinkling lights and a swinging bridge connecting it to a smaller guesthouse. "Not *home* home, just the resort my family owns." She laughed.

"We live in, like, a normal house. But I've heard every Swiss Family Robinson analogy," she said, taking her *Romeo* copy from her desk, holding it up. "Okay, who's first?"

They had declared each other scene partners (almost by default since Harlow and Alex had paired off) after spending the afternoon in the set workshop (him) and the costume shop (her). But now, surveying the artifacts of Harlow's stage prowess, she knew this wasn't going to work.

"Wanna—" she started. He looked up from his book.

"Get outta here?" he finished.

They found a shady spot on the Quad instead. Bradford had tasked each pair with switching audition monologues, coaching each other and performing them the next day. Midway through Mercutio's speech, she caught Ethan peeking at his watch.

"I know what you're thinking—you don't. Want. This. To. End. It's that good," she kidded, secretly embarrassed that she couldn't hold his attention.

"No, it's not you, it really *is* me—" He threw his arms up, in apology. "I have work in fourteen minutes."

"Oh." Relieved, she sat beside him. "Well, that's plenty of time for me to die and you to…live," she said, referring to their soliloquies.

"Is this really living though?"

"Is this still about the play or philosophically speaking?"

"I want to be in the moment, doing what I want to do."

"Okay…" She tried to follow. "You can go first—"

"But everything is a thousand times harder because I'm not doing what my family wants, not working for them." He patted the tattoo on his arm, which she could see now was a mechanical bull. "So I'm cut off, even though I created this merchandising offshoot that actually became profitable for them—"

"I'm getting the business-major vibes now," she said, nodding.

"So in between classes and auditions and set construction and rehearsals, I have to be at Poets & Pints," he sighed, ruffling the back of his hair, frustrated. "Sorry." He watched a group playing soccer across the way. "A long way of saying your thesis is looking pretty good to me right now." He picked a blade of grass and tossed it away.

"Sure, my thesis may seem sexy," she joked, and he suppressed a smile. "But you're the one who really has the right idea: everyone who's anyone waited tables, right? That's a well-paved path to success in the acting field." He shook his head, almost laughing. "And, by the way, you were pretty revelatory in your audition, so there's that too."

"This place is kind of intense, already, right?" he asked, like it was something not to be admitted out loud.

"Um, yeah. Have you met our roommates?" She checked her phone. "Not to be a downer, but we've got a solid nine minutes. Put me to shame as Romeo and then get out of here." He smiled, appreciative. She didn't mind tackling Mercutio on her own. She'd need more than a few minutes to stage her redemption, anyway.

11

IT MIGHT BE A
MONTAGUE-CAPULET-LEVEL SHOWDOWN

Charlie heard the bickering before she reached the kitchen, and it made her smile.

"…and even the market is more robust this year," the honey-smooth voice said. "Check out these tomatoes!"

"Matteo, do not make that lasagna," Danica scolded. "I'm not eating that, I told you. Every summer you do this to me."

"Dan, honey, if it wasn't for me you would *never* have any fun."

"Or any carbs."

Matteo Denali—summertime personified in his straw hat, rolled-up khakis and crisp short-sleeve linen button-down—unpacked overflowing burlap grocery bags as Charlie poked her head into the doorway.

"One more for dinner?" she asked.

"Charlie Savoy!" he bellowed as though announcing a winning game show contestant, lighting up with a wide grin. "Get over here, you!"

"If I'd known *you* were gonna be here, I wouldn't've needed a judge to send me," she said as he gave the kind of crushing hug that always made everything alright. She had forgotten that.

"Nick said you were moving in but, you know..." He didn't finish, just swatted the air, as though not wanting to bring him up so soon. Danica skulked off like a third wheel.

"Has it really been since—?" Charlie started.

"The year of *The Tempest*," he said, confirming. "Too long." They hadn't seen each other since he had starred as the sorcerer Prospero in the film and together they had been nominated for just about every award. He as lead, her as supporting. They drank champagne for months, that heady awards season buzz felt never-ending, and then went off in opposite directions, something you didn't think was ever going to happen while in the thick of all that celebration. "Chop these while you tell me what you've been up to." He tossed two tomatoes and she caught them.

"I don't sous-chef for just anyone," she laughed, recalling days of helping him in this very kitchen all those years ago, her first summer here. When she'd met him he was a soap opera heartthrob. He had to be, what, fifty...four now? But his presence felt as youthful as ever; he seemed not to age. Same boundless energy, same smooth skin, same shining eyes, same kindness and same devotion to the place that had helped him get his start. He still returned to the Chamberlain nearly every summer, despite having his own theater out west and a film career.

"We need you here," he said, slapping her shoulder. "And not just for your knife skills."

—

When Chase returned, the four of them gathered around the marble dining table—their spirit as lively as a chain restaurant commercial—feasting on Matteo's signature lasagna as Charlie's three housemates gave monologues on their recent credits and degrees of separation from each other. ("Charlie and I battled demons back in the day," Chase explained to Danica, referring to their teen movie. To which Danica replied, "Wait, are we talking about real life?")

Charlie felt her defenses rise up, waiting for inevitable questions about her accident, how she had been drafted into coming here, but to her housemates' credit, those questions never came. By the time they cleared the table, Danica (who had indeed sampled the lasagna) following Chase into the kitchen, Charlie had begun to feel at ease.

Matteo watched them go and then whispered, "So you and Nick? Things are cool now? Or cool enough?"

Charlie didn't mind this from him. Matteo occupied almost a paternal place in her heart. Maybe it had something to do with Matteo playing a young Miles Davis in one of his first films and Charlie's own estranged father, a jazz trumpet player, being hailed as the next Miles Davis when he began his career. That had been enough for her to always consider Matteo family.

She wanted to tell him that being back felt like crashing through the atmosphere of a distant, potentially hostile planet. But Danica returned before Charlie could answer, so instead she said lightly, "It might be a Montague-Capulet-level showdown, but we'll try to keep the bloodshed to a minimum."

12

SEE, I TOLD YOU: REVELATORY!

Wandering over from the cafeteria after breakfast the following morning with her fellow apprentices at nine o'clock SHARP—when the list was to be posted—Sierra couldn't take the charade of it all, knowing that within minutes of crowding around that terrible sheet of paper taped to the theater doors, they would no longer be equals.

She'd scored some solid roles at Wellesley, launched that theater workshop for at-risk kids in Boston, accomplishments she was proud of. But she still felt her most successful acting jobs were often just *acting* like she was okay with her many rejections.

By the time she made her way to the front of that buzzing, jostling pack, she was almost entirely unsurprised by what she saw. Beneath the heading, "Apprentices Selected for *Romeo and Juliet*," three names she knew—Harlow Hunter, Ethan Summit, Alexander Xing—and four additional apprentices, none of whom was her.

Sierra knew the drill: recover from the sting of public humiliation in a flash; reset; appear joyous for everyone else.

She hugged a squealing Harlow, or, actually, Harlow hugged *her* and everyone in her general vicinity, preemptively accepting congratulatory wishes. But Sierra was most anxious to find Ethan—he had skipped breakfast, texted that he had closed the pub last night and needed the sleep. She pulled out her phone, snapped a shot of the list, genuinely excited for him. So much so that it took a beat before she thought to worry: What if he got sucked into this new crowd?

On her way to seek out that *other* list, the one guaranteed to include her name—along with the other twenty-two apprentices left out of *Romeo and Juliet*—she texted: See, I told you: revelatory! and added a happy face emoji, theater masks and clapping hands and clapping hands and clapping hands again.

Just around the corner, through the doors to the backstage area, was the cast list for the Black Box productions. The Chamberlain's experimental, no-frills theater resembled, as advertised, the inside of a black box, with folding chairs for seats and a stage raised just a foot off the ground. *Sierra Suarez* was listed alongside someone named Tripp in something called *The Bachelorettes of Shakespeare: A (Sort-Of) Revival* directed by an apprentice named Fiona. Sierra wanted to be excited, feel a burning passion to give it her all and make everyone sorry they hadn't put her on the main stage. But she felt deflated.

"What the fuck is *Bachelorettes of Shakespeare*?" a voice behind her said, with mild disgust. She turned to find a tall, trim, excessively pretty boy—skinny seersucker pants, fitted T-shirt—the type who could be cast on a Bravo reality show where everyone's gorgeous and spends their time doting on tiny pets, planning elaborate birthday parties and getting in fights about nothing.

"I'm Sierra. Are you—?"

"Tripp, hi." He shook her hand. "And yes, it's Tripp as in triple roman numerals." He rolled his eyes self-deprecatingly. "But I'm *not* like that Blueblood bullshit. I'm a heart-of-gold type, you know? Fled the East Coast prep world for Oberlin even though my family is *nearly* disowning me for it. This *Bachelorettes* business has *got* to get me some cred or an agent or at least a boyfriend. Nice to meet you." He exhaled as though that was all something he needed to get off his chest.

"At least it's a two-hander," she said, attempting optimism. There was a small victory in their play being just the two of them.

"But look at these lucky bitches." Tripp pointed to the bottom of the list: under the category "Monologues" were the same seven apprentices who had been cast in *Romeo and Juliet*. He stormed off toward the rehearsal studio for their drama workshop.

"That's actually a good thing," she said, following. "Then they aren't taking Black Box roles from—"

"From those of us who may *never* get on the main stage all summer?" Tripp finished her thought.

"'No small parts, only small actors'…?" She quoted the famous line.

He sighed as she held open the studio door for him. He halted a moment, looked at her. "I swear I'm not always this moody. I already feel a total old Hollywood Rock Hudson/ Doris Day vibe with you, which is my *highest* compliment." He walked in ahead of her and she felt like this might actually be okay.

—

Nick was in one of his vortexes, second-guessing every little thing. Phone to his ear as another potential investor droned

on, Nick studied the table on the empty stage. Under the hot
lights, he wiped his perspiring forehead with his shirtsleeve.

"Well, I would respectfully disagree," he said into the phone.
"I'd argue this is exactly the time to take that chance. We sold
out the run when Chase Embers alone signed on. Then we
added Charlie Savoy and we added shows to the schedule. It's
unprecedented." He squinted; maybe they didn't need the lights
for this rehearsal. "Well, if only we could run the theater on
ticket sales alone, but it requires more than that to provide this
level of entertainment." He reordered the scripts, setting them
at different spots on the long table. He was sick of listening to
his own sales pitch. And also slightly terrified that the season
wouldn't live up to it.

The past six seasons—since he had taken over—had grown
more lackluster each year, if he was being honest. He knew the
common denominator was him. He hadn't even shown up last
summer, leaving the directing apprentices, Bradford and an ad-
junct Chamberlain professor to stage the entire season. At the
time, he honestly had felt like he wouldn't have done any better
than they did. He had begun writing yet another screenplay,
in hopes that it would mark his return to film at last. But the
road back had been so long—and riddled with so many dead
ends, cliffs and pits of quicksand. He felt like roadkill.

"Yes, we have some incredible corporations about to sign
on as top-tier patrons. I just can't share that information until
the ink is dry—" he lied. Though he was trying, no one was
even close to signing. "Yes, *The Tempest* will cap the season,
and I couldn't be more thrilled to reimagine it for the stage so
many years after my film. In some ways it's a reunion. We'll
have Matteo Denali… And Charlie Savoy? Well, I'm sure—"
That was another lie; Charlie's sixty days would be up by then.
"Oh, Sarah Rose Kingsbury, well, that would also be fantastic, wouldn't it? You'll be the first to know," he said, anxious

to stop the flood of untruths. "Let me know as soon as you can." He hung up, shuffled the scripts again, trying to distract himself from the fact that the theater would actually run out of money before *The Tempest*, the most highly anticipated show of the season. If a high-rolling donor didn't come through in time, they had only enough in the reserves to make it through the first two plays. He had exhausted every other scenario beyond sacks of cash dropping from the sky.

And while he waited for that miracle, he still had a first rehearsal of *Romeo and Juliet* to set up. Even that felt like a challenge. The names scrawled in Sharpie on each script no longer looked like words, but resembled abstract art, graffiti tags, hieroglyphs. He had now inadvertently set himself at the head of the table and Charlie at the foot, which looked too much like a dinner party thrown by the two of them. Too much like a scene that had actually happened, years ago, when they had that apartment in New York even though Charlie could never cook worth a damn and they all ended up ordering Chinese instead. And still it was the best dinner party any of them had ever been to, because it was that heady year when they traveled the world, premiering their movie and collecting awards, and he and Charlie were magic.

He walked offstage to the fly rail and kicked the back wall. He was reading too much into this seating arrangement. He grabbed the bottles of water, slammed one down at each spot along the table. So, maybe he wasn't a guy who could let things go. He switched Charlie's seat with Matteo's, placing the most esteemed cast member at the foot of the table. Yes, that made sense, and as an added bonus, he wouldn't have to look at Charlie and her electric-green eyes the entire time.

⁓

Nick found himself drifting during the read-through. He had forgotten how Charlie's voice, its timbre and tone on something like this, Shakespeare, could transform. It was elastic and alive, no trace of the barbs and bite marring her offstage interaction with him. More than a few times, he got lost in her lines, let them wrap around him—the way he imagined a pleased audience would. But he wouldn't permit his gaze to stray from the printed page. When he harnessed the courage, briefly, during one of the final scenes between Juliet and her nurse, he found Charlie—who had arrived ten minutes late, testy, climbing on the seats again—looking at him, *through* him, with those penetrating eyes, slouching, arms folded.

Her script *closed.*

She had been doing this all *from memory.*

His body processed that discovery as a surging heartbeat. And a rare feeling that he had done something right, for this place, by bringing her here.

13

HE DOESN'T BOTHER WITH
TYPES ANYMORE

The sun had just begun to set, the sky a perfect fiery haze that reminded Ethan of home, in a good way. Baseball games on the giant flat screens at Poets & Pints, happy hour in full swing, Ethan shot out of the kitchen, oversize bowl in hand, just as Charlie Savoy walked through the front door, followed by Matteo Denali and Danica Rainier.

And he promptly dropped Chase Embers's grilled salmon salad—dressing on the side, extra salmon, hold the croutons—onto the floor. He crouched down to scoop the greens back into the bowl (a challenge, this salad being particularly well chopped), as the trio walked past him to their costar. Chase had arrived minutes before, calling in his order on the way, then settled into the reserved table by the glass wall, as though on display to passersby, the best advertising any restaurant could hope for. There he sipped his iced tea, tapped away on his phone and looked up often enough to catch any eyes on him.

Ethan rushed Chase's replacement salad, took a deep breath and counseled himself, *Get back on that fucking horse.* What he always said even though the metaphor was fraught for him. He hadn't been on a horse since the first time he was bucked off—at age twelve—and vowed never to get on one again. During rehearsal he just sat at the end of the table with six other apprentices, he read his part, stayed in his lane. This would be the most interaction he had with the professional company so far and it was freaking him out.

He grabbed a pitcher of water and set off to their table, wondering if every day would be like this. Would the entire summer feel like one of those zoo parks where you drive through and the animals can walk right up to your car and lick the windshield, and you're supposed to play it cool even if they could actually eat you alive?

The four of them were all talking, and Ethan wished he could just stand there and listen, but unfortunately that wasn't his job.

"I'm Ethan. What can I get for you?" he introduced himself— mostly just to Matteo Denali, who, despite being a legend, ranked as the least intimidating. Ethan couldn't bring himself to look at the others, even as he filled their water glasses. He set the pitcher down and stared at his notepad, waiting for orders.

"I feel like I know you from somewhere?" Charlie said. Ethan didn't realize she was talking to him, until he finally glanced up to find her smiling at him.

"Oh, me?" he asked, embarrassed. "Probably, I guess, from… rehearsal? I wasn't wearing this…" He gestured to his burgundy Poets & Pints T-shirt. He felt like an idiot.

"It's Mercutio," Matteo said. "Nice work today."

"Yeah, I know, give me a little credit," she laughed at Matteo. "I guess that's it," she said, unconvinced, looking into Ethan's eyes in a way that made him wonder if she recognized him from her theater, even though he had only ever seen her there once from a distance. "Anyway—" she shook her head "—Mercutio is always the fan favorite, so lucky you. Own it, you know?"

All Ethan could do was nod, dazed. "Yes, absolutely," he said earnestly.

"I'll have the salmon salad too." Danica, who had not been paying attention, closed her menu. "And lemon for this." She pointed to her water. "Thinly sliced!"

—

Ethan realized he was *maybe* overattentive throughout their meal: refilling water glasses that were already nearly over-flowing; comping dessert despite being pretty sure he didn't have the authority to do that. And the rest of the time, he couldn't resist studying them from afar: Danica—whose hit sitcom had run for nearly a *decade*—was too stunning to be flirting so strenuously with someone like Chase. And Chase, not minding the attention, still kept an eye on the window and the many girls walking by. And Matteo and Charlie, so secretive in the way of actual, true friends. They ordered cheeseburgers—which felt so *human*—and occupied their own bubble, speaking in a low volume. Ethan happened upon only tiny fragments, but what he did hear fascinated him.

"Whatever, Nick canceled, no big deal," she said, dismissive.

"In his defense he's got a lot going on with this place," Matteo said.

"I texted this back." She held out her phone for Matteo to read, which he did aloud.

"'Never was there a story of more woe,'" Matteo laughed. Ethan recognized it as the last line of *Romeo and Juliet*.

—

As they left Poets, the others debating their next stop ("No, Matteo, we don't need ice cream, we need *wine*," Danica argued), Charlie breathed in the warm evening air, resetting her pulse to this new place.

Chase slowed to Charlie's pace. "I bet your vote is for music, like me," he said, in the way of someone who knew you when you were a different you. "Did you bring your sticks?" He beat the air as though at a drum kit.

"I'm a little rusty," she said.

But as they passed King's, Charlie halted, her gaze snagged on something—some*one*—in the window: Nick. Seated across from a woman.

The glass wall of the restaurant was set many yards back from their spot on the sidewalk, separated by the expansive and bustling outdoor lounge, plenty of camouflage.

Danica stopped beside Charlie, followed her line of vision. "That's funny," Danica said, watching the window—the couple's candlelit high-top table, bottle of wine—then looking Charlie up and down, as though in clear comparison. "She doesn't look like his type."

"I'm pretty sure he doesn't bother with types anymore," Charlie managed in a perfectly neutral tone.

Danica was right though: professional and formal, this woman definitely wasn't in the theater world. She wore a silk sheath dress, matching blazer draped on the back of her chair, defined arms and delicate hands leaning on the table, sleek golden hair. She looked to be Charlie's age but resembled an actual *adult*, who paid bills on time, had a healthy 401(k), knew how to cook, wore chunky statement necklaces. A sexy, successful business type—maybe real estate or investment banking, any kind of numbers-driven world that Charlie found vaguely intimidating.

"Men are literally The. Worst," Danica went on. "That's why I don't date them anymore." She said it entirely blasé, then walked on.

After a final glance to see Nick filling his leggy companion's glass, Charlie set off in the opposite direction. Her body knew where it needed to be.

As she walked to the end of Warwickshire and crossed over, passing the soccer field, she checked her phone and found a text from hours earlier from Nick, responding to her line from *Romeo and Juliet*: off-book already? i'm impressed.

His text disappointed her. *She* had disappointed *herself*. She had to remember to maintain her detachment. That was the most important performance she could give.

⸺

Ethan slung the last of the trash bags into the overflowing dumpster behind the pub and checked his watch—11:45 p.m.— when something caught his eye in the distance. Nearly all the storefronts lay dark on Warwickshire, bookended by the late-night crowd at the bar near Avon and a small group closing down King's. The figure cut through the back alleys. A woman entirely soaked from her long dark hair to her shoes leaving wet footprints glistening on the pavement.

If he wasn't mistaken, it was Charlie Savoy.

14

DO ME A FAVOR, DON'T GET ANY IDEAS

"...And I need final headshots by Monday!" Nick called out as the cast dispersed after rehearsal. Charlie had leaped down from the stage and was already halfway up the aisle when her name flew from Nick's mouth.

"Charlie!" he shouted. She stopped in the aisle, turned to face him. "King's. Tonight?" He hadn't thought it through, but they needed to talk, preferably in public where lingering hostility might be kept in check.

She paused, as though reading his hesitation. "Are you asking me or directing me?"

"Either way," he said, trying to sound nonchalant. "Eight o'clock?"

"I'll let you know." She smiled and walked out.

—

By 7:30 p.m. Nick still had heard nothing from Charlie but changed anyway: jeans, absurdly expensive T-shirt that didn't look expensive, blazer. Or no blazer? He couldn't decide. He brought it with him.

On the way to King's, the tangerine sky dimming to dusk, he swung by the farmers' market—which, truthfully, wasn't on the way; he had to *pass* King's to get to it, but he had time. Many of the displays depleted, merchants packing up for the day, he found a booth of locally grown blooms, grabbing a small bouquet of wildflowers. It looked thoughtful without trying too hard, just what he was going for. His phone buzzed. A text from Charlie: Okay Kings at 8. It was now 7:56 p.m. He was proud he had anticipated this.

He strolled back along Warwickshire, past the college kids, who looked so much younger and less tortured than he had felt at that age. He had reserved his favorite table—the high-top in the front window because it had a nice view and was set apart from the others inside.

The restaurant's longtime host, Alfred, greeted him outside with a handshake as he tended to the densely populated patio. "Aren't those lovely," Alfred said, pointing to the bouquet before returning to his patrons.

Perfectly congenial, but it made Nick wonder: *Too much?* He tossed them in a large planter near the front door and headed to his table.

—

Charlie burst through the door at five after eight as a raucous early contender for "song of the summer" blared from the speakers. Nick, facing the door, made eye contact with her then returned, poker-faced, to his phone.

Fifty-four days to go, she thought.

She was glad he had changed—his clothes, at least—because she had too, throwing on ripped black jeans and a black cami-sole at the last minute.

"Oh, you're here," he said, expressionless as she reached

the table. "Here." He kicked her chair out from under the table as though this was a new breed of chivalry, but used too much force on the top-heavy high-backed stool, knocking it over with a bang.

"Wow, a gentleman, thanks," she deadpanned, watching it fall then hoisting it upright again.

Nick hopped to his feet, but he was too late to actually help and instead kissed her quickly on the cheek, his hand landing softly on her back. She felt her skin flush—a reflex she wished she could ignore.

"Welcome to—" The college-aged waiter arrived as they took their seats.

"Wine," Nick cut him off, studying the list. "Red. White. No, red."

"Malbec, please," Charlie ordered, Nick's favorite. Another reflex.

The waiter nodded and disappeared. They both watched him go, as though willing him to move faster.

Charlie was on edge, like in the courtroom. Twitchy, she tapped the back of her neck, the lark tattoo, then shook out her hair to cover it.

"So… Charlie." Nick searched her eyes, as if he'd find the words there. "How's this going, so far? For you? The show, I mean."

"The show," she repeated. The flame of the votive on their table danced. She pulled her necklace—a golden pendant of a compass set at due north—across her lips, debating how honest to be. Then she said, "You're the director. You tell me."

"Well, I think—" he started slowly, leaning toward her from across the table. It took effort to not be drawn in by the way he looked at her, always as though she held the answers and they might reflect back to him if he searched deep enough. She had to remember to keep her guard up.

"*I think* I'm doing pretty damn well, actually." She didn't let him finish, leaned in, arms folded on the table, mirroring him.

"I was *about* to say I think so too." He laughed once.

"Oh," she said, surprised. "Then, thank you." Around them were full tables, energetic diners, the steady drumbeat of the music. But she felt like the two of them had been set in slow motion. Outside their window, streetlamps switched on, the sky dimming to a deep indigo.

"Then, you're welcome," he said, as the waiter reappeared with their wine.

Glasses generously filled, Nick held his aloft, but before he could say a word, she raised her own. "No toast necessary." She downed her wine, her heart souring as she recalled viewing this scene from a different angle just a couple nights ago. Him at this very table as she passed by on the sidewalk.

Somehow he seemed to sense this. He drained his glass, then changed tack. "So you know one of the directing apprentices is doing a revival of our old Black Box show, right?" The words seemed easier for him now, relief in the form of liquid courage and a noncontroversial topic. The fact that he called it "our show," not "his show," felt practically like flirting. It reminded her of how Nick had convinced her to star in it, and then told Grayson this was how it would be, not caring that technically he had been expected to cast an apprentice. It had always meant something to her.

"How old are we that we qualify for a revival?" She whispered it like a secret, hand through her hair.

"I like to think we were just prodigies then," he whispered back.

"Are you cool enough for this though?" she needled. "Can you summon the self-restraint to stay out of their way?"

"I'm good, I've got other creative impulses to stifle," he said, smiling, as though aware of how charming his self-deprecation could be.

"You're doing a spectacular job at that," she offered.

"Thank you," he said, seemingly sincere.

"But you've gotta shake up the parts," she almost purred, sneaking it in, an actual critique. The idea had struck her at one of the very first rehearsals. Much as she was relieved to be Juliet, she couldn't help feeling that there was a better way to do this.

Nick leaned back in his chair, sizing her up. "Here's the Charlie I remember," he said, gesturing for her to go on. "Hit me. How am I failing, already?"

"Put everyone on a rotation, the four of us, the company," she said.

"So you would be Romeo—"

"Sometimes."

"And Chase would be Juliet—"

"Sometimes. And other times Matteo and Danica or Matteo and Chase or me and Danica. Are you following? Do I need to mock up a flowchart?"

"There would be rewriting. Of Shakespeare."

"Barely. I can take care of that…" She shrugged. She needed some way to occupy those endless hours at night when she wasn't asleep, counting the cars on Warwickshire. The intense nighttime quiet of this place already had a way of turning up the volume on her thoughts.

"Then everyone needs extra costumes, extra rehearsals." He shook his head. "Your ideas are always expensive and impractical—do me a favor, don't get any more ideas." He laughed, filled her glass and his, again.

"Then just strip it down."

"Excuse me?" he asked, glass perched in the air before his lips.

"The production. Set it in the present day, stark backdrop, we'll wear our own clothes—"

"But, opulence, Versailles," he said, firm.

"Fuck Versailles," she said with a shrug. "Get some return on your investment. You got me for free, but I bet Chase cost more than Matteo and Danica combined."

He ignored her, which she took as affirmation. "So it's more *economical* to make everyone learn a thousand different parts?"

"'Two households, both alike in dignity, in fair Verona—'" She exhaled the beginning of *Romeo and Juliet* as if to say, *Challenge accepted.* Stretching her arms up, she twisted side to side, like warming up for a workout. "'From ancient grudge…'"

"I'm starving, let's order." He signaled for the waiter.

The waiter arrived, but she continued Act One. "'A pair of star-crossed lovers take their life—'"

"Are you going to order?" Nick asked, impatient.

"'I strike quickly, being moved—'" she went on.

"Just bring a couple of these." He pointed to the menu. "And we'll share them when she reaches the intermission."

"'…'tis known I am a pretty piece of flesh…'"

Nick looked Charlie in the eye once the waiter left. "Your point has been made."

But she just scanned the room, ignoring him and continuing on, "'My naked weapon is out; quarrel, I will back thee—'"

"Stop!" He seized her hand across the table, and her eyes snapped to his in response. She felt a charge, nerve endings sending a jolt from her fingers, up her arm, along her spine, as though she had been powered on. "Enough," he finally said, more calmly.

"Just saying." She watched his pale winter-sky eyes. "It's easy."

"Then why'd it take a judge to get you back into all this?"

She wondered if he realized he still grasped her hand. He locked on her eyes in a way of someone truly wanting to know.

"I'm here now," she said after a pause. It was all she could give just then.

He squeezed her hand once before letting go. "I have so many questions for you, Charlie." For some reason when he said her name, in that graveled voice, it felt like finding a post-card from a place you forgot you had ever visited. He squinted, considering her as he rested his cheek on his fist.

"I've got a lotta questions for you too," she said almost to herself, trying to pour another glass, but only drops remained. Probably for the best. This had been the first time she had drunk in years, not that anyone would believe it, and she already felt unsteady.

"Oh?" He had heard her, apparently. "Then shoot."

"Okay..." She straightened up in her chair, deciding where to possibly begin. "Why don't you tell me—"

"Look, if this is about last week here," he cut her off. "She's an investor."

"Who?" she asked, confused. "What?"

"Taylor. Matteo said you guys were walking by here and saw—"

"Ohh yeah. No, it wasn't about that... Since you brought it up though—"

"Long story, never mind." He shifted in his seat. "But, since you brought it up—" He pivoted. "What about you?"

"What *about* me?"

"Do you have any—?" He searched for the word.

"*Investors?*" she asked, in a loaded way.

"It's not— I told you," he said. He tried to refill his glass, forgetting the bottle was empty, and groaned. She eyed their waiter, grabbed the bottle from Nick's hands and shook it, signaling for more.

"This isn't what I wanted to talk—" He stopped. "I thought we should meet to clear the air."

"Ugh. Nothing good *ever* starts that way." She folded her arms.

"Just, you know, make sure we can…" He tapped his fingers on the table. "Get through these two months without you throwing anything at me. What do you think?"

"That'll depend," she said, remembering that night so long ago.

"On what?"

"On you. *Obviously.*"

"Me? You're the problem," he said like it was a fact.

Now she was frustrated. "The problem? Me? I'm the *solution.*"

"To what?"

"To *everything.* The problem is that you stopped *listening* to me."

"Oh, here we go," he said, dismissive, sitting back again. "Well, what do you want me to say, Charlie?"

"If I have to write your lines then it's meaningless."

"At least you've already answered my next question," he said almost to himself, head in his hands like people in commercials for pain relievers.

"And what question is that?" she shot back.

"Whether you're still angry."

"You fired me from a film that was supposedly inspired by *me*—"

"You walked off the set—" he countered.

She chucked her napkin on the table and got up. "No, *Nick.* I'm not angry at all."

15

I DON'T HAVE TO ASK HOW IT WENT

Charlie had taken to doing this, visiting the lake at all hours of night, which might have been dangerous, but she didn't care. Her body had remembered the way that first night a week ago without needing to consult her mind. Past the ice cream shop and the empty soccer field, through the line of oaks fencing in the campus, straight out to the clearing.

And there it lay. Peaceful and calm, aglow beneath a luminous sky obscene with stars. She had forgotten it was like this here. She didn't bother looking up in the city.

At the edge of the splintered pier, she pulled off her shoes and set them beside her. Didn't even roll up her slim jeans, just dipped her toes into the cool water, leaning back on her arms, eyes closed, as though sunbathing. Her head spun from the anger and the wine. She wished so deeply to not be here *now*, but longed to be in this space two decades earlier, to undo and rewind. To have no history. Because beneath the spikes and armor, there remained that lit spark. Somehow. Impossibly. She hated it. But she had felt it tonight. Reignited by this setting and by the grip of memory.

She could still see those long-ago mornings right here. That first bet of theirs: the race to the other side of the lake. If he won, she would star in his Black Box show. She had secretly let him win, but just beat him the next time and the next and the next until he'd realized it. There had been that one night too, weeks later, after his show—their show. The kind of night your mind returns to again and again for years afterward.

The show was a one-woman one-act comedy, monologues of Shakespearean women talking about their terrible relationships: Lady Macbeth, Ophelia, Juliet, a whole mess of them. Nick had written it and been awarded the fellowship for it. But she had rewritten it with him that summer. And he'd let her, bristling only a moment before acknowledging she was right, which she loved him for. She had crystallized for him what he hadn't been understanding from the resident dramaturge or even Grayson himself, with their vague touchy-feely direction: *Push it further, challenge yourself, and come back.* He had admitted to her, when they were on this very pier, in similar moonlight, still strictly friends, "I have no goddamn clue what they mean. If I did, I would do it. I feel like I reached a level I had no right to reach and now everyone will realize that."

"Relax. Everyone of any real value feels like a fraud 90 percent of the time," she had said like it was an artistic fact as basic as combining red and blue paint to make purple. "And the ones who don't are pretty much always self-obsessed assholes. My research has shown."

He'd smiled at this and let her read a few pages the next day.

"You're missing out. This should be unexpected, unhinged. You have Lady Macbeth but really *imagine* Lady Fucking Macbeth on a bad date," she'd told him. "It's the experimental, edgy part of this theater, not the stuffy part that *thinks* it's having fun if it does one play a season with no corsets." They had sat shoulder to shoulder on the rickety pier, its wooden planks worn down by time. A bright sun rising in the hazy morning sky, clouds burning off.

"I'm not edgy. Or fun," he'd admitted, toes in the water, eyes set in the distance. She'd let the silence wrap around them for a beat.

And then she'd pushed him in the lake.

One sharp shove.

When his head popped back up he was laughing. "Really? You just did that?" He'd shaken his head, water spraying, combed his hair back with his hands.

"See, you're fun."

"You're lucky I'm a good swimmer." He'd splashed water at her.

She hadn't flinched, just let it hit her, hadn't even closed her eyes. "*You're* lucky you're a good swimmer. *I'm* just lucky you stopped feeling sorry for yourself."

The next afternoon, after she had read it all, they had met at the coffee shop, Bard's Brew, a back table. He had nervously tapped his leg, shaking the table, and when she'd kicked his shin to stop, he'd tapped his fingers instead. He'd asked her to work on the play with him, looking through her with the same bright, intense eyes he'd had at dinner tonight. She had loved then that she could watch him think, could feel him listening.

She remembered it all, more clearly than she should. Lush, leafy branches rustled softly in the breeze, and she felt herself drifting off.

———

She awakened, surprised she had slept at all. She dug her phone from her pocket: nearly an hour; it was after 10 p.m. Texts from Matteo and Miles lit up her screen.

Grabbing her shoes, she took a few steps to leave. But stopped, not ready to go back yet, to the inevitable questions from her housemates. She let her shoes and phone drop from her hands onto the pier. A few paces back till her toes reached the edge, and she dived in, clothes still on. The crisp water enveloped her as she shot through it.

Then a flash of something else: that night in Boston Harbor.

She burst up to the surface, gasping.

Focused on her breathing, in and out, to slow it down, she treaded water. When she felt strong enough, she swam back to the pier and climbed out. She lay down on the grass now, her breathing still jagged. It was the first memory she had resurrected of the accident. Just slivers of sensation: bright streaks of city lights, the peace then sudden panic of waking engulfed by water.

Finally, wet feet shoved back into her shoes, she walked home.

Matteo was still awake, on the phone in his room, probably talking to Sebastian.

"Night, Charlie," he shouted as she walked by, popping his head out of his doorway. He had done this the past six nights and it only now occurred to her that he might actually be waiting up.

She stopped, turned around.

"Call you right back, love." He hung up on his husband. "The lake again?" he asked Charlie.

"Maybe," she said, still clearly drenched.

"I don't like this, just putting that out there, again. I get the baptism thing—"

"What baptism, it's not—"

"I get the whole water-is-life symbolism thing."

"No, that's not what this is."

"But I don't like you there alone and—" He stopped a second. "Unless—did you have company? After your dinner?"

She didn't answer, just exhaled, agitated.

"No. So I guess I don't have to ask how it went?"

"No. You don't." She walked on, waving over her head. "Good night."

"I do think he's trying, Nick is," Matteo called after her as she made her way upstairs to her room.

Well, Nick would have to try harder.

16

TENSION IS EVERYTHING

It could've easily been a horror story, Sierra thought, listening to Harlow tell this particular tale on this dark night at the lake. The full apprentice contingency and even the department heads had gathered for "S'mores under the Stars" as the schedule dictated.

The crackling flames of the bonfire lit Harlow's delicate features. "...and Chase sat down beside me...and his shoulder touched mine and I asked him about his ink." She slowly ran her hand along her own arm, took a deep breath. "It was *amazing...*"

Perfectly outfitted as though for Burning Man (hat, fringed metallic romper, white hiking boots), Harlow had been regaling their mostly female crowd with vignettes from the latest *Romeo* rehearsal for so long that her marshmallow actually caught fire without her noticing. While Harlow droned on, Sierra calmly took hold of Harlow's stick, blew out the flaming treat and placed it back in her hand. Ethan, just arriving on the other side of the bonfire, caught her eye, stifling a laugh.

Fiona, director of their Black Box one-act, turned to Sierra and Tripp. "I'm so fucking lucky you guys somehow aren't in the main stage show." Fiona had cropped pomegranate-red hair, clunky black glasses and strong opinions. Tripp bowed with his marshmallow stick like it was a cane. "Our show is gonna be fantastic once we lift it out of the Stone Age," Fiona went on. "People couldn't even text when this was written, so we've got our work cut out for us. But—fantastic."

"Company in the house," Alex, dressed in crisp, cool white linen, announced, joining them as he gestured to the actors along the pebbled path. Matteo chatted with Danica, and Charlie grabbed a marshmallow, walking ahead as a pack of girls swarmed Chase, snapping selfies.

"We had a definite *moment*," Harlow continued. "You know when you can just *feel it*?"

"Check this out!" Tripp interrupted, gesturing to his T-shirt as Ethan approached. Ethan had given Tripp, Sierra and Fiona each a soft cotton T bearing the Summit Rodeo logo: a cowboy on a bucking bronco. Sierra loved hers so much she had secretly ordered another online.

"Lookin' good," Ethan said, smiling as he took a seat on the sand beside Sierra. She gave up on the gooey marshmallow she'd been trying to sandwich between graham crackers and chocolate, handing it to him.

"He *made* these," Tripp reported proudly to an aloof Harlow. "They're at Urban Outfitters."

"The rodeo is my family—" Ethan shrugged, biting into the s'more "—but the merch is me."

"Wait, but, they're coming to *Romeo*, right?" Sierra asked without thinking.

"We'll see," he said in a way that sounded like *No*, eyes in the distance.

Sierra felt instantly sorry. "I didn't mean... Never mind."

"It's cool, Texas is a long way, and it's their busy season," he covered. "No big deal."

Sierra had already witnessed Ethan's frustration with his family and understood how hard he tried to bottle it up. Before she could console him, Tripp yanked her shoulder.

"Are you seeing this?" Tripp pointed to Charlie sitting atop an empty picnic table with a view of the lake, as Nicholas arrived by her side bearing a stick. "OMG. He brought her a marshmallow. Toasted. That is so sexy."

"Is it though?" Harlow questioned.

"It's an olive branch," Alex said, between bites of his s'more. "For freaking out on Charlie today."

"Charlie kissed Chase," Ethan explained.

"Traditionally that's what Juliet and Romeo *do*," Sierra laughed. "Unless I've been misinterpreting the play all these years."

"It was uncalled for, we were just blocking," Harlow snapped, as though this process of the director choreographing where his actors would stand onstage had been corrupted.

"Nicholas was jealous," Tripp said, lying on the ground, arms behind his head. "I didn't even need to be there and I know that. I'm a genius."

"Sure," Sierra had to admit, watching them. "There's this *tension* with Charlie and Nicholas."

"Tension is EVERYTHING," Tripp said, deliciously. "They were like *fire* a million years ago."

"Seriously though." Ethan leaned in to the group. "What is the *deal* with them? I mean, they make this genius, classic movie together, basically redefining the way Shakespeare is done on screen, right?" Everyone nodded. "Blunt's first movie, which is insane. There's all this folklore about how they were each other's muses, how she inspired him to rework scenes at the last minute, add these crazy badass stunts." Ethan started to pick up steam, as though telling the plot of a thriller. "They shoot it on a shoestring, then make, globally, millions. Win all these awards. They hook up allegedly after filming and Blunt gets all this cash thrown at him for the next movie, *Super Id*, and Charlie's the star and it's kind of about her and kind of a superhero movie and kind of a fantasy and kind of crazy—"

"And she's kind of rewriting *that* too," Sierra said. "*And* they're full-on *together* at that point—"

"Sure, and then first day of filming, just months after the Oscars—" Ethan snapped his fingers. "She quits."

"And they're over," Sierra said. "Broken up. Done."

"And they despise each other," Tripp added.

"And now, she's here. And he brought her here," Ethan went on.

"Look, it's like this," Alex began as though about to lay some major truth on them. "It's chemistry. Love and hate. They brought out an X factor in each other."

"Oooh, anyone wanna watch *Nicholas Blunt's The Tempest: Director's Cut* tonight?" Tripp proposed.

"All I know," Ethan said quietly to Sierra now, "is Blunt would have a lot less to worry about if he'd just cast you as Romeo. And it would be kinda nice to have a friend there." He elbowed her with his mechanical-bull-inked arm and Sierra felt herself blush.

—

Charlie wasn't wrong, which Nick found maddening.

"...so someone needed to resuscitate him. Chase was anemic," she said, twirling the stick he had brought her. Nick watched the lake shimmer. Chase did, in fact, seem terrible at this, at Shakespeare. But anything was better than talking about how their dinner had gone off the rails. "Iambic pentameter just ain't for everyone."

"But he was so excited about it." Nick had signed Chase without an audition—someone like that doesn't audition anymore. And Chase had said yes immediately. I'm down to rebuild my image. These new guys coming up are twenty-five and all muscle, so yeah, I'm in, he'd emailed with disarming candor.

"Timing is everything," she laughed, adding under her breath, "And he had the time, so I've heard."

Chase had indeed been dropped from an action film days before the start of production when that film's director discovered him having an affair with his wife. (Nick despised that director, so it gave Chase extra points in his book.) It all appeared serendipitous to Nick—until now. Maybe, since the whole season was built around this guy, an audition might not have been the worst idea.

"Shake up the parts," he sighed, recalling her unsolicited advice.

"You gotta do something." She slapped him on the back, took a bite of the marshmallow and hopped off the table.

17

YOU COULD DO THIS IN YOUR SLEEP

Nick wished he'd had the good sense to *not* answer the phone. He cringed at Taylor's voice as he pushed through the theater lobby doors, already perspiring from his walk under a burning June sun. A passing glance at the cast headshots he had arranged himself last night, he reached out, pure reflex, fingertips grazing that black and white of Charlie.

"Sooo, I'm still on the fence a bit with this, Nicholas…" Taylor cooed, needing to be convinced and enjoying the power that came with it. He hated this intense *selling*, but the number she had proposed was a hell of a lot of money. Enough to fund the rest of the season and then some. Enough for him to get the place back on track, in the spotlight, bring in new subscribers, new contributors, to do all the shit he should've been doing the past six years but hadn't, while trying to resurrect his film career to no avail. It was really a lot, juggling so much failure at once. "How can we set the theater world on fire?"

"Well, I'm glad you asked." He tapped his fingers on his desk, gazed out the window. Mercutio was outside, on the phone, smiling broadly. Something about Mercutio reminded Nick of himself his first summer here. Probably the way the boy had marveled at Charlie. He took a deep breath. "You'll love what we're doing with *Romeo and Juliet*..." He couldn't believe he was about to say this. "Our incredibly gifted company will switch parts throughout the run of the show."

"Nooo!" she said, enraptured. He wasn't sure which would be worse, having to stage the show this way or having to admit to Charlie that he had gone for her idea.

—

Charlie sprinted through the lobby doors, late as always, but halted at the sight of the framed cast headshots. Her photo looked so official beside the rest of the company, lights trained on them. This woman with the soulful eyes and hint of a smile in the eight-by-ten glossy—this polished version of herself—looked like she belonged here.

"Not a bad shot." Nick's voice broke her out of her thoughts.

"Could be worse." Charlie shrugged coolly. Secretly, she was pleased. She had used Danica's trusted local photographer: *He erases ten years but you don't look like a wax figure, he's a genius. But I'd recommend using one of my fourteen-karat-gold-infused face masks anyway, that morning, just to be safe.*

"You got my message about your wardrobe for the gala?" he asked. She remembered rolling her eyes at it late last night on her walk back from the lake.

"Ugh, LaPlage hates me," she groaned at the mere thought of the costumer.

"Great, you can go for your fitting after rehearsal." He ignored her, his voice tense. Mary leaned out through the box office window, not bothering to conceal her interest. Nick nodded at her, smiling, and patted his pockets. "I left my phone," he sighed, waving for Charlie to follow. "I have to run something else by you too."

"Why does that sound ominous?" She followed.

Once in his office, he crouched on the floor and located his cell by the door.

"Don't tell me you're throwing phones again," she said.

He ignored her. "We're doing your idea, switching parts," he said like it was no big deal, taking a seat at his desk and pulling up the spreadsheet. "But while I have you—"

"Wait, you're serious?" She wasn't sure she'd heard right. She sat on his desk, absentmindedly grabbed his iced coffee and took a sip.

"I'm always serious," he said.

"And usually that's one of my least favorite—" She stopped herself, and he looked up from his screen. "I mean—thank you. This might actually be good now."

"You owe me one, so you know that silent auction at the gala? Matteo's taking someone out for live music. Danica's making aromatherapy candles with her winning bidder. What do you want to do?" he asked, hands poised to type into a spreadsheet. "Do you still sketch? Wanna give someone a drum lesson? Passes to your art house? What do you do in your spare time when you're not pissing off directors?"

"This is mandatory?" She folded her arms.

"Perfect, you'll take people out for drinks," he said, exasperated, typing. He scrolled down on his screen. "Hey, does your mom have any memorabilia she'd like to part with or...?"

"My mom?" she said, irked, walking to the door. "I don't know, we're in a weird place right now. Do I have to do this?"

"Charlie!" he snapped, sharp enough for her to jump. "This is your community service. I'm sorry you're finding it so torturous here. Why is everything a *thing* with you? Why can't it just be easy? I need something to just. Be. Easy. For once.

Maybe you'll be lucky and this place will close before your sentence is over and then we can all leave. And never fucking come back." His voice had amped up to nearly shouting level.

"What's your problem? All I said was—"

"Do you think I want to beg like this?"

"Is this begging? This is supposed to be persuasive?"

"Begging you. Begging contributors, donors, anyone with cash. This place is going to *close*." He wasn't yelling anymore, his tone a mix of desperation and defeat. "Are you hearing me? Before the end of the season, before the last show of the season." He slumped back, eyes on the ceiling.

She collapsed into the chair in front of his desk, tone softened. "Is that true?"

He looked at her, expressionless, and nodded, his eyes weary. "I'm running out of time, I'm running out of money, I'm running out of ideas and I'm...sick of running."

"What are you gonna do?"

"Exactly. What am I gonna do?" he repeated, as though it wasn't a question he'd been asking himself for months.

"Who knows about this?"

"Just Matteo, and I want to keep it that way."

She nodded but said nothing else.

"So until some benefactor arrives with a check that has a lot of zeros, we're doing this," he sighed, sitting up in his seat again, back to his spreadsheet. "And you're going to be overjoyed to entertain three winning bidders with cocktails, coffee, whatever, and sparkling conversation, here or in Boston, I don't care." He typed. "You can go. Tell the others I'll be there in a minute."

She stood to leave, feeling compelled to say something more, but unsure what. She paused at the door, watched him typing. "And, I guess, you could toss in monthlong passes to the art house," she said before letting herself out.

—

Charlie slunk down, head over the back of her chair, staring up into the beams of the lighting catwalk. She tried not to think about what Nick had told her. She was only here for a fraction of the summer, it wasn't really her problem. Except, maybe it was: it tugged at her heart in a way she couldn't quiet.

It would've otherwise been a triumphant day. Nick had announced at the start of rehearsal that he was adopting Charlie's part-swapping idea, informing the cast that they would try it with Chase as Juliet today, and Charlie as Romeo. "It might be more work, but if anyone here is afraid of that then you're in the wrong place."

The arrangement showed glimmers of promise (she could feel a newfound spark, they had to pay attention, recalibrate, learn new lines, they couldn't coast). But there were speed bumps too and they grew impatient as the hours wore on well beyond their usual end time.

Nick had Chase in his crosshairs, past their dinner break. "You keep missing the heat," Nick interrupted him, agitated. "Again. You've got the poison."

"If only," Chase muttered.

Charlie, exhausted—she had been awake until dawn sketching on her rooftop—felt the same desire to escape she felt as a child trapped at her mother's rehearsals. She used to climb the ladder at the Globe up to the same little open-air cable car, the pulley system used to change the lights at the top of the stage. It freaked everyone out, her sneaking up there when she was ten years old to watch from above, but Charlie had always been one of those agile circus types. Until the day she jumped. She was thirteen. In the middle of her mom's rehearsal for *Antony and Cleopatra*. A clear twenty-foot drop. Charlie couldn't resist; she thought it might feel like flying. It did. Before she hit the stage with a crunch, sprained her ankle, skinned her knee and was never allowed up there again. She had been puzzled more than hurt. Accustomed to landing on her feet, it never occurred to her that stumbling was a possibility.

Charlie hadn't realized she had dozed off, slumping softly onto the shoulder of the castmate beside her, until she opened her eyes to find Mercutio—the apprentice Ethan.

"This is kind of a cure for insomnia, right?" he joked in a whisper, wide chocolate eyes.

"Something like that," she yawned.

Across the stage, Danica sat knitting, actually *knitting*, what looked to be a gray scarf, and Matteo scrolled on his phone. The apprentices beside them flirted quietly, bodies turned toward each other, as Nick and Chase continued to argue at center stage.

"I can wake you when you're on, if you want," Mercutio offered.

"It's okay." She stretched her arms over her head and for a moment wondered if she had dreamed her conversation with Nick. But she hadn't. And it seemed impossible that she could do anything in her brief time here to change the trajectory of this place. She almost didn't realize Mercutio was still talking to her. She caught the end of it.

"…you're a pro, you could probably do this role in your sleep, anyway," he said, watching Chase and Nick.

Where else had she just heard that? In her foggy haze, it took a moment to realize: that letter.

18

IT'S LIKE YOU, IT'S GOT NO EDGE

A week into the grueling, part-switching rehearsals that had left him questioning everything, an exhausted Nick opened the auditorium doors to find Charlie, alone onstage, slicing a sword through the air against imaginary assailants.

"Am I hallucinating or is Charlie Savoy actually early today?" he said.

"Don't get excited, just here for the swordplay," she said, thrusting, parrying, advancing, retreating, not even looking over as he walked up the aisle. "Can't believe Griffin is still at it."

The same fight instructor from their long-ago summer, now an octogenarian, would be training them today. A prospect that did nothing to alleviate Nick's overall dread.

"Solid weaponry," she continued. "Not aluminum anymore. Steel and carbon, I'm guessing?"

"So you got my voice mail?" Nick's phone buzzed. He

glanced at it, tucked it in his pocket as he hopped up the steps to join her on the stage. "About the gala?" He had put off asking her, but the only advantage of having told her the truth about the Chamberlain's abysmal financial straits was that she might be able to help.

"Yeah, I got it," Charlie said, still swinging.

"Oh," he said, equal parts surprise and trepidation. "What do you think?"

"Sure." She shrugged.

"Sure? Like, yes, you'll do the whole first act? What you did at dinner but more, reciting the entire beginning of *Romeo and Juliet*? At the gala?" he stumbled, not believing it.

"Sure," she said again, and so easily that he felt emboldened. He pushed his luck.

"There's something else I've been wanting to ask, another sort of favor." He tested the waters as she continued swiping at the air. "I wouldn't ask unless I thought it might really make a difference, to investors and things. It would involve, maybe, possibly seeing if your mother might be interested in coming here to—" He was about to finally spit it out but she lunged, thrust the rapier at his heart, halting mere inches from his chest. He took a step back, on reflex.

"Relax," she said with a smile. "See?" She pulled back her weapon, tapped the dull tip on her palm. "It's like you, it's got no edge." She stepped back, tossed the rapier at him. He barely caught it. The theater doors opened, Matteo and Danica leading the way into rehearsal. "Seriously? My mom? Here?" Charlie went on, puzzled, as though this proposition defied laws of time and space.

"Right," he said, like it was no big deal. "To send a message that we're doing exciting new things but remind potential investors of the foundation this place was built on too." He was actually giving her a sales pitch and it felt mortifying, so he tempered it with a casual, "Or, you know, that kind of thing." He tried to toss the rapier in a breezy way but it dropped on the stage, clanging and echoing just as the doors opened and three apprentice cast members walked in. "We can talk later."

"For *The Tempest*, you mean?" Charlie continued.

"Or *Midsummer Night's Dream* or anytime, really, but—not now..." He meant, he didn't want to talk about this *right now*, as the entire drama apprentice class presently began filing into the orchestra seats. He did not feel like having this conversation with an audience.

"Well, if you want anything from that woman you're gonna need to have your passport up-to-date because I haven't been back there in two years and she hasn't been here in six. So it'll take some major tap-dancing to make this happen."

"Okay, later, we'll talk later," he told her again and then turned to face the group, his voice strained. "Oh great, everyone is early today. We're so lucky..."

———

Somewhere outside the theater, sirens pierced the air, getting closer.

"At least that's fast," Ethan tried to comfort.

Three days before the gala, Chase Embers, the star of the summer, lay bloodied on the stage, the cast fanned around him. A hush enveloped the theater. The apprentices in the audience—who hadn't realized anything was wrong until Chase yelled, *What the fuck, man?*—had been stunned silent.

It was Ethan's first sword fight, obviously. Chase's too, apparently. And Chase, honestly, had been horrible: timid, useless. Ethan had advanced, thrust and then parried with too much force, inadvertently snapping Chase's sword and sending a sharp, jagged fragment of it flying right into Chase's perfect cheekbone.

"It's cool, you were too pretty before," Charlie offered, peering over the group huddled around Chase.

"Are your cheekbones insured, by chance?" Matteo asked.

Ethan had heard this of various celebrity attributes—legs, lips, asses, for God's sake—and found it ridiculous, but now he understood.

"Happens all the time." Griffin, their calm, aging fight instructor, reappeared fresh from calling 911. "Doin' great." He patted Ethan, who wished for more direction but remained crouched, holding his shirt against Chase's bleeding cheek to stop the flow, which seemed worthy of hemorrhage status, though Ethan was no doctor.

"It'll be okay, baby," Danica said, cradling Chase's head in her lap. "My son nearly split his head open at the playground—no, wait, better story, he was running with a stick—"

"Danica—" Matteo shook his head at her to stop. "Where the fuck did Nick go?"

"Waiting for the ambulance." Harlow knelt beside Ethan, leaned her face millimeters from Chase's. "You're going to make it," she said, as though auditioning for a medical drama. She kissed Chase on the forehead. "I'll be right there with you."

"Anyway, he's totally fine, Gianni is," Danica went on. "In fact, he'll be there opening night and—"

"Is his face his moneymaker?" Chase snapped at her. "'Cause I don't think you *get* it."

"Oh, well, not yet. He did some catalog work but we're taking it slow," she said. "My point is—it's a happy ending." Then, turning to Charlie, she said for all to hear, "This is *your* fault."

"Me?" Charlie laughed. "I wasn't even holding a sword when this—"

"It's just your general *aura* of *combustibility*," Danica said, accusatory.

"That's not even a thing." Charlie sipped her iced coffee.

"And if it wasn't for you and all the changing parts—you be Romeo! And *you* be Romeo! And *you* be Romeo!—we wouldn't all be exhausted and overworked."

"This is my fault, obviously," Ethan jumped in. Then to Chase he offered, "I'm sorry, man. I didn't expect it to snap like that."

"Dude, Mercutio was *not* supposed to win this." Chase glared at him.

Ethan caught Sierra's eye in the front row—because of course *today's* rehearsal was open for the whole apprentice class to watch—hoping for encouragement, but she just grimaced.

The doors flung open and two paramedics ran in, wheeling a stretcher, Blunt jogging behind them.

"Will there be a plastic surgeon on duty?" Chase asked as they loaded him onto the gurney.

The cast and apprentice class wandered outside to watch the ambulance pull away. Ethan turned to Sierra at his side. "Do you think I'll get kicked out?" he asked.

"For what? Overzealous fencing?"

Charlie walked past, smacked Ethan on the shoulder. "Chin up, Mercutio. Not your fault. He forgot how to take a hit."

19

TOM FORD ISN'T THE MAN
I HAVE A PROBLEM WITH

Sierra was the last one left in the costume shop, her work delayed when she briefly lost control of the iron—speed a factor in this accident—and burned her forearm in the shape of an arrowhead. Everyone else had moved on to their respective rehearsals, but here she was, touching up tuxedo shirts, in moderate pain, when Charlie Savoy bounded in.

"I'm here for my gala costume? Outfit?" she announced, seeming lost, probably at the sight of the empty room. "I know, I know, I was supposed to come days ago but—"

"Madame LaPlage had to leave early," Sierra began, turning off the iron to avoid another mishap, nerves rattled.

"Thank God. She hates me," Charlie laughed.

Sierra would've loved to convince her otherwise, but she suspected Charlie might be right. When they were calling in the gowns, Madame had rolled her eyes, frowning while giving Sierra the information for Charlie's, and said, *I used to joke with Charlie's mother that Charlie would prefer at all times to look like something rolled out of the 100 Club in 1976 and there is just no saving someone like that, sartorially speaking.* Sierra had just shaken her head, not understanding, to which Madame explained, frustrated, *The Sex Pistols? London? Punk scene? Never mind.*

"Sure. I can find it for you." Sierra led Charlie—who bit her thumbnail as though preparing herself—to a rack on wheels with a hanging placard marked Gala: Company. Sierra, who had been tasked with calling the designer showroom in New York and requesting to borrow the item, gently pushed aside the other garment bags to reach the one intended for Charlie. "I'm not supposed to tell you this," she said. "But Mr. Blunt chose this himself." Sierra unsheathed the black sequined gown, which shimmered, catching every bit of light. "It's really gorg—"

"Oh, hell no," Charlie said.

"But...it's Tom Ford," Sierra whispered, as though the designer himself might be offended.

"Tom Ford isn't the man I have a problem with."

Sierra opened her mouth to speak but had no words.

"I'm not wearing that," Charlie went on. "No."

"Do you want to see what we have for Danica, maybe you'll like that better?"

"Doubtful," Charlie said.

Sierra had to agree: Danica's dress was a lavender taffeta ball gown.

Sierra racked her brain for any solution: the gala was only two days away. What could she do in that amount of time with no budget? "Wait a second," she said, taking a seat before the laptop at Madame LaPlage's worktable. She brought up the site, a gallery populating the screen, and swung it around for Charlie to look. "What if I call in something else?"

But Charlie wasn't listening, hadn't even followed Sierra to the worktable; she still stood at the clothing rack, holding the dress with both hands, brow furrowed, looking as though she was trying to read invisible words woven into the fabric. Sierra wasn't sure whether to ask again. She wasn't sure if Charlie was upset with *her*, but any possibility seemed feasible. This was Charlie Savoy. Boldly, Sierra spoke again. "I have some other options, if that helps."

Charlie shook her head. "This—" she waved the dress on the hanger, the sequins producing a soft, cascading shushhh "—this is the entire problem, with everything, with the way Nick sees his world, me, this place."

Sierra wasn't sure what exactly Charlie was talking about, so she just smiled soothingly, as a therapist might. And Charlie went on, "This is beautiful."

"Yes," Sierra said. That made sense at least.

"But that's not enough. This isn't going to change anyone's mind about this place, convince them something revelatory is going on here. Nick is beat down, you know what I mean?"

Sierra nodded but still felt unsure.

"That's what failure does, you know? You get conditioned to sort of stop trying a little bit and go for what's—"

"Safe?" Sierra offered, surprising herself.

"Yeah, actually," Charlie said, looking at Sierra with newfound understanding. "And safe is definitely not enough to change people's minds or wake them up or make them give a fuck about something. That's not gonna save this place, you know? Everything counts now. If ever there was a time to take a chance…" Charlie trailed off, gazing at the garment again, entranced as though working something out in her mind.

"Absolutely," Sierra said. But she couldn't pretend this was all making sense. She worried she just wasn't a good enough actress to fake her way through an entire conversation like this with Charlie Savoy, and she didn't want to. How many people got to have seemingly meaningful conversations with Charlie Savoy? So *she* took a chance. "When you say 'save this place,'" Sierra started in her warmest tone. "Is that, like, I mean, it makes it sound like the Chamberlain is in some kind of trouble?" Sierra had read rocky reviews last summer, but she always assumed those were just critics being critics.

Charlie's eyes snapped up, the startled expression of someone caught. Sierra looked away, nervous, pushed her hair behind her ears. *Am I right? I can't be right, I'm never right*, she thought.

But then Charlie closed her eyes, sighed. "Fuck," she said. "Obviously you're not supposed to know this—"

Sierra's heart sank. "Know what?"

"Exactly, just like that," Charlie said. "I'm not even really supposed to know this. No one is. Matteo knows and no one else. I wish I could just *not* know." She put her hands to her temples, eyes downcast. "He'll kill me if he finds out I said this." Sierra knew the *he* was Nicholas. "But things like this gala are the only shot at keeping this place going all summer. So, yeah, Chamberlain is in trouble."

Sierra nodded, not wanting to pry but needing to know. "And it might close? Before the end of the summer?"

"Before *The Tempest*," Charlie confirmed quietly. "Unless some contributors step up."

If the theater closed before *The Tempest*, then it would also close before the Black Box show, before any chance for Sierra to get noticed by agents or casting directors.

"Okay," Sierra said, processing it all. "Then we really need to get you something better to wear to this gala." Charlie perked up, as though these words assured her that Sierra would keep the secret safe. Sierra snapped her fingers manically and walked back to the workstation. "I'll call them and make the swap. What about something here?" She swung the computer screen toward Charlie, a gallery of new options populating.

Charlie looked at her, a fiendish smile on her lips. "Madame will be pissed."

"Probably," Sierra said. "But desperate times?"

Charlie nodded, then leaned into the screen, pointing. "This one?"

It was a women's satin tuxedo, Sierra had seen it before, but it was missing something. "I like it a lot," she said, summoning the courage. "But if you like that, you might consider this..." She tapped and scrolled to another Tom Ford she remembered, which would make the swap easier.

"What's your name again?" Charlie asked, studying this new option.

"Sierra?"

"Sierra, I feel like you *get* me," she said. "Yes. Done."

When Sierra finished up the call to Tom Ford, she found Charlie browsing the costumes for *Romeo and Juliet*: heavy on denim and white.

"These aren't bad," Charlie said, nodding. It was the greatest compliment Sierra could hear.

"On behalf of the entire costume department, I should thank you. I think you're the reason Madame's mood board changed from French Revolution to a sort of old-school Calvin Klein ad? This was much easier." It was true, they had all been relieved by the shift from elaborate corseted gowns to white jeans, white T-shirts, white tank tops, and the occasional diaphanous scarf and drapey dress.

"My pleasure." Charlie smiled.

"So the suit is coming, but not until the morning of the gala, so if it doesn't work—"

"It'll work," Charlie said, unconcerned.

"You really don't get nervous. About anything, ever, do

you?" Sierra hadn't meant to ask out loud. "You don't have to answer that."

Charlie stopped, leaned against the doorframe. "I wouldn't say that's true," she started, thoughtful. "But I wouldn't admit it's not true, know what I mean?" She went on, slowly. "For instance, I didn't bother telling anyone that I was…thrown off…coming back to this. This place. The stage. These…*people*. And then I went from thinking *maybe I can't do this, maybe it's too much* to *maybe I want more*." Charlie smiled again. "Because seriously, even Juliet can get boring, if you've done it enough."

Sierra understood. She had begun to wish, for example, that she had had the guts to audition with Romeo in the first place; it might've changed her entire course here. She had been too, well, safe.

"Nerves are good, fear, it challenges your body to perform. People just don't need to know it's there." Charlie looked at Sierra now. "In my experience at least."

And with a wave and a plea—"You won't tell Nick, right?"—she was gone.

20

IT'S A ROLE-PLAY EXERCISE

Thursday night Ethan was surprised to observe Sierra arrive at the end of his shift and take a place at the bar.

"Someone is really anxious to run lines from *Richard II*," he joked. They had fallen into a solid routine running lines after class and rehearsal and before his shift. Sometimes she would even walk him to work and meet Fiona and Tripp there. Then they'd reconvene after work, back at their spot in the Quad, to tackle the next day's class assignment in the glow of the campus lights.

"Change of plans and we've only got half an hour, c'mon," was all she said.

He ducked into the clattering chaos behind the swinging kitchen door, returning with his backpack.

"This Charlie thing has me thinking we need to step up our game, you know?" she said, leading him into the evening excitement along Warwickshire, in the opposite direction of the dorm.

"I'm still processing your bonding session with her," he laughed. He had hung on every word of Sierra's encounter with Charlie. "And I still can't believe you *didn't* mention you're the one reprising her role in the Black Box—"

"I know." She face-palmed. "I was overwhelmed. I don't see her every day like you do."

"It's not like I talk to her though." He felt bad he had brought it up. Sierra had been so encouraging about his role in the show, he sometimes forgot how disappointed she had been not to be cast.

"My point is, let's look like we actually fit in tomorrow night at the gala."

"I was just gonna wear something of Alex's."

"And I'm saying, let's not do that." She held open the door to Ruffs and Cuffs, the priciest shop in town. He stalled, and she flung her head toward the store. "Closes in twenty minutes." Then, as though reading his mind, she assured, "We'll leave the tags on, return it after. C'mon, it's, I don't know, a role-play exercise. It's like extra credit."

"Role play," he sighed, dragging his feet as he walked in.

They found their sections on opposite sides of the store, but Sierra must've sensed he didn't know what he was doing. In no time, she had paired a dark suit, brightly patterned shirt, tie and pocket square (he had never worn one of those in his life) and shoved him into a fitting room. He tried it all on, begrudgingly, after a pained glance at the price tag, and emerged, looking uncertain, from the fitting room.

"Somehow everything fits?" he said.

She turned from the cocktail dresses she'd been browsing and smiled in approval. "At least my time in the costume department is paying off." She weaved around a few racks of gowns to straighten his tie. "Well, *you're* set." She pulled out one of the dresses, a pale blue, held it up and put it back, shaking her head.

"And where are you two going, if you don't mind my asking?" An older woman, big smile, tape measure around her neck, appeared beside them. "What a beautiful couple!"

"Oh, we're just—" Sierra started.

But Ethan remembered what she had said about role play and he grabbed her forearm, stopping her. "It's for our engagement party," he said. "This weekend." He looked at Sierra, whose eyes bulged a moment until she caught on.

"We're *so* excited!" she said, hand now on Ethan's lapel. "He always fights me on the pocket square, but look how perfect he is."

The woman clapped her hands and held them to her heart. "Michael!" she barked. "Get over here!" Sweet again, the woman asked, "Is the engagement party here in town? Don't tell me, let me guess, it's at King's? Or is it that new place down the road, nestled in the hills, that looks so romantic?"

"Yeah, that's the place," Ethan said. "Only the best for this one."

"It was his idea," Sierra went on. "I said, let's just do it at King's, where we had our first date and got engaged. It's our history. But he said, 'No—'"

"No, this is about our future, so let's make new memories," he said. "Right?"

"That is *just* adorable," the woman said. Michael, who had been at the cash register, joined them, and the woman put her arm around him. "Michael, these two are shopping for their engagement party this weekend."

"How nice," Michael said, far less effusive. "Looks like you'll be needing a ring too. We have some lovely options in our jewelry department," he added, gesturing.

"Oh, no, we're good, it was just too big," Ethan said, oddly offended.

"It's being resized." Sierra held up her bare left hand. "And then we also had that mishap—" She looked at Ethan.

"We were going over, on our way, to have it resized," Ethan started. "And it fell right off her finger—"

"Oh dear," the woman said.

"And got run over—" Sierra added.

"Oh my!" The woman again.

"By a truck," Ethan finished, shaking his head.

"Don't hear that every day," Michael said.

"It's being repaired," Ethan assured.

"We just hope it's not a metaphor for our marriage," Sierra said.

"No!" The woman grabbed her hands. "Forty years, me and this guy, so I know a couple with staying power when I see them." She looked at her husband as though deciding something. "We don't do this often, but we would love to give you a special discount. We're honored to be part of your story."

Once Sierra chose her dress, Ethan insisted on paying for both of their outfits—it seemed the kind of thing a guy would do for his fiancée. When they walked out, Sierra clutching his arm, he even kissed her hair without thinking.

They held hands halfway up the street until realizing simultaneously that they no longer needed to be in character.

"So the good news is we were pretty convincing," she said. "But the bad news is now we probably can't get away with returning it."

"Unless we want to stage a dramatic breakup," he laughed.

"I'm not sure I could do that to our audience. They're so invested in our characters."

Strangely, her words felt completely true. But he couldn't tell if she was kidding, so he just smiled.

21

CURTAIN UP!

Sierra shoved her bag—containing her clothes from her day of class/costuming/Black Box rehearsal/gala prep—under the table, smoothed her black beaded cocktail dress (chosen by Ethan) and shook her hair free from its ponytail. Ethan, in his new black suit, glanced over from the glass display case, straightening the signed scripts for the silent auction then locking the case again.

"You clean up nice, *Mrs. Summit.*"

"Really? I feel like we would hyphenate—Suarez-Summit? Summit-Suarez?" she said, taking her place beside him at the auction table.

"We'll figure it out in marriage counseling." He smiled.

The lobby of the Hathaway House Museum had been transformed for the gala. Doors set to open in minutes, tuxedo-clad servers hoisted trays of canapés, finished assembling champagne flutes into neat little rows and checked that bottle labels faced outward at all the bars. Nicholas Blunt—looking dashing, actually, like he had at the Oscars those years ago—crossed from the auditorium to the exhibition room for the thousandth time in the past half hour, this time carrying a stack of programs.

"What's Blunt so nervous about, anyway?" Ethan whispered, watching.

Sierra wished she didn't know, but it wasn't her secret to tell, so she deflected. "Who knows, but I'm sure Harlow is on it." She gestured to the lounge off the lobby, where their peers now gathered on the sleek-lined, modern couches and angular chairs, waiting to assume their roles as ushers and waitstaff and ticket takers. Harlow (poured into a vintage bandage dress) and Alex held court. Both had scored the plum assignments: Alex would be at the front of the auditorium guiding the most illustrious guests to their seats. Harlow would tend to the A-list donors in the VIP room, which housed the university's most treasured Shakespearean artifacts. By contrast, Sierra and Ethan had spent all day unloading boxes of donated costumes, props, autographed posters, photos and scripts for the silent auction, less glamorous than she had hoped. But still far better than Tripp's garbage duty.

"Is it just me, or do they have more free time than we do?" Ethan asked.

Nicholas appeared at the front of the lobby and clapped his hands. "Curtain up," he announced simply.

At once, the apprentices scattered to their places, string music piped in through the speakers, the glass doors opened, and the well-dressed, deep-pocketed guests flowed inside. Choreographed to arrive just five minutes later were the beautiful, talented creatures—the artists themselves—tasked with enticing the potential donors to part with their cash. Danica swanned in first, a lavender Cinderella. Then came Matteo, distinguished in his dark gray suit and splashy watercolor tie, followed by Chase in a cobalt tuxedo, the gauze on his cheek somehow adding to his allure, giving his perfect features rugged charm.

"That works on him, you're lucky," Sierra said, paying no attention to the people scribbling bids for the auction.

Ethan followed her line of vision. "The *two* stitches?" He laughed.

—

They had manned the table a solid hour—Sierra's feet aching in the strappy black sandals borrowed from Harlow, a half size too small—overseeing a steady stream of silent bidders, when Charlie finally wandered in through those glass doors.

She wore a cerise leopard-print satin tuxedo and stilettos, pausing just a moment to take in the scene and let the scene take her in. Then she made eye contact with Sierra, her arms out to her sides, as if to say, *Not bad, right?*, and disappeared down a corridor.

"Um, did Charlie Savoy just send you some kind of telepathic message?" Ethan whispered, adjusting his tie.

"Could be," Sierra said, proud. It was her greatest accomplishment in the apprenticeship thus far.

The lights dimmed, and a clinking of silver on crystal rang from the museum's second floor, which overlooked the lobby. Ethan stopped talking to a potential bidder midsentence. Everyone around them froze, their collective gaze lassoed by a figure leaning against the waist-high railing, champagne flute raised in the air.

There stood Charlie, commanding all those eyes.

22

I'M OKAY WITHOUT A NET

"Ladies and gentlemen, kindly take your seats in the auditorium, the performance will begin…" Charlie addressed the crowd from above. "As soon as I find the stage."

Everyone laughed, applauded, just as a tense Nick ran onto the mezzanine from stage left.

"Hi there," she said to him as he grabbed her forearm, gave a quick wave to onlookers, before escorting her into a hidden doorway.

"What was that?" he whispered into her ear.

She had gotten his attention at least.

"Thought it might be nice to welcome everyone." She smiled innocently.

He held open the door to the winding staircase that led directly into the auditorium's backstage. "The whole idea was for you to *not* be seen until the performance," he reminded her. "Build anticipation? We talked about this."

"Oh, you were serious about that?" She wasn't about to tell him that she had changed the plan after watching that investor Taylor glom on to Nick's arm during what little of the cocktail hour Charlie had witnessed.

Only forty-two more days...

He stopped now on the staircase, gave her a look as if to say, *You know we talked about that.* She responded with a sly shrug. "I just mean, this is kind of a big deal and I already feel like everyone can read my desperation, so give a guy a break and stick to the script. Okay?" He looked her up and down, noting her attire like a disapproving parent, but didn't say a word, just exhaled, walking again. She took it as a compliment. "Even the apprentices are looking at me weird tonight." He led them down another corridor and made a sharp turn to reach a door. He held it open for her, and she walked through then stopped in front of him:

"They're looking at you because you don't look half-bad and you were actually smiling at one point, which is like seeing an eclipse. Hold this." She handed him her champagne and untied and retied his bow tie. He let her fix it—as he always used to before all those awards ceremonies—making eye contact just a moment with her then looking away. "Perfect," she said of her work, grabbing the champagne back. "Thank God I'm here."

They continued into the dim lighting of the backstage, the minimal crew—just a few apprentice sound technicians—scurrying to prepare. Nick and Charlie halted at a marking on the floor in the wings where they wouldn't be seen by the audience. An all-black-clad stagehand materialized at Nick's side, reaching into his jacket and hooking a battery pack as Nick wound a small microphone in place.

"I'm doing this old-school," Charlie said, declining a mic. He pulled out note cards from his pocket, reviewing. Through a sliver between the curtain and wall, Charlie watched the audience file in, spotting Taylor in the front row between a pair of suit-attired men.

"Oh, look, your girlfriend is right in front," she said calmly.

"On in two," someone said behind them, followed by a brush of footsteps, tech crew rushing.

"I told you, she's not my girlfriend!" Nick said so loud it echoed all around them, a hush falling in the auditorium. He looked up from his cards. "And I don't know why it matters anyway."

"Who said it mattered? Not me." She sipped her champagne.

"Great! Then I don't know why I have to explain this to you, since you claim to not care," he said, his voice still raised. "And I'm a little busy launching our season here."

The stagehand reappeared, looking sheepish. "Sorry, Mr. Blunt, sir, that's a hot mic," she said. "And you're on."

Nick shot Charlie a look as the announcer's voice introduced him, applause ringing out.

"Good talk." Charlie slapped his back. "Go get 'em, tiger."

Nick sighed and stepped onto the stage. He really *was* nervous, more so than she had realized: he had certainly addressed more intense crowds than this. But he could perform too. She watched Nick walk the length of the stage as he introduced the three productions, unveiling them as though these were new technological devices everyone needed, not three centuries-old plays. She had forgotten he was capable of this kind of selling. This had been the side of him that had secured financing for *The Tempest* all those years ago and wrangled an award-winning cast.

Then she heard her name, served with such reverence she barely recognized it. "We're extremely honored to have her, bringing a fire unlike any the Chamberlain has seen—"

The applause again. Charlie closed her eyes, allowed herself the three-second flash of fear that assured her she was alive and then strode onto the stage.

———

The apprentices had all been granted standing tickets, lucky to attend without coughing up $250 for an actual seat. As Charlie, radiating complete calm—*joy*, even—took her place at center stage, Sierra whispered to Ethan, "It's like nothing happened!"

Minutes earlier, they had hushed—along with the entire room—to overhear Charlie and Nicholas Blunt sparring backstage. But now, Charlie greeted Nicholas with a handshake and winning smile. Then, as he made his way offstage, she stopped him. "Nick! Hang on."

He froze, turned, looking concerned enough that this felt truly unscripted. Sierra grabbed Ethan's arm as Charlie swiped the water bottle and script off the music stand and then held out the stand for Nicholas to take.

"I'm striking the set." Charlie shrugged, winking at the audience. Nicholas looked confused. Sierra was too. She had been to enough *readings* to know they were called that for a reason: even the most experienced actors still referenced the script, turned the pages, *read*. Charlie nudged his leg with her stilettoed foot as he took the stand from her. "This is a one-woman show."

Then Charlie walked to the edge of the stage. "And it's not a high-wire act, so I'm okay without a net." She fanned the pages of the script, then called to someone in the front row. "Sir!" Sierra stood on her toes, trying to see the audience member. "Hold on to this for me?" Charlie tossed the script at him, the whole room erupting into laughter, applause.

Alone now, under the lights, Charlie stood perfectly still, hands clasped behind her back, head hung, and when the room had quieted at last, she looked up: a peace washed over her, a new person. Transformed. "'Two households both alike in dignity...'"

Leaning forward on the railing, Sierra rested her head on her folded arms, the way she used to watch TV as a kid, instantly enraptured.

—

More selling to be done, bids to collect, but Ethan felt rooted. He hadn't moved for nearly an hour. His legs had stiffened, as if paralyzed, like after that last disastrous bull ride as a boy. But this time, he didn't mind.

He felt like he had been on some kind of journey with Charlie, everyone else in the room falling away. He could sense the shift at the end, the empty silence after her last line and then the change in her eyes when she became Charlie again. With the quick snap of a cursory bow, she was gone.

Ethan lingered in the auditorium, hopeful, the way you did at a concert, expecting the band to come back for an encore. From the corner of his eye, he caught Sierra watching him. She nodded at him with her kind eyes and he felt understood. He smiled in appreciation, nodded back just once, then led the way returning to their table.

23

I ALWAYS ACCUSED YOU OF
NOT BEING SPONTANEOUS

"So that's a *no*? Because we're not *cutting edge* enough?" Nick's postgala high was extremely short-lived. Saturday morning the good reviews were already flowing, just not the cash. He had been up all night, fearing this very scenario. This was the third conversation he'd had like this and it wasn't even 10 a.m. yet. He slouched, defeated, in his chair, looking out the window for answers. "I'll admit, recent years may have gotten a bit, to use your word...*commonplace*. But this is the new Chamberlain. We just need some new...dollars...to make it happen... I'm sorry too, sorry that you're not bold enough to join us on this journey, because many others will." He hoped, if nothing else, to inspire a fear of missing out.

He swung back around in his chair, tossing the phone on his desk, and found Taylor seated opposite him. He flinched, startled.

"Sorry, the door was open," she cooed.

False, it had been closed. "No, of course, always a pleasure—"

"I was brunching in the neighborhood." Doubtful. "Where'd you disappear to last night?"

"Did I? Disappear?" he asked, though she was right.

"I saw you before the show and then never again. I think that qualifies."

"Just *circulating*. How are you?" he deflected.

"Well, I suppose," she started. "I've been waiting for you to *circulate* that email to Jasmine Beijao. It's time."

The mere release of that name into their atmosphere made him feel he'd been poisoned and his organs were instantly liquefying, ensuring speedy death. "I can reach out and gauge... interest...but I can't make any promises." He lowered his voice, stern enough to convey what a last resort this was. He couldn't tell Taylor that he had vowed never to work with Jasmine again and that this would be suicide for him, personally speaking. Or that the theater company itself would suffer. It would be like injecting a foreign, toxic body into a unit on life support that had just begun to stabilize. "I've made no formal decisions yet." There was absolutely no fucking chance he could let this happen.

Mary knocked on the door, and he had never been so happy to see her. "Taylor, you'll have to excuse us, this is urgent," Nick said before Mary could speak.

"Of course, we can talk later." Taylor flashed her smile.

As soon as Taylor left, Mary looked at him, confused. "I'm just making a coffee run. Did you need another?"

"Not unless they have something stronger there," he sighed.

She smiled and closed the door.

He brought up his email, began typing: Jasmine, it's been a while, but a mutual friend asked me to touch base in the event this might be of interest... He stopped, hands through his hair, and opened his desk drawer, rummaging to the very back beneath pens and staplers and take-out menus until his fingers located it: the photo clipped from the back pages of the program that long-ago summer.

Charlie and him. Seated beside each other on the Black Box stage. She was watching him, listening. Script rolled up in his hands, he was repeating back to her one of her own ideas, probably, showing her that he understood, talking through how he could make it happen. But there was more there, an electric current. He could feel the telepathy between them. It was, for some reason, the only photo of them beside each other and looking at one another, from that entire summer. It had been snapped by his mentor, the theater's founder, Grayson, of all people. When Grayson sat in on Nick's rehearsals, it always terrified Nick. It was Grayson's approval he cared about more than anyone's in his entire life. He was the one Nick had learned everything from, had given Nick the opportunity that brought all the other opportunities.

So many years later, when Grayson grew ill, he summoned Nick to his Berkshires estate and told Nick he planned to bequeath the Chamberlain Theater to him. *The theater doesn't have to be everything for you, Nicholas, but it will give you dimension, remind you to give back, remind you of your foundation. No one is prouder of you and your film career than I am—I like to take some credit for it, in fact—but you began in this world and it's part of you and that's something not to be forgotten or taken for granted.*

"What did I do *now*?" Charlie asked, already defensive, as Nick pulled her offstage, fresh from setting Romeo's poisonous plans in motion. They had begun rehearsal without Nick, who had been nearly *an hour* late—completely unlike him.

Nick led her by the elbow all the way backstage, the rehearsal continuing without them. Finally he stopped in the bright corridor outside the greenroom, a manic smile on his face. "I think we need to do this." He produced his passport from his back pocket, like a magic trick, and held it up.

"You just carry that around with you?"

"I went home to get it."

"And I always accused you of not being spontaneous," she said.

"I'm holding flights. For Monday."

"Monday, as in the day after tomorrow?"

"What do you think?" He shook the passport again.

"Um, I think this is a little bit crazy, for lack of a better word. You, specifically, are crazy—"

"I know, true. I am. I was up all night. Thinking. Worrying. Worrying. Thinking—"

"You should stop that, I don't think it's good for you—"

"And I think it's led me to a place of clarity."

"And you need a passport to get to this *clarity*—"

"Because this clarity is just in London. At the moment. Do you think there's a chance your mom would say yes? To coming here? If we asked really nicely? In person?"

Charlie took a deep breath. She hadn't gone home in two years, in an effort to avoid her mother's frosty judgment at Charlie's imploding career and spiraling life choices. To avoid the inevitable guilt and aggravation. But for some reason, Nick seemed to have pinned all of his dreams for the survival of the theater—a place Charlie had to admit she may have missed, might actually be enjoying—on this Hail Mary of a trip.

Nick looked at her with that same intense hope he had decades ago when he asked her to star in his one-act, to polish it, make it shine. Those eyes, vulnerable and adoring, had a way of making her feel needed, even heroic. She snapped the passport from his hand, fanned its colorful stamped pages, considering it all. Could she do this? For the theater?

PART TWO

Lord, what fools these mortals be!

—WILLIAM SHAKESPEARE,
A MIDSUMMER NIGHT'S DREAM

24

THIS DAME IS GONNA NEED
TO BE WOOED

Two days later, Nick was on a flight to Heathrow with Charlie. This whole scheme was going to have to work because the
airfare alone cost more than the wardrobe for *Romeo and Juliet*.
The way Charlie had bristled when he brought up including
her mother in the season had convinced Nick that traveling
to London to ask in person was the only way to get Sarah to
sign on. *This dame is gonna need to be wooed*, Charlie had warned
him. *And she always liked you, possibly more than she likes me.*

They couldn't get seats together, but it might've been for
the best. He was *on edge*. He gave up on sleep and flipped
through the in-flight entertainment, slightly horrified to find
his *Tempest* in the "classics" section—was it really old enough
to qualify?—though he appreciated the status.

They touched down at 8 p.m. London time, strategizing

on the ride to South Kensington as though about to engage in guerrilla warfare.

"So how *is* your mom?" Nick asked lightly, pretending to make idle conversation.

"We'll see," Charlie said, exhaling.

"That's encouraging." He nodded, regretting canceling the hotel. "You're sure it's okay to stay there?" The cab drove too fast, winding and weaving.

"She insisted." Charlie shrugged. His body slammed into hers. "Ouch."

He watched the lights outside the window. They had agreed not to tell Sarah the real purpose of the trip yet and certainly not to let on about the theater's dire straits.

They reached the heart of the city, turning at the sweeping Natural History Museum, cathedral-like with its Romanesque towers and arches. Nick remembered Charlie taking him there once, playfully introducing him to the diplodocus commanding the main hall, which she said had been her favorite weekly excursion as a kid and one of the few times she remembered doing things that kids actually did. Most didn't grow up backstage at the Globe Theatre after all.

Minutes later, the cab arrived on lovingly manicured Sumner Place, where Dame Sarah Rose Kingsbury still resided.

Outside, Charlie stood rooted in place, gazing up at the pristine white-painted brick facade with its wrought-iron balcony and delicate gate. "Home sweet home." Her words sounded ominous.

It was easy for Nick to forget that Charlie grew up here, along this tony strip of townhomes a stone's throw from Kensington Palace, one of the most exclusive neighborhoods in all of London. But that was the point. Charlie wanted everyone to forget that. *She* wanted to forget that. Everything about her persona had been crafted to *not* fit that part.

But her mother, Dame Sarah—or Sarah or Ms. Kingsbury, he never knew what the hell he was supposed to call her—had always been intimidating: from that first summer at Chamberlain, even later when he was directing her on-screen in *The Tempest*, and absolutely when he and Charlie were officially together.

The scarlet door opened.

"Right on time, darling girl." Sarah embraced her daughter. Sarah Rose Kingsbury was in her sixties, elegant, with Charlie's slim build and bone structure but pale ivory skin. She had close-cropped gray hair and wore all black, with a vibrant patterned scarf, shiny earrings and bracelets he was sure would've set off Heathrow's metal detectors.

"And, Nicholas." She gave him a hug, not necessarily *warm*, but better than a handshake. He wondered how Charlie had characterized their working relationship, how much she might have embellished since one might be less likely to hop a transatlantic flight for two days with someone they despised. "The artistic director himself. How *are* you? It's been a while."

She ushered them in. The fabrics and color palettes may have changed in the many years since he was here at her home—was it the wrap party for the *Tempest* shoot? No, it was over the holidays that year and then again for the BAFTAs—but its formal air remained the same. The place was six bedrooms, three floors, probably 3,500 square feet and resembled a museum. He always feared he was going to break something, put something where it didn't belong; everything felt like an artifact or heirloom.

"So good to see you, thank you for letting us stay here—or me, because, of course, Charlie would stay, but thank you," he stumbled. "How long has it been?" He regretted this the minute he asked.

"Yes, I believe the last time we saw each other was at Grayson's funeral, wasn't it?" Sarah didn't say it in a heavy way, but still. "Six years."

"Right, of course, it was a moving service for an incredible man." This couldn't have been a worse start, really. That had been the most horrendous year of his life—not that things had been fantastic since then, but still: losing Grayson and inheriting the theater while he was struggling to release *Dawn of the Super Id*, which even he knew was lousy after years of turnaround and postproduction hell, drinking too much, abusing antidepressants, falling into a terrible relationship with a terrible woman, trying to win Charlie back at her movie premiere only to have a drink thrown at his head, and then it was all capped off with the complete bomb of his film and endless ridicule. Distracted by his failure, he didn't realize Charlie had taken over the conversation.

"...and Grayson would love what we've been doing, you know," she saved him. "I told you about everyone rotating through *Romeo and Juliet*. It's going to be amazing." As she talked *at* her mom about the summer, the plays, their flight, everything in that rapid-fire Charlie way, she strode through the well-appointed living room—delicate florals, furniture with feet that looked like animal hooves—to the updated kitchen, now even more suitable for catering large banquets.

"...so it's been going well, it's certainly brought back memories." Charlie opened the fridge, rummaging. "The place is completely the same and entirely different, if that makes any sense." She pulled out a half-eaten salad in packaging from the nearby Whole Foods, picking at it with her fingers. Sarah handed her a fork. "Sorry, we're *starving*."

"I'm fine," Nick said, to be agreeable. Even though he was, in fact, famished.

"I figured as much," Sarah said. "As you may recall, Nicholas, I was never the kind of mum who cooked." Charlie stifled a laugh, and Nick just smiled as Sarah continued. "But that charming Bumpkin is still open, shall we? You won't believe who I once saw there—"

"She can't go there without telling this story," Charlie said, taking another bite of organic greens.

25

YOU KNOW WHERE TO FIND ME

It had taken Charlie a full twenty-four hours to contact her mother after Nick had asked her to go to London with him. Finally she had sent the painstakingly constructed text.

I've been thinking, we have a quick break before the first show opens, how about that visit? Nick has a meeting in London, I can tag along. I know it's not long, but it would be nice. Okay? xx

Her mother's response had been instantaneous: Charlie, I had to read this twice to believe it. I don't know what's changed but I am over the moon! We will make the most of your time however short and it would be delightful to see Nicholas, as well. I always liked him, as you know. This is most exciting news! Love, Mum.

Now, as the three of them took their seats in the curated, faux-rustic haven that was Sarah's favorite eatery, Charlie tried to hide her unease, the rattled nerves that came with inhabiting her mother's realm, knowing that Sarah's charm could turn to dis-approval any moment. Nick seemed to feel it too, fidgeting with his silverware as Sarah spoke animatedly. "...so they had some kind of party in the private room and were leaving just as I was arriving and Will said, 'My parents always adored your work, you know,' and we joked that of course I suspected as much because his grandmother had made me a dame after all. And then he in-troduced me to Kate, who is just as lovely as you can imagine."

Charlie scanned the menu. She always ordered burgers when she was with her mother, asserting her independence by choosing something Sarah wouldn't.

"That's a good story," Nick said earnestly. "I can't imagine anything more flattering."

"You're a fine audience," Sarah said to him. "Much more patient than Charlie, who can't bear to hear the same tale more than once."

"Not true," Charlie barely defended herself, closing her menu.

"People need the arts," Sarah said, taking a sip of wine. "They speak to the soul, no matter who you are."

"Sure," Charlie agreed. "I just mean someone has to keep you grounded, so that's what I do."

"And I am firmly in your debt, as ever," Sarah said. "At the risk of oversentimentality." She put her head on her daughter's shoulder. "I am so glad to have you here. And grateful to you—" she gestured to Nick "—for dragging her back. So tell me, you two have plans tomorrow, then?"

"Yes, or I do. Our DP from *The Tempest*—remember Simon?—and film editor are still here," Nick said. "Haven't seen them in ages and I'm looking to get something new going."

Charlie glanced up, intrigued.

"Yes, well, I suppose it's about time, isn't it?" Sarah took another sip. It wasn't a very nice thing to say and Charlie shot her a look for it.

"As good a time as any," Nick said, kindly ignoring the slight.

"Well, darling," Sarah addressed Charlie now. "You're more than welcome to come to my classes, then." She proposed it in a way that sounded more like a command.

"Charlie tells me your studio is very popular," Nick said. Charlie had told him virtually nothing. "I'm not surprised, of course. And you're still consulting at the Globe too?"

Sarah smiled, clearly appreciating his homework. "I am, a couple of shows a year. It's nice to flit in and out of it. I'm having my 'second act'—isn't that what they call it?—with the drama studio, the coaching, the programs for children. It's great fun, and that wasn't always something I prioritized, as Charlie no doubt has told you over the years."

"Your students are lucky to have you," Nick said with true warmth, which was the most perfect response. Charlie could sense him finding a groove now.

"Thank you, Nicholas," Sarah said. "I am the lucky one. And they will adore having someone there to crawl on the floor with them without fear of injuring her knees." She said this to Charlie, who nibbled her fries, smiling nervously.

"I wish I could be there." Nick flashed Charlie a look that seemed to say, *Good luck with all that.*

"Well, we can all reconvene in the afternoon for tea," Sarah offered.

"Nick was just saying on the flight that he hoped we could do tea while we're here." Charlie returned his look.

⸺

The evening had gone well enough, so Nick didn't know why he couldn't sleep. He climbed out of the four-poster bed of the guest room, creeping down to the kitchen in his undershirt and sweatpants. As he got closer, he heard someone sifting through cabinets and clanging dishes in a way that seemed too cavalier to possibly be Sarah.

THE SUMMER SET • 141

"Jet lag is a bitch," Charlie greeted him in a tank top and boxer shorts.

"I always think I'll be exhausted enough to sleep anytime, but then it never works that way," he said, stretching.

"It never works any way for me." She spooned tea leaves into a small envelope. "I've been awake for, like, years. Do you want? It's kind of DIY here." She gestured to her make-shift workshop bagging the loose tea leaves.

He shrugged, pulled a mug—just like Charlie had, not a teacup—from the cabinet. "Hit me."

She tossed the bag she had made into his cup, then made another for herself, pouring the water from the kettle over both. "Just curious," she said. "You really seeing those guys tomorrow?" He nodded toward Sarah's room, and Charlie whispered, "Asleep."

He leaned across the island. "I wasn't going to be seeing them, but I sent a couple emails so now I am."

"So you *are* working on something?" She raised an eyebrow.

"We'll see," he said. "Anything you might be interested in?"

"We'll see." She matched his tone.

They stared at each other, neither saying another word. He had entered extremely dangerous—and exciting—territory. His gut told him just to savor the possibility that there could be something for them beyond sixty days, beyond the Chamberlain. Because if he knew anything, it was that he worked better with her. But he had to slow down. They still had a lot of history to right between them, and he worried the mere mention of a film, now, would be a trigger.

Somehow though, the complexity of their past and extremely fragile present and future could all be captured in a gaze. And so before he could speak again, she smiled and said, "You know where to find me if you need me." She took her tea, disappeared into her room.

26

SOME MIGHT SAY I'M ATONING

The Kingsbury School was a slim, glass storefront just down New Globe Walk from Shakespeare's Globe Theatre itself. Charlie had seen the school, which was a few years old, at Christmastime (two years ago), but it had been closed for the holidays, so she had never observed her mother in action— and she couldn't quite imagine it, honestly.

She had managed to sleep a couple hours and was surprised to discover Nick already gone when she came downstairs. On the kitchen counter, he had left a pair of coffees, assorted breakfast treats from the bakery down the street and a note.

Dear Sarah Rose,
Picked these up before heading out. Thank you again for the hospitality. Looking forward to tea this afternoon. Charlie can send me the time and place.
Until then,
Nicholas

Charlie got a kick out of the formal tone he took with her mother. She suspected his nerves had flared even more since last night. But she felt tense too—they would make The Ask at tea this afternoon.

When they arrived at the school, the teaching assistant— Lizzy, who apparently had a freshly minted master's in child psychology from Oxford—was greeting toddlers with their mothers for a class promising "make-believe, puppetry and dress-up," according to the brochure Charlie swiped from the front desk. It was full of photos of her mom encircled by groups of wide-eyed children.

"Summertime and we're at max capacity, so it gets pretty lively, just warning you," Sarah said, handing Charlie two plush puppets, a court jester and a horse. "Especially with this bunch."

"It's okay, I was a kid once…sort of," Charlie said, taking her place beside her mom in a playroom swathed in candy colors from the carpets to the walls, to the tables and chairs. The kids were already boisterous, running, playing. "Though this certainly looks like a group of hellions."

"You have no idea," her mom whispered as she clapped her hands, quieting everyone, and began to sing. "Let's pretend, let's pretend, let's pretend from beginning to end…" Charlie looked at her mother as though the woman's body had been overtaken by an evil spirit. "Everyone! I have a helper today," she said when the song concluded. "This is *my* little girl, Miss Charlotte! Can you say hi?"

"Hi, Miss Charlllaaahhh," the tiny voices yelled as Charlie waved awkwardly.

After some form of mass chaos called "What animal are you?" involving roaring and galloping and, inexplicably, some crying, Charlie and her mother manned the elaborate puppet show setup. They ad-libbed a play together—her mom had the king and queen puppets, of course—with suggestions from the audience, like a far less dirty version of the improv nights she'd been to.

At the end, the children rushed the stage, hugging the puppets and tackling her mother. Charlie smiled and chatted with the moms—many of whom were younger than Charlie but still knew of her and paid her compliments—and before she even had time to ask her mother how the hell it had happened that she, Sarah Rose Kingsbury, had become this maternal, they were greeting another class and singing and roaring and puppeting all over again.

"That's fucking exhausting," Charlie said after the second class, when they finally had a break.

"Totally true," Lizzy said, not even bristling at Charlie's word choice. "In a good way, at least."

Somehow her mother seemed more energetic than Charlie had ever seen her. She couldn't help but wonder if she had had *this* version of Sarah growing up, if she might have turned out differently: less restless, more sociable and steady. If she might've never had a reckless streak or rebellious years. And just as fast Charlie knew, yes, she would have had more of this and less of that and been cobbled together into another person. But she would've just as certainly missed out on a lot of what made her *her*.

"One more class then Lizzy takes over so we can have a bit of time," Sarah said. "Shall we go to your namesake, the Savoy?"

It hit Charlie like a quick jab but she bit her tongue because things had been going well. "Sure."

Sarah had Lizzy call in the reservation. "I trust you'll let Nicholas know," Sarah reminded Charlie, in a tone suggesting she had some questions.

"Of course," Charlie said simply because she didn't have any answers.

Class about to start, Charlie texted: Tea at the Savoy Hotel 4:30, and added, be warned: she might be in a mood.

—

When their last class wrapped, her mother hugged her and suggested they wander toward the river to see the Globe before tea. "It's always like visiting a childhood home for you, I feel," Sarah said.

It was true. Charlie had grown up as much there as anywhere. When they reached the grand Elizabethan landmark with its thatched roof, her mother found a bench nearby and grew pensive.

"You did well today," Sarah started as Charlie took a seat beside her. "Better than I might've even guessed."

"See, sometimes I do take direction well," Charlie said lightly.

"I was, truthfully, a bit nervous to bring you here, but wanted you to see it at work. I'm not sure if you'll understand or accept this, but some might say I'm…atoning," she said, a catch in her voice. She looked out at the river, then back at Charlie. "This is my way of saying that I realize how unconventional things were at home for you, for us. In retrospect, I see it. I hope you know I did the best I could at the time."

"I know, Mom," Charlie said, softly. "You did great. All that you had to handle and with a crazy daughter like me. You were amazing."

"I just needed to keep the work steady, to keep myself steady, after your father…" She didn't finish. "He's a genius, you know. Your fire comes from him. He's just not meant for a tied-down life. I know that now too. Wisdom comes with the wrinkles."

"What wrinkles?"

"Ahh, you're so kind now." She smiled. "It was probably selfish, keeping you at the theater with me so much. I just needed you close, as comfort. Even such a *free-spirited* daughter as you." She said it jokingly, warmly, then looked at Charlie. "This is why I've wanted you to come home. I worry there is nothing to steady you where you are."

Charlie gazed at the theater. After a long pause, she finally admitted it. "I know."

"It's hard for me to understand what's going on there, with you. Something has not been right, for some time, even before your…accident." She shook her head as though not wanting to even think about that. "Something is missing or haunting you. I only know what little you tell me. But I feel that this could be good for you, being at the Chamberlain. If I'm pushing you, it's only because I want you to feel your soul is full, as I do every day."

Charlie put her arm around her mom but didn't say more. She feared breaking the spell that had allowed her mom to offer this monumental admission. In this moment, Charlie felt understood, and that was more than enough.

27

I WON'T BE A SUPPORTING PLAYER
TO THIS ATROCITY

Nick paced the checkerboard floor of the legendary Savoy, trying not to appear anxious. He hoped his typical uniform—blazer, collared shirt, dark jeans—would satisfy Sarah's standards. It always startled him how Charlie and her mother could each be so intensely intimidating in such entirely different ways.

At last they breezed in, pleasantries and mild embraces exchanged. As Sarah led them into the hotel's tearoom, Nick whispered in Charlie's ear, his hand resting gently on the lark on her neck: "It's okay, I know you were really named for the French Alps."

It was his way of saying he appreciated what she was doing for him, and she stopped, looked at him just a moment, with the slightest smile. Charlie had chosen her stage name—making it legal at eighteen—as a way of emancipating herself. Even though Sarah remained offended by the change in last name, Nick knew Charlie had taken great care naming herself after one of their few family vacations, when they still *were* a family (the Savoy being a mountain range in the French Alps). She had told him so much that summer and later on in letters, actual letters on paper, in the years before *The Tempest*, when she was off doing theater and her first film on the East Coast while he was on the opposite coast, taking meetings, assembling the building blocks for his directorial debut, making ends meet doctoring scripts. Back when he and Charlie were so undefined but had so much quiet hope.

They took their seats now at a table beneath a bright skylight, near a glass gazebo that housed a piano, tender notes spilling from it.

"I hope your meetings were productive," Sarah said as they paged through the menu.

"Yes, thank you, always good to see old friends," Nick said, sipping his water. He couldn't care less what tea to order. If he could've gotten a scotch on the rocks without it looking like he was completely on edge, he would've. "But I'm sorry I missed seeing your school."

"It's really special," Charlie said sincerely, looking at her mom.

"Yes, indeed, we had fun." Sarah patted Charlie's arm across the table. "The children are going to be asking for my puppeteer, so perhaps you'll be back again before Christmas."

Sarah was easily as warm as he had ever seen her. So he decided to try. "Since we're sort of talking shop anyway," he began, smiling. Charlie tensed up beside him, her posture straightening and her lips setting into a firm line. It was now or never. "We've had a fantastic start to the summer at Chamberlain, thanks to Charlie." He looked at her, and she nodded, reluctant. "We've already got exciting things planned

THE SUMMER SET • 149

for *Romeo and Juliet*, which opens in just a few days, and then we'll be starting *A Midsummer Night's Dream* after that. And I thought, how thrilling would it be for audiences to see another adored Chamberlain alumna return?" He thought he had done well, but Sarah remained silent and Charlie just gazed from him to her mother. "Oh, and of course, I mean you!" Sarah's face had hardened, her eyes steely. "And, if this is too short notice, we're actually finishing the season with *The Tempest*—to have you for that would be stunning." Truthfully, it would be much more useful to have her sooner than *The Tempest*, but if he had to wait, he would. "You could have any role, obviously. Not just a cameo, this time. Unless that's what you wanted, like last time." Sarah had been the equivalent of an Easter egg in his film version. She didn't enjoy film work—*If I wanted to be a film star, I would have been one, I did it once and never again, it never fulfilled me*—she had told him back then, but she had offered to bless his project by appearing in the background of a crowd scene (requiring only one day of work), and her appearance (a close-up long enough to get attention) had succeeded in giving him cred and publicity.

"What Nick is trying to say—" Charlie started.

"I'm perfectly aware of what he's trying to say," Sarah snapped. Nick froze, felt a sudden unraveling. "Just as I'm well aware of how swiftly he has allowed his theater to wither on the vine. And you too. Both of you, completely and entirely ill-equipped to give it the lifeblood it needed to survive."

"What did I—?" Charlie was about to defend herself, but Sarah just cut her off.

"I know what's going on. News does make it over here, reviews. *You* took an active role in hastening the death of an institution," she barked at Nick, and then she turned to Charlie. "And you, my darling, took a passive role—just as worthy of blame—in allowing it to happen, when all it might have taken was a season or two of your work to help it regain its luster. Do you not remember when I suggested, after that last terrible movie of yours, that you devote some time to the theater, return to your roots, recenter yourself, when Grayson passed?" This was the first Nick had heard of it.

"It wasn't the right time for me, I don't see how—" Charlie countered, but Sarah interrupted again.

"You are both too foolish and selfish to care for anything properly. You deserve each other." Sarah gathered her glasses, her bag, stood up. "And I will *not* be a supporting player to this atrocity. This destruction of a man's legacy." Nick was sure the man in question was not himself, but Grayson. In one sweeping motion, before he or Charlie could locate any words, she was gone.

Nick sighed, head in his hands. "That went well." He peeked up at Charlie. "Is this a family trait, storming out of restaurants?"

"Apparently." Charlie tossed her napkin on the table as the server appeared bearing the tray with their tea. "I'm terribly sorry," she said in her sweetest voice. "We won't be needing those after all. We've had a sudden change in plans. We'll just take the check, thank you."

Nick watched from the corner of his eye as the server leaned in. "Ms. Savoy, certainly no charge. Please come back when you have more time. We would like to treat you to a proper tea."

"Thank you," she said kindly to the woman, not taking it for granted, it seemed. "I'll look forward to that."

Nick glanced at his watch as they crossed the lobby. "So we have exactly twelve hours. Enough time to salvage this?" he asked, pushing through the doors back outside.

"Did we just see the same show?" Charlie sounded defeated. "I don't think it's safe to even go home yet."

"We should've kept that hotel," he sighed.

28

I'M NOT UP FOR A TATTOO

In silence, Charlie guided them to the delicate steel curves of Millennium Bridge, that pedestrian walkway stretching across the Thames. When you stood in the center, as they did now, she always liked how London Bridge, Tower Bridge and the many offshoots lined up, extending over the water. They all gave the illusion of just barely holding London together, as though fastened with safety pins across the river dividing it.

Boats of all sizes passed beneath them, and a familiar gray hung in the sky. The sun was trapped behind storm clouds, but the warmth of late June still enveloped them. In the distance, Tower Bridge had begun to open, allowing a large tour boat through, the upper deck full of passengers taking in the sights.

"I still can't believe you jumped off that thing," Nick said quietly beside her, his eyes far away.

"Not my proudest moment," she said. "It was one of those things you do as a kid, or seventeen, whatever. To impress people. Friends. Who aren't impressed with things like performing at the Globe. Then it turns out you don't want friends like that, anyway. I could've been killed. Should've picked a warmer time of year. The Thames was freezing then."

"I think it's always cold, like even now it's probably just under sixty degrees," he said. "I remember from our shoot, stuff like that." Their *Tempest* had been set in present-day London and filmed here.

"I've only been back up there—" she flicked her head toward the bridge "—once since then, and I felt like they were eyeing me, like I was there to stir shit up again. But I was just there for a yoga class, up in that walkway." She pointed to the enclosed corridor stretching across the top of Tower Bridge.

"Of course you were," he said, arms folded, leaning on the railing.

"It's a legit thing you can do," she said. "There's a glass floor so you can see the whole way down, like 130 feet or something."

"That would be the last thing I'd want to do if I had jumped in the Thames."

"It was very pretty up there, actually," she said. "But generally speaking, I find yoga kind of boring."

"Of course you do."

"I've mostly given up on 'inner peace.'" She shrugged, making quotes around the term. Being on stage was as near nirvana as she ever got. The past few weeks had begun to remind her of that.

"What's replaced yoga?"

"Boxing," she said, shrugging again. "There's a place by the art house." She looked at him a moment, needing to say this. "I'm really sorry, about my mom and what she said, everything."

"It's okay," he said heavily, his gaze still steady in the distance. "She didn't create this problem."

Charlie led them back to the riverbank, the tube station at Trafalgar Square. But they let the station pass, continuing on through leafy St. James's Park, neither of them suggesting a cab or any way to get home more quickly. The sky darkened enough for streetlamps to flicker on, and a cool breeze blew through them, threatening rain. Their pace slowed, a calm settling between them—his hand in his pocket, jacket slung over his shoulder—as she wound them through the public gardens surrounding Buckingham Palace.

"The crazy thing is we were actually having a good day, before this," she said, trying to make sense of it. "My mom and me."

"She wasn't wrong," he said. "What she said about me. I let this happen. I have no one to blame—"

"But you're asking for help," Charlie cut in. "You're taking responsibility. And I don't understand why she won't try to save something she claims to love." A deeper disappointment nagged at her. "I know this is going to sound like I'm a pissed-off teen—again—but part of me really thought if I just came here, if I just said that this thing that was always important to her is important to me now too, then that would be enough, you know?" She shook her head, pulled her jacket more tightly around herself. "But that's insane of me."

"No, it's not," he said. "She's your mom. No matter what's gone on with you two, she should want to be there. I mean, hell, you threw a mason jar at me and I *still* never took off my Google alert on you." He glanced quickly from the corner of his eye with a small smile.

"Sure, that was easier than filing a restraining order. Then you could know, roughly, where I was and avoid me."

"It wasn't to avoid you," he said.

THE SUMMER SET • 155

"Well, maybe I've had an alert on you too," she said easily, pointing for them to cross the street, walk along the edge of Hyde Park.

He looked over, a flicker of surprise, but then said, "Fascinating."

She gave him the side-eye, advising him not to make a big deal, that he was lucky to have gotten that much out of her.

"And that *is* how I found out about your..."

"Dip in the harbor?" She kicked a rock as they walked.

"I was going to say 'accident,' but with you it could've been...a lot of things, but if it had to happen at all, I hope it was just an accident."

"It was," she said.

"Because you scared me, you know." He stopped walking, faced her now, serious.

"I'm sorry," she said and meant it. "Thank you."

"You're welcome." He looked into her eyes a moment—just long enough to seem significant, to remind Charlie for a flash what it felt like to matter to someone unconditionally—before setting off again.

Somehow, they had been walking an hour and a half, dusk setting in. She felt the first drops of rain on her arm, and he held out his hand to catch them.

"Just in time. Only a few blocks away."

She halted, even as the rain pelted them. "I don't want to go back there," she said.

"Neither do I," he answered in relief. "Your mom is fucking scary."

"I know," she said. "I have...*an idea.*" Her pace quickening now, she took a sharp right toward Kensington High Street, away from home.

"I don't think I'm up for a tattoo right now. I just don't know what to get or where, it would stress me out," he said, as though recalling the last time she'd had *an idea* in a summer rain. "Not that I regret that or anything." He put his hand to the lark on the back of his neck.

"Relax," she laughed. "This is entirely impermanent."

She had been shocked then that he had actually gone through with the lark—the bird that greeted them the morning after they had broken into the historic Chamberlain cabin and finally let things *happen* between them—and now even more that he'd never had it removed.

They arrived at the strip with Marks & Spencer and H&M in record time, jogging in the deluge, their clothes soaked through. At Derry Street, they darted around the corner, running halfway down the block to a bistro. Inside the shop, a handful of tourists quietly nibbled sandwiches.

"This looks so familiar," Nick said, but she ignored him, not wanting to give it away.

She grabbed a menu, seeking a girl in her twenties sweeping the floor, seemingly the only one working out front. Charlie could sense the girl trying to place her as she ordered.

"…and a couple of these and a bottle of this." Charlie pointed, then smiled the smile that had sealed many a deal. "And we'd like to take it up to the roof."

Minutes later, Charlie and Nick made their way six stories up with sandwiches, wine and explicit instructions to stay on the patio, not to leave anything behind and to be back downstairs in an hour, the shop's closing time.

Charlie pushed open the door onto the sprawling rooftop garden that had once played host to so many parties. Now it was shrouded in relative darkness, lit only by the nearby buildings and hazy moonlight behind thick, wet clouds, Kensington Garden and Royal Albert Hall barely visible in the foggy distance.

The once-vibrant patio of cozy lounge furniture lay bare,

save for an awning to protect against the elements and the empty bar. They sat down on the slate floor, surveying the lush green life: palm trees arched over stone paths; apple and pear trees still bearing fruit, which littered the grassy expanse; crimson roses dotting the bushes though the flamingos no longer roamed and the ponds had been drained.

"I *knew* I knew this place," Nick said, taking it all in.

"So, technically, it closed recently, but—" Charlie explained.

"Too bad, that was a pretty good party, as I recall," he said, a twinkle in his eye even in the dim light.

"It was okay," she said, smiling at the memory of the premiere for *The Tempest*: its after-party, held on this very rooftop, had been their official, public debut together for anyone prone to chronicling those kinds of things. After years spent on opposite sides of the country—or the world—constructing careers, too much time and too many miles to attempt a real relationship, they had fooled themselves into believing they were destined to be the kind of friends who remained friends after a dalliance. Only to then begin secretly dating toward the end of filming *The Tempest*.

After an all-night shoot riddled with problems, she had gone to comfort him in his trailer just before dawn and she had...*comforted him*, more than she anticipated, but he hadn't seemed to mind. It had been four years since Chamberlain, four years of diverging paths and drifting, four years of assuming this was friendship. And now this twist that somehow neither of them could have predicted. Still, they didn't let it happen again until the film was officially done, after weeks on end of Nick sequestered away, editing like a mad scientist in his laboratory, not to be disturbed. When he'd finally finished, and was actually pleased, they were inseparable from the autumn release straight through until the end of the awards season the following spring.

Their quiet stretched on, and she wondered if he was re-playing that night here also, the fizzy start of things, euphoric memories that felt like vivid dreams. A calm set in, the steady rain nearly lulling her to sleep. The day had been physically and emotionally exhausting, and she only realized now that she had stopped moving.

"Brace yourself for another disappointment," he said as he unpacked the items they had purchased, snapping her from her drowsy thoughts. He held up the bottle of wine. "Is there anything more heartbreaking than an unopened Malbec?"

"She said she'd throw in the corkscrew." Charlie grabbed the bag, flipped on her phone's flashlight to look. "Damn." She took the bottle from his hands, gazing longingly at it. "So much untapped potential in there."

"Sounds like one of the last reviews I got," he laughed, then groaned, leaning his back against the bar.

"Can we make a pact?" she asked.

"That depends," he said, wary.

"Can we, for the next—" she tugged his arm, glancing at his watch "—eight hours, forget our respective failures and not think about whatever fresh hell awaits us at Chamber-lain? Just handle…"

"The present?" he asked.

"Exactly." She stuck out her hand. After a moment, he shook it firmly, held on a second longer before letting go.

"Deal," he said, eyes shifting back from her to the shadowy garden. "It hasn't been that bad, so far, this summer—has it?"

She paused, watched the silhouetted palms tremble in the night breeze, as she summoned the courage to admit that it had been the best month in recent memory. She had quit act-ing in the all-encompassing, light-a-match-and-watch-the-house-burn-down way she did everything. But the feeling had crept back since joining Chamberlain. It was so much easier to inhabit someone else's skin than her own, so oddly freeing.

"You know what? Don't answer that," he laughed, leaning back against the bar again. "Look at this place. I mean, all these memories here, good ones, and this place has closed, but it's still *here*. It's alive, it's a little rough, but it's here. It can be restored. It just needs some work, right?"

"Definitely not a lost cause," she said to the weathered landscape. "There's still a heartbeat here." The air began to feel heavy with years of unspoken words, so she took the bottle from the bar, held it aloft. "I'm gonna take care of this, and be right back," she said, turning and taking a step in the direction of the stairwell door.

He lunged, catching her wrist. "Wait—" The bottle slipped from her hand, shattering against the slate patio. Neither flinched, they stood perfectly still, his hand gripping her. His translucent eyes pierced hers. She waited, barely breathing. Her pulse beat against his fingertips, so rhythmic she could almost hear it, like the clashing of drumsticks before the start of a favorite song.

"Sorry, I didn't mean to..." He finally spoke, slowly, as though searching for the words. He released her hand, his gaze pulling away, settling instead on the broken glass.

"Well, we got the bottle open, so that problem is solved," she said, crouching over the shards of glass and spilled wine, assessing the crime scene. "It's just a lot harder to drink this way."

He smiled, head hung in apology, kneeling across from her. "Maybe we do destroy everything we touch," he said lightly, paraphrasing Sarah's insults.

———

They swept up with a broom from the supply closet downstairs, finished their sandwiches in relative silence, seated atop the bar. When the rain finally began to dissipate, they walked home through the quiet, glistening streets, stealing glances at each other.

Sarah was already locked in her room, asleep or pretending to be, when they returned. Nick resigned himself to the fact that they wouldn't leave on good terms with her. Charlie, he could tell, felt responsible, though she shouldn't have.

"I don't understand her," she told him, frustration darkening her voice as they said good-night. "I honestly didn't think she could say no if we came all this way. But instead we've enjoyed a day of verbal abuse and inadvertent sightseeing."

"No, this whole thing was my idea, my problem, my mess, my...everything." He ran his hand through his hair. "I'll find another way, but it was worth a shot." He said it as encouragingly as he could, but she looked skeptical.

It was true though. Failed mission aside, as he lay in the guest room bed that night, replaying his day with Charlie, he couldn't help but believe the trip had been worth it. If nothing else, he felt a thawing had begun with Charlie, which would hopefully make their work at Chamberlain smoother. He felt more than that, but that was something.

Sarah didn't bother to see them off the next morning. Their cab arrived before dawn for Heathrow, and Charlie knocked once more, this time sending a note under the door.

Mistakes were made, but we're trying to rectify them and are asking for your help. If you care about the Chamberlain and Grayson's legacy as much as you claim, then come.
xx,
Charlie

It was late afternoon by the time they arrived back in Chamberlain. Nick parked outside the house on Avon and pulled

Charlie's duffel bag from the trunk of his dented ten-year-old Range Rover. He sensed a shift between them and wished they'd had more time away, wished they weren't being thrown immediately back into the reality of a failing theater, dress rehearsals and opening night two days away. As she slung the bag over her shoulder, he racked his brain for the perfect goodbye that would encapsulate all of this.

"I enjoyed our..." What would he call it? *Excursion* didn't seem enough. "...our 'bottle episode.'" He smiled, triumphant at this label. He liked that it recalled last night with the wine while also referring to an episode of a TV series that takes place with just a few of the main actors in a limited setting.

Before she could answer, he nodded, climbed back in his SUV. She shut the car door, leaned in the open window. "It wasn't *really* a bottle episode," she said, coquettish enough while also needing to be right.

"It was all in one location—London—" He was the one who had produced a (failed) sitcom after all.

"True, but it wasn't confined to one set."

"Though it included just a couple characters. Me. You. Us." He couldn't believe she was really challenging him on this. She was missing the entire point.

"But a bottle episode's purpose is actually to save money and our trip was, in fact, a tremendous expense." She smiled at this, adding with the right self-deprecation, "Not that I should be reminding you of that."

"So in that case—" he smiled "—maybe you could just say, for instance, 'I enjoyed it too.' Or, 'It wasn't so bad.'"

"It wasn't so bad," she said, but it sounded like more and he liked that.

"Agreed," he said, and with that she took the front steps two at a time and disappeared inside.

29

COME AT ME, BRUTUS

Sierra was still on the phone when Ethan knocked on the door a full ten minutes early to collect her for their usual afternoon scene-running on the Quad.

"I've gotta go, I'll let you know if it's assigned seating," she said, opening the door while trying to hang up. "…I think it's just, like, a general admission situation… Yes, there are chairs… You're thinking of standing room, it's not that… I will, it's, like, two months away."

She looked at Ethan, embarrassed, mouthed, *Sorry*. He shook his head, not seeming to mind, glancing at the photos on her desk, which he always looked at.

"I know, I'm excited too… Okay, love you too." She hung up, exhaled.

"So you do have a secret boyfriend," he said.

"My parents." She rolled her eyes. "They already bought tickets for the Black Box show."

"I didn't think those were even on sale yet—"

"They're not. But they begged the box office."

"Wow—"

"Exactly," she laughed. "And that's all you need to know about my family. Thank God I'm not on the main stage or they would find a way to move here all summer."

"Not the worst problem to have," he said, just wistful enough.

"Sorry." She felt bad, even though she knew he didn't mean for her to.

"Nah, it's cool. It would just make me nervous, anyway, to have the whole family here or whatever." He shrugged it off.

"If it's any consolation, they did harass me about my dissertation too, so that was annoying," she said, hopeful.

"Thank God," he sighed in mock relief. He pulled out his copy of *Julius Caesar*. "Ready?"

She grabbed her bag, and they set out to their usual shady spot on the Quad.

"Rehearsal ended early? Two days before opening?" she asked. "Guess the understudies have it all under control." Harlow had spoken endlessly about covering Charlie's roles during the *Romeo and Juliet* rehearsals while she was in London for three days.

"They're fine but nothing special." Ethan smiled. "Blunt and Charlie are back today supposedly. They'll be at the dress rehearsal tonight. What do you think that was all about, anyway? Kind of a crazy time for international travel, right?"

Sierra just shrugged. "Who knows?" But she did. And she hated keeping this secret from Ethan. If the theater closed before the end of the season, there would be no agents or casting directors coming to see the apprentices, no potential to catch someone's eye, launch a career. This place had to remain open long enough for that to happen. For their *lives* to *begin*. Hers,

Ethan's. Harlow's. Everyone had a shot. But Sierra knew better than to say anything. Instead, she pivoted. "You have to tell me what the vibe is like tonight, with them back."

"I'll tell you, but first you'll have to kill me," he joked, hopping to his feet, tossing his copy of *Julius Caesar* at her, which she caught. "Come at me, Brutus."

———

Cameras rolling on the cozy set of *Good Day, Boston*—the first stop on the company's media push the day before opening night of *Romeo and Juliet*—Charlie settled back between Chase and Matteo, attempting to project the necessary degree of sunshine for morning TV.

If she was being honest with herself, Charlie was possibly a little bit nervous about opening night. About the show. About everything. Nick was still the only director who had ever actually fired her—even though her other two film directors had surely wanted to—for being too vocal/hostile/opinionated/insistent/reckless. She had needed to harden her shell again as they drove back into town yesterday, and as she reentered that house on Avon.

Matteo had greeted her with a raised eyebrow. "How'd it go?" he'd asked, following her to her room. He was the only one who really knew the full financial mess that was the Chamberlain. Danica and Chase had been fed the same story as everyone else: Charlie went home for "family matters," and Nick had a previously scheduled meeting about a postseason project. No one should've bought those stories, but they had.

"Dame Sarah can't be bothered to return this summer. She sends her deepest regrets," Charlie had told Matteo in her mother's posh accent.

"No, I mean, how did it *go*?" he'd asked again, and she'd known he meant with Nick.

"It was okay, could've been worse," she'd said with a finality. Matteo had understood and nodded, polite enough not to ask more.

She reviewed the past few days in her head as she sat beneath the hot lights of the TV studio. Charlie had forgotten how much she disliked this part of every project: the selling part. Luckily, Chase had taken over, charming the host, doing most of the talking, letting the rest of them smile and nod. But it couldn't last forever.

"And, Charlie, this must be quite a change of pace," said the host, a perky blonde named Grace Garfield. "I'm sure many of our viewers are as familiar with your past films as they are with your movie theater—North End Cinema." Charlie smiled, nodded, took a sip of water from her *Good Day, Boston* mug. "But before joining Chamberlain, you were involved in a horrific crash, here in Boston Harbor…"

Charlie smiled again. After a long pause she asked, "Is that a question? Then, true."

"What has it been like recovering from that?" Grace leaned in, chin perched on her hand.

"I've been incredibly successful at not talking about that," Charlie said as her costars laughed nervously. She smiled, took another sip. "It was not the best night of my life."

"Would you say you've healed from that trauma?" Grace asked.

"I would say, I don't remember a lot of it."

"Fascinating. No memory?" she said, hooking on. "And you were more or less required to join the cast as a community service—"

"You know what?" Matteo jumped in. "We're glad she's okay, of course, and also just happy to have her here, despite the circumstances. When you see her in the show you really—"

"You had a famous relationship with Nicholas Blunt during his film version of *The Tempest*," Grace went on.

"Not so much *during*," Charlie felt the need to clarify.

"Well, even so, can we take this to mean you two are together again?"

Charlie, still smiling politely at Grace, rose to her feet, unclipped the mic from her shirt collar and calmly yanked the entire battery pack up through her black satin blouse and out at the neck, like a magic trick where a colorful scarf is pulled endlessly from a hat. Finally, she dropped the whole mess on the floor and strolled off set, continuing right out of the building and down the street, summoning an Uber and taking herself to the next meeting, arriving early at a *Boston* magazine photo shoot.

—

Nick hadn't planned to watch *Good Day, Boston*. He was in his office, avoiding everything he had so impressively pushed out of his mind in London. He had a lot to catch up on—emails, calls, inevitable new rejections—from the past sixty hours. And then there was tomorrow's sold-out opening night to prepare for. He had comped tickets to potential investors and would be there pleasantly harassing them with his sales pitch. It felt not unlike what everyone on stage would be doing, except he would just be playing a version of himself rather than a Shakespearean character. He needed the show to be good, he needed the reviews to be good, he needed it all to feel exciting enough that these potential investors in attendance would feel desperate to be part of this world.

When he stumbled onto *Good Day, Boston*'s website, streaming live, he knew from the host's first question to Charlie that it would derail. But Charlie being Charlie always made for the most compelling viewing.

Rehearsals for the play itself had actually been going *not terribly*. That frenetic energy and adrenaline had set in, as he remembered it could before a show run, all the performers

THE SUMMER SET • 167

clicking. Even Chase. He wouldn't win awards—his body and words still plenty robotic—but he was passable, and truthfully, it was enough just having him here to be worth the chunk of the budget that went to securing him.

Some duos were better than others: Chase was best as Juliet—which they renamed Julian—opposite Matteo. Danica had pleasantly surprised him, and when she played Juliet, she savored it like something precious and fleeting. Charlie could handle all of the parts, not just with skill and ease, but her wildfire. And while Nick would always prefer her as Juliet, he could agree that her Romeo—or Ramona, as they dubbed the character when she or Danica had the role—felt powerful and playful and free. Her Romeo made this old, weathered play almost shockingly new. Now, if it could just be enough to score some more hefty contributions. Weren't people looking for tax write-offs anymore?

With the costumes gathered—white on white on white, jeans and T-shirts and blazers and tank tops and leggings and dresses to pop against the minimalist black on black on black sets—and ready to go in dressing rooms so far in advance, Sierra had been moonlighting: first painting sets, and now inspecting each of the five hundred seats in the theater for damage, repairing tears in fabric, removing egregious stains.

She worked quietly, methodically and at a snail's pace, finding it impossible *not* to be drawn into the show's final dress rehearsal. Privy to the behind-the-scenes catastrophes—further swordplay injuries, major memorization fails (Chase had only just gone off-book four days before opening) and the sideshow fascination of Nicholas-and-Charlie's ups and downs—Sierra had expected it to be, well, rocky. But instead it fizzed, all chemistry and magic. She couldn't peel her eyes away.

Ethan especially—she had found herself captivated when

he was onstage. She forgot that he was someone she knew, someone she ran lines with in the Quad between rehearsals. That this was the same friend who joked about the terrible cafeteria food and never charged her for her iced tea at the pub and who liked to drop into her Black Box rehearsals to watch whenever he could. Which made her more nervous than she would ever admit, even though he only ever gave her the most glowing praise. Watching him now, she had another thought: if nothing came of this apprenticeship, professionally, she would at least be grateful for this friendship.

30

IT'S JUST SHAKESPEARE

Charlie still had her earbuds in—an aggressive, pounding soundtrack, the kind of thing athletes listened to before winning gold medals in fast solo sports like downhill skiing—when she arrived backstage to preshow mania. Tech crew zipping around in their shadowy black apparel, talking into their headsets. Stage managers and apprentices all boundless nervous energy. Fellow castmates sequestered in dressing rooms; apprentices buzzing in the greenroom where a TV showed live feed of the stage, the audience just beginning to trickle in. And Nick, who appeared to have nothing better to do twenty minutes before opening than to pace outside the dressing room Charlie shared with Danica.

"Almost showtime." Charlie smiled, about to brush past him to go inside, determined to appear calm, as she usually was on an opening night or a shooting day. Today though, the pressure of returning to this world for the first time in so many years inspired a greater fear than she had expected. You could do something perfectly a thousand times rehearsing in an empty theater, but it was terrifyingly easy to fuck it all up in front of an audience. Even the gala had been more under her control. Here though, there were so many moving parts. Every time on stage felt new and uncertain, this is *generally* what she had always loved about theater.

"Yeah, it *is*, thanks for joining us." He folded his arms across his chest. She pulled out her earbuds, even though she wasn't sure she wanted to hear him. "Call time was, like, days ago. Maybe come a little earlier tomorrow, before they start dimming the lights."

"We'll see." She winked, earbuds back in, and sauntered into the dressing room.

As soon as she shut the door, she closed her eyes, deep breath. Charlie took opening nights seriously, that was why she arrived when she did. She couldn't get there a minute too soon. Too much time was poison for her. She needed to breeze in, hair done, makeup almost all on, throw on her costume, touch up her face and land on stage, all in one sweeping motion like an uninterrupted tracking shot. You wouldn't catch her doing tai chi backstage two hours before showtime like Danica, who did this even for dress rehearsals. (The woman sat on a magenta ikat-patterned floor pillow in full costume now, meditating in a corner of their tight dressing room. She opened one eye briefly as Charlie entered. They exchanged respectful nods.)

A bouquet of long-stem roses in an open box lay at Danica's vanity. Charlie tried to peek at the card, but Danica's eye opened again.

In front of Charlie's own mirror: more roses, twice as many, of all hues, fanning out from a crystal vase. And a note.

Girlie,
Break a leg (I hate even saying that to you with all the
trouble you've gotten into, but you get it). Wish I could
be there. But these flowers are almost as pretty as me.
Kisses and see you soon,
Marlena

Charlie had to smile. Marlena Andes was that best friend you
didn't need to see often to still feel protected by: she always para-
chuted in at the right time and had called her theater immediately
upon hearing of Charlie's accident and getting no response on her
drowned phone. Marlena could be a tough person to get a hold
of now that she was living the quintessential LA actor's life on a
hit Hulu show: as fan favorite Dr. Stevens on *Terminal Earth ICU*,
the edgy, soapy medical drama set amid the ravages of climate
change on a planet on the verge of death. Charlie and Marlena
had been connected like long-lost twin siblings ever since hitting
it off on that teen angel film when they were nineteen, back when
Marlena was still Marlon. They had been through a lot together.

Charlie tucked the card back into the blooms, reminding
herself to call Marlena after the show. She flipped on the lights
around her mirror now, surveying what work needed to be
done. The mirrors, scratched here and there, had not changed
in all these years—only the reflection staring back at her had; it
had lived. Charlie felt the full weight of being back. It mattered,
being here. This place mattered to her; what she did here mattered to her. She turned up her music to drown her thoughts,
trying to remain in the zone.

She pulled on her "Ramona" jeans and T-shirt—designed
by Sierra to embody a sense of danger, it was shredded and
torn and safety pinned and tied, as though ripped off someone's
body by a savage animal, which Charlie loved. As she lined

her eyes again, smoothed her foundation, Charlie kept coming back to what Nick had said to her yesterday at the last rehearsal.

He had already shocked Charlie when he told the cast opening night would feature her as Ramona and Chase as Julian. After he had given his notes and dismissed them, he chased Charlie down the aisle. "Hang on, Charlie," he shouted for her to stop. They were the last two left in the theater.

"I'm not sure about any of the rest of this," Nick said, true concern in his eyes. "But you are this show. In case you wondered." These had been the same words he had said to her the night before his student show all those years ago too.

It had all flooded back for Charlie in that moment, down the rabbit hole: getting to know him here, the first time, how Nick had been on his own like her; his rank above the other directing apprentices meant more work, greater opportunities. How he didn't like to talk about himself, but Charlie drew his stories out: Nick as a kid who could've used a spotlight but didn't find it in any sport. Nick as a tortured teen, who would've liked to create but couldn't act or sing or dance or paint, finding his way only in college, in his native Indiana, as a psychology major/ English minor who happened to take a theater class. He was still that boy.

And so at last night's rehearsal, Charlie had nodded at his revelation and then did what she had always done: defused his worry.

"We got this," she had said with a shrug. Then she'd kissed him quickly on his stubbly cheek, whispered in his ear. "It's just Shakespeare."

Charlie changed into her cocktail dress and heels—she had enlisted Sierra to acquire an outfit for the after-party, a black Rag & Bone minidress with a keyhole cutout at the solar plexus—but urged Danica to go ahead with her family over to King's. Charlie just needed a minute. Alone. She had forgotten this, the sublime autopilot of being beneath the lights. A switch flipped on and she didn't have to do anything. Her body carried her through the scenes.

During intermission she had changed swiftly then escaped through the stage door out into the warm night air. She had needed to protect the space around her, to not have to talk to anyone, to not shatter the bridge she had constructed to the world of the show. When it was time, she returned, finding a spot shrouded in the stage wings until her next scene, hungry to get out there to a place that felt easy, that pulled her from her own universe into one she could navigate better than real life.

It had gone perfectly. She wished she could skip everything that stood in the way of the next night's show, fast-forward to it, get lost in it, do this again *now*. She needed that pure escape again.

Though Charlie hadn't anticipated the thrill to flood back so intensely, one small part of the night she *had* foreseen: she had suspected that, if the show had gone well, she would feel compelled to make an effort and show up at the opening night party at King's. Whenever she felt certain she performed her best, she didn't mind a gathering like that. She almost craved the outlet, to come down from that high.

Before leaving, she pulled out her phone: Opening night, she typed to her mother. Reminded me of Much Ado. Full house. That buzz like everyone's plugged into the same power source. Went well. You were right, should've come back here sooner. You should come see for yourself. xx, Charlie.

———

Ethan was the first of the cast to arrive. He couldn't help it. His veins buzzed. He felt drunk on the thrill of the night. He was glad Alex and Harlow had told him not to wait for them. He had too much manic energy to burn off, the flip side of what he'd felt the entire course of the show. He had been terrified actually, but he had done pretty well, could breathe now.

He walked over to King's with Sierra—who had hugged him the minute he stepped out the stage door—and Fiona and Tripp. Music and the roar of conversation spilled out at them at once. The low-lit lounge and the twinkling outdoor patio had been engulfed by the after-party. Members of the show's audience, local townspeople, all invited to celebrate.

They posed for a photo on the way in, not realizing at first that they qualified for that kind of attention, and staked out a spot by the bar where they could watch the room. Danica arrived with a woman as statuesque and stunning as she was, but brunette, and a young boy. Soon after, Charlie, Matteo and Chase. A man with dreadlocks in a crisp white suit stood opposite the bar, waving the actors over and giving Matteo a kiss.

"Matteo's husband is a super famous artist." Fiona nodded. "Like Banksy but not a secret."

"How amazing would it be to live in that world where everyone is some kind of creative genius?" Sierra said, longingly.

"I mean, that's what we are, am I right?" Tripp joked.

Ethan was distracted, looking for an opportunity to say something to Charlie, tell her how amazing she had been tonight. He watched her group, searching for the right break to dart over, but the dynamic now seemed off: Matteo and his husband appeared to be arguing. Meanwhile, Charlie was ignoring Chase, and instead Charlie's eyes speared the front of the room, where the photo shoot was set up. Nicholas Blunt had arrived with a blonde woman Ethan didn't recognize. When he looked back to Charlie, she had started walking away, toward the kitchen. Ethan set off through the crowd, keeping her in his sights until she was close enough to reach with his fingertips. He tapped Charlie's bare shoulder.

"You were amazing," he said, cursing himself for not coming up with something better.

She smiled, squeezed his arm as though in appreciation and then kept on.

On his way back to his group, Ethan glanced out the front window just in time to spot Charlie emerge from an alleyway. Something in her eyes had looked defeated, which surprised him given the successful opening night, so he ducked out the front door, past the throngs still coming in, and onto the sidewalk. But as he stood there watching her walk away to the end of Warwickshire, someone brushed past him.

Nicholas Blunt, running after her.

Ethan watched until the street grew too dark, wondering if Nicholas had caught up.

—

Even as Charlie marched on, heels stabbing the sidewalk, she felt ashamed to care this much. The night had been good. She had felt enveloped by her castmates, bonded after making it through this together. She had even spotted the TV interviewer whose show she had walked off. The woman, Grace, gave her a wave and a smile from across the room, and Charlie had returned it. But in the few minutes when Matteo and Sebastian were in deep conversation and Chase flirting with the blonde apprentice, Charlie's eyes had set on that step-and-repeat backdrop bearing the Chamberlain Shakespeare Summer Theater logo.

There, Nick stood still long enough for a solo photo, all smiles in a blazer and jeans, looking relieved the show had gone well. The seemingly perpetual crease between his brows, eased. But in the next camera flash, Taylor stepped from the sidelines into the shot, attaching herself to him, as though taking a prom portrait.

Charlie's eyes met Nick's just a moment. She drained her champagne and, pausing only an instant with kind Mercutio, she found the hallway past the kitchen and out the back door, into the warm, cruel night.

31

THE LADY WANTS AN EVEN
PLAYING FIELD

Halfway down the block, Charlie heard her name, or a close enough approximation.

"Romeo!" that voice called. Over her shoulder, she saw Nick following. "Where are you going?" he shouted.

But she walked on, not expecting him to keep trailing her. It wasn't until she crossed the street to the field that she noticed he was still there, closing the gap between them. He picked up his pace, jogging now.

"That was my exercise for the day," he said, catching up to her at last.

"You should be doing more than that," she said, her tone flat.

"Chasing you is a solid daily workout, so I'm good."

She stopped to slip off her heels, let them dangle from her fingers, the soft grass brushing her feet. He didn't ask where she was going, but when he walked ahead of her through to the clearing, she realized he already knew. He led the way to the end of the pier, sat at the edge.

"It's more peaceful without a hundred wild apprentices," he said, recalling the bonfire.

Sitting down beside him, she dipped her toes in the warm water. Moonlight ricocheted across the waxy-leafed trees.

He pulled off his shoes, dipped his feet in next to hers. It was too quiet, but she didn't feel like filling the emptiness. "So why'd you leave?" he asked finally. "By my calculations you were there for five and a half minutes. I saw you guys walk over."

"Yeah, I don't know." She patted for that small pile of pebbles she had collected a couple nights earlier and skipped a smooth stone across the water's surface. "Maybe I'm just a really efficient partygoer, so five minutes gets the job done."

"Maybe you just don't like King's. Note to self, find new location for *Midsummer Night's Dream* opening party."

"You can go for the *Midsummer* closing—I'll be gone by then," she said, like she was doing him a favor.

"Don't make me think of that *now*," he said with a sigh, like he had forgotten. "I've only got you for, what, just eight days of that three-week run?"

"Something like that." She couldn't tell if he was put out by the thought of recasting midshow or if it might be something more.

He stood. From the corner of her eye, she saw him shrug off his blazer, unbutton his shirt. Then he pulled his shirt and undershirt over his head all at once, tossing them on the pier.

"What are you doing?" She tried not to watch, which took some effort.

"I didn't want to have to do this now, but you started it."

"Started what?" she asked, eyes on the lake.

"And you've left me no choice but to challenge you, Charlie Savoy, to a race."

"A race? Like, right now?" She looked at him. It was impossible not to notice, even in this near darkness, that somehow he looked better than she remembered. Ripples of definition carved where there had been none.

"Yeah. Right now." He sounded serious. "And if I win—or if you forfeit—then you're stuck here through the full run of *Midsummer*—all twenty days."

"And if *I* win?"

"You get to leave at your court-appointed date—"

"Wow, enticing. I'm already planning to do that—"

"Okay, you can leave a day early," he offered. "I should've bribed the judge or something to keep you longer than sixty damn days. But I don't think things through lately. Which is kind of what's been getting me into trouble," he added, the last bit under his breath. "So." He shook his head. "You, me, race, now. Or maybe you're afraid I'll win?"

"*Definitely* not," she said.

Silence as they watched each other, cicadas chirping around them, the faint hum of the party in the distance, Warwickshire thriving. She felt it in her veins. Just as she had in London when he had reached for her and his eyes had tunneled into hers. Without another thought, she hopped to her feet. Maybe it was the champagne. Or maybe she had spent too long looking at him looking at her.

"Well, fuck, I borrowed this and allegedly it's silk, so—" She rolled her eyes, then pulled the dress over her head, chucking it onto the pier.

Nick followed its trajectory, poker-faced, pretending not to notice how little she now had on. He stood, arms folded across his bare chest, calmly waiting for this swim meet to begin.

She pointed to his jeans, still on his body. "Go on, level the playing field."

"Seriously?" He looked surprised.

"If we're doing this, then we're doing this," she ordered.

"Some might say I'm actually at a *disadvantage* since you'll be far more water-resistant in your...uniform," he said, clearing his throat.

"Uniform," she said, skeptical.

"But, what the lady wants," he said, pulling off his jeans and tossing them beside her dress.

She stared him down, steely. "The lady wants an even playing field."

"So we're even." He took his place beside her on the pier's edge. Both now attired strictly in underthings, unmentionables. "Where are we going?"

They both leaned forward as though in position on a narrow starting block, shoulders touching.

She pointed. "Swim out until we're in line with that tree, the one that's jutting out, and then come back."

"No, it should be to the one that's arching over, see?" He gestured.

"That's exactly what I said."

"No, you said—"

"Whatever, it's the same fucking tree. You can call it arching, I'll call it jutting."

"Jutting is more aggressive, so I'm not surprised—" he said.

She turned to face him. "Are we doing this or not?"

He looked her in the eye and said stonily, "Go." Then he took off, diving in ahead of her.

"Always a cheater," she said to herself, launching in after him.

A flurry of kicks, splashing, arms and legs chopping at the water as they sped off, but in no time she caught up. She was about to overtake him when that feeling coursed through her again, a scene flashing: her body being tugged down into the murky depths of the harbor. So real.

She gasped, taking in too much water with her next breath, but kept fighting, as she had that night.

She remembered, then, still afloat, where she was: the lake, Chamberlain, with Nick. Forcing herself onward, making the turn, still in time with him, she found power enough to propel herself, clawing the water, back toward their finish line.

She slapped her hand on the warped pier, just a beat before him. Physically spent and immediately disappointed, wishing she had thrown the race, been forced to stay. Deep breath, she smoothed her hair back away from her face.

"You still got it," he said, panting. "And, embarrassingly, I was actually trying to win." He held his hand up as though taking an oath, then ran it through his wet hair. "What's wrong? You're not gloating."

The milky light shimmering on the water, the tone of his voice, something about it all: she felt a pull to him. "Sportsmanship," she said, a little breathless, not entirely from the race.

His eyes, glowing iridescent in the moonlight, locked on hers too long in that way of his. The silent seconds stretched past the point of innocence crossing a threshold, and she couldn't look away. Didn't want to. Returning his gaze, she let herself fall, made the choice. He seemed to understand, but waited another moment still, as though to be sure there was no mistake. She glided mere millimeters nearer in the water, a barely detectable movement, fingertips still gripping the pier, and finally, he leaned closer, close enough to breathe his words into her. "In the name of good sportsmanship, then—" But he didn't finish his thought. His lips landed on hers, an electric jolt unlocking a time capsule.

Back then it had taken nearly all summer to let this happen. They had been so young but so oddly sensible, flirting intensely while working together but waiting until after his show to take that chance. She had kissed him first, surprising them both. But then he had made it up to her.

Now, just like those years ago, their scene felt shrouded in a haze. She didn't know how or when they ended up back on the pier or on the grass or with their remaining layers peeled off. But she did remember his hands tangled in her hair and that rough scar on his chest and the taste of the back of his neck and his lips on her skin and the way his palm fit between her rib cage and hip. And how the sky glowed a deep velvet sapphire, starry, afterward.

—

Charlie awakened to Nick beside her, birds announcing morning from the treetops, a bright sun already overhead, not a single cloud. She wasn't sure if he was awake yet, wasn't sure how to play this, whether last night was casual or if she could admit that it meant something. She spoke first, lightly.

"So *this* is camping," she whispered, eyes barely open. Her body still, she patted blindly at the grass in search of her dress.

"We need a rematch because I don't like these terms we agreed to." He swept her still-damp hair to the side, kissed that lark imprinted beneath.

"We'll talk," she said in a tone that signaled another race might not be necessary. She had missed this, all of it. The stage last night, being part of something again, that feeling that each night would be different, that the show itself was something alive and breathing, that she was alive and breathing. And him. Them.

His hand traced that groove on her thigh. "I don't remember this," he said. "And I remember a lot."

"I'm flattered," she said. "And that's new. Souvenir from

the harbor." She tossed it out easily enough, hoping he would let it float by. But his hand froze there.

She thought back to last night's swim, how vividly her mind had called up the accident. Why had that memory chosen *that* moment to reveal itself? She had visited the lake almost nightly since arriving.

"I don't like how you got it," he said, his eyes downcast. "But it suits you." He planted a delicate, healing kiss on that ragged slash. And then on her lips again. "If only the theater was dark today." He sounded pained. They had a matinee, a Q&A and an evening show. "But reality starts—"

"Imminently?" she asked, without urgency. She grabbed his hand, checking his watch, which had survived the swim: 8:13. "Not imminently." She sat up anyway, disengaging from him long enough to slip her dress back on and for him to do the same with his jeans and T-shirt. His phone rang, chiming offensively at them. He silenced it.

"Imminently enough," he said, with even more regret. "Alarm," he explained, flashing the screen, and tossed the phone onto the grass. "I'm awake."

He pulled her to the ground again, entwined once more. She felt entirely swept up, couldn't envision any scenario that would involve either of them leaving this isolated perch until showtime (so long as it remained unpopulated).

Until his phone disturbed them again.

"You're busy," she whispered against his lips. "This is literally why the voice mail transcription feature exists."

He kissed her neck again and her forehead, reaching over her for the phone, missing its last ring. He collapsed onto his back, eyes set on the screen, squinting in the sunshine. She lay on her side, her hand beneath his T-shirt, resting on his chest.

"I do have some meetings, phone calls," he said, defeated. "Stuff that has to happen before the matinee."

She looked at him, waiting for him to say more. He didn't. She scanned his eyes for explanation, finding none. Her heart started to turn. "Oh, you're serious," she said, more hurt than she could ever admit. "Meetings or whatever. That's what you're going with? Okay, well, I'm super busy too." She rolled her eyes, shoved her hand against his chest, using it as leverage and pushing herself up to her feet.

"Hey," he coughed at the impact, like he'd been punched.

"So I'm gonna find the rest of my clothes and my misplaced judgment and then I'm bolting too." On her feet now, she took a step, but he lunged, just catching her fingertips, then gripping her hand in both of his to stop her.

"Wait, what are you talking about?" He rose to his feet, still not letting go of her.

"Let's not do this." She waited. He said nothing, just looked at her, confused. "You need your lines," she said almost to herself. "Here's where *you* say—'This shouldn't've happened/can't happen/won't happen. I'm with someone,' et cetera—"

"Taylor?"

"Right, sure, whatever." She threw her arms up, not caring about the details. "You say, 'Last night was fun, thanks for the memories—'"

"But I'm not with Taylor or anyone and this isn't a one—" He shook his head. She looked away, but he found her eyes again. "No, you're going to listen to me. This place—the theater—is still going to close. And I still need to try to keep that from happening. Even if it's inconvenient and gets in the way of the best thing that's happened to me in years." He paused a moment. She focused on the lake. "I meant *you*, in case you didn't get that."

At this she glanced at him.

"I'm trying to make up for lost time, but…it's a lot…lost… here." He scanned their surroundings. "And here." He put his hand to his chest, and then gestured to her, his eyes trying to catch hers. "Believe me that I do have meetings and phone calls even if they're with people I'd honestly rather not have to deal with. And the last thing I want to do is…basically everything I have to do today." He picked up his blazer, his buttondown, stepped into his shoes. He exhaled, hand through his hair. "This is an epically bad time for me to have this place falling apart and so few weeks to pull it together and then also to have this *emotional chaos* of you…and me and us. Amazing chaos. This is why I was about to kiss you on the rooftop? In London? But then I didn't, but then maybe I should've." He seemed to forget he was saying this out loud. "And you're completely freaking me out right now. Why aren't you interrupting me? You're always interrupting me. You're just gonna let me keep talking?"

It was probably the longest she had ever allowed him to speak without cutting in. But she had no words.

"I'm just, I'm a couple revelations behind," she managed, dazed.

His phone rang, and he closed his eyes like he had been shot. "I have to—" he said, walking away, pulling on his shirt, answering his phone after a few paces. She watched him go.

Thirty-four days. It didn't feel like enough now.

32

THEY'RE MADLY IN LOVE AND DON'T KNOW IT YET

The theater was packed, with the full audience of the matinee staying behind for the TalkBack: a question-and-answer session with the four *Romeo and Juliet* professional actors and Nicholas. A collective rustling broke out as at least a dozen theatergoers left their seats to line up at the microphones.

Sierra and her fellow apprentices pooled near the far left orchestra seats. She wanted to ask about Charlie and Nicholas, who sat beside each other on the stage. In the rare instance they made eye contact, both would look away instantly. Was Sierra reading too much into it? Willing something that wasn't there? It was odd to feel like you could understand the motivations of two people you really didn't know at all. It was possible to *think* you knew them, knew what was best for them, just from reading about them, from clips of them together when they had actually been together, from quotes given about each other in articles. All Sierra really knew for certain, she realized, was that the kind of chemistry Charlie and Nicholas had didn't happen to everyone.

"Are they or aren't they?" Sierra whispered to Ethan beside her while the actors took turns answering an inevitable question about "process."

"Are they or aren't they what?" he whispered back.

"Like, you know, *together* together."

"How would *I* know?" he asked. And then said, "How *would* I know?"

Because right now Charlie and Nicholas seemed entirely unlike what Ethan had reported from rehearsals. As Matteo Denali discussed character development, on the other end of the stage Nick leaned into Charlie's ear to tell her something, one hand covering his microphone, the other hand on her back. Charlie smiled, nodded, their eyes connecting a moment, silently, before they returned focus to Matteo.

"Ohhh," Ethan whispered.

"I can't take this anymore." Tripp, who had been listening to Sierra and Ethan, stepped over them to get to the aisle and the microphone with the shortest line.

After a question from one of the directing apprentices about the challenges of switching parts, Sierra heard Tripp's voice booming:

"This is for Charlie and Nicholas," Tripp started. "What's it like working together again?"

As Nicholas snapped forward, Sierra and Ethan, both horrified, exchanged glances, like they had been caught, guilty of something.

"Maybe you should take that," the director said to Charlie with a nervous laugh that the audience echoed. "I know my answer, but I'm curious if it matches yours."

Charlie shrugged, not shy. "I'd say it's good." She looked at Nicholas, and everyone held their breaths for more. But there was nothing else.

"That was my answer too, so that's a relief," Nicholas said to the audience. Then to Tripp, he murmured, "Thank you."

"They're madly in love and don't know it yet, bless their hearts," a wise Tripp whispered to Sierra and Ethan when he returned.

"Another question for Charlie," a directing apprentice asked next. Charlie nodded. "You were here last when you were with your mom. Any plans to work together again? She's such a legend."

"That's true. And you'd have to ask her," she said. "I would love to but she never comes 'across the pond' these days. She's very devoted to her theater school for children and she doesn't like to leave it. So it would have to happen there, I guess."

—

As soon as their talk wrapped, Nick ushered Charlie away quickly, backstage and up the staircase to avoid the crowd. "I have an idea, I think it's a good one actually—" He swooped her into his office, swung the door shut.

"Really?" she said, a saucy inflection. They hadn't had even a moment to talk since he'd left the lake, but during the Q&A, when the attention was on Matteo, Nick had whispered, *I'm sorry about this morning.* She had whispered back for clarification, *And last night? Are you sorry about that?* To which he'd replied firmly, *Absolutely not, that was no mistake.* "So, what's your idea?"

"It's about your mom," he said.

"Oh, okay, *not* what I was thinking." She shook her head, resetting.

"Sorry, no, I know. I have other ideas, that don't involve your mom, you know what I mean, never mind, but first," he sighed, starting over. "What if we sent her the clip of that question today? Wouldn't she be flattered that she's being thought of independent of us? Do you think she's cooled down?"

"Honestly." Charlie sat on his desk, thinking it through. She so wished that she could give him the answer he wanted. "She's just stubborn, even irrational."

His phone rang, and he glanced at it.

"It's okay," Charlie said, glad to have a way out of the conversation.

He kissed her quickly, glancing at the door as though they might get caught, but then kissed her once more as if he didn't mind. Finally, rolling his eyes at his ringing phone, he picked up as she let herself out.

—

Sierra had to skip the *Romeo and Juliet* matinee to rehearse for the Black Box one-act. She couldn't tell yet how it would come together, but at the very least, she worked well with Fiona and Tripp and knew her lines. Now, attired in her jean skirt and fuchsia Chamberlain T, she had to miss the evening *Romeo* performance too, to man the gift shop—which wasn't so much a *shop* as just a pair of large carts packed with Chamberlain T-shirts, sweatshirts, magnets, tote bags, tumblers, autographed cast photos and a phone with a credit card scanner.

All the apprentices had to rotate through these stations, but observing Tripp brave the nonstop chaos of the concession stand made her actively dread her stint there next week. She wished she could just watch the show every night. She still couldn't quite reconcile the Ethan onstage with the one who routinely stole her bacon at breakfast and stayed up late Netflixing favorite old movies on their laptops (the indie beginnings of Cameron Crowe and Spike Jonze and Baz Luhrmann and Catherine Hardwicke and Kathryn Bigelow and even Tarantino). She studied that cast photo again—Ethan smiling shyly like he wasn't sure he belonged—then swiped her own credit card, rolled up the photo and snuggled it into her bag.

Midway through intermission, she finally had a lull in customers and spotted Nicholas Blunt, in his usual Chamberlain shirt, blazer and jeans, wander inside from the warm night and roam the lobby, shaking hands, talking to the audience, asking how they liked the show. (He had cleverly placed the intermission early after Romeo and Juliet were married, rather than after Mercutio's and Tybalt's deaths in the stagings Sierra had seen elsewhere. This made for a more upbeat audience at intermission time.) He was smart: Nicholas knew the power of letting people be near him, giving them a chance to feel part of this place. As someone who often felt a step outside the circumference of the spotlight, Sierra understood on a molecular level how this mattered, this inclusion. Something about Nicholas's warm smile and slaps on the back felt genuine too.

She didn't know him, only what she had seen of him at their lectures and events, but now that the season had launched he looked more *alive* for some reason—or maybe it was just that she knew how much was riding on this kind of outreach. She couldn't understand how anyone with the funds at their disposal could be immune to that kind of charm. The theater was worthy of investment too, this show proved that art was being made here that deserved to continue. Maybe Nicholas and the cast just needed more significant time, a more intimate gathering with the people with the cash, the people who could change the fate of this place. More than meet-and-greet minutes between acts. Even the gala, which had been perfectly exciting to someone like Sierra, was still just a large event, a performance. What they needed was something more personal, that let donors feel part of this club. Would it be too far outside their established boundaries for Sierra to talk to Charlie about this? she wondered.

The lights flickered, signaling intermission's end, and as the crowd trickled back in, a statuesque woman in a gauzy minidress and heels cut a quick path through the front doors, stopping in the dead center of the lobby and shaking out her bouncy caramel mane as though wanting to give everyone ample time to notice her. And they did, staring and whispering, doing double takes.

Jasmine Beijao had just strolled into the lobby of the Chamberlain Summer Theater.

Sierra's mind almost couldn't compute it. This was not the kind of place you expected to find Jasmine Beijao. A Hollywood premiere? Sure. The Oscars after that movie she really wasn't so great in? Yes. The set of the next Bond movie? Absolutely. St. Bart's in a string bikini? Totally. But a Shakespeare summer theater? Never.

The only person who didn't seem to notice this strike of lightning was Nicholas, currently preoccupied with a gray-haired couple.

Jasmine sailed straight through, seas parting for her, walked up to Nicholas, wound one arm around his neck, her other hand on his chin, and planted a kiss on his lips. Interrupting his conversation and the conversations of everyone around them and seemingly stopping time for several seconds. Sierra hoped her jaw hadn't actually dropped. Without a word, Jasmine continued on toward a woman Sierra recognized from the gala. "Right this way, Ms. Beijao, we have a seat in front," the woman said, leading her into the auditorium.

The chattering began again, the flow of guests, the last blink of lights. And a final glance at Nicholas, the shock still on his face.

33

THOUGHT I'D GIVE YOU THE
FULL GROUPIE EXPERIENCE

When Charlie skipped the curtain call, Nick knew she had seen the third row.

He spotted Charlie in the backstage hall, grabbed for her hand as she walked by, already apologizing. "I don't know why she's here, believe me." But Charlie shoved him out of her way, pushing her hand into his chest, his heart, strong enough to slam him into the wall. Without even slowing down, she walked past her dressing room to the stage door and outside. The cast disassembling after their bows, the stagehands, the end of show chaos quickly engulfed him, erased him, and he couldn't get to her. By the time he made it outside there was no trace of her.

Matteo caught his eye as soon as he came back inside, yelled from down the hall, "Nick, man, what the hell?"

192 • AIMEE AGRESTI

"I know, it's a long story. I have to find her."

"Give her space…"

But Nick didn't hear the rest. Over Matteo's shoulder in the distance, Nick spotted Jasmine Beijao, being led backstage by Taylor. Nick ran in the opposite direction, weaving around apprentices, stage crew, and up the side staircase to the safe confines of his office. He locked the door and called Charlie. And texted her. And called her again. Each time it rang and rang. He left voice mail after voice mail. Apology after apology.

And then he made another call, to another voice mail box. "I *never* agreed to this, Taylor. You're not the artistic director here. I am." He hung up and threw the phone at his desk. He couldn't remember the last time he had behaved as though this place was actually *his*. It was time.

A knock rattled his locked door, the knob shaking.

"Niiiiick? It's me. Are you there?" Jasmine's voice oozed. "We have sooo much catching up to do!"

He didn't answer. Didn't move. Didn't breathe. He waited until she left, until the crowd flowing out of the lobby had died down, and then, just to be entirely sure the path was clear, he opened the window of his office and climbed out.

It was just half a story, eight feet max. But this wasn't the sort of thing he did on a regular basis and he landed poorly, twisting his ankle, hobbling all the way back into town, to the house on Avon.

—

All around Ethan, the greenroom buzzed with the night's gossip. "Jasmine Beijao!"

"OMG, did you see her?"

"OMG, did CHARLIE see her?"

"She was in the middle of the third row, who could miss her!"

"What is she doing here?"

But Ethan tried to ignore it. He didn't want all the noise to bring him down from that high. He let Alex and the others go ahead, told them he would catch up on the apprentice bar crawl, though he wasn't sure it was true. He just needed a few moments alone to fully absorb the charge of playing Mercutio opposite Charlie Savoy's Tybalt tonight.

His pulse *still* raced. Battling Charlie was so unlike battling Chase or even Matteo, and certainly Danica. It required everything he had, every bit of fire in his veins, there could be no holding back with her. If not for the rounded tips, she really might've killed him. The adrenaline of that scene had been otherworldly, addictive. And, it had played out like all the best experiences in life: your body knowing what to do and your mind content to let it happen. He wished he could be killed by Charlie's Tybalt every night for the rest of this run. For the rest of his life. It pained him that he knew of only one other night like this on the schedule. Charlie had passed him in the hallway immediately after, slapped him on the back. "Nice. You sure you're not a professional fencer?" She kept walking before he could even formulate a "thank you," but her praise meant everything.

He opened the stage door at last, stepping out into the clear night, shocked to find Sierra on the bench by the loading dock.

"I thought I missed you." She hopped to her feet. "But I took a chance."

"You waited. For me?" he asked, a pang in his heart. Tonight had broken him open, like a dial turned up so high he quaked from the feedback.

"I thought I'd give you the full groupie experience." She smiled, holding out what appeared to be a photo. "Well, not the *full* groupie experience," she corrected, embarrassed. "But you know what I mean. The *partial* groupie experience."

He laughed. "I'm honored. Either way."

"Glad to hear that because—" she waved the photo as they began walking to the dorm "—I couldn't help but notice, in my important, vital artistic work tonight, that you didn't sign any of these."

It was the cast photo autographed by the four main stars. He shook his head. "Oh man, I'm lucky they even let me into this picture." He remembered the day of the shoot: trying to draw as little attention to himself as he could, feeling completely unworthy of his place in that group.

"You think I'm kidding but—" She uncapped a Sharpie. "I'm totally not."

He looked up from his feet long enough to be ensnared by her bright, sincere eyes, which shone on him in a way he couldn't deserve but felt lucky for. "I can't believe you're making me deface a perfectly nice picture." He took the Sharpie, scribbling an arrow to himself and a message.

"See, is that so bad?" she joked, then read aloud, "'How'd this guy get here? Thanks for running lines with me, best scene partner anyone could hope for.'"

He tried not to blush hearing his own words.

34

NOTHING I HAVEN'T SEEN BEFORE

Charlie felt like she had when her harness broke midflight in
the teen angel film and she had crashed to the ground, wind
knocked out of her, two cracked ribs.

Her body had absorbed the sight of Jasmine Beijao—seated
front and center in the third row—like a sucker punch. A betrayal. Again. Charlie had lain on the stage, dying as Tybalt
freshly stabbed by Romeo in Act Three, when her eyes flickered out to the audience, trying to comprehend the presence of
this creature there, Jasmine Beijao: the model-turned-actress-
turned-Bond-Girl.

Who also happened to be Nick's ex-wife.

Still wearing her bloodied Tybalt costume, Charlie stood
at the edge of the pier, about to dive into the lake, hoping it
would free her. But gazing out at the shimmering water, she
felt none of the usual calm. This place felt ruined for her: she
could only see last night, with Nick. So she left.

The front door was unlocked, and she let it slam shut behind her. Jazz music, a sizzling stove, voices spilled out at her. She strode through the kitchen, head down, pace quick. But had to stop, not sure she had seen correctly:

A young boy in striped pajamas stood on a chair in front of the stove, flipping a grilled cheese sandwich in a pan. No one else there to watch him, she was overcome with an ill-timed flare-up of *responsibility*.

"Um, are you allowed to do that?" she asked the boy she recognized from so many photos in Danica's room. She didn't, in fact, know if it was alright to leave a child of six, seven, eight, whatever he was, alone at a gas stove. "Where's your mom?"

"What? This?" The boy laughed, flashing his jack-o'-lantern smile: three missing spaces where baby teeth must've fallen out. He had messy white-blond hair and Danica's face in miniature form. "Please," he said. "Who do you think does the cooking at home? That one—" he pointed upstairs "—is always on the raw food diet." He held out his hand. "I'm Gianni."

"Charlie." She shook his hand, still suspicious.

"I know. Charlie Savoy. Cool sword fights. Sorry you had to die tonight." He flipped the sandwich again then waved the spatula like he was fencing.

"It was twice," she said under her breath, counting seeing Jasmine.

"Really?"

She could see him trying to figure it out. "Never mind."

"Midnight snack?" He plated the sandwich and held it out to her.

Charlie looked around, as though Danica might appear and scold her, then shrugged. "Split it?"

"Okay." He hopped down from the chair, grabbed the knife from the butter dish and sliced the sandwich diagonally. "Crusts?" he asked, cutting off his own.

THE SUMMER SET • 197

"They're okay," she said. He left her half on the plate, took a bite of his and returned to the chair, tossing another already-assembled sandwich onto the pan. "Not bad," Charlie said, mouth full, hopping to sit on the counter.

"I was worried about you." Matteo swooped in, gave her a hug. "I can't believe she's here. I'm in shock, so I don't have better lines right now. I've only got clichés."

"I thought you were staying at the inn with Sebastian."

"I need to focus," he said.

"Since when?"

"Since last night." He opened the bottle of wine on the counter, taking a swig. "It's not important. Did you talk to Nick yet?" he deflected.

"Absolutely not." She grabbed the wine bottle, took a big gulp.

"Maybe he didn't know—"

"If fucking Jasmine Beijao was here— Sorry." She looked at Gianni, who just shrugged like he'd heard it all before and plated another sandwich, handing it to Matteo.

"What is a Jasmine Bay-Jow?" Gianni asked, doing his best pronunciation.

"If Jasmine Beijao is here then I don't want to be." Charlie took another bite and added, still chewing, "As soon as my sixty days are up. I'm out."

"Jasmine Beijao. I mean, how? Why?" Matteo said.

"What is a Jasmine Bay-Jow?" Gianni asked again.

"The woman has literally never done theater in her fucking life. Sorry," she said. Gianni tossed another sandwich in the pan, hopped off the chair to grab something from the kitchen table.

"And after last night." Matteo shook his head in disbelief.

"I know. I'm just mad at myself. I shouldn't have trusted—"

"My advice, talk to him. He's been in a bad place." She gave him a look. "I know, I know. I'm just saying, the Nick

I know would not have wanted this to happen. I know London meant something to him too," he said gently. "If Jasmine Beijao is here—"

"Siri, who is Jasmine Beijao?" Gianni said into his phone, back at the stove.

"There must be some reason. Let him explain," Matteo went on. "You do know he was the one who ended it with her, back then."

"I didn't know that," she said, coldly, trying not to care, trying to make it not change anything, so she could rebuild the walls she never should've taken down in the first place.

"I just always got the feeling that was some temporary insanity—his time with her." He shook his head. "Like he was a rebel teen for whatever that was two months—"

"*Two* months, though—"

"—that he was married to her during that terrible *Super Id* movie—"

"It *was* terrible," she said, confirming.

"—that he should've obviously waited for you to rewrite and fix," Matteo continued.

"Yup." She threw her hands up, drank from the bottle again.

"And he certainly should *not* have replaced you with her as the star because that was ridiculous."

"Whatever, I didn't care then and don't now." She lied.

"Although, the last time you saw her, you threw a drink at her—" Matteo said.

"No," she cut him off, pointing. "*Near* her. Not even her. Nick. Near Nick. Over their heads. Over his head. Just to make a point. I'm not a monster, I just had to—"

"Is this Jasmine Beijao?" Gianni interrupted, looking stricken as he flashed his phone at them. "Why isn't she wearing any clothes?"

Charlie ripped the phone from Gianni's grip as Matteo threw his hands over the boy's eyes.

"Yes," Charlie said flatly, staring. "Why *isn't* she wearing any clothes?" She held it out to Matteo, still shielding the boy's eyes.

There on Instagram, in a photo snapped earlier that afternoon, stood Jasmine Beijao, all five feet eleven of her, taking a selfie in a full-length mirror and wearing *nothing* but a ruff—one of those accordion-style collars aristocrats wore at their necks during Shakespeare's time—and a gleaming white smile, her cascading curls everywhere.

"No big deal, guys, I'm in the middle of a classical art unit at camp, so nothing I haven't seen before," Gianni said calmly, eyes still covered.

"'Found this must-have accessory at the most charming shop #ruffsandcuffs in Chamberlain'?" Charlie read the caption aloud as though it was a long, offensive question. "'Catch me here in the upcoming *Midsummer Night's Dream*'?" She looked at Matteo, disgusted.

"Ohhh, man," Matteo said, leaning in to read it himself.

"'Tickets available now. Link in bio. #theatergoddess #berkshiresbabe'? *This* is why I'm not on Instagram." Charlie shook the phone.

"It's not *all* like that. Did you see the filters on my photos from Hopkins Forest? Magical," Matteo said.

"No," she deadpanned.

"Is something *burning*?" Danica barked, interrupting them in her matching striped monogrammed pajamas.

"Hi, Mom!" Gianni said, eyes still covered, waving anyway.

Charlie and Matteo whipped around to the stove, where the grilled cheese sizzled to a carcinogenic lump. A thin veil of smoke began to coat the room.

"Fuck!" Charlie lunged to turn off the stove but was too

late: the smoke detector blared on. She jumped at its deafening screech.

"Gianni!" Danica yelled to be heard over it. "What have I told you about being careful when you're cooking?" She fanned the burnt pan.

"They covered my eyes!" he shouted back, pointing at Charlie and Matteo, the latter of whom had leaped onto a chair, trying to dismantle the smoke detector.

"I don't know *what's* going on here," Danica scolded. "I literally left for, like, five minutes to say goodbye to Sally."

"It's okay, Mom, they just didn't want me to see the naked lady—"

"That sounds worse than it is," Matteo said over the still-piercing alarm.

"I thought Mr. Chase was watching you," she said to Gianni.

"You left him with Chase?" Charlie laughed, and Danica shot her a look. "I mean, he's great with kids. Mr. Chase."

"He's on the phone," Gianni explained. "It sounded important, so I told him to take his time."

"C'mon, sweetie." Danica put a protective arm around Gianni, as though cocooning him from so much moral corruption. "Time for bed."

Gianni glanced back at them and mouthed, *Sorry.*

At last the alarm quieted, but Charlie barely noticed, too preoccupied with another siren as she scrolled the many images of Jasmine: Jasmine arriving at Hathaway House in a lime-green Ferrari; Jasmine allegedly wearing no makeup; Jasmine at various premieres and awards shows. Every inch of her life—and her figure—documented. Charlie couldn't help it. She had spent so much time pretending this woman didn't exist in real life, off-screen, but now here she was again, unavoidable, and Charlie felt hurt and just masochistic enough that she kept swiping this endless photo stream. It felt like a scab that had somehow begun gushing blood again with no warning.

"No-no-no-no, no good comes of that, trust me." Matteo pried Gianni's phone from her hand, tossing it facedown on the table, its Pokémon case staring back at them.

The doorbell buzzed. And buzzed again. And again. And again. Leaning toward the kitchen window, they saw Nick in profile at the door. Buzz. Buzz. Buzz. Knock. Knock.

Matteo looked at Charlie. "Do you want to—?"

"I don't want to talk. Ever. No. But could I punch him?"

"I'll tell him you're asleep."

"I don't care what you tell him, I don't want anything to do with him." She passed Chase on the stairs, hanging up a phone call.

"Is something burning?" he asked.

She just walked up, straight to her balcony, took a deep breath. Thirty-three days to go. It felt like a life sentence.

—

"Is Charlie—?" Nick started the second Matteo opened the door. But instead of inviting Nick in, Matteo stepped outside, closing the door behind them and gently pushing Nick farther back on the porch.

"Look, I'm supposed to tell you she's not here," Matteo said. "Nick, help me here—what were you thinkin'?"

"I was young and I needed the money?" He tried the classic line, defeated, then clarified. "Or, I guess I was old and I needed the money."

"I know better than anyone what trouble this place is in, I get it. But there has got to be a better way."

"Don't you think I'm trying? I didn't even do this. This was the last thing I—"

"It's not fair. To her." Matteo looked over his shoulder as though Charlie might be watching, lowered his voice to a

202 • AIMEE AGRESTI

whisper. "I thought you loved this girl." He gestured toward the house.

"I know, I do," he said, sighing.

"Then you don't do this. Not to that girl."

"No. I know, I'm just... I don't know what I'm supposed to do." He took a seat on the top step.

"Get creative," Matteo said, walking back to the door. "And get outta here. For now."

Nick watched as he disappeared inside, then closed his eyes, pulled himself up and limped home.

By the time Nick got back to his place, he was fairly certain he'd had what could be categorized as a slight psychotic break. It had just started to rain, managing to soak him before he reached his bungalow four blocks from Charlie's house.

Yes, he had sent that initial email to Jasmine, and received a "Maybe, let's talk" response, which he had ignored, and that was it. He had hoped Sarah Kingsbury would change her mind in the meantime and that her presence would be enough to get Taylor to forget all about Jasmine. But that had all been wishful thinking. Taylor had just gone around him and hired Jasmine herself, a stunning abuse of power, power she didn't technically have. Nick wasn't an idiot. He knew what Taylor was doing. He knew the kind of drama, offstage, she was hoping to manipulate with this casting. The attention she hoped to garner. Taylor was successful, wealthy, powerful, and used to getting what she wanted, she didn't believe in boundaries. He felt trapped in a game he had no interest in playing.

Midsummer rehearsals weren't set to begin for another week. It was time he could have used to try to run out the clock, find a way to *not* hire Jasmine. Or, at the very least, time to prepare Charlie for Jasmine's arrival. But now all he could do was damage control.

35

GIVE HER THE LINE!

The water rushed over Charlie, not unpleasantly, at first. She floated.
Too free and weightless to be bothered by the biting chill. River and
rain aswirl around her. The words came to her, as though from another
world, from her past: "We are such stuff as dreams are made on, and
our little life is rounded with a sleep." Yes, sweet, elusive sleep. Was
she actually sleeping? Finally? Was she breathing?

Or was she on set, her director barking at her?

"Give her the line!" the voice shouted, urgent. "Give her the line!"
She could hear it, but the words arrived fuzzy in her ears. She listened again for the director's deep, rich rasp. Her body tumbled over
and over, spinning. Then the fierce tug decidedly down.

No, it wasn't her line, was it? The voice had been right. That line
was Prospero's. She was playing Ariel. "Our revels now are ended.
These our actors, as I foretold you, were all spirits and are melted into
thin air," she thought.

"GIVE HER THE LINE!" She heard it again, angry now.

She had the line, but when she opened her mouth to say it, water flooded in, choking her. Eyes opened to soggy flashes of light against a black landscape; her limbs flailed, understanding before her mind did.

She was drowning.

Her right thigh stung, but still her legs kicked, struggling to push to the surface of the water. She sucked in the air, desperate. But it was wet, suffocating. Too much water.

"Grab the line!" a man shouted, not the voice she thought. Gasping, her head bobbing under, she reached, stretching her fingertips to find the life preserver on the rope. Hugging it to her chest, panting, she let herself be dragged back to dry land. Her eyes set on the contemporary art museum gleaming along the darkened riverbank, Long Wharf, the lights of Boston twinkling beyond, as she tried to steady her jagged breaths and racing heart. She had never seen her world from here, from the water. It had never looked more beautiful…

—

Charlie awakened on her balcony, lightning illuminating the sky, thunder crashing, a storm raging. And Chase kneeling above her, in the downpour, white T-shirt and plaid boxers sticking to his body as he shook her.

"Charlie? Heard you yelling all the way in my room. What're you doing out here?" he shouted over the cascading rain. "Is this about *The Tempest*? This some kind of 'method' shit? I really don't get you guys."

"I wish," she said, sitting up now in her Tybalt costume. She remembered lying down when she grew weary of the Warwickshire crowds below. She smoothed her wet hair back from her face.

"Let's get you inside." He pulled open the trapdoor, gesturing for her to go in first, then yanking it shut behind them.

"Sure you're cool?" he asked, soaked now too, standing in her doorway before crossing the hall to his room.

She nodded. Across the way now, leaning against the doorframe, she saw a woman's figure—Harlow—pushing the golden hair out of her eyes. Chase swung Charlie's door closed with a nod goodbye. From the other side of it, she heard Harlow's silky voice: "What's going on? Everything okay?"

"Yeah, it's nothing," he said, protecting Charlie. "Back to bed, c'mon."

In the suffocating quiet of her room, Charlie peeled off her wet clothes, leaving them in a heap on the floor, and climbed under the cool sheets of her bed. For what felt like hours, she lay awake, listening to the rain beat against her window. And replaying, over and over on a loop, that dream. But it wasn't a dream at all, but a recollection of what had actually happened. All the missing pieces assembling themselves into a full picture of that night she had driven into the harbor.

It was that memory of Nick, directing her, *The Tempest* shoot, that had shaken her out of her sleep as her car drifted to the depths of the harbor. It seemed unfair that it had been Nick's voice in her head awakening her that night, signaling her body to fight, reaching into her deep subconscious and pulling her back to life.

36

WE'RE TEAM CHARLIE

Sierra, Fiona and Tripp were already at their regular table at the pub when Harlow swanned in with Alex and announced grandly, "Listen up! I have it from a very well-placed source. Jasmine Beijao is trying to win Nicholas Blunt back!"

"Yeah, we know, Sierra saw her kiss Blunt," Tripp said, no big deal.

"Oh." Harlow deflated, the wind sufficiently let out of her sails.

"Hi, stranger. You would've known that sooner if you'd come home last night." Sierra smiled at Harlow and innocently sipped her iced tea. She hadn't seen her roommate in two nights.

"The plot thickens!" Tripp leaned in. "But I do love Jasmine Beijao!"

"No! You can't love Jasmine Beijao," Sierra said. "We're Team Charlie."

"Why do we have to choose?" Alex asked. "And why does everyone use her full name all the time?"

"They hate each other—Charlie and Jasmine Beijao," Sierra said.

"It's over Nicholas," Harlow said, dismissive.

"Charlie should be pissed, especially after whatever went on in London," Tripp said.

"We don't know that for sure," Sierra said.

"It doesn't matter." Ethan appeared, tray in hand. "And it's not just about a dude. It was about a role that was Charlie's that he was forced to give to Jasmine."

"A role in a terrible movie," Harlow said.

"A terrible movie that would've been great if they had let Charlie do it," Ethan said. "She would've fixed it. It was rushed."

"Why do you people know all of this?" Fiona asked, typing on her laptop.

"Am I the only one who watches *E!*?" Sierra asked, embarrassed.

"You might be the only one who watched it a million years ago when all that went down," Harlow said.

"It was, like—" Ethan paused, mouthing numbers like he was computing a math problem "—over a dozen years ago, factoring in the many years between recasting, filming and the release of the movie, which was in postproduction for ages. And released years later, probably because everyone involved knew it was so bad. Anyway, where's your sense of history?"

"Of course we're Team Charlie," Tripp said. "But Jasmine is *such* a diva—we don't have to *like* her in order to like her *drama*."

"Jasmine Beijao is a bombshell of the highest degree," Harlow defended. "And almost won an Oscar—"

"That wolf movie was awful," Ethan interrupted, notepad

out to take orders. "It's fine to make a pretty girl ugly if the story is a good one, but there was nothin' else going on. An empty ploy to get awards."

"All costume and makeup," Sierra agreed.

"I totally want to be her," Harlow said.

"Why?" Sierra asked. "I would want to be Charlie."

"It would just be a lot more *work* to be Charlie," Harlow said. "But Jasmine seems like everything comes easy."

"Easy is boring," Ethan said, getting called away to the bar.

"Easy *is* boring," Fiona confirmed, scrolling through her phone.

"I'm always whichever team had to work harder," Sierra said, nodding.

"Speaking of hard work, I'm so spent with *Romeo and Juliet*," Harlow said. "You guys have no idea how emotionally exhausting it is to perform on the main stage."

"It can be intense," Alex said, stretching his arms over his head. Sierra sipped her drink, trying not to let on how supremely left out and *less than* she felt.

"You guys are *so* lucky to have extra time to prep for the next auditions. *Midsummer Night's Dream* is just around the corner," Harlow said, turning to Sierra. "There are more apprentice parts for that one."

She had possibly intended to be encouraging, but to Sierra's ears it sounded condescending. "I know, I'm working on it." Sierra tried to be breezy.

Ethan listened in as he refilled sodas at the next table. He leaned over to her. "Yeah, get on that, Sierra," he said, rolling his eyes. Harlow was too engrossed in her phone to notice, and Ethan glanced at her screen. "Making plans for New York?" he asked.

"Maybe," Harlow snapped, shielding the phone against her chest.

The apprentice trip to see *Abby's Road* was just a few weeks away, but Sierra hoped it would light a fire in her to be there.

"The after-party with Bronwyn and the guys?" Alex asked, always at the center of everything. Harlow nodded. "A mutual friend from Juilliard is in the chorus," he explained. "You guys should come."

"Alex," Harlow said, as though scolding him for inviting everyone.

"We're there," Tripp said, agreeing on behalf of the table.

Sierra didn't mind: she could think of worse things than hanging out with cast members from the hottest new Broadway show.

37

YOU STILL ARE A CHILD

Charlie sat beside Gianni on the porch steps, which were still damp from last night's storm. Her hair had dried in wild, beachy waves. She sipped her coffee. After sleeping so soundly for the first time in ages, she now felt in a fog, her body not entirely awake.

"…and also if you want me to start an Instagram page for you—or Twitter, Facebook, Snapchat, what have you—let me know," Gianni offered, waiting for Danica to finish packing him up to head back to camp. "It could be beneficial, I'm sure you have fans who would like to correspond with you. And me too, I write great letters."

"Thanks, little man," she said. "I think I'm good for now on all the pages. But I'll take you up on the letters." He threw his arms around her, surprising her with a warm, puppyish hug, then pulled away just as fast, loading an enormous *Star Wars* backpack onto his back. "And good luck with Sparky."

She patted his backpack, which held parts of the robot he was building and programming.

"You'll get to meet him when I'm back for *Midsummer*, that's one of my favorites," he said as Sally and Danica emerged from the front door saying their goodbyes with tender kisses. Danica's sentimental side made such rare appearances, Charlie almost couldn't look away.

"Can't wait," Charlie said, sincere, raising her hand for a high five, then low five, then her left hand high and low, then both hands. She and Gianni had devised the secret handshake during breakfast after he had admitted he didn't want to go back to camp. But now, he seemed fine. She wished she could overcome setbacks so swiftly.

"You're good with kids," Danica said to Charlie as the car pulled out. "Which shouldn't surprise me since you kind of still *are* a child even though you're forty?"

"Thirty-nine," Charlie corrected, waving to the black Lexus as it rolled down the driveway.

"You should think about freezing your eggs." Danica dispensed the advice like the doctor she had once played in an ad. "Now. *Immediately.*"

"Yeah, no, I think I'm good." Charlie patted her belly like it was a foreign object not attached to her. "I'm not cooking anything up in here. It's just not my thing, I don't think. But… I'll keep it in mind?"

"Good, glad to help." Danica smiled, letting herself back inside.

Charlie's phone buzzed: Nick again. can we meet before the show? She hadn't returned any of his texts. She didn't see the point. But she wanted this to stop: do NOT talk to me today. or ever. just let me do my fucking job until my sentence at this prison is over.

Chase bounded up the steps, in his yoga gear, squeezed

Charlie's shoulder. He let himself inside as her phone buzzed once more.

sometime when you're ready, i need to explain. it's important to me and then those three blinking dots: YOU are important to me.

She shoved her phone in her pocket without responding.

—

Knowing the basics of what had gone on the previous night—that Jasmine Beijao had thrown herself into Charlie's world like an ax into a tree—Sierra dreaded the costume assignment Madame LaPlage had saddled her with. But Charlie had apparently run off in her Tybalt costume last night and it needed to be returned, cleaned and prepped for the next time Charlie would be playing that role.

They had a matinee today. Sierra arrived backstage early, lingering near Charlie's dressing room. When Charlie did show up, it was earlier than Sierra had expected. The actress nodded a hello to her, her expression tense.

Sierra gathered her courage. "Madame LaPlage was asking about your Tybalt—"

She sighed audibly. "I'll bring it back tomorrow," she said like a kid without her homework.

"And there's one more thing. Something I wanted to talk to you about, an idea, for this place." She whispered the last part.

Charlie looked at her, curious, and opened the dressing room door, flicking her head for Sierra to join her. "I needed to get the fuck out of the house, you know," Charlie said, taking a seat at the mirror, flipping on the lights and digging through her bag.

"I get that." Sierra wished she could ask if Charlie was okay, after Jasmine and whatever it was that had gone on last night, but it felt too personal, invasive. Charlie said nothing, just tied back her hair into a low ponytail and pulled out a compact, sweeping a bronzer across her face, all business. "I was thinking about ways to help this place, you know, stay open."

Charlie sighed. "Let's hear it, I guess."

—

When Charlie finished her makeup and Sierra finished her pitch, Sierra was shocked to find Charlie lead them out of the dressing room and straight upstairs to Nicholas Blunt's office. Charlie knocked once and opened the door, not waiting for an answer.

"Charlie." Nicholas stood up at his desk when Charlie appeared in his doorway. "I was hoping we could—"

"I don't have anything to say to you," Charlie said, flatly. "But Sierra does and I think you should listen. She knows this place is in trouble." As she said this, his face dropped. "I didn't mean to tell her, but you're not entitled to be angry with me after what you've pulled in the past twenty-four hours." He nodded at this, and she went on, "So Sierra seems to think people—the kind who have dollar signs attached to their names—would like to see more of us. You're on," she prompted Sierra, leaving her there alone.

Sierra nodded, taking her cue, fingers fidgeting until she mentally told them to *stop*. She felt as she had before her audition, as Nicholas sat there with his arms folded watching her, but reminded herself there were no lines this time. She was actually doing him a favor. "Well, I was just inspired seeing you greet guests at the show," she began. "You may not realize it because you're...you...but it's a big deal to people, audience members, to come here and get to see you and talk to you and be heard by you and be near you. And that's true of all the company members. That time, one-on-one, those microconversations matter but—"

He nodded slowly. "Like the gala."

"But that was so many people," she said, gently. "I was

thinking, what if you hosted something more intimate, for a select group who are most likely to invest significant amounts of money? Give them attention and time with you and the company actors? Maybe a small dinner, somewhere that feels exclusive, a place most people don't have access to. Honestly, I can't imagine anyone saying no to, like, all of you guys," she said, sincere.

"I suppose we can be charming when we want to be," he said.

"It's more than that though." She couldn't quite describe what he and the professional actors had, the allure, the ability to command attention. Perhaps it was something that came organically from years of being watched. Nicholas began clicking on his keyboard, eyes on the screen. She felt she had lost him, so she said simply, "Thanks for your time," and took a step toward the door.

"So it's decided," he said, and she stopped. He swung the screen around, the July calendar. "We'll do it next week— July Fourth."

"Seriously?" she asked, not believing it.

"It's the only day the theater is dark before the money runs out," he said, almost to himself, swinging the screen around again. "They do fireworks in the field behind the museum, we can even see them from Hathaway House. We'll do it there. I'm pushing back the *Midsummer* auditions a week." He continued typing, not looking up.

"Really? They're not tomorrow now?"

"Feel free to tell your friends. I'll have Bradford announce the change at tomorrow's workshop." He said it all stream of consciousness and continued typing. "I just can't deal with rehearsals and any of it this week, I just—" He stopped himself, as though realizing he was speaking this out loud. He looked up a moment. "Thank you," he said, sincerely. "Your idea is a good one."

On her way out, Nicholas called after her just before she closed the door. "And, Ms. Suarez, I know Charlie mentioned our situation here is a little…" He searched for the word but she understood.

"I won't tell, I promise," she said.

He looked instantly relieved. "Thanks." And then before she left again, he added, "And you know." She looked back. "I wondered if you could tell Charlie that I appreciate her bringing you and your idea to me. Let her know I said yes? And that I was encouraging—I think I'm encouraging, right? Like in a mentoring kind of way?"

She smiled, warmed at the thought that even someone like Nicholas Blunt could have the same difficulties navigating relationships as she did. "Yes, I'll tell her."

38

ACT LIKE YOU'RE A NARCISSIST

It helped that Sierra had never planned to go on the July Fourth trip to Boston: a day of touring historical sites—*Like where Charlie Savoy drove into the river!* Harlow had said—shopping, fireworks and catching the last bus back. Most of the apprentices, who hadn't been drafted into service for the contributors' dinner, would be going. Luckily, Ethan was among those staying behind too. Sierra wished she had been allowed to tell him that this whole dinner was actually her idea, that she had found a way to be part of the theater, despite not earning a role on the main stage. But she kept quiet, as promised, and kept busy until she was needed for dinner prep.

While Ethan worked the early shift at the pub, she escaped into the lush thickets of Hopkins Forest in search of that elusive, endangered plant species. Hiking with her notebook and map, snapping photos on her phone of any plant life worthy of a cameo in her thesis. The hours trickled by as she roamed the well-trodden dirt paths, listening to the stark quiet, letting the calm envelop her, fully at peace even in patches so densely canopied the sun's rays barely broke through. It had been a long time since she had been alone. The frenetic pace of the apprentice program had gotten her accustomed to so much multitasking. Here she could hear her own thoughts again, and they told her there was still time to make waves. That was easy to forget when everyone was so focused on *Romeo and Juliet* for so long, but auditions for *Midsummer Night's Dream* were now just one day away: a new chance to be on the main stage. And there was still her part in the student Black Box show—Fiona seemed happy with Sierra's work there; maybe one of the agents would notice her at that performance. It was just over a month away now. Still time to turn the summer around.

Completing the trail's loop, she finally made her way back toward the park entrance, where she was greeted by a pack of footfalls and the faint buzz of conversation. At once, they flew by her like a track team: a dozen college-aged girls led by Chase Embers.

—

At 2:30 sharp, Sierra waited on the manicured lawn outside of the theater—which was dark tonight. She took a seat beside the stone sculptures of comedy and tragedy masks roughly the size of stallions. A honking horn startled her, and she laughed when she saw the old red pickup truck. "Hop aboard, these flowers ain't gonna pick themselves," Ethan greeted her with a smile.

"Awesome, my Uber's here," she said, leaning in the open window.

"Nice, right? Mason's wheels," Ethan said. Mason was the Chamberlain's longtime set designer. "Looks just like mine used to, only difference is this one actually runs."

"They have these in Oregon too, you know." A wave of nostalgia hit her, a touch of homesickness. They had a green truck at the resort that she would use to drive guests' luggage to their rooms. "Do you mind if I—?"

"Really?" He sounded intrigued. "So you can take the girl out of the tree house…"

⸺

Windows rolled down, sunglasses on, her hair blowing, Sierra sped into the mountains in search of the farm supplying the wildflowers for the night's dinner party. Ethan navigated on his phone, and they found the weathered barn in the middle of nowhere, just a half hour out of town. The proprietor, a woman in denim and chambray whom Sierra recognized from her favorite flower stand at the farmers' market, had gathered bunches upon bunches—black-eyed Susans, New England asters, fireweels, cornflowers, lilies in violet, golden and cherry hues—all bound and nestled in buckets, ready for transporting. Ethan and Sierra simply needed to load them into the truck.

In the distance, Sierra spied the fields where the flowers had been plucked.

"You're welcome to have a look around," the woman told them and then went back into the barn.

They had time, so Sierra drove them up the dirt path, arriving at the field of lilies and sunflowers. They ran through, holding out their arms on either side, fingertips grazing the blooms, like athletes low-fiving fans as they rushed into a stadium.

Ethan stopped after what felt like half the length of a football field. "So, I'm generally emphatically anti-selfie," he called out.

"Same," Sierra agreed, turning around and stopping herself.

"But…wanna make 'em sorry they're not here?" He meant Harlow and Alex.

She smiled and pulled out her phone. "Challenge accepted. Act like you're a narcissist who doesn't know he's a narcissist," she joked.

They snapped themselves with the barn and mountains in the background, and lay on their backs laughing as they took shots in the sunshine, flowers surrounding them.

"You know…" Ethan said, beside her in the field, the sky bright blue with streaks of cirrus like swipes of paint. "I probably shouldn't say this because she's your roommate and all…"

"Harlow," Sierra said to the sky.

"Yeah, I hope you know, she just, she doesn't *think*, that's why she says some of the stuff she does. And I think it's very… generous of you to not, like, want to knock her out half the time."

Sierra laughed. "Well, what kind of roommate would I be if I did that?"

"A perfectly justified one."

For a few peaceful moments, Sierra forgot about auditions or expectations or pressures or falling short.

Before they left, they raced, climbing to the top of the tree beside their truck. Perched on the branches beside him, she could have stayed there all day.

39

WHY CAN'T YOU JUST
STAY AWAY FROM ME?

Though she admired Sierra's initiative dreaming up this fund-raising dinner, Charlie had been actively dreading it all week. The only brief respite in Charlie's daily misery had come when Chase yanked her into the living room Tuesday morning to watch the Emmy Award nominations live and they had cheered to hear Marlena's name announced among the contenders for Best Actress in a Drama Series. Charlie had called Marlena immediately, not caring that it had been 5 a.m. in LA, and Chase grabbed the phone right out of her hand to congratulate Marlena himself, whom he hadn't spoken to in so many moons. They had never been close on set those years ago. Chase had kept to himself while she and Marlena—or Marlon, then—had been inseparable, just like their characters. But she supposed sometimes you didn't need to have been especially close years ago to feel a kinship when your paths crossed again. To hear the two of them catching up as though no time had passed had warmed Charlie. Even more surprisingly, they had kept talking.

"So she's in New York taking meetings and wants to come see us," Chase, hands in the pockets of his dove-gray suit, updated Charlie as they walked to Hathaway House, trailing Danica and Matteo. "Next weekend maybe? She's working it all out."

"I think you've talked to Marlena more in the past week than I have in the past year," Charlie joked. She wore the items that had unexpectedly materialized in her closet—black tuxedo pants, lacy camisole, strappy heels—courtesy of Sierra. A welcome find after a tense run in Hopkins Forest with Matteo, who'd dragged her along to keep an eye on her, she knew. Chase had told Matteo of her night on the balcony.

"I had about two decades to catch up on," he laughed.

"She's not usually so easy to get a hold of, she's pretty in-demand." Charlie smiled, proud.

"I know, good for her." Chase was pensive for a moment. "She did this all her own way, you know?"

"She's got it all figured out," Charlie agreed, adding, "Wonder what that's like." As they reached the gothic stone mansion— all gargoyles, pointed archways, turrets and parapets—she felt her skin crawl. "This'll be fun," Charlie sighed as Chase held open the door.

Inside, they were greeted by the buzz of conversation, pulse of dance music, clink of glasses and crowd of a few dozen of the most generous donors. Chase quickly dissolved into a group of chatty patrons, shaking hands, smiling, patting backs, expertly accepting the compliments they lavished on him. He was good at this.

Years earlier, Charlie would've loved to have been here: she and Nick had walked past the building a million times, always speculating about what lay inside. She would've marveled at the vaulted ceilings, intricately patterned floor with that crest in the center of the foyer, ornate woodwork in dark mahogany and rooms upon rooms. Now though: not so much. She noted the land mines to avoid—Jasmine circling Nick, Taylor circling them both—grabbed a glass of wine from the bar and slipped out, down a long corridor, to a study adorned with floor-to-ceiling built-in bookcases.

Alone, she felt a brief calm. She scanned the shelves and found the complete works of seemingly every notable playwright from the beginning of time through recent Pulitzer winners. She had just pulled out *A Midsummer Night's Dream* when she heard footsteps.

Nick appeared in the doorway: dark suit, no tie, drink in his hand and a sheepish expression.

She said nothing, eyes back on her book.

"I was hoping I'd see you here," he said, trying a smile but giving up when it wasn't reciprocated.

"I'm legally obligated to be here, so here I am." She glanced up only a moment.

"The *Boston Globe* called our staging 'inventive and surprising' and called you 'an exhilarating Romeo,'" he said cautiously, an icebreaker.

"That's nice," she said flatly, not wanting to give him the satisfaction of knowing she cared. Secretly though, she tucked those words away to come back to—as she had that letter from the drama student—the validation sweet and unexpected.

"Look, I need to say…" She turned away and crouched to read the spines nearest the floor. But he knelt beside her. "This is not at all what I—"

With a bang, she slammed shut the book in her hands, making him jump, to her pleasure. "I'm not listening to this." She stood again. He did too.

"But—"

"Not now. I'll leave." She walked away, toward the shelves beside the window. "You're lucky I'm here at—"

"Okay, okay. No talking." He appeared beside her again, ruffled his hair, the way he did when he was exasperated with her. Which usually made her smile. "What about a tour, then?" he asked. That golden haze of dusk filtered in, giving him a warm glow. "This is a historical landmark, you know."

"I'm *so sick* of the past," she said, almost to herself, even though she had always been curious about this place. The mansion belonged to the university, often serving as an event space, but Grayson used to rent it for the entire summer theater season, rather than staying at the small house in town that the theater owned and reserved for the artistic director.

"Unless you'd rather converse with all those lovely people?" He tugged her by the elbow, leading her out again, gesturing to the crowded foyer. "Which is probably what you should be doing." He did have a point, unfortunately.

"Fine." She rolled her eyes. "Tour."

"Great." He set off down the corridor. "So here's where we're having dinner." He opened the door to the ornate banquet room, with a long oval table set as though for kings and queens. Velvet drapes, wall tapestries, more tall, narrow windows. And in the corner: Mercutio and Sierra, deep in conversation, holding baskets of rolls. "Ever the devoted apprentices," Nick said as they quieted.

He walked ahead, looking over his shoulder to be sure Charlie was still there. She opened a door, peering down into a pitch-black abyss. "I think I was wrong about this place. It's actually creepy." She opened yet another door: "Yep. That's where the bodies are buried for sure."

"Here's the kitchen," he continued, tuning her out. "There's some way to get outside. There's a fountain out there. But I'm not sure, how to get to it…" He shook a series of stuck door-knobs that opened into closets. "Are you enjoying this at all?"

"Is there a ballroom?" she asked.

"I'm not sure—"

"A screening room?"

"Doubt it."

"A billiard room?"

"Yes, let's find that—"

"What are the bedrooms like?"

"I don't know, I guess they're up there somewhere." He gazed up the grand staircase, stopped in his tracks, faced her. "Is that an invitation?" He tried to be funny.

"No. It was a test," she said, frosty. She had been hoping to trip him up.

"Shoot," he said. "I was thinking you were letting me off the hook." And then, understanding. "Ohhh. No. I have *not* seen the bedrooms. See, I passed—didn't I? Your test?" He leaned against the banister, arms folded.

"You didn't fail, I guess," she sighed, winding her hair into a loose topknot. She had, of course, been subtly trying to find out whether he had visited Jasmine's bedroom specifically, since she had rented a room for the show's duration.

"I know you're angry," he whispered from behind her, standing very close.

"I am," she said, with cold certainty. Just as she was angry that his eyes were so iridescent today and his voice so deeply graveled, as it had been in her dream of the harbor. She was angry that when she looked at him she saw *their* history and worse, the false promise of finding true purpose again, instead of seeing the betrayal and confusion. And she was angry that when he stood this close to her, she still had an impulse to believe whatever he told her.

"You're allowed to be. Angry. Charlie… I didn't want her here either. You've gotta believe me."

"Why have I *gotta* believe you?" She drained her wineglass and left it perched in the hand of a statue of a naked woman, breaking away from him. She ducked into the first empty room she found.

"Believe me because the lake meant something, London too." He stepped into her line of vision again, but she averted her eyes. She ran her hand along the smooth marble shelf above the fireplace, studied the black-and-white photos, surprised to see one of her mother and Grayson, arms around each other, circa sometime after Charlie's summer there; she could tell by the length of her mom's hair. Nick stopped to notice it too, then looked at her again. "Believe me that I want *you* here——" He stopped as an apprentice came in, setting up the billiard table. Nick ushered Charlie out again, hand on her back. "I want you here." He lowered his voice, tried to slow their pace, but now they were being trailed by a pack of guests pretending to admire the art. "And not just for sixty days. And it wasn't me, it was Taylor who brought Jasmine, unauthorized——"

"Ugghhh, I need another fucking drink for this." Charlie darted away to the foyer, but he kept pace. "It's never your fault, it's never *you* making the decisions." She spoke too loudly, grabbed a drink and tossed it back. "You *never* used to be like that. And I can tell you exactly when——"

"Listen, this isn't the time to rehash everything." He tried to quiet her.

"So now he *doesn't* want to talk. This is *exactly* what I'm talking about."

"I just meant that *the investor*," he whispered, looking to be sure Taylor wasn't within earshot, "the investor, who you are also right to dislike——" He tried to guide her back to the study, but they had drawn a crowd blocking the way.

"Oh, thank you," Charlie said, as though it was a news flash.

"*She* brought Jasmine, before I could stop it." He sounded

vague, which she didn't like. "I was trying to have that *not* happen. Despite the trouble this place is in."

"Why can't you just stay away from me?" Her voice too loud again, guests now watching.

"That's what I'm *trying to tell you.*" Now he raised *his* voice to get her attention. Then quiet again, he said, "I can't stay away from you. And I think you might feel the same way—"

"Wow," she cut him off, offended, partly because she thought she had been a much better actress than what he was accusing her of. "Is that right?"

"But that is *not* what I wanted to *say* right now—"

"Then just tell me and then leave me alone!"

A hush fell over the house now, just the two of them and the music, everyone listening. Except Taylor, who seemed to think the party had silenced for her. "Welcome! Dinner is now being served in the banquet room!" she announced, as though nothing could be more thrilling.

Some began to clap. Charlie was unsure why until a petite older woman, clasping her husband's arm, came over and said, "You two were brilliant, brav-o!"

Nick shook his head. "No, we're—"

But Charlie shushed him. "Thank you, ma'am," Charlie said with a bow to get rid of them.

"Oooh, is this going to turn into one of those murder mystery nights where you have to figure out who the killer is?" another woman said to her husband as they made their way to the dining room. "I love those!"

"Or maybe it's one of those escape rooms where everyone is locked in and has to get out?" a gentleman, dapper in a three-piece suit, asked a similarly attired man. "This house would be sheer perfection for that."

"This whole fucking summer is like an escape room," Charlie said into her glass, taking a final swig.

40

WE'RE ACTUALLY A LOT ALIKE

Ethan poked his head out of the dining room, exchanging glances with Sierra, who stood across the hallway ushering people in. She fidgeted with that necklace—a shooting star pendant, the center of intense drama—and Ethan felt for her as he turned over in his mind what she'd started to tell him before Blunt and Charlie interrupted them. Apparently the necklace was Harlow's—but Harlow had left it in Chase's room last night. Chase brought it with him, thinking Harlow might be at the dinner, but since she wasn't, he gave it to Sierra to return instead. And completely ruined Sierra's night. She still looked shattered.

Ethan wasn't sure whether it bothered him more that Chase had unwittingly broken Sierra's heart or that Sierra had enough of a crush on Chase to be upset by this. That afternoon at the farm had felt so comforting to Ethan, it had taken him away from the pressures of this place. Of performing, of being worthy of the part he'd been awarded, of trying to fit in.

One of the caterers summoned him now, pulling him from his thoughts and his station outside the dining room. "We need you washing dishes, stat."

———

For some reason, once Charlie got outside, she wished to be back *inside*. Not so much at the torturous dinner now in progress, but she itched for another take of her scenes with Nick. She sat on the front steps of the mansion. She couldn't bear going home, alone, waiting for her housemates to return with stories of what had transpired after she'd left.

If only they could've just had a show tonight. That made sense to her, *that* she could do, there she felt at ease. The hours onstage were the only hours she could be sure she was navigating her life properly, doing what she should be doing.

Fireflies sparking in the air around her, night descending—soon the fireworks would begin in the distance—she tried to place this sensation gnawing at her. It had been a long time since she had felt she was missing out on anything. You have to care about something to miss it. She walked around the side of the mansion to the wall of stones sealing the perimeter of the backyard and the iron bars of the gate. She tugged: locked, of course. It wasn't terribly high, six feet maybe? So she slipped off her heels, tossed her stolen book through the gate and grabbed the bars, climbing up. The crosshatch pattern in the ironwork offered easy footholds, so she made it over without too much difficulty—she had always liked doing her own stunt work.

Walking along the inside of the walls, she ducked as she passed the long windows of the banquet room. She peeked in just enough to see the smiling faces. Only one exception: Nick, who sat drinking something amber, tense eyes focused in the distance—his typical brooding pose, which made her smile. As though sensing this, his gaze shifted in her direction. She hunched down again, wondering if he had seen her.

Not chancing it, she crawled to the back of the building, where she found a partial moat, which was more like a narrow half-moon-shaped pond with an arched bridge leading to the fountain: a monstrosity of cherubs spitting water and playing harps. Standing beside the fountain, in a slinky scarlet gown with her back to Charlie and a thin plume of smoke winding up above her, was Jasmine.

Charlie turned slowly, intending to creep away as silently as she had arrived. But it was too late.

"They won't let me smoke in the house, those fuckers," Jasmine said, her back still to Charlie. "Want one?" She turned around now, her expression stony.

Charlie couldn't fault anyone for being wooed by the voluminous hair, the luscious curves. Jasmine was all Amazon Woman-Goddess. Charlie hadn't smoked in years, but tucked the book under her arm and plucked a cigarette from the pack anyway.

"The dinner is pretty boring, you're not missing much," Jasmine said, dully.

Charlie smiled. "Glad to hear."

"But that's not to say that *you* weren't missed." She took a puff. *Unusually generous*, Charlie thought. *There must be a catch.* "It's probably just that he's drunk and you have extremely loyal housemates. Wish I could stay in that cozy little shack with all of you."

"You're welcome to take my room in a few weeks when I leave," Charlie said.

"I'll be taking plenty when you leave." Jasmine smiled. "But not your room."

Charlie sat down on a large rock and took another drag,

grateful for the calm it brought her body; she had forgotten that. She had also forgotten that Jasmine always thought they were in a battle for Nick's affections. But that hadn't been the source of the problem Charlie had with her at all. It was about being cast aside midcollaboration, being seen as easily replaced—as confidante, counsel, muse, when Charlie thought she held an unshakable permanence in his heart. And it didn't help matters that Jasmine had mentioned "Charlie's meltdown" in every interview she did for that film, as though Charlie had been some kind of lunatic leaving that role. When Charlie walked away, she had honestly believed Nick would follow her, hear her out. She had hoped to get his attention, make him understand he needed more time to shape his script. But it hadn't worked out as she'd planned.

"This place is so cut off from civilization, don'tcha think?"

Charlie looked out into the mountains, their silhouette still visible against the night sky. Her gut told her not to speak, to just finish her cigarette and go. But she felt compelled to defend this place that had been sheltering her. "I think it's within the realm of reason to look out there and see possibility and mystery and endless restlessness." She pointed to the mountain range with her lit cigarette. "Or I think you could look at that." She inhaled again. "And that." She pointed to the range on their left. "And that." The one on her right. "And feel trapped by it. But I think that would be a shame." She paused. "I see possibility, but that's just me."

"Maybe some of us have more endless possibility, or whatever, in ourselves," Jasmine said and paused a moment. "Do you ever get nervous—" she looked at Charlie in the dim glow of the lights strung along the trees, electric torches flipping on "—knowing you'll be forty someday?" Jasmine deployed the words in a manner between bullet-to-the-chest and taking-an-informal-poll.

THE SUMMER SET • 231

"No," Charlie said easily. "You?"

She let out a laugh. "Terrified." She breathed deeply, trapping the smoke from her cigarette. "But I wouldn't admit that to anyone."

"Why are you telling me, then?" Charlie was truly curious.

"Because you're terrified too. Of something," she said, uncharacteristically thoughtful. "I just can't figure out what. Not age. But something."

"Let me know when you decide," Charlie said. "So I can sufficiently freak out."

"We're actually a lot alike," Jasmine said, eyeing her.

"Oh?" Charlie couldn't quite conceal her skepticism. "Enlighten me."

"Just trying to capitalize on our assets before we're washed up at thirty-five."

"No, not really," Charlie said. "And I'm thirty-nine."

Jasmine whipped her head around to Charlie, appearing devastated. "My condolences." She looked Charlie up and down like she had a disease she didn't want to catch, dropped the cigarette, smashing it out with the toe of her stiletto, and breezed back inside without another word.

Charlie flicked her own cigarette into the fountain, waited a beat, then swept in through the door before it locked behind Jasmine.

Music, conversation, the clinking of plates. As soon as the silky train of Jasmine's gown slithered away, presumably into the hallway and back to the banquet room, Charlie emerged into the bustling kitchen, tossing the book back and forth in her hands. Waiters whisked dirty dishes into the sink as white-jacketed caterers plated slices of a fruit-filled cake. A handful of apprentices had an assembly line washing, drying and stacking dishes in the cabinets, Sierra and Mercutio among them. Charlie grabbed a piece of cake off a plate, took a bite and made her way to Sierra's side by the sink.

"Hey, thanks for this." Charlie gestured to her outfit, leaning against the counter.

"Ohmigod!" Sierra nearly dropped the soapy plate from her hands. "I mean, you look amazing, I knew you— Wait." She stopped short, looking down. "Where are your shoes?"

"Possible health code violation," Mercutio said, injecting himself into the conversation. "Hi."

"Hey." She tapped his shoulder, then focused on Sierra again. "The shoes are outside, long story…"

"Were you in there? Not that it's my business, but you know I switched the place cards and put you next to Nicholas and put Jasmine way on the other end of the—"

"That's sweet. But, no, I'm not going in there."

"Oh." Sierra sounded disappointed.

"Just had to give you this." Setting the remainder of her cake slice on the clean plate Ethan was holding, she wiped the icing from her hand on his dish towel. Charlie fanned the pages of the book until she reached a spot near the end. "Auditions for *Midsummer* are soon?"

"Tomorrow actually, one o'clock," Sierra said, like it was burned in her brain.

Charlie pointed to a passage, dog-earring the page. "Do Puck's monologue."

"You came back just for that?" another apprentice asked. "I'm Tripp, hi! Nicholas said you had food poisoning."

"Wow, he's even less creative than we feared," Charlie said, almost to herself. "Yeah, pray for me." She smiled with a wink, walking away, then turned around again in the doorway. "If you want to work on it together…"

"Yes!" Sierra practically yelled.

"Tomorrow at the lake, 11 a.m."

On her way out, Charlie overheard Mercutio say, "I think that was actually meant for all of us? Me and Tripp, we can come, right?"

Charlie slowed her pace by the banquet room, catching Nick just as he glanced over midbrood. She saluted him, and he looked like he'd seen a ghost, which felt gratifying to her.

She let herself out the front door, collecting her heels at the gate, and walked home, fireworks bursting in the sky behind her. She didn't bother to watch.

41

WHY DO YOU WANT TO
DO THIS, ANYWAY?

Sierra arrived early to the lake, skipping their morning lecture to be there. She found a spot under a shady elm and tried to keep from jumping out of her skin at the thought of having to perform for Charlie Savoy. She had stayed up half the night practicing, memorizing, trying to make these few lines her own.

When Charlie emerged from the break in the trees, only ten minutes late, Sierra exhaled.

Charlie took a seat beside Sierra on the grass. "Showtime, Puck," she said, no small talk, stretching her legs out in front of her.

"Absolutely." Sierra bounced up to her feet, shaking out her limbs, closed her eyes, opened them again. And she began, eyes on a knobby tree in the distance, "'If we shadows have

THE SUMMER SET • 235

offended, think but this and all is—'" She made the mistake of glancing at Charlie midperformance. Her stare was so penetrating that Sierra stopped herself. "Just real quick—"

"*Whoa*, what are you doing?" Charlie asked, sitting up now.

"I just had a question," Sierra tried again.

"No. First, go. Questions later."

Sierra nodded and began again. She made it through the entire thing—that whole long minute—and thought she had done not terribly. But Charlie said nothing, just wound her hair up into a loose topknot; it had already grown hot, even in the shade. Sierra, standing perfectly still, interpreted the action as a bad review: your audience should forget whether they're hot or cold or hungry.

"Why do you do this, anyway?" Charlie asked, squinting in the glare of the late-morning sun, hand shielding her eyes.

"Me? Theater?" Sierra asked, watching a group of students setting towels on the slim strip of sand near the water.

Charlie just nodded.

"To feel...at home," she said, hoping it sounded important enough. It was the purest truth. "Or more than that, somewhere between comfort and thrill or adrenaline and escape. I can't explain it." She shook her head, embarrassed not to be able to put something that should be so obvious into words.

"Sure, transcendence," Charlie said easily. "That's why I'm here. That's what I'm chasing too. Every damn day." She tossed this out, breezily, but it felt profound to Sierra. That was exactly what she searched for and, on the good days, could find.

"Yes," Sierra said solemnly.

"That's a good reason, by the way," Charlie went on, slapping Sierra on the back. "Again." She gestured. Then, remembering, "Wait, you had a question."

Sierra feared it would sound too rookie after this moment of deep understanding between them. But she asked anyway,

gently. "It's just, you do know that this is on every list of audition monologues to avoid because they're so overdone?" Sierra had discovered that during some research.

"Yep," Charlie said, dusting some dirt off the leg of her
jeans. "I know."

"Then why—?"

"If you can do something like this and turn heads, then you
can do anything," she said. "And if you saw those lists then so
did a lot of other people, so there's a good chance you could
be the only one gutsy enough to try this."

"Ohhh." It was like a light bulb exploding. "Counterintuitive.
Reverse psychology. I like that."

"Just like, do we think Nick Blunt is the first guy to ever
think of staging *A Midsummer Night's Dream* in the *middle* of
the *summer*? No," Charlie laughed. "So we're all just fucking
hoping he's got some new ideas for this thing. Think of it this
way—we need to inspire him. *You* need to inspire him. Inspire
me." She shrugged, like this was an easy request.

"Got it," Sierra said, though she wasn't sure she actually
did have it.

"It's okay, use your neuroses—"

"Absolutely, neuroses." Great, now Charlie thought she
was crazy.

"—or whatever you've got." Charlie leaned back on her
elbows.

Sierra closed her eyes, thinking of the last time she felt true
peace. *Transcendence.* She started again, those first two lines, but
on the third—"'That you have but slumbered here...'"—her
body propelled itself, without a plan, up into the elm tree,
nestling on a low branch just above Charlie. "'While these
visions did appear...'" Stretching out like a sleeping cat, taking her time before the next line.

Sierra had sufficiently blacked out in the middle, which she hoped meant that that part had worked, and by the time she reached the end—"'Give me your hands, if we be friends…'"—she was back on the ground beside Charlie, who had held out her own hands for Sierra to take. On the final line, she looked in Charlie's eyes. They were a lush green she had never noticed before, probably because Sierra had been scared to look directly at this woman—much like the sun—for too long.

Charlie smiled in a serene way that made the world stop. "Nice," she said.

It was one word but so much more. Sierra remembered Ethan describing a compliment from Charlie that way, and now she understood.

"I told you. Do it again and then I've got a stand-in for the tree. We'll talk after…" Charlie said, anticipating Sierra's next question: how to translate this to a theater devoid of leafy vegetation.

As one o'clock approached, they walked back into town together, Charlie telling her simply, "Just do what you just did."

"If I could only remember that every time then it would be so much easier," Sierra said. "I should tattoo it on my arm."

"Not a bad idea." Charlie smiled, watching the shop windows along Warwickshire.

"Did this one hurt?" Sierra touched the nape of her own neck.

"Oh, this."

"I have no ink, so I know nothing," Sierra went on. "But maybe if I ever get the nerve…" She felt less cool the more she spoke, so she stopped.

"It did hurt, actually," Charlie said like it was a secret, tapping the bird delicately. "But I never tell anyone that."

"Nicholas has one too." Sierra shocked herself by mentioning this.

"See, *that* was great acting," Charlie laughed. "I almost

believed you thought it might be pure coincidence that we both have these."

Sierra watched Charlie from the corner of her eye, worried she'd offended her. "Sorry, if I—"

"Nooo," Charlie said, buoyant enough. "It was a long time ago, first time I was here. We met here." She put her hands in her jeans pockets, slowed her pace. "It was kind of a secret. We snuck off campus. It was sort of to commemorate the end of that summer…" She trailed off.

"I think that's amazing and romantic."

"Or maybe insane," Charlie said lightly. "Either way."

They had reached the theater, too soon for Sierra.

"Do it like you just did," Charlie said again, turning to leave.

"Thank you, Charlie!" Sierra called out, though the words didn't seem enough. But there was one more thing she had to ask. "Wait!" She took a few steps as Charlie faced her again. "Why did you want to help me?"

"Why did *you* help *me*?" Charlie asked, rather than answer.

"I'm fascinated by how you do what you do. How you make these lines I've heard a million times sound new, how somehow there's you in these parts even though they were written a million years ago when no one like you was around."

"No one like me?" Charlie seemed surprised.

"Fiery and commanding and not caring—"

"I care—" Charlie said, a statement, not a defense.

"No, I know, I mean, not caring about what anyone thinks, doing everything your own way."

"For better or worse," Charlie laughed.

"I once read that experiences, even ugly ones, are useful, a well to draw from—" She had read it in an interview of Charlie's referencing her arrest in her late teens.

"True," Charlie said, appreciative, as though recognizing the words as her own.

"And also, I don't know if you know this, but there's something that happens when you and Nicholas are together, an energy or something—"

"That's probably just years of unresolved issues. We should be in couple's therapy even though we're not actually—"

"No. It works." Sierra felt it was important for her to know. "He's excited around you—he's boring anytime he's ever lectured. But when you're around, it's different. It's the kind of thing I always thought happened all the time in theater, but I've never actually seen before now." She felt she was talking too much. "So anyway, I'm here for anything that facilitates that."

Charlie nodded, looked away a moment. "Thank you," she said sincerely. And added finally, "Now don't be late. He hates when people are late."

42

YOU'RE BEING EXTREMELY RUDE
TO YOUR CAST

Charlie slouched in her chair beside Nick, who felt *tooclose*. But maybe it was just the way they were all crowded around this table. Or perhaps, Charlie could admit, she might be feeling a bit *claustrophobic* in general. This first *Midsummer* read-through was barely underway, and already she was convinced of one thing: she could not share the stage with Jasmine Beijao.

At least Charlie was Puck (at her own insistence). And Sierra—who had delivered a fantastic audition, according to Nick—would be the fairy Peaseblossom and Charlie's understudy, which filled Charlie with as maternal a sense of pride as she had ever felt (with the exception of the brief time she had that French bulldog, before she lost him somewhere between Tower Bridge and Hyde Park).

Charlie's phone vibrated, and she flipped it over in her lap as Chase's Lysander stumbled through Act Two.

Nick's name popped up on her screen: Are you going to keep ignoring me?

She didn't respond, instead taking a long moment to wind her hair up into a topknot, securing it with a pen—his pen, which she'd grabbed from the table. The beak of their lark curving around her neck, visible to him now, she imagined.

Indeed, from the corner of *her* eye, she caught him looking from the corner of *his* eye. He watched as though willing her to text back, she could feel him waiting. She always liked pretending not to notice his eyes on her and for a moment she forgot that she was angry. But as he turned the page of the script, she remembered and concentrated on the words again.

He inched his arm closer to hers, his left forearm touching her right elbow. She moved immediately, typing, I'm literally midrehearsal here.

He glanced at her, and she glared back.

He typed again; her phone buzzed once more: Can we talk tonight?

She looked directly at him, shook her head. What was there to talk about?

Nick focused on Chase, reading so terribly, and then swiftly pulled his pen out from Charlie's hair so it fell to her shoulders.

She exhaled, blowing a wisp of hair away from her face, folded her arms.

He scribbled onto her script, "please?"

She yanked the pen away. "You're being extremely rude to your cast right now," she wrote on his script.

"There's exactly one cast member I care about right now," he wrote on hers.

"'Right now' = the operative term," she wrote back.

"No. I mean: AT ALL." She didn't write again, she took the pen, put the cap back on, set it between them.

By the time they reached the play's end, Charlie was so desperate to escape, she couldn't stop her leg tapping up-down-up-down, manic. She recited those final lines—the same she had assigned to Sierra to audition with—hardly getting the last word out before Jasmine stepped on them.

"That felt *so good!*" Jasmine announced, nearly orgasmic. "I can't believe I haven't done theater before!"

A few apprentices, who didn't know any better, cheered.

"Yep, it's pretty damn amazing," Matteo said, expressionless.

Nick hopped to his feet. "I know this is a tough part of the season, finishing up *Romeo* while staging this—"

But Charlie couldn't take another minute. She shoved her chair back with a screech. "I have somewhere to be," she said.

Nick reached out as though to grab her arm but she slipped ghostlike through his fingertips and jumped off the stage, bursting through the side door toward the workshop. The buzz of circular saws was soothing after that read-through.

—

Yes, that went well, Nick thought, as he swallowed two codeine tablets (left over from his ankle injury post-window-jump), washed down with cold, bitter coffee in his office. This new show was already as brutal as any of Shakespeare's most violent tragedies.

A knock rattled the door. He hoped it might be Charlie, manifesting from his thoughts, but it opened to Mary instead.

"Hello, hello!" she chirped, ignoring his grim expression. "So I have a special request from the silent auction winner for Friday night's show—the one who bid to choose which actors would play which parts at Friday's *Romeo and Juliet?*" Nick nodded, scrolling through his emails, barely paying attention. "They called with an *unconventional* casting option—"

He pulled up the schedule on his laptop. "Sounds promising," he sighed.

—

"I feel like I should be bringing you coffee and answering your phone," Ethan joked, as he walked Sierra to her Black

Box rehearsal on the other side of the theater complex. "Now you're the one with the killer schedule."

"I'm just glad I'm finally doing more acting than, like, seat upholstery and costume wrangling," she laughed.

"Can we *please* talk about the drama at that rehearsal?" Tripp caught up with them, kissing Sierra on the cheek. "It is by far better than the show."

"I'll leave you to your work husband." Ethan smiled, letting himself out the side door, a little disappointed to go.

He hadn't been able to stop thinking about Sierra's *Midsummer* audition. They had run lines together daily since they'd met. But in all that time, she hadn't shown a glimmer of her first audition, when she had conjured Romeo. Until yesterday.

The moment Sierra began Puck's monologue—the one that people who have never read Shakespeare still know—Ethan had reflexively shifted forward in his seat, rested his chin in his palm. Perched on the edge of the stage, she spoke to the audience as a friend, then leaped off, making her way to where Blunt sat beside two directing apprentices. She crept atop the table to kneel before them, grabbing their hands and talking just to them, but somehow Ethan still felt like she was speaking to him too.

When she'd finished, she sat there a beat and then smiled and said, *Thanks*. Not *Thank you*, but just *Thanks*. Slid off the table, walked up the aisle, right out the doors and into the lobby. As she passed Ethan, rather than returning to her seat beside him, she shot him the quickest glance. A flash of a character-break that made him shiver.

His phone buzzed with a text: SOOO excited for next week, Miles wrote with a smile emoji and theater masks. Get ready, Romeo. Break a leg!

As if on cue, the stage door clanged open on the other side of the loading dock, and Ethan peeked around the corner to spot Charlie. She darted across Stratford, dodging cars, as she

244 • AIMEE AGRESTI

walked away from the main drag and marched past the hotel and finally to that historic log cabin: the first thing anyone saw upon arriving into town, the last thing they saw before leaving.

Charlie hadn't planned to go to Chamberlain Cabin; her body had just taken her there. The darkened sky, threatening rain, suited her mood.

Even though it was late afternoon, it looked like dusk inside the cramped wooden dwelling. Same dirt floor, same fireplace, same wooden loft with its rickety ladder of chopped branches. She climbed up there now, the rungs creaking under her feet.

The rehearsal had been miserable, but when she thought of that fast-approaching date—July 30—when she would be free to go and have her previous life restored to her, she only felt worse. She liked so much about being here: the work, the stage. She sensed that something once lost had been returned to her and she wasn't sure she could give that up again. She didn't want to share the stage with Jasmine, but maybe she didn't have to *physically* be on that stage.

She had resigned herself to a cold war with Nick, but it didn't feel like a solution. Maybe there wasn't one. Maybe she had come to the cabin for answers.

She could feel that night again, all those years ago, here in this cabin with Nick. It had been the night after their tryst at the lake, and they hadn't known yet whether it had been an experiment, a mistake or the beginning of something. So she had kissed him again, here. And again it had led to morning. And this time to their lark in the window. And to the larks on their necks the following night. And to an imprinting upon each other that they wouldn't be able to shake.

She drowsily recalled it all, until her phone buzzed, signaling showtime.

43

THAT'S WHERE THE ZIP LINE WILL GO

Days later, Nick opened the auditorium doors and found Charlie already there, early for their blocking rehearsal. She walked up the aisle toward him, smiling in a way that made no sense based on their extremely frosty week. He looked behind him, in case her warmth was intended for someone else.

"You know what this production is missing?" she launched in.

"Uhhh, nothing?" he asked, hopeful.

"Aerial work," she said as the side door opened.

"Excuse me?" he asked as their set designer, Mason, jogged over.

"This show is gonna rock," Mason said in greeting, tying his shoulder-length hair back with a rubber band. "We've got some great stuff cooking. I was stoked when Charlie told me what you wanted. So I'm thinking the zip line goes up—"

"I'm sorry, did you say *zip line*?" Nick cut in. "Charlie, what the—?" She just smiled, mischievous, as Mason kept talking.

"—right, so we'll install it right there, by the lighting booth." Mason pointed to the ceiling. "We'll do a lot of wire-work—I'm an amateur flight instructor, so we can do this all in-house," he said proudly. "Then some trapdoor stuff, dust off that pop-up toaster." Mason tapped his fingers at the air, all manic energy. "I'm gonna set Charlie up in the rehearsal room now, we rigged up the wires there, so she can start getting the mechanics down."

Charlie nodded, began to walk away with Mason.

Nick, processing it all, lunged to catch up with her. "Um, yeah, what's the deal with all—?"

"Sierra's on board running lines while I spend the next week or two, whatever, downstairs on the wires," she said. "You *know* it's a good idea."

"I'm not saying it's not," he said. "It's just…a lot…and who's going to do this when…?" He didn't want to remind her that she would be leaving nine days into the run. "I worry it's just going to make you irreplaceable or something…" As soon as he said it, it sounded much more naked than he'd intended.

"Not my problem." She shrugged. "I've gotta fly." She walked away, adding over her shoulder, "But you know where to find me."

"Unless…" He said it too softly to be heard. "Unless you're planning to stay."

—

Walking home with Matteo and Chase in the soft summer drizzle, Charlie felt more renewed with each step and every word.

"Jasmine started asking around immediately, 'Where's Charlie? Did she leave?'" Matteo reported of the rehearsal. "And one of the apprentices who's in the workshop—"

"Ethan, it was Ethan," Chase said, as though keeping track of him ever since their sword fight.

"Right, so he was like, 'No, man, Charlie's doing this whole aerial thing on wires, it's gonna be awesome,' and that did it." Matteo clapped, laughing.

"So Jasmine says, in front of everyone, like LOUD—" Chase stepped in.

"But in that voice, you know, the one that she thinks sounds sweet—" Matteo added.

"But really sounds like right before the serial killer murders someone in the movie?" Charlie asked.

"Like that," Matteo said, as they reached their house, unlocking the door. "Jasmine says—"

Danica piped up from the kitchen. "Are we talking about, 'If you really care about me, you'll put me in a wire?'" she asked the three of them, stirring in a spoonful of honey into her preshow tea, delivering the punch line of their story.

Matteo clapped, slow, reverent, and Charlie couldn't help but smile. The goal had simply been to spend as little time as possible physically on stage with Jasmine, so this reaction was a bonus, like finding deleted scenes on the DVD of your favorite movie.

"Okay." Charlie pulled a soda from the fridge. "But the real question is—"

"What did *he* say? Right?" Chase hopped on the counter, unwrapping a protein bar.

"He says, loooud—" Matteo bellowed.

"Like to the whole group," Danica clarified.

"—'Last time I checked, there's only one actress here who hasn't ever relied on stunt doubles,'" Matteo said.

"BOOM!" Chase said.

"Honestly." Danica furrowed her brow, considering something. "I don't know why Jasmine would even *want* to do wirework. It's just asking for trouble. Especially with the terrible stagehands they've had the past couple seasons," she went on. "Remember last year the whole fly rail was fucked up, they forgot to weight it properly and the lights came crashing down and the stagehands flew up to the rafters. People could have *died*." The three of them just stared at her as she casually grabbed her tea. "But you'll be fine," she said to Charlie. "You seem to know what you're doing, more or less." She slipped out of the kitchen to begin her preshow ritual.

"Thank you?" Charlie scrunched her face.

Matteo snapped his fingers, remembering. "So you're good on next Friday's show?" he asked Charlie.

"Fine by me, he's got it." She shrugged. By then she would have only fourteen days to go, she could roll with anything.

"Mercutio as Romeo." Chase whistled. "I'd love to know who the anonymous donor was that just had to see *that guy* as the lead."

44

BLINK TWICE IF YOU'RE OKAY, ROMEO

Ethan couldn't believe this was really happening. He replayed the afternoon in his head, again, as he walked back to the dorm to prepare for the night's performance. He wasn't even technically an understudy for Romeo, but Miles had hatched this plan weeks ago, so Ethan had learned the entire Romeo part, studied how Chase played it opposite Charlie, memorized every movement down to the detail, in order to seamlessly assume the role. Nicholas Blunt had even held a special rehearsal to run the major scenes—balcony, sword fights, death, the usual suspects.

But it was Act One, Scene Five, that first kiss at the Capulet ball, that had been the most invigorating. Or at least, as invigorating as something could be when it was also terrifying and choreographed and the director watching them was his costar's ex-boyfriend. In his very limited stage career of student productions, Ethan had never kissed anyone onstage on whom he'd had a crush offstage. He always wondered if the heart would understand that this was acting or be fooled into believing this was real. The answer, he discovered, after the wave of fear as he leaned toward Charlie and the shock of his lips connecting with hers, was that the heart—his heart—was smarter than he'd expected. It knew and was swiftly over-ridden by his brain, which instructed his head to lean to the right so as not to block Charlie from the audience's view and that he should hold her hand and that it should last approxi-mately four seconds and that he had a line immediately after, and she did too, and then another kiss, and that above all, he had to do this *well*. The Actor Ethan had to remain present and in control and active in order to appear worthy of performing opposite someone like Charlie. The heart knew.

When Miles had informed him that he'd taken up a col-lection among the employees of North End Cinema to raise funds to install Ethan in his dream role for a night (it had cost $501, a dollar above the second-highest bid), Ethan was touched. *But why would you even do that?* he had laughed. He couldn't resist asking.

Because I think you'll remind her of herself, when she started out, Miles had told him. *And I think it would do her some good to re-member that. Things like passion, you know?*

Ethan felt like there had to be more to it than that—it was a lot of money—but he let it go. He didn't want to talk Miles out of it.

—

Sierra thought Ethan was kidding when his text popped up on her phone just fifteen minutes before showtime: are you busy? can you come back here a minute?

backstage???? Sierra typed.

yes. greenroom. closet.

She excused herself from Fiona and the intense debate the directing apprentices were waging about the most overrated auteurs of the twenty-first century, and slipped out the main doors to the corridor that fed like an artery into the back-stage maze.

In the greenroom, Harlow, Alex and the other apprentices in *Romeo* laughed and talked, spirits too high to even notice Sierra. She rapped on the closet door and then opened it: Ethan sat on a backward folding chair. Makeup on, hair slicked, in costume.

"Well, you look good at least, and that's, like, half the battle," she said.

He wore jeans, the requisite white button-down, open collar, sleeves rolled up above his elbow. The same shirt that she was so used to admiring on Chase. And the very same one that she had ironed crisply only hours earlier. The ink of his mechanical bull half-sleeve tattoo—which she had learned was meant to imply the intersection of old and new, a metaphor for the expansion of his family's business, because this was the fascinating way Ethan's brain worked—visible through the translucent broadcloth. He still said nothing.

"Okay, blink twice if you're okay, Romeo." She leaned down, looking in his eyes. He blinked once. "Good enough." She sat on the floor in front of him. "They're still making you change in here?" she asked, to lighten things. "Don't they know who you are?"

"Exactly." He spoke finally. "I'm nobody. What am I doing here?"

"No, what am *I* doing here? You're about to go on in—" she glanced at her watch "—seven minutes?"

"Is this crazy?" He looked at her now, serious.

"Which part?" she whispered. "The part where you somehow got friends to put up the cash at the silent auction to request you to star opposite *Charlie. Savoy. Tonight?* As Romeo? Or…"

"Yeah, all of it," he said. "And I'm paying them back. Somehow." He was on his feet, pacing now, which was hard to do in such cramped quarters. "And I've spent *a lot* of money at that movie theater, so it's sort of even anyway—"

"Listen," she cut him off, grabbing his shoulders to stop him, looking into his dark eyes as she had that very first day on the field. "I'll tell you the part that *isn't* crazy, and that's you as Romeo. You know how to do that, no matter who's starring opposite you."

A sudden scurrying and calling out of directions and names filtered through the walls.

He took a deep breath. "Text me at intermission and tell me if I'm a complete disaster?"

"No." She smiled. "You got this. Break a leg."

Ethan had never experienced this. Had never had his own emotions bleed so completely into a role that he had to continually remind himself that what happened onstage wasn't real. But even though his heart might've known he wasn't Romeo and Charlie wasn't Juliet and they weren't star-crossed and weren't in love, something about it all *was* true: within the confines of this specific performance, under those particular lights, on this night, there were *sparks.* The professional sparks, the necessary ones that the audience feels when everyone is doing their job. *Chemistry.* He had known it in his first scene with Charlie. He had known it without having to glance at the second row during the curtain call to find Miles, wiping a tear. Or when he saw Sierra standing in applause. Even before Charlie had whispered into his ear, "Nice, Mercutio," as they took their bow.

After the hugs and the molting of the costumes and the

greetings of the audience and the harboring of secrets and the introductions, they walked to the Fourteenth Line all together. Miles had advised him to pretend they *didn't* know each other and he would call him "Ethan" instead of "Rob." "I think we should forget about that letter, trust me, you're doing fine without it," Miles whispered on the way there. "And I'm not sure it would help her to know you wrote it."

"No, it's supposed to help *me* for *her* to know." Ethan was confused. For some reason he had expected tonight would finally be the big reveal. "I spilled my guts out in there and my heart and…everything. I thought you thought she should know that."

"No, I think you should just keep your guts and heart where they are now." Miles said it kindly, with certainty, and made his way into the Fourteenth Line. Ethan followed the group, trying to make sense of this, but didn't understand. He felt deflated. His truest self was in that letter and he had spent so much time imagining Charlie reading it, and those words meaning something to her, that he wasn't sure he could just let it go.

Charlie was surrounded by her castmates and friends, including Marlena Andes. (*The* Marlena Andes—Ethan almost couldn't fully absorb that another star of that wattage had watched him tonight and she had even told him, *You were beautiful.*) But now Ethan felt his postshow luster and confidence rapidly fading as he retreated to the periphery of Charlie's circle, watching instead of participating. Back to himself. The thrill wearing off, leaving him only with a sense of disappointment. A swift mood swing and adrenaline crash as epic as the surge he had experienced preshow.

He guzzled his beer then switched to a Vodka Red Bull.

"Not the ending you hoped tonight?" Sierra asked, knocking her shoulder against his.

He shook his head. "You know when you build something up in your mind?"

She smiled and exhaled. "Yeah, I get it."

"Of course you do, sorry." He thought back to that night Chase had given her Harlow's necklace. "You always get it. Thank you for always *getting it*, not making me feel like a total idiot."

"I'm an idiot too, so it's cool."

⏤

Walking back to their dorm, Ethan's hands buried in his pockets, he struggled to find the words. "I'm not sure what I expected," he said, still embarrassed.

"I'm familiar with that feeling," she said.

But he couldn't stop himself. "I wrote Charlie a letter."

"Like tonight? On a cocktail napkin or something?"

"No," he said. "Before we got here, before I even knew she would be here."

"Wait, what?"

"For this drama class we had to write to someone we admired and tell them why."

"A fan letter."

"Yeah, but, I don't know, more about art and the imprint it makes on your soul kind of thing."

"Wow, okay."

"So, you know, she owns that movie theater in the North End."

"I guess I heard about that. I don't really get out much," she said, softly.

"So I go there all the time because it's close by and I have, like, no friends—"

"I'm sure that's not true—"

"Trust me," he said. "I never see her there, but I got to know Miles pretty well, and mentioned to him that I had this letter and I wasn't ever going to actually give it to her, but then he told me I should because that would be good for her to hear, so I showed it to him—" they reached the Quad and he lay down on the ledge surrounding the flower beds, still talking, as though on the couch in a therapist's office "—and Miles decided he would give it to her, and vouch that I'm not crazy—" He paused a moment, looked up at her. She had sat down beside him on the ledge and smiled at this.

"I know, debatable—" he said.

"No. You're the least crazy person I know," she said.

"Anyway, he gave it to Charlie."

"And she never said anything?"

"I don't know if she ever even read it. If she did then I don't think she knows it's me. I signed it Robert, you know, before I tried to become this *actor*, or whatever," he said. "But anyway, the day Miles passed it along to her, she had the car accident that night."

"Wow, that sounded really horrific, but somehow she was completely okay—"

"I know. And there was never the right time for—"

"You've gotta tell her—" she cut him off.

"Wait." He sat up. "I mean, you think?"

"I don't even know what it said, but I know you and yeah." She nodded. "If you were, you know, creepy or ugly or something, then I'd be like, 'Hey, maybe just forget that note.'"

"Thanks—" He lay down again, this time his head on her lap.

"But I just feel like, people should know they matter to you," she said. "I mean, wouldn't you love to, matter to someone?" She paused a moment, her eyes up at the stars. He felt himself drifting off to sleep, listening as she went on. "Maybe that's not the best example, because you know, you matter to me, or whatever. You know what I mean, I don't know…"

—

Charlie and Marlena closed the place down, outlasting even Chase, who tried to walk Marlena to her hotel but was thwarted. "Girl talk," Marlena explained.

As soon as he took his leave—kissing Marlena on the cheek—Marlena, all six feet of her in heels, looked at Charlie from the corner of her eye. "Chase is still *annoyingly* gorgeous."

"True," Charlie said, as though it were fact.

"Anything there?" Marlena asked, an eyebrow cocked.

"Oh, God, no!" Charlie said. "We were destined to be just a one-night stand."

"Good to know," Marlena said mischievously. "In that case—" But she was interrupted by a trio of drunken collegians spilling out of King's.

"We love you, Marlena!"

"Are you gonna live? PLEEEASE!" They all shouted over each other, referencing the season's cliff-hanger.

"Love you too!" She waved as they walked on. "We'll see! Keep watching!" She blew them a kiss.

"See, *you* are so good at this," Charlie said.

"Not really, just in the zone right now." She smoothed back her blond curls. "But, you know the real me is like, 'Do *you* love me? Do *I* love me? Please love me! Keep loving me! Someone!'" Marlena laughed at herself and Charlie did too.

"*That* I get," Charlie said, speaking for herself. "And I love you."

"You better." Marlena linked arms with her. "And while we're on the subject—as I was saying, if you all are strictly platonic—"

"Chase? One thousand percent yes—"

"Then I have to tell you—" She turned to face Charlie, her eyes brightening beneath luscious lashes. "Chase totally held my hand! Tonight. After the show!"

"What? Tell me everything," Charlie said, excited.

"No, that's everything, but, like, backstage. I mean, he. Grabbed. My. Hand. And held it. Like this." She took Charlie's hand in both of hers. "And said he was glad I was here…" Marlena started walking again.

"*That* is *very* interesting," Charlie said, wheels turning.

"Do *not* tell him I told you." She pointed at Charlie.

"And, he kissed you."

"Just on the cheek," Marlena said.

"You've had a crush on him since we met—"

"Guilty. But, I mean, nothing could happen. Unless…" She trailed off. "But, no, that's a big *unless*."

"He's changed, I think, actually." Charlie had felt a shift in him ever since that night on her balcony. "So, you just never know, is all. Unless you go for it."

"We'll see. I'll be back to see *Midsummer*—you're turning me into such a Shakespeare junkie," Marlena said. "And in the meantime, your costar is delicious. In case you hadn't noticed." She meant Mercutio, who had played Romeo opposite her Juliet tonight, and gave Charlie a look.

"Overlooking the fact that he's young enough to be my child, if I had been a teen mom—"

"You with all your excuses—" Marlena cut in.

"I just think I already have enough extracurricular drama with the people in this production," she laughed, holding open the door into the hotel lobby.

"Just have fun," she cooed. "I mean, *act* like you're having fun. Get me?"

"Ohhh." Charlie stopped, a revelation. "Like, in front of Nick?"

"Seriously, you didn't think of that on your own?" Marlena shook her head, curls bouncing. "Where's your game, girl? Thank *God* I'm here."

45

THIS IS YOUR CALLBACK

The music pulsed at the Fourteenth Line—*again* Sierra and Ethan's second time there in a week, they were almost regulars haunting that same corner of the mahogany bar—as the cast, apprentices and audience from that night's show flowed in, this time to celebrate the end of *Romeo and Juliet*'s run.

"You still haven't told her," Sierra said to Ethan, accusatory, as Charlie walked past with Matteo and settled at a table near the stage marked Reserved. Chase was already there, chatting with Danica and her girlfriend.

"Maybe I did tell her and it didn't go well, so I didn't bother telling *you*." He practically inhaled his Vodka Red Bull. "What is Alex doing?" He was distracted by the stage, where his roommate now stood at the microphone, apparently for an impromptu performance. The familiar music kicked in: *Hamilton*. "Of course."

"That guy is *not* throwing away his shot," Sierra replied with the song lyrics. A commotion at the front door stole their attention from Alex as Jasmine Beijao swanned in barely wearing a coral sheath halter dress. She pressed through the crowd, pushing her assistant as a human bulldozer clearing the way. She immediately found Nick, kissed him in greeting, which he seemed startled by, and installed herself at his table up front. "You know what?" Sierra said, thinking. "You're not throwing away your shot either."

"Are we drinking shots now?" Ethan asked, confused.

"No, with Charlie, because she is over *there* hating life right now, because of what's going on over *there*." Sierra pointed to Jasmine. "Go talk to her."

"What am I supposed to say?" Ethan said, hand through his hair, entirely lost. In the background, a young, scrappy and hungry Alex rapped his song. Ethan watched and Sierra could see an idea strike Ethan. He nodded as though accepting it and said to Sierra, eyes still on the stage, "You're right. I'm gonna sing."

"Ohmygod, what?" It was all Sierra could do not to spit out her drink in shock.

Ethan took off, cutting through the crowd to the stage. He said something to the drummer. Then the guy with the acoustic guitar handed it over and suddenly Ethan was at the microphone with the guitar. His body haloed in the spotlight, he began to strum.

Ethan didn't introduce the song, didn't dedicate it. He didn't even so much as look in Charlie's direction, where she stood huddled with Matteo. But the moment he played those first few chords, she turned toward the stage, cocked her head, intrigued, and watched with a coy smile.

Sierra was riveted. She had heard the theme song to *Midnight Daydream* many times before—it was a solid semi-hit, doing better on the charts than the film had at the box office—but never on acoustic guitar. Never like this. She loved how Ethan talked his way through the song as though he had written it.

She wouldn't have thought she would be able to look away, until someone sat beside her at the bar. "I owe you a long-overdue apology," the voice said.

It was Chase Embers.

—

Ethan couldn't bear to even glance at Charlie. He would've been too destroyed if she wasn't listening or didn't seem to like what she'd heard. He wasn't that great, but he could play, and it was the kind of song you could almost just recite; it didn't require a whole lot. And it was short, which was a huge selling point. It hadn't gone so bad. People clapped, some even cheered, and as he stepped off the stage, intending to walk all the way to the back of the room, reclaim his spot by the bar, Charlie yanked his arm.

"Mercutio, you're full of surprises." She actually smiled.

"Am I?" he asked, shaking his head. "Well, it's a good song from a great film."

"Brought back memories, thanks for that." She looked over his shoulder, a mischievous glint.

Ethan could imagine who she might be watching. He glanced in Sierra's direction for encouragement and, finding her *still* talking to Chase, felt unusually empowered.

"So, just wanted to mention," he started. "In the event you're ever looking to make him jealous, Nicholas—"

Charlie's focus snapped to Ethan. "Oh?" she asked, an intrigued inflection.

"—then I would be honored to audition for that role." He couldn't believe he had said it and feared he might have actually offended her.

But a slow smile curled her lips. "And what exactly would that role be?" She sipped her drink innocently.

He shrugged, smiled, as if to say, *You tell me.*

"You seem too sweet for anything I'd have in mind." She looked toward Nicholas and Jasmine again.

"I can play against type," Ethan said.

"How old are you?"

"Twenty-one."

She nodded. "Dating anyone? I don't need any drama."

His eyes landed on Sierra and Chase. "No," he said, firmly. Then to Charlie again. "Is this an audition?"

"That was the audition." She flicked her head toward the stage, where another group belted a song from *Rent*. She circled him now, arms folded. "This is the callback."

"What do I need to do to land the job? Do you need me to fall in love with you?"

"Absolutely not," she snapped.

"Okaaay. I promise *not* to fall in love with you."

"You're on," she said easily. "Act One, Scene One." She grabbed his hand, leading him past Matteo—who shook his head at them—and Nicholas. She stopped near enough to the stage to catch some of the light, and pulled him into a kiss. He kissed her back, in keeping with his role, and when he nearly drew away, she locked him in again.

He'd expected it to feel more real than it had onstage when it had been choreographed, part of the show, but it felt...the same. It felt like performance instead of truth. Still, he had no doubt it appeared plenty believable to anyone bothering to watch. And when she did finally inch away, she left her hand on the back of his neck, stared in his eyes. He noticed her glance over his shoulder a second and then she whispered in his ear, "We're leaving, *now.*"

He wasn't sure where exactly they were going, but he didn't ask questions. He just smiled, stared back into her eyes, nodded, and then at once, swooped her up, throwing her over his shoulder and carrying her through the crowd and right out the door. As soon as they got outside, he put her down, and she laughed, pulling his arm to tug him around the corner and out of sight. They crouched down in the alleyway, peeking from the side of the building.

"Nice ad-lib," she whispered, impressed.

"What now?" he asked.

She grabbed his forearm to quiet him. "Wait for it," she said, confident.

Moments later, the door to the bar flung open and Nicholas ran out onto the sidewalk. He stopped halfway down the block, not far from them. Then turned to look the other way, into the darkness. They slunk back farther, swallowed up into the shadows, stifling laughter. A few minutes later, she nodded that it was clear.

Ethan offered to walk her home, but she said she would be fine. She gave him a hug and a peck on the cheek, thanking him, then gently cradled his face in her hands.

"You're good at this, Mercutio," she said into his eyes. "Not just this," she laughed, referring to tonight's charade. "But all of it." And with a wave, she disappeared back toward Avon.

—

That was what Nick got for moving the party from King's? He had done that for *her.*

She probably hadn't even noticed. She had been *busy.* He kicked the rocks in his path as he walked away from the bar. The kiss shouldn't have bothered him, he had seen that before—last week on stage, for instance. But there had been costumes and sets and other actors and a script and it wasn't really *them.* Tonight though… He'd seen this kind of thing plenty: two actors have a good night on stage and that mess of magic and magnetism bleeds offstage. Excess energy in search of an outlet. Nothing more. Hopefully.

Meanwhile, he had gone out of his way to not even so much as shake Jasmine's hand tonight. He hoped Charlie noticed how he'd worked to distance himself from Jasmine, as much as humanly possible.

The streets vibrated with so many people out enjoying the summer night. He wasn't ready to go home and found himself walking toward the edge of Chamberlain village.

At rehearsal, Charlie had taken to wearing her hair piled on top of her head, and their lark always seemed to be *staring* at him now, judging him, questioning his life choices. It was all he could think about when he would steal into the rehearsal room daily to watch her float up toward the ceiling, gliding and flipping as she delivered her lines. Each day stronger, more effortless.

If he watched that lark on her neck, as she swept through the air, it almost looked real. It reminded him so much—too much—of that night, and he wished he could tell her that, wished he could ask if she remembered it too.

Maybe that was why he now found himself standing at the tiny log cabin, a very sparse museum really, that they had broken into those many years ago. It had been her idea, of course, as everything the least bit illicit always was.

It had played out like a fever dream.

That next morning, Nick had awakened minutes before Charlie. Time fleeting, he had committed it all to memory: the single ray of sun streaming in that window, her hair fanned out, the soft rise and fall of her breathing. She wore his T-shirt, perhaps putting it on in the middle of the night when the air had grown cool. He felt her move, yawn, stretch her arms. The lark had flown in the window just as she'd opened her eyes.

46

IS IT OKAY IF I SCREAM?

"I feel like we're betraying Charlie just by being here," Sierra whispered to Ethan in the back of the auditorium at Jasmine Beijao's sold-out Q&A. The Chamberlain had even brought in that talk show host from Boston, Grace Garfield, to moderate. The event had been mandatory for apprentices, or technically, it was considered a perk. But Sierra didn't see it that way.

"…and I'm so glad you asked." Jasmine fluffed her hair. "For a long time it really was a curse, looking the way I do. It's a struggle, beauty. And then I got *Canis Lupus* and my entire world changed—"

Ethan rolled his eyes at Sierra.

"This, of course, was the film about a woman in the Alaskan wilderness who's essentially raised by wolves that scored you an Oscar nomination," Grace said, as applause broke out. Jasmine put her hand to her ample chest, mouthing thank-yous as though winning a pageant. "Tell us how you were able to get into character."

"Well, Grace, it wasn't easy. She was very…ugly, frankly. It was really out of my comfort zone—"

"The character is actually quite warm and loving though, which is the point of the film—"

"No, I mean, *physically* ugly. I had to dig deep to imagine what it might be like to not be as blessed as I am. It was a lot of work, especially with the prosthetics. But you know, a rewarding journey."

Sierra looked at Ethan. They'd both had enough. Without a word, they quietly left their seats and the theater.

—

Charlie had missed her days of solitary flying sessions so much that she had been arriving early ever since moving to the main stage to rehearse with lighting, sound and set pieces. The pendulum with her wires and harness was already attached to the flight track above the stage—evidence that Mason was here, somewhere—and she'd started to strap herself in when the doors flung open.

"Look who I found!" Mason called out as Danica trailed him with Gianni at her side.

"Sally had a meeting, so he's coming to rehearsal," Danica said, frazzled.

"Hey, buddy." Charlie crouched down on the stage, holding out her hand for a high five, which turned into their secret handshake.

"I brought Sparky," Gianni reported, hitting his enormous backpack.

"Welcome, Sparky," Charlie called as though the robot might be able to hear.

"Can we see you fly?" Gianni asked, unzipping the bag, taking out an iPad.

In no time, Charlie was buckled into her harness, Mason at the wires hoisting her up. Gianni stood in the aisle, not even taking a seat, yelling up question after question as he watched her flip and soar.

"How do you do that? Have you ever gotten stuck? Can I try that? Is she heavy?" he shouted.

"Let's see, to answer everything," she started. "You arch your back and dive. Not really. No, you can't try. And—Mason?"

"She's pretty light, mostly because of the way the system is weighted so I'm lifting half of her weight instead of all of it," Mason called down to Gianni.

"Can I see? If I promise not to touch?" the boy asked.

Mason allowed Gianni to stand beside him and watch, prompting even more inquiries. Gianni even programmed Sparky to roll to the center of the stage and wave at Charlie as she hung upside down like a bat.

As the cast trickled in, Charlie grounded herself, slipping out of her harness. Nick still hadn't arrived. It would be a long day. When she looked down at Gianni, already bored and tired, playing a game on his iPad, which he would be doing for the next five hours, it felt like watching her own childhood, electronics aside. At least this wasn't typical life for him. He seemed to have so much more stability than she'd had. Charlie thought of every actor who had ever been kind to her.

"Have you ever seen a trapdoor?" She knelt beside Gianni's seat. He perked up, shook his head. "Ask your mom if it would be okay."

Two minutes later, Charlie and Gianni were running through the halls down to the storage room under the stage, with Mason. Danica had been highly suspect when Charlie had asked permission.

Charlie helped Gianni step up into the pop-up toaster, a

clear cube, no top, set on a hydraulic lift directly beneath the trapdoor. She crouched down, holding his hand as Mason slid open the passage above them.

"So curl up like this." Charlie folded herself into a ball. "And then it'll toss us up into the air."

"And then we'll be on the stage?" he said.

"Exactly."

"On three," Mason said. "One—"

"Is it okay if I scream?" he asked.

"Absolutely," she said, then muttered to herself, "That's a question I ask myself daily."

⸺

As they waited for rehearsal to start, Harlow gabbed on and on. She seemed on edge.

"I just think maybe they shouldn't have scheduled the New York trip so close to opening," she said.

"When else would it be? It's like the only day the theater's dark," Alex said.

Sierra wondered if Harlow was concerned less with scheduling and secretly about seeing supposed friends of hers on Broadway, celebrating *their* success.

"Sorry! Let's get started." Nicholas jogged up the aisle now, fifteen minutes late.

"Is it just me or has he been kinda weird since closing night?" Ethan asked Sierra, sounding guilty.

"Maybe it has to do with whatever happened with you and Charlie." Harlow turned to them, overhearing.

"Tripp was on his morning run and said he saw Nicholas coming out of that log cabin thing," Sierra reported.

"Tripp runs?" Harlow asked.

Tripp appeared beside them now, slinking into an aisle seat. "Yes, Tripp runs," he said, offended. "A body like this doesn't just happen through sheer force of will."

"Last day of dress rehearsals, so, we gotta focus today," Nicholas announced to them. "Who are we missing?"

As he scanned the group, there was a BOOM and a scream, as Charlie and Danica's son, Gianni, shot up through the cut-out and landed on the stage.

47

YOU'RE GIVING ME VERTIGO

Nick was spent. They had run the entire show. Twice. Lights, costumes, wires, turntable, smoke, effects, everything. A *lot* had gone wrong, but enough had gone right that he felt confident wrapping for the night.

"No, that's wrong," he said into the radio, trying to resolve a lighting glitch. The lights beaming on stage grew too bright, too red. "No, this looks like a circle of hell, which, while accurate for me personally, is not in tune with this particular play."

When he turned around, Charlie dropped in front of him, upside down—"Hi," she greeted him, as he jumped. "Sorry!" She turned right-side up, landing on her feet. The lights around them came up vibrant blue this time, as though underwater.

"What's going *on* up there?" he said into the headset.

One of his directing fellows sat in the booth, the other in the audience.

"Just wanted to do a few more of these before calling it a day," Charlie answered him, lifting off the ground again. "What's the problem?"

"Not you. Up there." He pointed to the lighting booth. "Them." The lights burned violet now.

"They're probably exhausted, go easy on 'em," Charlie said, flipping to his other side.

"Wrong again," he said into the mouthpiece. "But closer."

"Too close?" she asked, hands on his shoulders to propel her next flip.

"Not you," he said again. "But while I have you, sort of— did you get my text?"

She floated back down into the space just above him again, patting at her pockets. "Um, no, I don't have my phone on me." She flipped over his head again to land on his other side.

"I'm gonna need to know if you're staying," he said, curt.

"Right now?" she asked, another rotation in the air.

"Soon. Like, in two days, by opening night." He watched her. "Do you have to keep doing that? You're giving me vertigo."

He scribbled in his notebook, ripping the sheet out as she flipped over him. He grabbed her midflip, stopping her again. "Read this." He held up a folded piece of paper, tucked it into the sleeve of the bodysuit she wore beneath her gauzy costume. "And see you tomorrow."

He stepped offstage to consult with his directing fellow. He didn't want to watch to see if Charlie read the note or not.

—

Hovering in the air, Charlie turned once more and stopped upside down to read the note Nick had just slipped her. An invitation of sorts.

Avoiding the actual onstage rehearsals for so long had at least calmed the ferocity of her anger toward him. But she wasn't sure how she felt yet. For now, she crumpled the note, intending to shove it back into her sleeve...just as she was jerked upward.

"Whoa!" she shouted at Mason, the paper falling to the stage as she grabbed the wires on either side to steady herself.

"Sorry!" he shouted back. "Muscle cramp."

But he had been at this all day: through two full run-throughs of the show. "It's okay, we're good here," she said as he lowered her, only now realizing how much her body ached after six hours of flying. Her numb legs barely felt attached to her anymore. *Nine days left.*

PART THREE

We are such stuff as dreams are made on...

—WILLIAM SHAKESPEARE,
THE TEMPEST

48

IT'S, LIKE, AYAHUASCA 2.0

Their buses arrived late into New York, torrential downpour slowing their progress, but Sierra didn't mind. Like everyone else, she had slept nearly the entire ride, the intensity of the past few weeks catching up with her. She had awakened to a soundtrack of honking horns as they swerved into Manhattan, Ethan's head on her shoulder, peaceful, while cars and taxis zipped between swarms of pedestrians and bikers. She felt the pace instantaneously enter her bloodstream.

They stashed their bags at their Times Square hotel—assigned four to a room, in the same pairs as the dorms, unfortunately—and changed. ("Is that what you're wearing?" Harlow asked of Sierra's satin tank and pleated skirt, which did seem tragically demure alongside Harlow's little black dress.) Then they embarked on a preshow whirlwind: touring the Winter Garden theater—home of *Abby's Road*; a Q&A with the writer/director/ composer himself; dinner at a hole-in-the-wall pizza place; and back for showtime. They slipped into their balcony seats minutes before curtain.

Sierra clutched her program the entire show, feeling every note echo in her heart, reverberate through her veins. She had been to a Broadway production only once before—a *Phantom of the Opera* revival—but this felt so brand-new, exotic. And to be just one degree of separation from three cast members—two of the soldiers in the chorus and the girl in the lavender hoop skirt were Harlow and Alex's friends—gave Sierra a shot of inspiration that felt like pure adrenaline. This kind of life was possible. She had never been in such close proximity to people her age, living the life she dreamed of. This, all of it, was what she, Sierra Suarez, wanted.

Ethan and Tripp watched beside her just as rapt. Harlow, seated a row in front of them, shifted endlessly. She swung her leg, tied her hair back, took it down, tied it back again. Scowling during John Adams's death scene, she whispered something to Alex, then perched her head on her fist, looking bored.

After the curtain call, they were invited into the tight corridors of the backstage to meet the cast. Sierra hung back in the pack, but loved viewing these creatures up close. They looked even younger, slighter, and it was hard to fathom that those voices had come from some of those bodies.

It was midnight when they returned to the hotel and 12:01 when Alex pulled Harlow, Ethan, Sierra and Tripp aside. "Still in for the after-party?"

Ethan and Sierra raised their eyebrows at each other, lucky to be included.

Alex and Harlow—quieter than usual, still scowling—led them to the fifth-floor walk-up their three friends shared above a Greek restaurant in Hell's Kitchen. The grimy shoebox of a two-bedroom apartment, posters and playbills taped and tacked onto the walls, was nothing short of thrilling to Sierra. These three were living an artist's life, here in the middle of this chaos and madness. It seemed incredibly romantic, gutsy, intoxicating, and any bit of supposed suffering just made it all the more alluring. Sierra was almost too excited to speak.

⸻

Ethan was still in a heady fog—from the show, which had infected him, and the lights of Times Square and the energy and the *everything*—when they arrived at the after-party, music spilling out, along with an herbal, musky, charred scent he couldn't quite place.

Alex led them straight through the dim-lit, thumping-bass dance party to the kitchen, like he owned the place. Tripp peeled off from their group, beelining for the runway-model-looking guy who had played Charles Adams. In the kitchen, they found several pots on the stove top, a bearded, skinny hipster in thick glasses stirring them with the care of a DJ spinning. He and Alex shook hands, slapped each other on the shoulder. "Looking good," Alex said to him. Then to the group he said, "This is Stone."

Stone nodded, Ethan reciprocated.

"And you guys know each other? And all these people?" Sierra asked, in awe.

"Juilliard." Stone pointed at Alex and himself. A man of few words.

"Wow, so this is Juilliard Drama." Ethan surveyed the room.

"I'm ballet," Stone said. "He's drama." He pointed at Alex.

"And also a lot of NYU. Harlow knows everyone too."

Sure enough, Harlow already stood at the center of a group, drink in one hand, cigarette in the other, chatting and looking relieved to be *home*. Ethan could only imagine what she was telling them about her summer. He suspected a lot of exaggeration.

"This ready to go, man?" Alex asked.

Stone shrugged, nodded. "Let's do it."

"So what's goin' on with all this?" Ethan asked, aware he was confirming his utter lack of cool.

"Oooh, is this ayahuasca?" Sierra leaned over Ethan, peeking into the pots, which bubbled like three soups of varying consistencies.

"Seriously?" Ethan looked at her in disbelief. "What do you know about ayahuasca? They do a lotta this at Wellesley?"

"What do *you* know about ayahuasca?" she laughed. He was 99 percent sure she knew as much as he did, which was nothing.

"Ayahuasca is over," Stone cut them off, expressionless.

"Good to know." Ethan nodded.

"*This* is what you need to be doing now," Alex said. "This is, like, ayahuasca 2.0." Stone combined the three saucepans into a larger pot, ladling the concoction into disposable coffee cups. "It's, like, next-level stuff. It's, like…" Alex put his hand to his head to signal an explosion and mouthed *BOOM*.

Ethan and Sierra looked at each other like they had walked into some kind of college drug-movie shoot. "It seems kind of complicated," Sierra said. "For something that's ultimately supposed to be *freeing* or whatever."

"It's cool, it's herbal, so it'll blow your fucking mind but it won't kill you or anything," Alex said easily.

"Bonus," Ethan said.

"It's all natural, and practically FDA approved," Alex went on, handing them cups.

Ethan held it near his lips: it smelled like dead flowers and gasoline.

"Cheers," Stone said, tapping his cup to Ethan's and Sierra's, then slipping into the low lights of the living room, the throbbing music, the roar of chatter, the party respectably raging.

Ethan watched him and Alex get swallowed into the dancing crowd, and when he turned back around, Sierra was knocking back her drink.

"Wait!" Ethan grabbed her forearm. "You really think it's okay?"

"It's weirdly delicious." She shouted to be heard over the music, which had cranked up. "And I feel like, I don't know, maybe I'll make tonight a night I'll remember in twenty years when I'm old and probably boring—especially if this whole acting thing doesn't work out—and I'll be like, *damn, I was exciting once when I drank that crazy poison during my seventeen hours in New York.*"

"Is this absorbed immediately into the bloodstream or what?" he asked, laughing.

"Here's hoping," she said, drinking the rest.

He held up his cup, deep breath, and downed it.

Sierra *felt* like she should be *feeling* more by now. She had been so game to drink the stuff, shake up her world, *for once*, but she had been hoping for…*more*. So she chased it with a beer and chased that with a shot—and another and another and another and another—of something, anything that was circulating. Ethan did the same. They threw themselves into the party, jumping, jumping, jumping, arms in the air, dancing for what felt like hours but may have been minutes, who could tell? Until the room finally started to look like something being constructed in real time on a pottery wheel, spinning too, too, too fast. While their bodies seemed to be moving tooooo slooooowly, and they collapsed beside each other onto the faded sofa, laughing about everything and nothing.

Just a breath later, something, *someone* hurtled at them, smashing through the glass coffee table before them. At the crash, they rose to their feet, Ethan yanking Sierra away as fast as his dulled reflexes could manage. Tripping over the feet of whoever sat beside them, they stumbled together into a wall as the room's collective screams modulated to cheers when Stone—it had been Stone, so ungraceful for a dancer—sprang right up, dusting shards of glass off himself.

Still wobbly in the chaos, people jostling them in the dim hallway, Sierra steadied herself, clasping what turned out to be a doorknob behind her back. Someone pushed past them, shoving Ethan against her in the process, and as she looked at him in that tenth of a second, it was as though that drink *finally* kicked in. His lips just millimeters from hers, she closed the distance, kissing him, and he kissed her back, arms wrapping around her waist. Dizzy all over again, she somehow twisted the doorknob open and they fell into someone's empty room, nearly pitch-black, music still playing. She shed her satin camisole. He pulled off his button-down shirt. Or maybe she pulled off his shirt, and he hers. It was impossible to know and unimportant to her: what mattered was the impulse felt equal—mirrored—and relentless in that way of anything left simmering too long.

49

I NEED TO WEAR A CATSUIT AGAIN

Nick checked the time again—7:42 p.m.—as he stood shirt-less before his closet, pulling out a blue seersucker shirt and a crisp T-shirt. He didn't want to seem to be trying too hard but...he was. And maybe he *should* try too hard, maybe that made sense tonight. He held both shirts in front of himself in the mirror. At least tonight had to be better than last night when, after that endless rehearsal, he had to take his old pal Ron—from Chamberlain First Bank—to dinner to investigate how the hell to *not* have the theater shut down immediately after this summer. The infusion of funds from Taylor—who contributed under the condition that Jasmine be cast in the show—would sustain this season, but it was still a Band-Aid on a hemorrhage.

The theater was dark tonight. The apprentices were in New York, giving everyone a necessary breather before *Midsummer*'s opening. Including Nick. He hadn't heard from Charlie since

282 • AIMEE AGRESTI

he had slipped the note to her yesterday at the end of rehearsal, which wasn't surprising: she liked to make him fret, it was sport for her. But he hoped she would be there.

Seersucker, he finally decided, nodding at his reflection. Tonight mattered. Before he could pull it on though, he heard the knock at the door. They were due to meet at eight—and not here. But he felt a thrill at this change of plans: she had come to him, the surest sign that she felt the same pull he did, no matter how rocky things had gotten. That these weeks in each other's orbits again had reminded her that there *was* something between them, a magnetism, a lightning that perhaps didn't strike as often as books and movies and song lyrics had you believe. At least that's what he had discovered in these intervening years between meeting her, falling in love, having it blow up and reuniting by an act of law. Maybe she was ready to hear him out, finally, and then move forward…together.

The knock again. But first, he needed to answer the door. He started to pull on his shirt then thought, *Maybe not, actually.* He hadn't spent the weeks between her sentencing and arrival doing all those crunches for nothing. And wasn't this how it always was in those prime-time soaps? Someone always showing up at the door when someone else is getting dressed. He even had their soundtrack playing. One night when he couldn't sleep, he had made a mix of songs from their time together—that summer, the *Tempest* shoot in London, the awards season—and had it on to rev him up.

He swung open the door, without looking out first, realizing too late that this was exactly how so many horror movies began.

—

Charlie arrived early. To the lake. She hadn't planned to, but she needed to escape the pervasive *joy* of the house: Matteo and Danica each had nights out with their visiting loves, Chase was getting ready for *something*—music thumping in his room, humming along, a spicy cologne misting through the door.

After more thought than she usually dedicated to these matters, she had pulled on a strappy silk tank and her ripped jeans and snuck out without anyone noticing.

—

Jasmine launched herself at Nick the minute the door opened, wrapping her arms around his neck, pressing herself against him as though trying to clothe him with her own body.

"You dressed up," she said, planting a kiss on him, then walking through the open door and taking a seat on the sofa like a new pet.

He closed his eyes, as though watching the train that carried the evening's vast possibilities suddenly derail and plunge into a ravine. "I was just on my way out, so I can't—"

"Like that?"

"I was just getting dressed and *then* on my way out," he sighed. "So this is a bad time for…whatever *this* is." He gestured to the open door, signaling for her to go.

"But I got your note," she purred, innocently, unfolding a familiar slip of paper and flashing it at him.

"How'd you get that—?" He tried to swipe it but she pulled it away too fast.

"What do you mean?" She smiled, fluttered her lashes. "You wanted to meet, so I came to you."

"That's probably because you don't even know where the fucking lake is."

"Get *over* here," she said, in a way that would have been alluring to the vast majority of the human population, man or woman, but not to him anymore. "I'm sure I can change your mind about wherever you think you're going."

He stepped forward, pretending he might sit down but instead grabbing the paper from her hands.

"Hey!"

"You can't really think this is yours," he said with a laugh, inspecting the jagged edge, "because it had the letter *C* here and now it's clearly been ripped off."

"Why didn't we work out?" she said in a dreamy tone, stretching her tanned legs out on his sofa.

"I was high—literally—when we got married and you were a rebound," he said, monotone. "Worst mistake of my life." He had given in to Jasmine, and a lot of things that were bad for him, because he was heartbroken over Charlie walking away from his film and his life, and his heart refused to heal or even to scar. His producers had hired Jasmine and he had had no choice but to accept it or walk away himself. It had marked the start of a downward spiral that included their short-lived, miserable relationship and shorter, more miserable marriage. When he left Jasmine, she claimed she'd only attached herself to him in the first place expecting the film to be a hit (it wasn't). "And you know that. I've told you that."

"I think we should work together again." When he just stared blankly, she changed tack. "I want to help you get back on the map."

"No." He folded his arms across his chest. Something wasn't right. He had read that she had dropped out of a couple of projects.

"Can we do another superhero movie—but a good one?"

"No."

"I need something sexy again," she whined. "I'm just getting all these weird ugly parts—tired moms with no makeup, people 'hitting rock bottom.'" She cringed.

"That means you're good at what you're doing," he said. His problem with her was never about her acting. "People are giving you more Oscar bait, enjoy," he said, dully.

"I *need* to wear a catsuit again," she said as though it was the most delicious secret. Her costume for his movie had been the only aspect of the production nominated for any awards—Razzies notwithstanding. "My boobs aren't going to be like this forever," she said, gazing longingly at them. "I'm sure you're working on *something*. Other than this theater stuff."

"I am," he said. He hadn't told anyone except Charlie, but he was going back to his roots, taking something time-honored and making it shiny and bold and palatable to a new audience. He had been thinking it over for a while but just needed the courage to take that chance. He had such hopes for it but hadn't secured the most vital parts, the people, the magic, yet. "It's not your kind of thing," he said dismissively, hoping to deter her. "And besides, I like this theater stuff—"

"It could *be* my thing," she cut him off.

"It's not."

"It could be."

"Jasmine," he snapped. "We're not good for each other. You don't care about what you're doing, you care about how many people are seeing it, and that's fine." It really was fine, it just wasn't for him. "I'm just not about the popularity contest."

"Spoken like someone truly unpopular," she said.

"Exactly my point. We're incompatible in, basically, every way."

"Yes! Like yin and yang," she said like it was a good thing. On her feet now, she walked toward him.

"No." He looked out the still-open door, wondering if he could just run away. "Yin and yang are counterparts, they form a unit, they fill in each other's blanks—"

"I can fill in your blanks," she whispered into his ear.

"No, thanks." He put his hands up, not even touching her. "I'm good. You gotta get outta here. *Now*, Jasmine." She stood still, not accustomed to being denied—especially not twice by the same man, which he realized was probably no small part of why she was interested in him. "The show is great, you're great in it, it's all…just great," he said. "But I didn't hire you, I'm making the best of this, that's it."

She took a deep, slow breath, exhaled, eyes closed as though finally hearing him. When she opened her eyes again, she stepped outside the door, then paused once more, tracing her fingers along his bicep. "It's okay," she said quietly. "We can talk later." And she walked out.

"No!" he called out after her. "That is *not* what I meant."

But she was gone. He checked his watch: 8:32. He grabbed the seersucker shirt and ran out the door, putting it on as he flew through the streets.

———

Charlie sat on the pier, shoes still on, not wanting to get too comfortable. She had been so oddly moved by Nick's note. By its punctuation, all the question marks. "C—Meet me at our lake tomorrow night? 8 p.m.? Please? Love, Nick." The collective ownership of the lake. The closing: "Love." The subsequent text message had been identical to that slip of paper she had lost at rehearsal.

She had decided, while still upside down over the stage, that she would go. She just didn't need to tell him then, did she? Maybe she had actually played too many games. She pulled out her phone—8:15 p.m.—and bit her lip, hating every minute of this. But she would do it, just in case there had been any doubt about whether she would be here: she snapped a picture from her spot on the pier, the water shimmering in the moonlight, and sent it with the caption: am i at the right lake? Then, feeling unusually hopeful and even sentimental, she added, xx, c.

The truth was, she had been thinking that maybe the statute of limitations had expired on his being classified as an asshole in her mind. She had been no angel either. He seemed to have changed, seemed to be trying. Something was there, locked away in her subconscious, *somewhere*, that had conjured him up—of all people—to save her life that night in the harbor. And so she would trust that, that instinct. This was a wave she had decided she was willing to ride.

But when she checked again—at 8:35 p.m.—and still heard nothing, the hurt began to poison her heart again.

—

Of course, Nick groaned, discovering the missed text from twenty minutes earlier: Charlie.

He tapped out a response as he ran: Heading over now—an unexpected delay. still there?

Finally he reached their spot and found it empty. He took a seat on the pier anyway, and snapped a photo of the same view in her picture.

Looking for you... he wrote, and then, because it was obvious: Missed you. I'll come to you, anywhere. He waited a few long minutes but nothing, not even ellipses, came across the screen, so he took off, heading to Avon.

Sweaty and sticky in the humid, heavy air of late-July, he ran all the way up to her front door. He rang the doorbell, knocked, peered in the window, nothing. He tried the door-knob: thank God no one locked their doors in this town.

"Charlie?" he called out as he crept inside. "I think you're here?" He walked through the kitchen and living room, all empty, though he heard music somewhere above. "I hope you're here because otherwise I don't know where you are." He looked up the stairs, and decided to climb, still narrating. "I was at the lake. Late. Which I know isn't like me." He reached her room, but she wasn't in there. He clanged up that spiral staircase that led to the balcony and poked his head out: nothing.

Back in her room, he continued narrating. "Maybe you're

here and just don't wanna see me." He scanned the room—unmade bed, clothes in heaps, books. "Sorry about tonight, it's kind of a long story. I know everything is a long story with me." He browsed the stack of books, the *Romeo and Juliet* he'd given her was on top. "But, even though I keep fucking everything up, with us, with this place, this is still easily the best thing I've had going in years. And that's because a whole string of unlikely events brought you back here. So, in case you're here somewhere listening to this, just wanted you to know that. And it's my hope that you feel the same way about some of that. I'm sure you'll at least agree about what a fuckup I am, but, you know, the other stuff too."

Beneath a copy of *The Tempest* that he recognized as his own, swiped from his office shelves, he found that photo from the liner notes of a CD: her father with his trumpet on an otherwise empty stage, her mother pictured in the background. And then, fanning the pages of the book, Nick came across another photo that was being used as a bookmark: the one from their own Black Box rehearsal that summer they met, Charlie and Nick sitting on stage, looking at each other. The shot that had been used in the program that summer. It was the same photo he had tucked away in his office. But this wasn't a stolen copy of his photo—the edges were rough, like it had been torn out, whereas his he had cut from the program lovingly, precisely.

A door opened across the hall, and he shoved the photo back into the book.

"That was a motherfucking great speech," Chase said, standing in his doorframe, shirtless. "I don't think she's here—"

"Yeah, I'm kind of realizing that," Nick said.

"I just felt bad letting you keep talking. But I can tell her—"

"No," he said. "It's fine, no big deal."

"It sounded like a big deal—"

"I'm just, you know, I'm gonna go now, but see you tomorrow night," Nick said, waving as he walked by and glimpsing another figure inside Chase's room. "Hi, Marlena."

⸻

The next morning, Charlie woke up inside that log cabin, alone—she had retreated there after Nick never showed up at the lake—and made her way back to the house. She debated whether to bother texting Nick back before showtime, but she wasn't even sure what to say at this point. Her mind was so clouded, Charlie could've sworn she saw someone who looked exactly like Marlena turning the corner out of sight as she arrived on Avon, even though Marlena wasn't due until right before the show tonight. She could've used her friend right now. She needed someone to make her feel like less of a sentimental fool for going to the lake, for giving Nick another chance, for having let herself open that window into her heart.

Matteo greeted her in the kitchen. "We got a *lot* to talk about, am I right or am I right?" he said, emptying every vegetable from the fridge in a manic frenzy.

"I know, Nick and—"

"Fuck Nick—no offense—"

She put her hands up. "None taken."

"Sebastian went home last night."

"What do you mean!" She grabbed his arm in shock, unable to compute his husband going home before the show.

"I mean, he left the hotel and got on a goddamn plane and went back to San Francisco is what I mean."

"No, but, what *happened*—?"

He sighed, put down the carton of eggs and a trio of red peppers. One pepper rolled on the floor and he left it there. "He found out about this little hiccup I had with one of his assistants—" He looked away a moment.

"Matteo," she said, too stunned to form words.

"I know, I know, we were having a rough patch, it happens, you know—"

"You're supposed to be relationship goals for me—"

"And apparently for Chase too," he said. "And Danica and everyone. I'm flattered you all think I've got all the answers but I'm just one damn man."

"Wait, Chase?" She was just catching up. "With who?"

"You won't *even* believe," Matteo said, cracking the eggs into a bowl now.

The front door creaked open, and Chase appeared, seemingly fresh from Pilates, mat under his arm. "Morning, all—hey, is that a frittata in the works?" he asked. "Where were you all last night? Had the place to myself."

50

WHAT DO YOU REMEMBER?

It felt unlike any hangover Ethan had ever had. All numb. The room still and silent except for breathing. His eyes flickered, opening finally to chestnut locks cascading over his face.

He tried not to panic.

He had assumed it had been a dream. It was just so...*vivid.* Too vivid. He felt like he might be sick, but he wasn't sure if it was physically or just mentally. This was *not* supposed to happen. He wasn't the type of guy who had a lot of friends who were girls or a lot of friends at all, and Sierra was the only one this summer who *got* him. She had always relegated him to the friend zone, so it had been easy to assume there was nothing there and to turn off all non-friend-like impulses.

But it hadn't been pure coincidence that he had wandered in her direction that first day on the football field. Sure, he was lucky she was standing there in need of a partner, but even if she had already paired up, he would've still placed himself within a short radius of her. Honestly, he had been ensnared the moment he saw her swim by, coolly mimicking the "crawl" stroke out the theater doors after that first apprentice meeting when everyone else was crawling on the floor with no imagination whatsoever.

He didn't want to be thinking of this right now. He couldn't have *drama* with her. Was he a good enough actor to play it cool? Doubtful. That one day he had seen Charlie from afar at her theater after her car accident, he had tripped over his own feet when they unlocked the lobby doors and cut his forehead from hitting the newsstand inside.

Why did he remember *everything* from last night? Shouldn't he have blacked out at some point? Instead, he could call up the full play-by-play. He remembered that Sierra had kissed him first, even though he had wanted to kiss her and just hadn't orchestrated his move yet. For some reason, kissing Charlie onstage—and offstage—had been so much less world rocking than all this with Sierra. With Sierra, it felt like everything around them went out of focus and the camera moved in and this was *their* scene now.

Sierra stirred, but still lay on her side, her back to him. He moved his arm—the one he realized was flung over her shoulder. If he tried to crawl out from under the sheet to find his clothes—because that was another thing, he wasn't sure where they were—he would undoubtedly fully wake her. He heard her yawn, but he could tell her eyes weren't open yet.

Her hair was impossibly shiny and smooth like corn silk, and these were exactly the thoughts he didn't want to be having. She combed her hand through her hair now, groaned—that was how he felt too—and moved just centimeters. He remained frozen, closed his eyes.

She gasped, whispering, "Ohhhmygod...are you awake?

Don't be awake. Don't be awake. Don't be awake," she said, her back to him, both of them perfectly still.

"Not awake," he said, unsure.

"I'm awake." A head popped up from the floor at the foot of the bed. They both screamed, grabbed the sheet. It was Alex.

Then another voice, male, beside Alex, yawning. "Coffee. Need coffee." It was Stone.

"None here, there's a food cart across the street or a Starbucks a block in any direction," another voice croaked. *How many people were in this room?* At least everyone else was on the floor.

The door opened: Harlow in a bathrobe, as though she lived there. Behind her was the guy who, Ethan was almost positive, had played Abigail Adams's son Charles last night, his arms wrapped around Harlow, kissing her neck.

"Players," she announced, like a stagehand calling the actors to their places for the curtain opening. "Listen up!" She nibbled on a chip from the bowl in her hands, the party snacks left out overnight. "Just a PSA—it's 11:07 a.m., bus leaves from the hotel in twenty-three minutes," she said calmly, yawning. "We're gonna miss it if we don't rally." It took a beat for it to register. If they missed the bus, they would miss the opening night of *Midsummer*. Terrible scheduling, for sure, but apparently Bradford had bought the block of tickets before Blunt bothered to tell him he was extending the *Romeo* run. But that didn't matter now. What mattered was they had to GO. At once, they burst from their places, too manic to even be embarrassed.

—

Their cab inched along too slowly, so Alex flung open the door, and they all ran through Times Square to their hotel, grabbed their bags from their rooms and then raced back out to the bus idling on a side street. Its doors had already closed as it began to pull out, and they sprinted toward it, Ethan ahead of the pack. He smacked the door with his palm just in time, and the driver opened up.

"Nice of you folks to join us." Bradford smirked at them.

It wasn't until they found their seats, Ethan and Sierra sitting one in front of the other this time, that they looked at each other.

"What do you remember?" he whispered.

"What do *you* remember?" she asked.

"Nothing," he lied, testing it out. But actually: *everything, everything, everything.* He couldn't stop seeing the flashes of what had gone on between them last night.

"Oh, good, me neither." She looked relieved, so he went with it.

"Absolutely nothing," he said, sounding somewhat believable. *Everything.* He pretended to sleep the rest of the way. *Everything.*

———

Sierra could not sleep, exhausted as she was. Ethan had dozed off before they'd even gotten out of the city, but every time she closed her eyes, she saw another scene from their night. There were a *lot* of them and they were all good, really good, that wasn't the issue; the problem was that it had happened *at all.* If she was being honest with herself then, sure, she had kind of been looking for an excuse to kiss Ethan anyway.

But what were they supposed to do *now*? She wondered if he really didn't remember anything. That drink did *not* do what she'd expected. She thought she might remember sensations, maybe, but details, no. She had full recall of those. And now she couldn't help feeling drawn to Ethan, which was not helpful because she really loved their friendship. But how do you just forget a night like that and move on? She supposed the answer was act like it never happened. That felt achingly unfair. Why couldn't Ethan just have been a terrible kisser and terrible *everything else*?

These thoughts were exactly what she didn't want on her mind as the bus rattled back to leafy Chamberlain for opening night of her first main stage performance. But she wanted to be an actor, and actors had to put on a good show despite what was happening in their real lives. Sierra would simply have to don her flower crown and become the fairy Peaseblossom.

—

Charlie was glad Jasmine had worked it into her contract to have her own dressing room. It meant the other four of them now shared the room that had previously been just Matteo and Chase's, but she welcomed the company. In a rare turn of events though, no one seemed to want to talk about themselves (except for Danica and no one cared since she appeared happily settled), so they grasped for neutral ground.

"I heard the apprentices had some kinda drug-fueled orgy in NYC," Chase said.

"No way. That group?" Matteo asked. "Though I did hear there were hookups."

"Good for them, they should've already been doing that," Charlie said. "They're too damn young to be so serious."

"But that's the whole purpose of being here," Danica said. "To be serious."

The three of them stared at her, but Danica surprised them all by being first to laugh at herself and they all joined in.

As Mercutio and Sierra passed by in the hall just before Charlie was due on stage, she couldn't suppress a smile. "I hope every last rumor is true."

51

I'M NOT PLANNING TO
COME TO MY SENSES

Ten minutes until opening, a full house, and Nick knew the best thing he could do was table the personal matters until later. Charlie refused to talk to him—again—anyway. And he had forgotten entirely about Jasmine, who had been sequestered in hair and makeup with her own team for eons. Until she'd emerged from her dressing room right when he happened to be reviewing a last-minute change with the prop team.

"So, have you come to your senses?" Jasmine cooed, grabbing the lapels of his blazer, effectively chasing away the small crew. "About last night? Working together."

"Jasmine, no," he said, annoyed, extricating himself. "I told you, I'm not *planning* to come to my senses. My senses are indicating that this—" he pointed to her and himself "—is not happening in any way beyond this production." But there was still, in fact, a show to do, so he added, hastily, "Let's just focus on tonight's performance."

He could've said more, but she smiled her gleaming red carpet smile, wound up and sank her fist smack into his left cheek with surprising force. He cradled his face in his hands as she continued on toward the wings.

As he walked away down the hall in search of his dispersed props crew, tapping his cheek, checking for blood, another door opened into the hallway, and Charlie breezed out of the company dressing room, costume, makeup, ready to go. He stopped, so much he wanted to say, and yet she looked up at him, her expression transforming from stony to confused to smirking.

"Looks like someone beat me to it," she said to him.

"Luckily I have another." He turned his uninjured cheek toward her. "How's your left hook?"

"We'll see, but I'm busy till intermission." She patted him on the back and continued on to the wings.

⏤

They hadn't yet reached intermission when Charlie saw the first sign of trouble. Jasmine, who was indeed as beautiful and bold a Hermia as Charlie had seen, became shrill, testy in a way she hadn't played the part in rehearsal. It was around the time Lysander falls in love with her rival Helena that Jasmine began to lose it, screaming her lines.

The audience shifted in their seats, the quiet slowly shattering. And then the full breaking point: when Hermia was to go searching for her love, Jasmine stood at center stage, beginning her monologue then shaking her head, looking directly into the orchestra seats.

"You know what? I don't know why I should bother looking for Lysander, anyway," Jasmine told the audience. Anyone who knew anything about Shakespeare began whispering.

"What's the fucking point, anyway? He's not going to want me when I get there because now he's in love with Helena for reasons that make *no sense* whatsoever. I don't get it. I do *not* get it. I hate this fucking play…"

She went on like this while Charlie was literally trapped in the air above the stage, waiting to fly back in, Mason too transfixed by Jasmine's tirade to notice Charlie flailing to get his attention, to bring her down. That's when Charlie heard it. "Maybe Lysander really needs someone like Charlie SAVOY! Maybe THAT would just solve EVERYTHING!" Jasmine shouted, a mocking, vitriolic tone, thrashing her body, pulling off pieces of her costume and throwing them at the audience, who gamely caught them, still confused.

"Enough, Jasmine." Matteo appeared behind her like a human straitjacket, trying to drag her into the wings, but she put up a fight, swinging her arms and kicking her legs.

Where the hell was Nick? He was the only audience Jasmine seemed to care about.

"Because Charlie Savoy is just SO SPECIAL…well, let me just tell you…she's *not*… I don't see what the big deal is…anyone can do what she does but she's just got everyone fucking fooled…" Jasmine went on.

This was only going to get worse. Desperate, Charlie—out of sight behind a screen and at least a dozen feet up—took a deep breath and unclipped her harness. Down she fell, landing on her feet at the back of the stage. She ran into the wings in time to see Jasmine headbutt Matteo, giving him a bloody nose and forcing him to release her. The audience gasped, murmured, unsure of what they were watching. On stage, everyone stood frozen in shock except for Chase, who took Matteo's place attempting to restrain Jasmine.

"And let me tell you another thing about Charlie…" she began again.

Charlie ran to Mason, who looked shocked to see her not in the sky and let go of the ropes. "Go help Chase, pull Jasmine over the trapdoor," she ordered him, then ran down through the twisting corridors, to the greenroom.

Charlie ducked her head inside long enough to gauge whether the actors were positioned over the trap yet. The apprentices not currently onstage watched the video feed in silence as Mason and Chase held on to a bucking Jasmine. It would be only a few more steps.

Charlie sprinted to the room beneath the stage, where an apprentice sat glued to a soundless monitor, likely wondering what was happening.

"Open the trap!" Charlie yelled at him now.

"Seriously?" he asked, calm. "It's not that easy, it's not like a sunroof. It's a fairly antiquated system. I need a minute."

"Open. The trap. NOW!"

He flew out of his chair, frantic, and together they shoved a crash mat in place beneath the hinged opening. Quickly, he unlatched the locks so only a large pin held it in place. Then he pulled that pin, and at once, all three of them fell to the mats. Jasmine was still shouting as they landed in a heap, groaning, wind knocked out of them. Chase and Mason had lost their grip on impact, and Jasmine scrambled to her feet and ran off, a blur of her sweeping gown, like a wild animal suddenly freed.

"I just saved you from yourself," Charlie yelled after her, offering a hand to the men.

Above them all came another crash: the curtain falling too fast, and screams. She glanced at the monitor to see a few fallen actors flat on the stage, not having moved out of the way fast enough.

Finally, *finally*, Nick's voice over the speaker, attempting to sound calm. "Due to unforeseen *issues*, we are unable to continue tonight's performance. We will reschedule on a later date."

As Chase and Mason rehashed the trauma like survivors of a natural disaster, Charlie slipped away. She replayed Jasmine's words—*Charlie is nothing. Not anymore. She has everyone fooled. Every last one of you*—as she crashed open the stage door and out into the steamy night. She shed the gauzy layers of her costume as she ran, until she was left just in her bodysuit underneath, like a ghost haunting the town. She jogged all the way home, so much mad energy, her blood, bones, muscles, every nerve vibrating with anger...and with the fear that those words were true.

She shook the front door, locked—it was hardly ever locked but at least it wasn't the dead bolt. Her bag was still at the theater, so she kicked open the door, strode up to her room, flung her duffel onto the bed and began shoving her clothes inside. She didn't care about her sentencing or Nick or anything. She was done here.

52

AT LEAST NO ONE'S
TALKING ABOUT US ANYMORE

Sierra had never fully grasped the meaning of the word *pandemonium* until now. She and Ethan had been in the wings, providing a full view of the audience, the stage and even backstage. When Charlie had crashed to the ground like a fallen angel, they had traded looks as though unsure they had seen the same thing. Then all hell had broken loose: that trapdoor swallowed her castmates with a thud, closing behind them, and Jasmine's madness seemed to transfer to the theater, permeating everyone's *being*. The audience, furious and in utter disbelief over the cancellation, streamed out of the auditorium in a roar. The rest of the cast on stage, recovered from the falling curtain, finally snapped to, erupting into chaotic chatter and speculation as they flowed backstage:

"Who knew Jasmine Beijao was crazy?"

"Maybe that wolf movie fucked her up, like De Niro in *Taxi Driver*?"

"She sure hates Charlie Savoy."

"She kind of has a point."

"She's just bitter because she knows she doesn't have the chops Charlie does."

"It's the love triangle, it's always about a love triangle."

And on and on.

Now Sierra and the group—Ethan, Alex, Harlow, Tripp, freshly changed—emerged from the greenroom.

"I actually don't mind ending early tonight," Alex said, stretching his arms as though just waking up.

"I'm basically sleepwalking," Ethan said.

Sierra was about to agree when Nicholas stormed straight down the middle of the hall, parting their group. A directing fellow, a stage manager and Matteo Denali all trailed him. He ignored the questions, looked at Matteo. "You okay?"

"I'll live," Matteo said, holding a fistful of paper towels to his bloodied nose. Then Nicholas raised his hand, barking at the hallway, "Everyone, go home. We're done here tonight." He whipped around the corner, no one daring to follow.

"You heard the man," Alex said, waving their group out.

"At least no one's talking about us anymore," Ethan said, holding the door for Sierra. "And by us, I mean all of us. Who went to New York. And maybe partied too hard."

She was glad he was still thinking about it too. But something else nagged at her. For instance, as a *friend*, she would normally tell him that tonight was the time to say something to Charlie. Charlie would never be a better audience for his confession about that letter than now, after being made a verbal punching bag by a gorgeous, heartless superstar. Sierra felt for Charlie and what she had endured coming back here, that was not an easy thing to do. But the other part of Sierra cared only about finding a way to repeat last night with Ethan and mean it.

She hadn't realized that this intense internal debate had slowed her pace, the rest of the group now several yards ahead, cutting across the dark and leafy Quad to the dorm. Ethan looked around as though he'd lost something.

"Hey, you really are sleepwalking," he called out, jogging back to her. "What's with you?" He grabbed her bag, slinging it over his shoulder with his. "Don't say 'nothing.'"

She stopped walking, looked in his heavy, questioning eyes. "I think you should tell Charlie," she said, though it pained her.

"The letter? Now?" he asked, stunned. "I was just gonna forget that whole thing, like Miles said?"

"I know but if it was me, then I would want to hear from someone like you, on a night like tonight. Like, immediately."

He exhaled, but she just nodded, pulled their bags from his shoulder.

"Good luck," she said, kissing him on the cheek and walking alone to their dorm. When she looked back, he still stood there for a moment, then, finally, set off into town.

53

I NEED THE LIGHT BULBS THAT
LOOK LIKE IDEAS!

As he stomped down that backstage hallway, dodging a sea of people looking for answers, Nick's first inclination was to hide in the broom closet, wait for everyone to go away and then leave the theater and Chamberlain itself and never be heard from again. He imagined the story of his disappearance might get covered somewhere, maybe the *Boston Globe*, since the incident might be mistaken at first for local crime.

Oscar-nominated director goes missing after nightmare show. But a quick investigation discovered him to be missed by, really, no one, and the search was instantly called off. "He's done us all a great service, disappearing like this," said a source, who worked with him, echoing a number of other sources. "His first movie was a brilliant fluke. Not the sign of greatness to come,

like everyone thought. It was beginner's luck, the equivalent of
a viral video. Good riddance."

But Nick passed the broom closet and knocked on the door
just beyond it. Not waiting for an answer, he threw open
the door, and found Jasmine yelling into her phone, makeup
smeared from sweat and tears. Her assistant fanned her with
a program.

"Consider yourself fired, effective immediately," he told
her. "You've got ten minutes to get your stuff or I'm sending security."

"I'm on with Taylor *and* my agent, *right now*," she barked
at him.

He smiled, felt himself actually growing a backbone as he
stood there, even sensed his posture straightening. "Fantastic," he said. "Tell them both to call me when you're done.
Ten minutes." He slammed the door shut and went straight
to the neighboring dressing room, knocking. Invited in, he
found only Chase and Marlena.

"If this is what you all are doing with Shakespeare these
days then I am *here* for it!" Marlena greeted him.

"Thanks," he sighed.

"Seriously though, it was really revelatory until, you know,
all hell broke loose," she said, earnest. Nick had always liked
Marlena. He had lost custody of their friendship when he and
Charlie split.

"I think she went home," Chase said.

———

Nick shot across the stage, hoping to avoid the minefield of
those hallways and to get outside faster, and ran right into
Mary from the box office.

"Oh! I've been looking for you!" she said. He grimaced.
"Everyone wants to know—"

"Mary. I have so many fires to extinguish that—" But his eyes drifted stage left, the corner of the wings: a sea of black where there should've been a tiny beacon. "Where's the ghost light?"

"The ghost light?" She looked side to side. "It's around here somewhere."

"It's supposed to be right there, in that corner, quietly keeping the evil spirits at bay." He charged over to the spot, moving carts and equipment. Finally he saw the small, lonely stick lamp with the broken bulb. "This is *never* supposed to go out."

"I thought that was just a superstition—"

"That's exactly what it is," he said, walking away. "We've gotta replace this."

She followed him to the closet in the greenroom but all he could find were tiny bulbs that didn't fit or the coiled ones. "We use those coily ones in the office," Mary said gently.

"Those just aren't right." There was *history* to this light, it had been there when he was an apprentice and certainly long before. "I want a bulb that looks like a fucking idea, you know what I'm talking about? Like a normal fucking idea-looking light bulb."

"I think we're just out of ideas, right now, idea-light-bulbs," she said, calm.

"I don't know how to make this fit into my life." He waved a coiled bulb at her.

"Well," she said slowly. "You could try it. And maybe it'll even be better. Sometimes change is good—lighting technology changes, people can change…"

"I see what you're doing." He pointed the bulb at her. "And I'm going to put this in here for now," he said, screwing in the energy-efficient bulb. "But I don't necessarily like it."

"It bears mentioning, I believe," she began, "that, tonight aside, there have been some genuinely exciting things happening here this season. That's not something I've been able to say in many years. And that's because of you being here. Being present."

He shrugged.

"Well, you and maybe some help," she amended with a wink on her way out.

54

I HATED YOUR LETTER

No one answered the front door when Ethan rang the bell at the house on Avon. The lights were out on the first floor, but when he walked around to the side, he noticed one light upstairs and saw Charlie inside, shoving clothes in a bag.

What Sierra had said had surprised him. The truth was that after last night, he wasn't really thinking about Charlie in quite the same way anymore. Instead, he couldn't stop thinking about *Sierra*. But he couldn't tell *her* that. And worse, it seemed that if he didn't talk to Charlie tonight, Sierra was going to be disappointed in *him*. He imagined Sierra might think he was the kind of guy who didn't have the guts to tell someone how he felt. But then, he kind of *was* that guy, wasn't he? Because he sure as hell didn't have the guts to tell *Sierra* how he felt about *her*.

All he knew for sure was that Charlie was in there and he had promised Sierra he would do this. So despite the twisted logic of it, he took a deep breath and climbed onto the dump-ster in the alley and up to the fire escape that led to her win-dow. Then he abruptly got a debilitating case of cold feet, changed his mind and moved to climb back down, when he heard: "*Ohmigod*, what the fuck."

He looked up to see Charlie staring right at him through the glass. Startled, Ethan stumbled and nearly fell right off the metal landing. She opened the window.

"Um, hi," he started, still crouched on the fire escape like a cat in a tree.

"I don't know what you're doing, but I cannot deal with you getting killed tonight, so get in here," she ordered. He hesi-tated then did as he was told, since it was easier than climb-ing down. "What is *with* everyone tonight?" She wore part of her costume, a full-length black bodysuit that made her look like a dancer. The entire contents of her closet lay on her bed as she stuffed them in her bag. "Everyone is fucking crazy."

"I just, I came to check on you, and I saw your light on and no one had answered the door and I wanted to make sure—"

"Look, Mercutio," she said, chilly. "You're really sweet, but I'm just not in the mood for, like, *anything* tonight."

"No, I know, that's why I just wanted to say, real quick, then I'll go... I just...wanted to tell you—" She sighed, and he blurted out the rest. "I wrote you a letter, at North End? Way back, in April? It was this class assignment—write a let-ter to someone whose art has mattered to you. Anyway, I wanted you to know that *Midnight Daydream* got me through high school. You got me through high school. You gave me hope that there was more out there for me, that maybe I was 'sleeping through the good parts.'" He made quotes around the film's tagline. "I needed to open my eyes, see something new. It's why I left home and applied to transfer east to do something that made no sense but made me feel something. I said it better in the letter." He needed to stop, felt disappointed to not be delivering this speech as effectively as he had envisioned. "I signed it 'Robert.'" A flicker in her eyes showed the blanks being filled. "My real name. But when I came *here*, I decided to make my middle name my stage name—the way you named yourself. I thought this place would be a new start. But I still don't really know what I'm doing. Clearly."

He was nearly panting now, he had said it all too fast, in too few breaths. She stared at him, eyes squinting as though processing it. "So, that's all," he said, highly embarrassed. "Now I can leave you to…whatever you're doing." He began to climb back out.

"Wait," she said softly. "I hated your letter."

Her tone sounded just the opposite. He froze, not sure he'd heard correctly. "Excuse me? You read it?"

"Your letter." She smiled, and in that same dreamy inflection, murmured, "I hated it."

"Okay," he said almost to himself. "That must be why Miles told me to forget about it. He told me to leave it for you. Then he told me not to say anything." He crept out onto the fire escape. "Very confusing, but now I get it."

"No!" She leaned out the window, grabbing his arm to stop him. "I mean, wait. So much is making sense now, with Miles…" He could see her putting the pieces together. "He was asking me about getting back into this, acting, taking a break from the art house. Even before the harbor. He was weirdly worried about me."

"The letter was supposed to be inspiring, make someone feel like their artistic contributions were important. Sorry if that didn't really come through—"

"No, I got that," she said slowly. "It reminded me of everything I wasn't anymore. How I sort of gave it up and stopped trying."

"Oh…" he said, "Yeah, not my intention."

"No, that letter was the best thing that could've happened to me, in a lot of ways, actually. It shook me up in a way I needed. I probably didn't need the accident part of that night so much, but the rest…" She didn't finish her thought. Instead she just said, in a deep, meaningful way, "Thank you." She sifted through her stack of books and there it was, the letter, nestled in among them. "See?" She held it up. "I've been known to reread it from time to time."

Ethan felt a wave of shock from those words. It meant everything to know that she still had it. He didn't know how to convey that, so he just smiled, nodded in respect. Before climbing back out, he said with care, "One last thing that's not in the letter." He looked at her clothes and duffel bag. "Wherever you're going now. Don't. Okay? Things are just getting good here. Don't leave before the last act."

55

MAYBE IT'S TOO LATE

When Marlena appeared in her doorway, Charlie, lying in her clothes-strewn bed, just threw her hands up. She had entirely forgotten that Marlena would be in the audience tonight.

"So, how's your night?" Marlena kidded.

"Yeah, it's great, whatdidya think of the show?" Charlie answered in the same loaded tone. She wanted to laugh and maybe cry, though she wasn't really a crier.

Marlena just stepped in and wrapped her arms around her. Nothing more to even be said.

"Don't tell me you believe a single word out of those over-injected lips," Marlena said. She looked around. "And what's going on over here?" She gestured to the bed. "This is where you say, 'It's not what it looks like.'"

"No, this is exactly what it looks like. I'm getting the hell outta here," Charlie said, on her feet to continue packing.

"Okay." She nodded. "Or, alternatively, you could *not* do that and instead you could listen to what this guy has to say."

Nick appeared outside her room now.

"No, thanks." Charlie resumed throwing clothing into her bag item by item, with greater force than necessary. Marlena tiptoed out, grabbing the door to swing it shut.

"Ohhh no," Charlie called after her. "You're staying, this won't take long."

Marlena looked like she was about to object but instead sat back on the bed.

"Listen—" Nick started, tentative.

"I'm sick of—"

"I have done almost every single thing wrong since you got here," Nick cut her off.

"That's a good start," Marlena said under her breath.

"I say *almost* because the things I got right were pretty much exclusively the things *you* told me to do." Charlie still didn't look at him, just continued throwing clothes in the bag, while Marlena took them right out, folding them. "I fired Jasmine—" At this, Charlie glanced over. "And I fired Taylor. Or, I mean, I told her we don't need her cash if it comes with strings." He paused for that to fully sink in.

A smile curled Charlie's lips but erased just as fast. "No." She shook her head, tossing clothes again. "You can't. There's no way—"

"I can find another Hermia—"

At this, Marlena cleared her throat in an exaggerated way, still folding. He and Charlie looked at her.

"I know that, technically, you can't afford me," Marlena said. "But I'd be willing to do it for scale…or, you know, maybe pro bono, because that's just how I am." She added in a stage whisper to Charlie, "And, you would not *believe* the dollars those cosmetics companies are throwing at me."

"Done," Nick said to her. "Thank you."

"But you still need Taylor's money," Charlie said to him, unemotional.

"Maybe I can't afford to say no to it…but I can't afford *to take it* either. It would cost me too much." He said it with a heaviness, kneeling on the floor near the bed now, trying to force her to look at him. She just continued folding, her mind turning it over. Her heart too. It was simple, really: tonight had wounded her. To have those words said by that woman felt like a perfect storm, all of Charlie's fears and failures, converging. "You are all tied up in this place for me, in the way I work here, in the way I work at all, and—"

"I don't want to do this right now," she said slowly, icy enough to stop him. If Nick said the right words to her right now, she feared she would cave again and she wasn't yet sure she should. She had opened her heart up to him this summer, not something she did easily, only to have it torn out of her chest. How many times can you let the same person hurt you? How many times can you take the same risk?

This is why she always needed to be the one to walk away—from a relationship, from a career—and not look back: to give the illusion of power and control no matter how quietly broken she remained inside.

"I don't…understand…" He paused, body slouching, as though knocked out by her words. "I thought we were in this together? I'm trying to tell you I need you here—"

"I'm trying to tell you, you should've thought about that. I'm trying to tell you I have seven days left and that's literally all I owe you. And I don't even want to give you that much." *I'm trying to tell you I've always loved you but I'm in pain*, she thought but would never say. Vulnerability was not something she condoned in herself. Ever. Like that day she walked off his film set. She had told him to delay, that the script wasn't ready, he told her she was fired if she didn't shoot that day. So she said that was fine and walked away and didn't look back. He let her go. It played out in front of a stunned cast and crew but the scene was eerily calm, final. Each assumed the other would apologize. They had too much pride, of course. It was so much easier to just blame the other for everything that went wrong that day, before that day and after that day. So they did.

"I know that," he said softly now, as destroyed as she had ever heard him.

"I'm trying to tell you maybe it's too late." She struck a tone that cut so deep that Marlena, silently folding all this time, looked up, reaching her hand out toward Charlie, then, as though instinctively, setting it down again.

Nick looked away a moment. "I know that," he repeated, sitting back on his heels. "I understand." It came out defeated. He ran his hands through his hair, as if trying to reset. She got up to avoid looking at him. Marlena shot her a quick questioning glance, brow furrowed in concern, but Charlie just grabbed the handful of books from atop her dresser and returned to the bed, placing them in her duffel bag.

"Wait," Nick said, as she nestled his copy of *A Midsummer Night's Dream* in the bag. "What about this—I know you still care about this place at least. I don't know if it will survive this summer, but I am *certain* it won't survive if you go now. Stay for the seven days, for the full twenty of *Midsummer*'s run? Don't do it for me, you're free to hate me and I'll leave you alone, whatever you want, honest." He held up his hand in oath. "But give this place—this place, that I know you love— one last chance." It was a statement, not a question, but one that trembled with hope and fear. She lay back on the bed, looking at the ceiling.

Charlie thought of how heavy it would weigh in her heart if the Chamberlain closed without her here, trying. The the-

ater world—here, London, New York—had always been there
for her, before film, then in between the films—because she
never much cared for the dull film scripts that came her way
after *The Tempest*, passing on them all in favor of theater for
years, until *Midnight Daydream*, which had potential but had
ultimately faltered. It was Shakespeare and Tennessee Williams
and Ibsen and Albee and Tony Kushner and Sam Shepard and
Chekhov who had caught her when she had fallen, after losing Nick and his film.

She never cared that her star, her status, had fallen so immediately when she walked off that film set, when she chose a film
few liked—*Midnight Daydream*—as her cinematic follow-up to
the film everyone adored—*The Tempest*. When she walked away
from everything after *Midnight Daydream*, to show the world
she didn't care and didn't need that career, rather than be hurt
by the sting of failure, she had overcorrected. She had under-
estimated how much she would miss the part of it she loved:
being a conduit for a story, giving a room full of strangers permission to gather together, put their lives on pause, get lost in
someone else's plight and feel something. Her spirit and body
and soul craved that and missed it. And she would always miss
sharing that with the rare, perfect collaborator.

Theater was the one thing that always wanted her, had always pursued her, appreciated her, taken her back, no questions asked. And this place had been a cherished part of it all:
here she had become something independent of her mother.
Nick's Black Box one-act that long-ago summer had been her
first role outside the Globe Theatre, the first role that sought
her out for *her*. Her first New York theater work came from
an agent in the audience at that performance, her first film
too. Her roots truly lay here.

"This is it, this show—" she said.

"And *The Tempest*? If we can afford to stage any of it?"

She exhaled to the ceiling, then nodded.

Still seated on the floor, he reached for her calf. "Thank you," he said solemnly before getting back on his feet.

He lingered at the door of her room. "You and me and our memories and this theater and our lives all just feel intertwined to me." It sounded like an apology. He left, not waiting for a response.

"What just happened," Charlie said after she heard the front door close. She felt spent. She turned to Marlena behind her and now noticed all of her clothes expertly folded and piled up, her duffel bag empty, even her books returned to the top of her dresser.

"You did the right thing. We have the whole run of the show to 'unpack'—metaphorically—everything." Marlena kissed her on the cheek. "Now, if you need anything else," she said, on her feet, glancing at her watch, "I'll be across the hall—" Charlie flashed a curious look. "I know, that's a whole *other* thing, but I'll save that for later. You've got a lot on your plate right now."

Marlena closed the door behind her, but Charlie crept over to open it again, in time to see Marlena disappearing behind Chase's door.

—

The idea struck Nick the moment Charlie had given in and agreed to stay, as though the instant thrill of that news—coming on the brink of nearly losing her *again*—had jumpstarted his mind. He jogged the whole way home, in an almost dreamlike state—so much so that he nearly got hit by a Ferrari speeding out of town.

As soon as he got back to the house—which he appreciated more knowing it might not be his much longer—he found what he was looking for in his suit jacket pocket—he had swiped a photo from the mantel the night of that painful dinner at Hathaway House. Something about this photo of Grayson and Sarah, arms around each other, was intimate in a way he couldn't explain. He had heard rumors before, but now felt like he finally had begun to understand.

He took a seat at the desk in the study and grabbed a leaf of his personal Chamberlain stationery and his nicest pen. She was the type to appreciate things like penmanship. He began to write.

> Grayson had told me at the end of that summer to make a place like this thrive, you need it not just in your heart but in your blood too, it has to flow through your veins, it takes your entire being. And it helps if you can find kindred spirits: those with the same bloodtype, if you will. It's not easy. He said it after the Black Box Showcase, my show with Charlie, and I've thought about those words a lot recently and now maybe understand them for the first time. Grayson also told me he was proud of me. That I worked harder than any directing fellow he had known. I'm not sure that praise would still apply, but I am hoping to be worthy of it again.

He wrote a little more, enclosed the photo and sealed it all in an envelope, then loaded it up with stamps, not knowing how many he would need to get it there, and went outside into the night to put it in the mailbox, not wanting to wait another minute.

Back inside, he tried to sleep, but couldn't. It hurt, for so many reasons, to remember Grayson, that year he got sick. Nick had been in a fog, mired in reshoots upon reshoots for *Super Id*, the Band-Aid put on a film when it really needed a DNR. He hadn't cared about it anymore, about anything, and it was then that he'd succumbed to Jasmine. He always suspected she made a play for him only because she thought a relationship—and an absurd drunken elopement—would get the film more press. But he wasn't thinking at all, he was dangerously overmedicated. He saw Charlie at Grayson's funeral, spoke only to her mother, but seeing her reminded him of how he used to feel about work, life, love, everything.

When he'd arrived at Charlie's premiere a month later, he had already told Jasmine he wanted to separate. Jasmine followed him there anyway.

By the time *Super Id* came out he was divorced, thank God, but as lost as ever.

56

ANY CHANCE YOU'VE GOT IT ON VIDEO?

It was strange how little Ethan wanted to talk about his conversation last night with Charlie. The text message he was reading aloud at the moment was the first he had mentioned of Charlie all day—which seemed like a tremendous amount of self-restraint considering how monumental it should've been to tell her about that letter.

"It's from Miles," he said now, scrolling on his phone, scanning it himself first.

Sierra sat beside Ethan in the auditorium with the rest of the *Midsummer* cast and crew and the entire apprentice class, waiting for Nicholas Blunt to inform them what was happening to the show in the wake of Jasmine Beijao's "breakdown," as they had taken to calling it. Sierra had heard that including everyone at the meeting was Nicholas's way of taking hold of the runaway train, all the rumors flying. Sierra had no idea what was going on. Life had been a blur pretty much since their trip to New York.

After the show last night, Sierra had returned to the dorm with the others, tried to watch something, one of their favorite movies, anything to pass the time until Ethan returned. She even invited Harlow to watch, though they never really hung out like that.

"Are there any movies about backstabbing roommates?" Harlow had asked.

She'd scanned the Netflix options on her laptop. "I don't know, like *Single White Female*?" and then she realized. "Ohhh. Everything okay?"

"I know about you with Chase at the Fourteenth Line during the *Romeo* closing night party." Harlow said it as though declaring a murderer, weapon and location in a game of Clue.

"Nothing happened," Sierra said, actually laughing. "He apologized for messing up my audition and he gave me, like, a peck, that was it." That was the truth. Sadly.

Harlow squinted her eyes, trying to determine whether it could really be the full story. "Well, fine. Just don't let it happen again," she threatened, pointing her finger so it nearly touched Sierra's nose. It was all Sierra could do to keep a straight face. Sierra was the least of Harlow's competition, from what she had heard: one of the costume apprentices had accidentally walked into the company dressing room and caught none other than *Marlena Andes* alone with Chase as he was getting changed.

Sierra had been halfway through *Midnight Daydream* by the time Ethan knocked on her door. His report of what had transpired between him and Charlie seemed so anticlimactic. This was probably the same way Harlow had felt about Sierra's own recounting of her interlude with Chase. At last she could relate to Harlow on some level.

"So check this out." Ethan read aloud now: "From Miles, 'Heard about Jasmine: WTF? She was always fucking insane, IMO, just got away with it because gorgeous. Is Charlie okay though? Not answering texts. BTW do you know if there's in-house video of last night, better than blurry audience phone video online that—'"

Sierra had stopped listening. "Maybe Charlie's not answering because she's been busy finding Jasmine's replacement." Sierra shook his arm. "Look…"

He glanced up from his phone as Marlena Andes walked down the aisle, taking a seat in the front row, followed by Matteo, Danica and Chase. No Jasmine.

But no Charlie either.

"She was packing," Ethan said, his voice and spirit low. "I told you."

A hush fell as Nicholas stepped onto the stage.

"Thanks, all, for this emergency meeting today," he addressed them, as serious as Sierra had ever witnessed him, yet somehow more powerful too. "I wanted to get you guys up to speed on some changes in the main stage show and in our schedule the next few weeks, since this pertains to everyone—" The doors opened with a creak, soft footfalls jogging up the aisle. "I'm sure you all have a lot of questions about last night—"

Sierra squeezed Ethan's arm, pointing as Charlie ran past them and took a seat beside Marlena, who whispered to her.

Nicholas nodded to Charlie. "First order of business," he went on. "Jasmine Beijao is no longer with our show." Gasps broke out. The idea of someone of that magnitude, who seemed so untouchable, getting fired felt shocking. But, also, it gave Sierra faith in humanity that even someone like that couldn't get away with the kind of cruelty she had pulled last night.

"Apprentices, let this be a teachable moment. We are artists and as artists we need to support each other. Jasmine Beijao's behavior was entirely unprofessional. And not in keeping with the spirit of the Chamberlain. That's all I'll say on the matter. Onward…"

⌣

Charlie was a full twenty-four hours behind on the onslaught of texts from Miles, who seemed shockingly well-informed on everything that had gone on here. She skimmed them while walking to the football field for the outdoor all-apprentice screening of last year's Black Box show—or as she dubbed it, The Mandatory Bonding Replacing Tonight's *A Midsummer Night's Dream* Performance. (The *Midsummer* run was postponed two days for Marlena to prepare to take over Jasmine's part. Tomorrow's matinee was rescheduled so the cast could rehearse together.)

Charlie planned to avoid Nick for the duration of her remaining weeks there but Miles's text intrigued her. She caught up with him walking ahead of the company en route to the field. "Got this from my staffer at North End," she launched in, no greeting. He looked up from his own phone, an expression of mild shock that she was even talking to him. "'Question about Jasmine's breakdown: any chance you've got it on video? Professional quality, in-house crew?'" she began to read. "'Friday night crowd already clamoring, could be a moneymaker, tell Nick…'" She trailed off a bit when she hit the speed bump that was "Friday night," having read it aloud without thinking, but in true actorly fashion, she committed and saw it through. "So I'm telling you."

He had that crease between his eyebrows he got when he was considering anything business related. "We do have video of that," he said. "I record everything and—"

"Do you think it's legally—?"

"And as you may recall," he cut her off, reading her mind. "You signed a number of documents when you started working for me, everyone does, and one was, indeed, a release to use their image in photos and videos to promote the theater, et cetera, et cetera. Jasmine signed this, as well."

"Well, then." She nodded, as though admitting he was smarter than she thought. "The couple of phone videos that have posted have actually gotten a ton of hits, maybe something like this could possibly be a good thing if—"

"Friday night crowd, huh?" He said it in a way that made clear he knew this was her theater's weekly showing of his bomb *Dawn of the Super Id*. He stole a glance from the corner of his eye as they crossed the street past the gym. The sports fields were located just beyond, and they could see the lights. The sky glowed midnight blue, night just falling. "You're the reason I despise Fridays now, did you know that?" he asked. "I have this, like, sick dread every Friday night." He clutched his stomach. "I'll never understand why you would screen that movie—the one that basically broke us up—every Friday night for the past five years. Like it's a joke that you refuse to let just die?"

"So, you did notice?" she said. She assumed he never knew, or she would've heard from him.

"What's that supposed to mean?"

"I mean, I don't know what you would call it exactly." She scratched her head, looked away, caught off guard. "But I guess, I was flirting?" she said flatly.

"I can't ever tell when you're serious," he said, impatient, like this couldn't be the answer he'd been waiting for all these years.

"I'm always serious," she said lightly, a line he had said before.

"I was supposed to get *flirting*...from that?" He looked entirely dumbfounded.

"It was like..." She searched for the proper analogy. "Sending flowers but more personal."

"Oh? Okay. Right," he laughed, looking straight ahead.

"The way I see it, how much cash have you made off that film since its initial run?"

"Well, it's not like I have any sales figures in front of me, but,

off the top of my head, I guess, I don't know, it's probably—"
He was stalling.

"We sell out every Friday night. And we have for five years.
I'm sure you're seeing some checks from that. It's not *nothing*.
But nothing is probably what you're getting otherwise. So,
therefore—flirting. And paying you for it."

"Thank you," he mumbled, after a pause, clearing his throat.
"Despite the humiliation and repeated sting of failure that
comes with it."

"You're welcome."

"I'd hate to see what it would look like if you really liked
me. You'd probably hit me with a car or something."

"Lucky for you, mine was totaled a few months ago."

He halted in his tracks just before heading onto the field,
stared at her a moment with his transparent eyes and, without
a word, kissed her forehead. Kindness and care transcending
any history or anger, messiness or complications.

—

Sierra knew this was coming, tried to brace for it, but she
couldn't calm her nerves. They had watched the three one-
acts and assorted monologues that comprised last year's Black
Box production and now Nicholas introduced the main event.

"Just a few short years ago," Nicholas started in, a rare
glimpse of his sense of humor, "yours truly had his Chamberlain debut as the writer-director of a show that I'm thrilled
to see getting an update this summer. I had some help in the
form of an accomplished, headstrong, intensely gifted star,
whom you may recognize…"

As Nicholas spoke, Sierra's mind raced, manically, and she
inadvertently consumed the entirety of her popcorn and what
was left of Ethan's.

"You okay?" Ethan whispered to her.

She looked at him, exhaled in an exaggerated blowfish

way and mouthed, *I'm. Nervous.* She was as nervous as a person could possibly be who wasn't actually performing but was merely watching a video of someone else's show.

They were seated side by side on the turf, and he nudged his shoulder into hers as if to say, *Hang in there.*

It was a tall enough order knowing she was filling Charlie's shoes, but now the entire apprentice class *and* Charlie *and* Nicholas would have this performance fresh in their minds when they watched Sierra stage the updated version in just a few weeks' time, with Tripp.

"Thank God it was just a one-woman show back then," Tripp whispered. "If I had to watch someone rock the part I was supposed to perform, I would go freaking crazy."

"Don't listen to him," Ethan said and put his hands over her ears.

As soon as Charlie arrived on-screen, the entire lawn cheered. Charlie, seated on a Chamberlain picnic blanket beside the rest of the company, shook her head and proceeded to throw popcorn at her image, jokingly.

Somehow, Charlie looked nearly the same on-screen, same glow, same ferocity; the passage of time had barely left a mark on her. If anything, she just seemed more powerful now, in greater control of her performance, emanating a greater wisdom.

Sierra soaked in Charlie, making mental notes of all the ways she, Sierra, needed to not impersonate but to *be* something else. Though she studied the show as an actor, Sierra, the human, found the most compelling part to be the very end: Charlie bowing, modestly, barely, before dragging a very reluctant Nicholas onto the stage for a moment he never would have taken on his own. That gesture said everything anyone needed to know about the two of them.

57

FOR YOUR CONSIDERATION: US

The crowd had cleared, equipment was packed, and the field lights shut off. The quiet of the empty sports pavilion and abandoned fields made Nick feel at peace, isolated, as though they were miles away from town. He had lingered talking to the company about the days ahead, and now as they wandered into town, he hustled to catch up to Charlie, at the back of the pack.

"Better or worse than you remember?" he asked her of their old show.

She slowed her pace as the trio of company actors continued on a block ahead. "Jury's still out," she said, not entirely frosty but still cautious. "Could've been worse."

"A rave." He smiled at her review. He didn't often see video of himself from past chapters of his life; he saw the films he made, had the memories of making them, but *seeing himself* was entirely different. He felt like that same guy now: completely unsure, working hard, trying to make it, with no idea what the world might have in store for him. On paper, he had done a lot since then: he had made films (good and bad); he had tried TV; he had written things. This place was now his. But after all that he didn't feel *different*. That realization struck him as too much to share right now, so he said instead, "We do give good curtain call." He had recalled that ending especially vividly. It sometimes played in his mind on the highlight reel of their summer, encapsulating the full sweep of their collaboration: her pulling him out of his comfort zone, into the light, and creating a moment that people could feel, react to, that they would remember.

"I mean, that was mostly me, but okay," she said, still guarded, but almost matching his light tone.

"I will say, it actually *worked better* that you had to pull me up there." He wanted to keep talking, overcome with the sense that she didn't completely hate him right now. "If I had just gotten up there myself it wouldn't have been as rich or raw, dramatically speaking."

"Whatever makes you feel better."

"You know what would make me feel better?" He took a chance because it had bothered him since their talk before the screening. "I was thinking about what you said earlier about *Super Id*—" He noticed her tense up, folding her arms as they walked now.

"'She can leap tall buildings in a single bound but her psyche is scarred by what it all means.'" She quoted the tagline with an eye roll.

"I never got to tell you that—obviously—you were right, that movie did need more time. To become something." He glanced at her, but she still didn't say anything. "And maybe a director who was more sure of himself would've shut down the production before you had to walk away." Now she looked at him. "Maybe it would never have been any good and I just needed the time and the guts to scrap it and start over. All I know is it didn't occur to me then that I might've had that power. It didn't really occur to me until now, when I feel like I have no power and everything to lose."

"I tried to tell you," she said softly. "It was the first time you didn't listen." She sounded hurt. "You just told me to show up on time on the shoot date." They had been on opposite coasts, him preparing for the shoot, her in New York reading scripts, doing a Tennessee Williams play. "And I *did*. I showed up in the suit. Most of it, anyway, but I just couldn't let you start filming that movie. So I walked up and told you it wasn't any good, *yet*, but that it could be in time, and instead of agreeing you said—"

"'Shouldn't you be wearing a cape.'" He sighed, ashamed of this and also recalling her greeting him this way in the courtroom. "I was out of line. And in over my head. And worn down from producers trying to convince me my star wasn't insurable and was a risk based on her reputation—"

"You never told me that." She stopped him.

"Because I didn't want that in your head."

"Oh," she said quietly, as though stunned that he had tried to protect her. "Maybe it didn't help that I had a track record of fighting to do stunts to the point of halting production for days and getting in screaming matches when my advice wasn't taken," she said, referring to her teen film and then her last one, he knew. "And the arrest from the bridge, I guess, didn't help." She almost smiled.

"Well, maybe I got into some...bad stuff, with Jasmine, and when I tried to get back on track, I didn't know how," he offered, to match her candor. "And maybe when I showed up at your premiere, she followed me there. I was trying to get you back... It just didn't go as expected." Charlie had been so incensed at the sight of them, she had thrown that glass and had to be physically led away by a production assistant. "And maybe it was easier to blame each other for our failures all this time."

"Imagine the drama we could have saved ourselves if we just, I don't know, talked at some point in the past decade," she tossed out. "At least we're not boring."

"It might even be said we're entertaining to watch, for better or worse." As he said it, his wheels began spinning. Had he hit on an idea that might actually make a difference to this place? Was it possible? He wasn't sure whether he should broach it, the evening had been unusually encouraging. He watched the glimmering night sky as they crossed over to the strip of Victorian homes along his block, so many people gathered on their porches, sipping drinks in the warm air. "I know you don't watch your work unless forced to at a premiere or something—" he started.

"True—"

"And I don't really belong on any kind of screen," he said, deeply hoping to be contradicted.

"True," she said. And then added, "You're not bad," with just the right inflection.

"And despite the fact that we both despise that sort of thing on principle—" He couldn't believe he was even considering it or that she was still listening.

"True—"

"There are plenty of other people who might actually want to…watch us and it might—"

"It might be good for this place," she sighed, finishing his thought.

"Despite it feeling—"

"Like a form of prostitution—"

"Okay, sure," he said. "Or I was going to say 'despite it feeling empty,' but you know, either way." He smiled, shuffling his feet. "Desperate times, right? Maybe we should sell tickets to our own drama."

"Let people watch us fight and make up and fight again and try to figure our lives out," she said slowly.

"But only what we want them to see," he said.

"Scripted reality…"

"As little as we can possibly give—"

"While still generating enough buzz—"

"To get some attention here."

"Fascinating," she said.

They turned onto his street, too soon despite how slowly they had been walking. Cicadas chirped, as though in approval. They were, appropriately, the ultimate comeback story of the insect world.

"For your consideration—us," he wrapped his pitch.

She smiled at this. "On a related note, watching tonight, it reminded me that I always thought I'd have my shit together by this age, know what I mean?"

"Um, yes," he said, as they reached his place, which was on the way to hers from the field. "So… I would invite you in…" He paused.

"You *would*?" she asked, intrigued. "What's the qualifier?"

"I…actually don't have one," he admitted because at this point, he had no game left. "I hadn't planned to finish that sentence at all. I figured I wouldn't need to, that you would cut me off—which you did—and then supply the reason for me." He walked up the steps, unlocked the door.

"This is the problem, you're so used to me doing your work for you," she said, walking in ahead of him as soon as he opened the door. "Solving all your problems."

He was so surprised, hopeful, cautious, that he instantly vowed to himself to keep this professional, to sort out a plan for the theater with her, pushing aside thoughts of *them*.

58

WE ARE CROWNING A NEW KING

Marlena had been the lightning bolt they needed, as Charlie knew she would, generating so much excitement—fans of hers coming in from New York and even her castmates surprising her from LA—that any refunded seats for *Midsummer* had sold out immediately. (The only ticket holders demanding money back after "Jasmine's Bei-breakdown," as it had now officially been dubbed by the media, had been from diehard Jasmine fans—self-proclaimed "Bei-watchers"—and/or friends of Taylor.)

Nick had been consumed with a new problem: the growing waiting list for *Midsummer* and even *The Tempest*. "When you come up with a way for me to sell more tickets while lowering overhead costs, let me know," he told Charlie, daily.

Nick was singularly focused on the theater to the point Charlie wasn't quite certain where they were, in terms of their relationship. They had precious little real time together—with the exception of the night he'd shown up at the house on Avon after the evening's *Midsummer* performance just minutes to midnight and announced, "Just under the wire, today's your sixtieth day—still staying?" And she had said yes, of course, and had given him a kiss on the cheek. Smiling, relieved, he had then left immediately, as though not wanting to rock the boat, not even trying to be invited in.

Charlie let him have his space, remembering how all en-compassing work could become to him when he let himself care enough to be immersed. Through the years he had fallen out of touch when he was trying to make himself into some-thing, no distractions, all or nothing. She understood this about him, the artist side of him. And loved it, though she secretly hoped she wasn't far from his mind.

Charlie kept busy, as well. Sierra had asked Charlie to watch her audition monologue for *The Tempest* and Charlie was proud to tell Sierra she needed no instruction from her. The appren-tice had earned a small part and would be Charlie's understudy. And Mercutio, too, would be in the production. Charlie con-tinued to reread that letter, and had told him days after their talk, as a thank-you, *You're right, I did need to stay for the last act.*

The Tempest cast had gathered for the first table read and Nick should've been admiring how far they had come this season. How this group had learned to work together, how even Chase seemed to know what he was doing now. His apprentices, too, Sierra and Ethan among them. And Marlena had been an in-vigorating force. (If only there were more shows, more seats, more time.) He just wished all of that was *enough*. Instead of listening to them, admiring them, Nick was plagued by so many still-unanswered questions, worry drowning out the lines being read. He could only see the ticking clock, march-ing on to the end of August. Many of the investors who had been circling now seemed content to wait this season out and "strongly consider the Chamberlain" during their next fiscal year, as he had been told too often. He was running out of time and ideas.

The doors crashed open and shook him out of his thoughts. All heads turned in the direction of the commotion.

For a beat, the entire table remained still, too stunned to speak, trying to process this sight as Sarah Rose Kingsbury strode up the aisle. A messenger bag on her shoulder, looking ready to work.

"Sarah." Nick rose to his feet, finally, greeting her in shock. Charlie bolted from her seat. *"Mom?"*

"Greetings, all." Sarah waved, as a queen might.

Charlie leaped off the stage and threw her arms around her mother. "What are you doing here?" she asked. She looked to Nick, but he had no explanation. He could only hop down from the stage and dart up the aisle in a delayed reaction.

"Hello, up there, so sorry I'm late, hope you'll pull up an extra seat at the table." Sarah projected to be heard by the cast onstage, many of them now standing too.

"I had no idea," Nick said when he got close enough. Sarah surprised him, again, by embracing him with true warmth.

"Of course you didn't," she said to him. "And neither did you, darling," she said to Charlie, her hand on her daughter's cheek. "Because what good is it if I can't make an entrance?" She smiled. "Now, where do you want me, Director?"

"Right this way."

As he and Charlie escorted Sarah to the stairs, she informed the two of them, "You know, I received the kindest letter and I couldn't stay away any longer." She looked at Nick. "I just had to be here."

"Wait," Charlie said to Nick. "When? What did it say?"

"That's between us," Sarah said.

The rest of the cast stood to receive Sarah as they might a visiting dignitary. Since Nick hadn't known she would show up, he had cast *The Tempest* without Sarah, but the idea struck him at once. He looked at Matteo, who nodded in understanding. He had dual roles, anyway.

"So, I think we're going to be crowning a new king for our production," Nick said to Sarah as he pulled out his own seat for her. She set her bag gently on the floor beside her. "From the top, now that we're all here," he directed.

Nick stood behind them all, a sublime peace: his cast was complete, and this show could now be everything he needed it to be. Maybe it still wouldn't be enough, in the long run, who could say now, but this meant something to *him*.

Charlie caught his eye with a look of appreciation. He nodded back and then, not to get sentimental, brushed off his shoulder, as though it had been no big deal.

—

"I need to know what you said," Charlie whispered to Nick as they carried her mom's suitcases upstairs to her room at Hathaway House. She would be sharing the posh accommodations with Marlena, whom Sarah adored. Marlena, who could afford the place on her own but was thrilled to have company, had moved in within hours of Jasmine leaving town.

"I can be very persuasive, you may have forgotten," he said.

"Maybe, maybe not." Charlie had barely so much as texted her mom since their failed trip to London and yet Nick had somehow managed to get her back to the States for the first time in six years, to perform for free at the theater she had accused him of running into the ground.

"Just ask your mom," he said, setting two suitcases down in the second grandest bedroom there. Charlie tossed her mom's satchel and messenger bag on the bed, just as Sarah appeared in the doorway.

"This place really is just as I remember it," she said.

"You've had a long day," Nick said to her, hand on her arm. "So I'll leave you ladies to it. Until tonight's show." He ducked out the door, but Sarah rose to her feet.

"Oh, Nicholas, you left something though," she called out.

He reappeared patting his pockets, checking for his phone. But she walked toward him, holding out the weathered messenger bag, as though bestowing a prize.

"But this isn't—" he started.

"It's yours now," she said. "It was his—Grayson's. I gave it to him." She looked at Charlie, whose mind worked to connect so many dots. "And I took it back when he passed. As you'll notice, I even had it engraved for him inside. It should be yours."

Nick took it in his hands with great care, smoothing its cognac leather. "Are you sure?" He looked to Charlie for help, but she just shook her head, equally taken aback.

Sarah clasped her empty hands in front of her. "I am too close to it. It's why I was hesitant to come back at first too. I needed distance...from him."

"I'll take good care of it," Nick said, holding it to his chest. "And I'm trying to do the same with this place. From now on. As well."

Sarah closed her eyes a moment. "I know you are. And I owe it to you to tell you." Concern swept her face, and she looked at the floor. "The Chamberlain was failing for him too, at the end." She said it like the words were too painful to get out. "He just poured his own money into it until he passed."

"None of that is visible in the books—" Nick said, clearly in shock.

"Of course not, he covered it up. He felt ashamed that he couldn't figure out how to monetize what he loved anymore," Sarah went on. "The truth is, the odds were stacked against you in a way you didn't realize. I didn't want to have to tell you that because it meant admitting that that man—a man I loved—" she looked at Charlie, to see if she understood "—was part myth too. But we all are in some way, aren't we? We tell ourselves what we need to just to get through the days. You know why I'm really here now?" Nick waited a moment and shook his head. "Because through all of this, you never asked me for money. You asked me only for time and craft—"

"Honestly, money from you wouldn't solve the real heart of the problem," he said, choosing his words carefully. "We need to expand our reach, speak to new audiences and new donors in order to sustain this place. We need to reach beyond people who just loved Grayson if we're going to really thrive and be viable here. We need to evolve."

Sarah closed her eyes and nodded. "That is exactly what I hoped you would say. You're worthy of this place, I hope you know." She touched the bag once more. "Now, go on and take this before I change my mind."

59

I SAID TOO MUCH

The cast began rehearsing *The Tempest*, and when Charlie and Nick weren't at work on *that* show—which involved constant hushed meetings with Mason to devise effects so special few would be permitted to even *know* about them—then they were preparing another show entirely.

Charlie couldn't believe she and Nick were actually doing this: they would shoot a few behind-the-scenes videos to send to media and post online. They had tapped Fiona to help them, pairing her with Simon, who would be pitching in long-distance from London to edit the project. They could only trust a few people. What they had planned for opening night was so elaborate that even Charlie was nervous.

The final show wasn't the only thing on her mind.

"Brace yourself," Charlie said to Marlena as they walked back to Hathaway House, bags slung over their shoulders, stage makeup still on, fresh off yet another full-house standing ovation for the night's *Midsummer* performance. They had just a week left of the run. "I'm about to get freakishly emotional." She glanced at her friend from the corner of her eye.

"Are we talking tears here?" Marlena said lightly. Charlie gave her a look that said, *Absolutely not.* "Kidding. I'm the crier here. We all know that. But, okay, ready for it."

"You know how Nick's been doing so much and we only see him at rehearsals and he has a lot on his mind—" she said, tense. It was nearly midnight, fireflies lighting the way as they passed the museum.

"Yeah, but *The Tempest* opens in one week, so that's kind of intense—"

"I know, I get that, I'm great at *getting that*, but last time he did this—"

"Dawn of the Super Id."

"—when he resurfaced, he had this plan devised that I couldn't go along with—to do this terrible movie without reworking it, without taking the time, without the collaboration. And I had to walk away."

"You guys literally weren't on the same page of the same script."

"Exactly," she said, as Marlena unlocked the door of Hathaway House, letting them in. Marlena went straight for the bottle of rosé from the night before. "He had all the wrong ideas. And then we were over and the movie happened and Jasmine happened and we had this cold war. And our careers fell apart in the process. Because you're only as good as your last project, et cetera, violins, cautionary tale, the end."

"Wow, that's a hell of a montage when you lay it all out like that," she said, pouring their glasses. "I would say you've just been taking an intermission."

Charlie sighed as though not buying it.

"And I would also say," Marlena went on. "Sure, so you don't know what happens after *The Tempest*, at all. You don't know where he goes, you don't know what you're going to do. Status quo or something gutsy." She took a gulp of her wine. "Here's the only thing that matters—do *you* know what you want? Just for you. What Charlie wants. Not about him. About you, about your life, your career, things you haven't bothered considering for a while. And I love your movie theater, you know, I love everything you do, but you know what I'm talking about."

Charlie took a deep breath as though about to dive from a cliff, studied her glass then looked at Marlena. She nodded. She did know. For the first time in years.

"Then *that's* what you do. Scary as it is. And after this is over, then you'll see if his script looks like yours." She shrugged, took a sip of wine. "Can I rock a pep talk or what?"

"Not bad. So Dr. Stevens does make house calls?" she joked of Marlena's TV character.

"Listen, this is a totally radical concept called friendship, not sure you're familiar with how it works. You were there for me, you know? Remember *my* intermission? And *my* montage becoming me?" She topped off Charlie's wine. "It was you holding my hand, talking and listening and researching and deliberating and scheduling and comforting and convalescing and encouraging and then finally, thank God, celebrating. So I'm here. For whatever's coming at you." She said it all easily, glossed over, in her way.

"That's good because I have no idea what's coming in the next fucking act." And she was nervous, for the first time in years, but it meant that she cared.

"Cheers to that." Marlena clinked her glass against Charlie's.

—

Two days before opening, Charlie had a very different role to play. She sat down on a wooden stool before a camera set up in one of the rehearsal studios.

"So Nick did this? Already?" she asked Fiona.

"He did, indeed, just yesterday," Fiona said, adjusting the camera on its tripod.

Charlie pulled her hair up in a topknot. She and Nick had discussed doing a few "very short confessionals" talking about each other, but she realized now that they had neglected to go over what each of them would *say*. It was Charlie's inclination to skim the surface, play it safe—exactly the *opposite* of how she behaved on stage. This just wasn't her kind of performance. Nick's either. She inhabited *other people's* stories. She didn't share her own. But to preserve this place, she would make the sacrifice.

"Ready when you are," Fiona said. "I'll get that—" she pointed to Charlie's lark tattoo "—at the end."

"So he *did* talk about that..." Charlie said to herself. "Any chance I could maybe—?"

"I know what you're asking," Fiona said, still setting up her shot. "We'll make a deal." She spoke directly to Charlie now. "After we shoot this, I'll let you see his clip. Then you can even reshoot if you want."

Charlie exhaled, tentative. "Okay, fine."

"Rolling." Fiona signaled. "Total softball question. Why do you think you two work well together?"

"I guess that sort of presupposes that we *do*," Charlie laughed, looking away a moment; this was going to be harder than she'd thought. She drummed her fingers against her lips. "He can do things I can't, which is always exotic and mysterious. He's all structure, foundation. Where I jump first and just explode at everything." She considered their years. There was so much she could say, but not here, not like this. "He hears me and listens too—and those aren't the same. Many directors do neither." She stared off, smiling softly. "If I had words for it, then it wouldn't be very special, would it? I can't define it. But it's always been there. And it's unlike anything I've found anywhere else." She paused a moment, looked not at the camera, but at Fiona. "What?"

The girl seemed disappointed in some way. "I think you're holding back," Fiona said, boldly. "There's got to be an example you can give or something. All your history together…"

Rather than bristling at this, Charlie actually felt proud: Fiona sounded like a director, a good one, one who wasn't afraid to challenge Charlie. And also, if Charlie could admit it, she knew Fiona was right. She looked at the ceiling now, big surrendering exhalation, and back at the camera. For once Charlie truly thought about what she was going to say before she said it. Turned it over in her mind, smoothing it like a river rock, deciding it was something a person deserved to know, that Nick deserved to know. And this might be as good a place as any to share it.

"Well, there is one thing," Charlie started slowly, her tone heavier now. "I heard Nick's voice, that night in the harbor… that night, you know, the night of the car accident." She looked away. "I know, he wasn't there or anything, but I heard him anyway and it sort of…woke me up. That night. Got me back up to the surface. You know what I mean?" She worried she wasn't making sense but it was the best she could do. She hadn't realized how hard it would be to hear those words out loud, to admit that he had remained part of her all that time, even while they blamed each other for downward-spiraling careers, even when they weren't speaking.

Fiona looked directly at her, asked in a soothing voice, "Does he know that?"

"Not yet," Charlie sighed. "But he will when he sees this."

"Is that okay?" Fiona asked, making sure.

"I guess it's gonna have to be."

—

True to her word, Fiona sent Charlie the clip of Nick, or a link to access it. She watched it that night on her phone, up on her balcony overlooking the town.

"What's special about Charlie…?" Nick had repeated Fiona's question on the video, grimacing. "I can't believe we agreed to this. Okay. I hope this is gonna be okay with her." He looked worried, which made Charlie smile because she still couldn't believe she had revealed what she had. "She brings the life to everything, in case you hadn't noticed. And without fire, you have nothing. It's not something as readily available in the world as you might think. Plenty of people think they have it—and are wrong. If you have it you probably don't even know. It's definitely not something that I have." He laughed at himself. "I mean, obviously, these—" he slapped his neck as though killing a mosquito there "—these were her idea, a long time ago. And it reminds me every day of what I could be…" He trailed off, changed course. "I'll just say this, there is no one like her. If you've been near that and you somehow lose it, you do everything you can to get it back and then you don't let go." He folded his arms across his chest, gazing at his feet. "She's the voice in my head. Even in those years when she wasn't really speaking to me, she was still the voice in my head." He ran his hand through his hair, looked up and stared right into the camera. "I feel like I said too much. I'm not good at this."

Charlie had been so taken with his video—comforted by his words, set at ease by the raw candor that seemed to match her own—that she hadn't realized the next clip loaded automatically: it was Sierra.

"This is going to sound crazy," Sierra said into a mirror, wiping off her stage makeup after what must have been the Black Box dress rehearsal. "I never thought I would have people like Marlena Andes and Chase Embers and Charlie Savoy and Nicholas Blunt clear their schedule to come to some show that I happen to be in." She whispered, shaking her head, "I'm terrified of messing everything up. Which I *did* at the start of the summer and I do *not* want to do that again. But if I'm being honest, like I'm supposed to be, I guess…" She looked to the side of the camera, as though for prompting from Fiona. "Then, weirdly, seeing Ethan out there opening night is going to be even more terrifying. I want him to think I've done something this summer, because I remember how I felt watching him the first time as Mercutio, you know? And I want him to feel that too. A version of that, because that feeling is, like, life-changing. Don't tell him," she said and then laughed at herself. "Well, I guess he'll know at some point. Obviously. Unless this gets edited out." Her eyes lit up, as though an idea struck. "Wait, what did *he* say?"

Ethan's clip was there too, and now Charlie had to watch. Fiona had recorded it during his shift at the pub. She asked him about the future.

"Back to school in a couple weeks and then, I don't know, more of this," he said. "I mean, the drama part, not the waiter part. Although, that too, actually."

Fiona's voice asked about Sierra. "I don't know what she's thinking but…between you and me and whoever watches this, I guess I'd say…well, one of my first nights as Mercutio, she made me sign a photo, which was so kind but I always got a solid *friend vibe* from her, so, you know, anyway, I signed this thing and it was after this night onstage and I was just feeling, *everything*, and I started to sign it 'love,' without thinking but then caught myself, and sort of fixed it, but anyway, this summer has been…*everything*. We go to school just miles from each other. And I'm hoping maybe she needs someone to go to Cape Cod with at the end of the summer…" He trailed off, wistful.

That was the end of the footage. It had gotten Charlie thinking about opening night for *The Tempest*. Maybe there was time to make one more change.

60

YOU STOLE MY LINE

"You can't really be asleep." Sierra heard Ethan's voice and popped her head up from the bar, where he had just set her iced tea.

She yawned, laughing, "Actually, I can." She glanced at her watch. The madness had set in, everyone afflicted now. One night until the Black Box show *and The Tempest* opening. Either one would be huge enough, but they were happening on the same night, in rapid succession. So much needed to be done before then, it could barely fit in the remaining hours. Sierra felt like a time-lapse video of a skyscraper being built. When she wasn't onstage performing in *Midsummer*, rehearsing *The Tempest*, fine-tuning the Black Box show or in the costume shop, she was either asleep or she was awake working herself into a frenzy over the agents and directors expected to descend upon the theater on that one all-powerful night.

Scoping out new talent and possibly extending invitations for meetings, auditions or even representation.

"You might actually be the luckiest person around tomorrow night," Ethan said. "Between the Black Box and *The Tempest*, all in one night, that's a lot of stage time."

"Only if I actually do okay." Sierra had gone from Least Likely to Succeed to as close to ubiquitous as she would ever be. "Otherwise it'll be like, 'This girl again? Make it stop.'"

"Good attitude," he said. Then paused. "And—same. Not to freak us out, but this could be life-changing—"

"Tomorrow night is kind of the point of the whole summer," she said, exhaling. "I feel like I already need a paper bag to breathe into."

"You know what though, it's not…the whole point," he corrected. "Even if we crash and burn—"

"This is not the encouragement I was looking for—"

"No matter what happens, there are people like Nicholas and Charlie who know what we can do, right? That's something. And being nervous, that just means you're alive, right? Unless you're—"

"Harlow," she said. Her roommate had been in a hyperfocused zone the past week and had barely spoken to her, but seemed totally calm to an otherworldly degree, not the least bit bothered by this date circled in neon on their calendar.

"I was going to say Alex."

—

The night before *The Tempest* opening, their dress rehearsal ended early, so the professional company had dinner together at the pub, jovial in the way of a family gathering at the end of that kind of feel-good film you watched on repeat. Afterward, Charlie, Sarah and Marlena deposited Chase, Danica and Matteo at the house on Avon with shared wishes of good rest and sweet dreams.

"Especially you," Chase had said, knowingly, to Charlie. And then to Marlena, lightly, with a wink, he added, "And you too."

After, at Hathaway House, where her mom and Marlena were staying, Charlie said, "I still need to know how this all happened with Chase."

"I'm a woman of mystery," Marlena said with a laugh as she lay on the bed in her room.

Sarah, at its foot, raised her glass of pinot noir as though toasting. "And don't act like you don't know about that kind of thing yourself, Charlie."

"Me?" Charlie asked, coy, sifting through Marlena's closet.

"I think you and Marlena have a lot in common," Sarah said, which Charlie ignored. "Not to bring up London, but there was much time unaccounted for, take it from a mother who waited up for quite a while—"

"You first," Charlie said to Marlena.

Her friend sat up, leaning on her elbows. "Fine. So, you know how I always thought during our shoot those years ago that Chase didn't like me *at all*?"

"Yeah, he was pretty cold." This had been the subject of daily discussion back then.

"Thanks," Marlena laughed. "But, no, you're totally right. Well, turns out he liked me *too much*. And he was *really* confused back then. And I was a different me, or you know, figuring out how to become the true me."

"We were all so young too, eighteen, nineteen." Charlie still couldn't believe it was that long ago.

"I know, *please*, I feel so damn *old* all the time." Marlena went on, "Anyway, it's been a lot for him, know what I mean? So it was just recently that he started…figuring things out…" Charlie could tell Marlena didn't want to share too much, since it wasn't her journey. "Anyway, totally worth the wait is all I can say."

"Cheers to you both, finding each other again," Sarah said.

"Thank you," Marlena said, her hand on Sarah's arm. "I feel like we should be brushing each other's hair, it is *so nice* having you here. And I still feel bad you let me have this room, Dame Sarah. I try to make her switch every day," she explained to Charlie.

"No, truly, the accommodations down the hall are much better suited to me, and full of…greater memories," Sarah said, looking at her manicure—always the lightest pink—demurely.

Marlena picked up on the subtext. "Grayson?" she asked gently.

"Mom! I am *not* hearing this." Charlie stared at them in the mirror, where she had been sorting through Marlena's vast array of beauty products, spraying perfumes on herself, testing lipsticks. "Don't make me leave."

"You're no fun, darling," she said, then leaned into Marlena. "So, we would steal away here from time to time. We had a very loose arrangement, dictated by the fact that his wife was often around. Which could be somewhat problematic."

"Did she know?" Marlena gasped.

"I always suspected she had her own…supporting players, if you will."

"I can't believe I missed all of that." Charlie looked at them now, a soft pink lipstick on, entirely unlike her usual crimson.

"That's lovely on you," Sarah said as Charlie cringed, wiping it off. "Help her, please," she said to Marlena.

"I've tried." Marlena shook her head.

"She doesn't need help," Charlie said of herself. "And she doesn't need to know anything else about your…*liaisons*."

"Well, you might've known back then if you weren't so busy swimming and running off to get tattoos and enrapturing a young director and antagonizing me. All your favorite hobbies."

"Memories," Charlie sighed.

"I like it here," Marlena said. "Everyone's hot. Everyone's sleeping with everyone. I'm so glad you convinced me to do theater. I had no idea."

—

Before midnight, Charlie walked back to the house on Avon. Everyone was still awake.

She poked her head into Matteo's open door. "Did you know about my mom and Grayson?" she asked, grabbing popcorn from the bowl on his bed. He had FaceTime up on his laptop.

"Well…" He thought about it. "Yeah, I always kind of suspected."

"Really?"

"Really, you didn't?"

"You never think your mom is capable of that kind of thing, you know, it seems too sordid and…*interesting*," she said with a shrug. And then, because she spotted Sebastian's name at the top of the list of calls: "Speaking of…"

"He's coming to *The Tempest*," Matteo said. "Talked him into it. He's gonna come to one of the last shows and then we're going to Maine. It's so gorgeous there. We need some time together. Hit the reset button."

She squeezed his shoulder, nodded. She did understand, but he seemed to read her hesitation.

"I know, I mean, supposing the dates at the end of the season actually *do* happen." He smiled. By now they all knew what was riding on this.

Once in her room, Charlie climbed straight up to the balcony, watched the street until the storefront lights went out one by one. She texted Nick, who had spent hours running through the effects with Mason.

Tomorrow might be an epic disaster, so get some rest. Kidding. You've done everything, know that. These are such stuff as dreams are made on...

The ellipses flashed immediately: You stole my line. That is so like you. And WE have done everything. Thank you, Charlie (this medium is completely inadequate for what I want to say, so more after our three perfect acts)...

The video—with their confessionals—was due to post the next morning. She wanted to ask if he had seen it yet, but she lost the nerve.

—

After his closing shift, Ethan and Sierra walked back from the pub, stopping at their favorite spot on the Quad under a starry sky. He knew they still had three weeks left—the few apprentices in *The Tempest* who were still college students, like him, had to get clearance from their schools to stay on past Labor Day—but he felt their days and minutes and seconds slipping away. Sierra seemed especially nervous, even wanting to run some of her understudy lines for Prospero's part ("Whatever makes you happy," he said, though it seemed unnecessary).

When he walked her back to her room, she opened the door to Harlow's side, entirely empty. No clothes, no sheets on the bed, no posters, no nothing.

"Yeah, she left," Alex said, unimpressed, when they found him with his entourage playing video games in their room.

"What, why?" Sierra couldn't hide her shock.

"She said she had to get back early for an audition," he said, clearly skeptical. "Personally, I think she just felt things had gotten, like, static for her. She kind of likes to be the epicenter of the universe, in case you hadn't noticed."

"I guess none of us would be here if we weren't a little dramatic to begin with," Sierra said.

"Exactly," Alex said, eyes on *Fortnite*. "So don't get *too* crazy tonight, kids, big show tomorrow. Even *I'm* staying in."

"Right," Ethan said, kind of annoyed that no one would let New York go. "No ayahuasca 2.0 for sure."

"That's hilarious," Alex said dryly. "I'm gonna whip up some now if you want."

"Good one," Ethan said.

"No, really, it's an acquired taste but soothing, you know?" Alex said, hand to his throat.

"Maybe that's not the best idea," Sierra said, sensible.

"Dude, you know it's just, like, a bunch of different herbal teas and some sage and licorice root and ginger and shit? It's good for the throat," he said, confused, taking in their blank faces. "Why are you guys looking like…?" And then he realized. "Ohhh." He started laughing. "No, guys, I thought you already knew. It's what Stone and a bunch of them like to do at parties with a lot of new people," he explained. "They convince them they're drinking something 'dangerous and crazy.'" He made quotes. "Then they watch the placebo effect take over. It's like an acting workshop for them. But wow, okay—"

"We totally knew that—" Sierra started.

"We just didn't know if you knew…that we knew that," Ethan said.

"You're welcome to stay and have some more of our totally natural, totally noneuphoric, nonhallucinogenic boring tea but—"

"We're good," Sierra said, walking away.

"Thanks, anyway." Ethan followed.

They walked in near silence back down the hall to her room. They had planned to watch a movie, and Ethan wondered if that was too weird now. He wished he knew what Sierra was thinking, but he couldn't bear to ask.

In her room, she grabbed her laptop and let him choose.

(Not that he cared what they watched.) She cued it up, setting it on her desk as always, and they took their usual places side by side, shoulder to shoulder on her bed.

She didn't seem to be watching the screen at all. And he wasn't either, because he had been watching *her* to see if *she* was watching the screen. They spent the entire movie like this. Then, at the end, gave each other hugs good-night. It was excruciating.

61

I FORGOT WHAT A GOOD SHOW
YOU MADE

Sierra still had time to pull herself together before curtain.
Their show was third in the lineup, which, she had been told,
was traditionally the positioning reserved for the best of the
Black Box offerings. All of the female apprentices shared one
dressing room and the guys another, but she had sought out
the restroom, needing time away from the chatter and mad
energy to focus. She looked at her reflection in the mirror
and, once she confirmed she was alone, talked herself down.
"Frankly, it would be super weird if you *weren't* freaking out,"
she said to herself. "Own that. Use it. And just don't pass out
or anything."

But she had peeked out from behind that shabby curtain
before the show began, in time to see *all* the reserved rows in
front filled—saved for the scouts. And, if that wasn't enough,

another row for the actors in the company. Charlie Savoy and Nicholas Blunt took seats dead center. It was almost enough to forget she would have a cheering section too: her parents and brother.

When Sierra returned to the dressing room, she found a single sunflower waiting at her mirror, with a note scribbled on Chamberlain paper: "Break a leg! Love, Ethan."

A knock shook the door, their stage manager's voice ringing out. "Five minutes!"

—

The Black Box auditorium pulsed with the collective energy of all those nerves, all that joy, all that fear, every apprentice from each program (set design, costumes, business, drama) gathered. They had ownership over tonight. Charlie and Nick and their fellow actors fanned out in the audience, only guests.

Fiona had invited them to come to rehearsals anytime, asked them again at dress rehearsals, but Nick and Charlie had dropped in only once, wanting to give them freedom. *You don't have to please us, do what you think is right*, Charlie had overheard Nick telling Fiona once. And Charlie had said to him afterward, *That was actually very cool of you.* To which he had responded, *Occasionally I know what I'm doing with this whole mentoring thing.* But it was more than occasionally. He had a much more open heart than she ever gave him credit for.

"He is selling these babies, look at him." Marlena leaned forward, pointing to the huddle in front of the stage.

Charlie watched Nick, in his blazer and Chamberlain shirt and jeans, kneeling on the floor in front of a handful of talent reps. At least a dozen of them had already settled into their prime seats. Nick was animated as he flipped through the program, pointing to names and faces as though they were his own children.

As soon as the lights dimmed, loud screeching ambient

music shooting through the speakers, the first show starting, Charlie felt her mind drift. She remembered how Nick had been frantic, pacing backstage, to have Grayson at his show. To have Sarah Rose Kingsbury. To have Matteo Denali, that year's resident young Turk. To command their attention for an hour and ten minutes had felt game-changing, door-opening for him then. It had been the start of everything.

—

For better or worse, some things hadn't changed since Nick's day. The first show was always the experimental one. Nick had outsourced the job of choosing which apprentice submissions to stage to Professor Bradford, who was either trying to sabotage the entire program by selecting this first production or else just had worse taste than Nick remembered. This show was apparently a comedy about artists staging a coup in a fictional place that looked a lot like Elizabethan England, featuring two mimes, a king, a bunch of people dressed in hoop skirts (men too) carrying torches, someone in a horse costume and one poor guy who spent the majority of the show nude for no discernible reason beyond the obvious sight gag. Charlie had whispered at the end, "If nothing else, this oughtta get that guy some dates."

The second show—an overwrought meditation on the meaning of an artistic life—wasn't bad. Its heart was in the right place, it just took itself too seriously, in the way of most student productions. People at a party debating a play they'd just seen—heavy in themes of Shakespearean tragedies—with the playwright himself, who becomes infuriated when everyone has universally loved it but misunderstood every element.

Both shows had their moments though. He was proud of the apprentices and felt newly connected to them. He remembered well the exhaustion and the fear of being responsible for bringing something to life from nothing, of entertaining a theater full of people he desperately wanted to please.

When Fiona introduced their revival, calling Nick and Charlie "together an inspiring force," Nick squeezed Charlie's wrist. Her pulse had always calmed him, the best way he had ever found to reset himself. But from the very first line, his fear dissipated. The words transported him to that night so many summers ago, all of the nerves he had watching his show for the first time. This work of his wasn't perfect, but it held a special place in his heart like a first kiss or a graduation.

Everything rushed back at him: watching from backstage, Charlie giving his words life before a crowd of people he adored. The relief he felt the moment the spotlight set on her. As though his future was in her hands. It almost didn't seem fair, how much weight rested on her shoulders—he had written it and staged it, devised the tricks and twists and turns, but she was the messenger, she made it more than it had been on paper. It had been so easy to fall in love with her, for that alone.

At the end of the show, Charlie pulled him to his feet to applaud. "I forgot what a good show you made," she said into his ear. "Thank God they didn't fuck it up."

When Sierra and Tripp arrived onstage for the curtain call, rather than bow, Sierra put her palms together, nodding toward Nick and Charlie, and then held her arm out, redirecting the applause their way.

—

Ethan waited for Sierra outside the stage door behind the Black Box. There wasn't a cast photo for the Black Box shows, no merchandise, but he had planned ahead.

The apprentices who had been in all three main stage productions appeared with asterisks beside their names in the info packets prepared for the scouts, and Ethan felt extremely lucky for that distinction. So much felt entirely out of his con-

357 THE SUMMER SET • 357

trol in this world: he couldn't be sure they would see in him what he wanted them to; he couldn't know if he was enough. It was like falling in love in that way. He could only do his best, put his heart on the line, try not to get in his head too much, and hope.

After they'd finished their own monologues, Ethan had watched the rest of the Black Box performances beside Alex. Ethan thought his had gone well, and Alex had even given him a hearty congratulatory slap on the back. Though Ethan was grateful for Alex's approval, he'd almost wished he had been seated alone to absorb the final show, and Sierra's performance, without having to keep his emotions in check, without worrying that Alex was making any more assumptions about them. Sierra's command and her power had gripped him, like her auditions had but now dialed all the way up. By the end of her one-act, he hadn't cared what anyone thought. He'd stood up and shouted her name over the applause. He wanted her to know, without a doubt, that he was there.

Now he waited outside, sky darkening, as nearly two dozen of his fellow apprentices trickled out in clusters—some heading to the other side of the complex to the main stage door, others heading back to the dorms to change and return as audience members or to work concessions, box office, ushering.

Even Tripp had already come and gone, along with his new crush, an apprentice named Declan—who had, for some reason, worn absolutely nothing during the role in the first show. *But, at the same time, good for him*, Ethan thought. He clutched a Sharpie and a photo he had snapped himself: Fiona, Tripp and Sierra during one of their many afternoons at the pub. He had it printed at the CVS on Warwickshire as a glossy black-and-white eight-by-ten.

He waited, waited, checked his watch and finally convinced himself he must've somehow missed her. Maybe she was already in the greenroom of the main stage, prepping for *The Tempest*. Which upset him; she needed to know how well she had done. Or, what he really meant was, *he* needed her to know how blown away he had been. It felt urgent. His mind fast-forwarded to weeks from now, when they would go back to school, and what would happen then? To not see her every day? He rolled up the photo, put it in his back pocket, Sharpie in his mouth. He took out his phone, starting a text to her, and then he heard the door open.

"Hey!" Sierra sounded genuinely surprised to find him there. "You've been waiting here? For me? All this time?" She smiled as he looked up. She had her duffel bag slung over her shoulder and had changed into a tank top and jeans, almost herself again except for her stage makeup. "Fiona had this video thing she had to do. It's a long story but—"

But he wasn't listening. His eyes not leaving hers, he walked right up to her until their lips met. His hand clutched her waist, the other webbed in her hair. She let her bag fall from her shoulder to the ground and pulled him closer.

62

WALK DON'T RUN
TO THE NEAREST EXIT

It happened at the beginning of the third act, just after inter-mission—because *The Tempest* was, of course, five acts.

Everything had been going so well. The first three acts had been perfection: the storm raging in the theater, the lightning effects, the lasers, the wind tunnel, the shaking chairs rigged throughout the audience, the wirework, the zip lines and the water cascading in torrents on stage. The actors too—every one of them: transformative.

Every minute, every inch, had been grand and luscious and moving and spiritual and arresting in the very best way. A show that would wake you from your dreams weeks later recalling the water and fire and smoke. Charlie almost won-dered if their plan had been the right thing to do. But *they had to*, she reminded herself. There had been no other way.

People tended not to come to the aid of anything failing until it was failing in a dramatic, dire enough way. So they were just providing that impetus when, during that quiet, reflective scene, Charlie as Prospero imprisoned in her jail cell…

An explosion.

A fiery, charring *BOOM* ignited the back of the stage and sent Charlie flying several feet in the air, landing on her leg with a scream. Fire alarms blared, emergency lights flashed in the auditorium. Sprinklers flickered on, shooting water at the stage and the audience. Matteo ran out first. The lobby doors at the end of every aisle flew open, the ushers then the others—actors, stagehands—anyone in the wings flowed out toward the side doors. Sarah ran to Charlie's side, with Chase helping her up, hobbling with her.

Nick's voice called out from the lighting booth, "We need to safely evacuate the theater. Please walk, don't run to the nearest exit. We apologize for the inconvenience." He repeated it over and over as the audience scrambled out the doors, the crush of bodies, the stampede of feet, the sirens and sprinklers. Ushers and apprentice stagehands led the crowd into the Quad as they had been trained to do, coincidentally, in a refresher emergency preparedness seminar a day earlier.

Once the theater was checked, everyone accounted for, the masses safely outside, firefighters inside assessing everything ("It's the strangest thing, we can't find the source of the fire, we think it was just a burst light, some kind of flare? We're continuing the search to be sure the place is safe," the fire marshal said), Nick addressed them all.

He stood atop a bench at the center of the Quad, shouting to get the attention of the hundreds of audience members still milling around, expecting to be let back in. Off to the side, Fiona recorded on her phone. "Ladies and gentlemen, I'm terribly sorry, the fire department is investigating. We suspect things will be just fine," he said, calm. "However, we do owe you a show. We would like to complete this remarkable performance out here on this beautiful night. Our cast is present and accounted for—"

"Nick! Wait a minute, man," Matteo yelled out from behind him, walking up to the bench. "Charlie may have a broken ankle. She's got some smoke inhalation, they're checking her out, but she gives her blessing for her understudy, Sierra, to go on."

"Wait, is she okay? As long as she's alright?" Nick shouted back to him, taking a few steps in his direction.

The audience around him pressed in closer, conversations halting, everyone hanging on these words.

"Yes, she doesn't want anyone to worry," Matteo told the group, which seemed to sigh in relief at this.

"Okay," Nick addressed them all again. "Then, we'll stage the rest of the show, right here, if you all give us your blessing. We could put everyone over here." He pointed to the great, vast lawn. "And up front here," he said, pointing near where he stood, "will be our stage. We apologize for our technical issues. We're grateful everyone is safe, and I don't want to say the show must go on, but you know what I mean." They actually laughed at this. "The role of Prospero will now be played by Sierra Suarez. Sierra?"

Sierra jogged out from her place amid the pack of apprentices toward Nick as a voice cheered in the back.

Nick waved to the actors to assemble, and they took their marks. "I give you the conclusion of *The Tempest*."

Applause welcomed the show's return. The audience, many of them bedraggled and damp from the sprinklers, had found places to sit on the lawn, seemingly invigorated to be part of the adventure. A hush fell and Sierra's voice, the actors alongside her, carried to Charlie, and she felt at ease.

Charlie watched it all from the street. The ambulance had parked on the hill, giving her a nice perch.

"Remember," she told the man wrapping her ankle, "the second anything real happens, you guys get outta here."

"You got it," he said. "You all picked a good night, it's been quiet." He gave her ankle a pat. "Think you're set here." He winked.

"That looks legit," she said, stretching out her leg to admire her bandaged foot.

"That's because it is," he said. "I don't know how to fake it."

"If this place stays open, you all have some free tickets coming your way." She hopped down from the back of the ambulance, set to limp to Nick's side.

Nick was supposed to be standing along the periphery of the Quad closest to the street where she was. But she couldn't find him. This was, so far, the only thing that had *not* gone according to plan tonight. She couldn't walk too far or too fast or risk being seen by the entire audience, so she hobbled, lurking along the edges in search of him. Whispering to anyone who asked, "Just a sprain, it turns out. I'm just fine, thank you, enjoy the show." She returned to the street just as the ambulance was ready to roll out.

"Can I bum a ride?" she asked, to keep up appearances. "It's on the way."

63

ARE YOU ACTING RIGHT NOW?

The ambulance dropped Charlie off as close to the log cabin as any vehicle could get, situated as it was in the center of a grassy expanse set back from the main road. But it was dark enough, save for the nearby hotel and the fireflies, that she felt confident walking the rest of the way without being seen. For some reason she thought to come here first: not his office or his place or even the lake.

As she walked to the cabin, she felt soft raindrops against her skin and hoped the show would wrap in time. Their plan, roughly sketched that night after their walk from the football field and brought to life with Mason's technical wizardry, played out exactly as they had dreamed. Three perfect acts, a fake electrical malfunction to clear the place out, and the show completed outside with no special effects, nothing expensive, everything completely low-tech, back to basics but just as affecting, even more so.

The great hope now was that tonight's show might score them some attention once they cut together their behind-the-scenes segment—thanks to the added drama of the "explosion," Charlie's "injury," the show continuing outside and having one of the greatest Shakespearean actresses of all time, Sarah, there too. If all that didn't bring new eyes and fresh clicks and page views and excitement and ultimately investors, nothing would. Meanwhile, tonight's electrical wiring "incident" would "shut down" the theater for the remainder of the season and they would be "forced" to perform the show outside every night. After all, even the Globe Theatre itself was partially open air.

Sure, they would risk having ticket holders demand refunds, but the show would absolutely go on, for a fraction of the overhead costs, in the Quad every night, where there was plenty of room for everyone on the lawn. If need be, there would even be space enough to add seats, sell even more tickets. And if any theatergoer needed reassurance of just how special this could be, there would be that web series, where Nick and Charlie would be laying out just how touch and go things were at the Chamberlain and what a struggle it had become to keep the theater afloat. And then continue to shed only the slimmest slivers of light on their own relationship, just enough backstage drama and intrigue.

The rain picking up, she began to run, her chiffon cloak—Prospero's cloak—billowing behind her until it became too soaked and clung to her like her dress beneath. They had told as few people as possible of the details. There were easily a million different ways they could be sued if anything went wrong, and it was safer that way. It had been Charlie's idea to give Sierra this moment at the end of the show. She had earned it.

The first behind-the-scenes segment—featuring her and

Nick, and Sierra and Ethan, all coyly dishing on each other—had gone live just this morning and already racked up hundreds of thousands of views. She wondered if Nick had watched it yet.

The door to the log cabin had been left open. She knocked anyway, just twice, her hand trembling. No response. Her nerves more intense than any she had ever had onstage, she poked her head inside the shadowy room. The lights from the hotel in the distance cast a honey glow, and she made out Nick leaning against the ladder, gazing out the window.

"You missed your mark, you know," she said in greeting. He looked over, not surprised to see her, not moving. She walked toward him anyway. "This is *way* off from where you're supposed to be."

"Yeah," he said, darkly. "That's why I'm not an actor."

"You haven't been brooding again, have you?" she asked, leaning beside him now, too close to be ignored—though he was doing a fairly good job of it.

"Maybe," he said, still so heavy, that voice.

"In case you didn't notice, this has all gone pretty perfectly. Tonight. There's a chance this will actually work."

"I know," he said, angry, eyes set above her.

"Then what's your problem?" She raised her voice too, matched his tone.

"My problem is it doesn't. Change. *Anything.*"

"It could literally change *everything*—"

"It won't change the most basic thing—the season will end, you'll leave, everyone will, it's a summer theater, but you'll leave and—even if the Chamberlain manages to open again next summer, it almost doesn't matter now because I don't know if I can do this next summer and the summer after that, without you…here…*fighting* with me," he said, as though it was being beaten out of him. "How fucking crazy is that?"

"Not crazy at all," she said. "Maybe I feel the same way." She felt him take in those words. They had focused only on the show these past weeks. She had been too proud, desperate to play it cool—and she suspected, he had been too wary of her walking away from everything.

"Your video—" he started, quieter now. "Was that true? What you said about me? About that night in the harbor?"

"Yeah." She softened, had to look away from his piercing eyes. She gave him a moment to absorb it, then nodded slowly as she looked in his eyes to be sure he got it. "And you, did you mean what you said?"

"Of course," he said, serious. "This couldn't have happened without you—"

"Then ask me to stay," she said with a shrug.

"How?" He sounded defeated. "This place doesn't even operate most of the year, so I don't understand...the logistics... of what it would encompass to—"

"Ask me to stay," she said again. "Like in the overall, metaphysical sense."

"Stay," he said, barely looking at her.

"Ask me like you mean it," she said, annoyed. "Why do I always have to do so much directing for you?" She lunged for the door.

"Please." He reached for her, catching her wrist. "Will you?" He stepped closer, said it again, sweeping her damp hair to the side. His hand resting gently on her neck, her pulse beating beneath the lark's wing, he said softly into her ear, "Stay."

In the background, she swore she could hear the lines she knew, her lines, the final words of the show, and she nodded her head toward the lawn. "'Please, you, draw near,'" she quoted. She could hear the applause now too, enough to know the audience had remained until the end. A victory.

"That's the last line of our show," she whispered.

"That's not what I asked," he whispered back.

Instead of answering, she pulled him close, kissed him. They would miss tonight's curtain call but there would be plenty more.

EPILOGUE

The climb here hadn't been what Charlie had expected, but nothing ever was. The path had been well marked, the map accurate, and she had given herself plenty of time to hike the steep trails to the top of Mount Greylock, the range she was used to watching from the confines of Chamberlain. All in all, an orderly, organized endeavor; not the way she generally operated.

She found the perfect spot, a fine view of the surrounding peaks, and took a seat amid the rocks. The day was still warm, though the end of summer neared. This, in so many ways, was not where she thought she would be now—and she was glad for it.

Tonight was their final *Tempest* performance of the season. The show had moved from the Quad to the college's football field. They set up folding chairs for ticket holders close-in surrounding the stage, turning it into a theater-in-the-round for the duration of the play. The regular theater crowd was game for the change of scenery, eager to find their seats out in the warm night air.

Sarah had gone home for now (with the promise of returning next season), and she'd left only after they began hearing from a series of other luminaries offering their services— Kenneth Branagh had taken over the role for a few days, Judi Dench, Idris Elba, Hugh Grant—which kept the box office phones ringing. New audience members showed up on a whim. Others stopped by multiple times a week to sit in the field's bleachers for a fraction of the cost of a standard ticket. It had rained every night at that same time for days on end, just before the bows, but no one seemed bothered by it.

Just as Nick had almost, almost, stopped minding that Charlie breezed in so late every night before showtime. He still paced, but he seemed to know she would make it in time. Even if barely.

Charlie breathed deep, the cool mountain air, took one last look, then was back onto her feet, dusting the dirt off. The curtain would rise at 8 p.m.—figuratively, at least—and she would be there among the fireflies, with her favorite lark.

★ ★ ★ ★ ★

Charlie Savoy - ACTRESS

Charlotte "Charlie" Savoy is a stage and screen actress and coartistic director of the Chamberlain Summer Theater. She is also a star and producer of the Emmy-winning reality series *Backstage at the Chamberlain*. Daughter of famed Shakespearean actress Dame Sarah Rose Kingsbury and jazz trumpeter Reggie Fairfield, she was born in New York, New York, but grew up primarily in London with her mother after her father left to pursue his music career. She won a host of supporting actress awards (British Independent Film Award, Independent Spirit, Critics' Choice) and even more nominations (Oscar, BAFTA, Golden Globe) for her plucky Ariel in *Nicholas Blunt's The Tempest*, but took a hiatus ("a self-imposed exile," she later said) after creative differences caused her to drop out of Blunt's psychological action film *Dawn of the Super Id*. The indie *Midnight Daydream*, in which she starred, has since gone on to achieve cult status. Her next film is Nicholas Blunt's as-yet-untitled, highly anticipated return to the big screen, a project shrouded in secrecy and scheduled for release in time for awards season.

TRIVIA:

In a longtime relationship with director Nicholas Blunt, coartistic director of the Chamberlain Summer Theater

Best friend of Emmy winner Marlena Andes-Embers and served as maid of honor in Marlena Andes-Embers's wedding to actor Chase Embers

Mentor to *Backstage at the Chamberlain* costars Sierra Suarez and Ethan Summit

Survived near drowning in Boston Harbor

Reputation for being a wild child (arrested after jumping off of London's Tower Bridge on a dare as a teen)

Legally changed surname to Savoy at age eighteen

Owns North End Cinema movie theater in Boston, Massachusetts

FILMOGRAPHY:

1. Untitled Nicholas Blunt Film (in postproduction)
2. Backstage at the Chamberlain, Season 2 (self; reality TV series; in production)
3. Netflix Presents: Live from the Chamberlain Theater, Much Ado about Nothing (Benedick)
4. Netflix Presents: Live from the Chamberlain Theater, Hamlet (Hamlet)
5. Netflix Presents: Live from the Chamberlain Theater, Macbeth (Macbeth)
6. Backstage at the Chamberlain, Season 1 (self, 13 episodes, reality TV series)
7. Netflix Presents: Live from the Chamberlain Theater, The Tempest (Prospero)
8. Netflix Presents: Live from the Chamberlain Theater, A Midsummer Night's Dream (Puck)
9. Netflix Presents: Live from the Chamberlain Theater, Romeo and Juliet—A Four-Part Special Event (Romeo, Juliet, Tybalt, Paris)
10. Midnight Daydream (Charlotte)
11. Nicholas Blunt's The Tempest (Ariel)
12. Illuminate (Haven)
13. Law & Order (Stacy; 2 episodes)
14. A BBC Presentation: Live from the Globe Theatre, Macbeth (Lady Macbeth)
15. A BBC Presentation: Live from the Globe Theatre, Hamlet (Ophelia)
16. A BBC Presentation: Live from the Globe Theatre, Romeo and Juliet (Juliet)

ACKNOWLEDGMENTS

I'm so lucky to have the most wonderful cast of characters shining their light on this book. Thank you, thank you, thank you:

To Stéphanie Abou. If my life were a play, you would be that actor who shows up on stage in a million different roles, all brilliant (agent, friend, reader, therapist!). You're fantastic and I'm so grateful for you! And a huge thank-you to the team at Massie & McQuilkin.

To Melanie Fried, the most patient of editors! Thank you so very much for your guidance, laser-sharp eye and encouragement over so many reads. And an extra thank-you to the lovely Justine Sha, Lia Ferrone and Pam Osti, and the whole gang at Graydon House, Harlequin and HarperCollins. I so appreciate all you've done for this book!

To Margo Lipschultz for your early support before this book was even a book!

To Richard Ford for always telling me to keep writing.

To the theaters that inspired me. I loved quietly skulking around the incredible Williamstown Theatre Festival in Massachusetts, seeing shows, touring backstage, getting a feel for how a legendary summer theater operates. And to the Olney Theatre Center in Maryland, where I spent my high school years volunteering (offstage, way offstage) and going to a *lot* of free plays. And a shout-out to Bill Evans for casting me in those musicals at Sherwood High, where I had so much fun (despite being extremely pitchy).

To my squad of pals and moms, with an extra thank-you to Rachel Paula Abrahamson, Jami Bjellos, Jenny Laws, Jessica Lucas, Ryan Lynch, Poornima Ravishankar, Anna Siri, Jennie Teitelbaum and Kate Ackley Zeller.

To my truly amazing family and cheering section, fabulous parents, Bill and Risa; awesome sis (and beloved first reader!), Karen. And supersupportive in-laws Steve, Ilene, Jill, Lauren, David, Gabrielle and Alexander.

To Brian, of course, for the love and endless encouragement and for corralling our wild guys while I wrote. And to sweet Sawyer and Hardy for your excellent writing tips and beautiful artwork for my office!

And, finally, thank you, dear reader, for taking some time to peek behind the curtain of the Chamberlain. I so hope you enjoyed the show!

THE
SUMMER
SET

AIMEE AGRESTI

Reader's Guide

GRAYDON
HOUSE

QUESTIONS FOR DISCUSSION

1. In what ways are many of the characters (Charlie, Nick, Chase, Sierra, Ethan) "acting" in their *real* lives? What are they trying to project about themselves and how does it differ from how they feel on the inside? Can you think of times in your own life when you've tried to appear a certain way to hide your true emotions?

2. Which characters are reinventing themselves and embarking on a "second act"? How do they feel about their journeys? How successful are they? What does *The Summer Set* reveal about failure, second chances and reinvention? Have you ever made a major life change? How did it feel?

3. Charlie talks about "returning to her roots" as a metaphor for returning to theater work. Matteo mentions water as a symbol of life and rebirth. What role does the natural world play in the novel? How are certain characters reinvigorated by their landscape and inspired by the world around them? (Or in Jasmine's case, perhaps just the opposite!)

4. Charlie and Nick have so much history—good and bad. Why do you think they still have sparks when they meet again? Do you think it ever works to get back with an ex? Can people change?

5. What does *The Summer Set* have to say about the passage of time? What role does time play in the relationships in the book?

6. How do the three Shakespeare plays staged at the theater—*Romeo and Juliet, A Midsummer Night's Dream* and *The Tempest*—reflect what's going on *offstage* at the theater?

7. Charlie had an unconventional childhood. How does her upbringing shape her interactions with Danica's young son, Gianni? How does Charlie's friendship with Gianni help her understand her relationship with her own mother?

8. How do the characters' opinions about fame differ? For characters not as interested in fame, what motivates them instead? What is the book's message about fame and stardom?

9. In what ways do Ethan and Sierra remind Charlie and Nick of their younger selves? Though Charlie and Nick should be the mentors, how do Ethan and Sierra perhaps help them? Do you have a mentor? How have they helped you navigate different times in your life?

10. Do you think Charlie and Nick stay together after this summer? Why or why not? If so, what do you think their first creative project together might be?